NEVER SEND ROSES

ROSES

HARMONY BLACK, BOOK SEVEN

CRAIG SCHAEFER

DEMIMONDE BOOKS

CONTENTS

THE STORY SO FAR

Harmony Black was never a big fan of Las Vegas.

The lights were too bright, the sounds and smells overwhelming, and she preferred cold calculation over gambling. Duty called, though, after stolen financial documents drew a dark outline of the demon *Najidanere*'s criminal empire. Harmony's nemesis, known to mortals simply as Nadine, holds sway over the House of Dead Roses: an infernal cult offering murder, sabotage, extortion, and chaos to the highest bidder.

Nadine's right-hand man, a former German intelligence agent known as the Basilisk, was on the move. He'd been sent to Sin City with five million dollars of Nadine's money, intent on claiming the top bid at a secret auction. Harmony and Jessie went undercover, infiltrating the event and digging for clues about Geordie Tynes, the mysterious auctioneer whose entire history was a nest of lies.

The artifact up for grabs was a stolen battlesuit capable of jumping between parallel worlds, and Tynes — desperate, cornered, and on the run from the "lawbringers" of his world — aimed to trade the nearly-depleted suit for the funds he needed to escape. Hunters from Tynes's world soon arrived in hot pursuit, competing for the prize. And that wasn't all: the mutant assassins known as the Sisters of the Noose were on the scene, trying to force Tynes to build a gateway home for them. And finally, an old familiar face appeared: Bette Novak, an Air Force officer who Harmony's team had encountered during the Red Knight incident.

Bette had shady connections and a shadier mandate. She raided the auction with her team, posing as FBI agents, and nearly swept Harmony and Jessie up in the dragnet. Harmony escaped, only to be captured by the Basilisk. Thinking quick, she transferred the Basilisk's money — *Nadine's* money — into a locked account with a scrambled password. Terrified at the idea of disappointing Nadine, her henchman brutally tortured Harmony; she held out just long enough to slip loose and turn the Basilisk's deadly magic back upon himself, killing him and his hired guns, before escaping into the night.

The battlesuit was returned to its rightful owners. And Geordie Tynes died to a single bullet, an act of mercy at Harmony's hands.

Now Nadine is rolling up her operations on earth and burning her paper trail, desperate to escape capture. Not this time. Harmony and her team are airborne. They're hunting big game tonight, preparing to face their greatest challenge to date, and their greatest enemy.

CHAPTER ONE

They gave Harmony pills for the pain. She didn't take them.

The first two toes on her right foot were useless, their shattered ruins swaddled under rolls of white bandage, demanding time to heal that she couldn't afford and jolting her awake every time the plane's thrumming engines lulled her to sleep. Every step was agony, but she wasn't afraid of agony: she was afraid the painkillers would slow her down, gunk up the whirling gears of her mind when she needed them most. The pain kept her sharp. That was part of it. Then there were the visions, memories coming on strong every time she closed her eyes.

She had killed a man in cold blood, shot him dead on the tarmac. He'd begged her to do it. He had good reason: they couldn't harbor him, couldn't hide him, and if they handed him over to the interdimensional cops on his trail, he faced a fate infinitely worse than a quick, clean death. The closest thing he had to a good option was a mercy bullet.

"You should have let me do it," Jessie had told her.

"It was my job."

"You don't kill cold," Jessie said. "It's not in your nature, hon. It is in mine. You leave that kind of work to me, okay?"

Harmony just thought about the dog she had when she was little. How it ran off into the woods, got savaged by...*something*...and came back rabid and frothing. Her father loaded his service revolver and led it into the backyard. Then she heard a single gunshot. He explained to her, after, that this was how it had to be: nothing was going to cure Pacer, he had nothing ahead of him but madness and pain. There was only one kindness, one act of love, her father could grant him.

"It had to be me," Harmony tried to explain. "Tynes trusted me. In his last moment, I... I didn't want him to be afraid."

She hadn't told anyone about that final fatal second, when Tynes turned from the trunk, only to find Harmony squaring him in the sights of her pistol.

He smiled. Sadness in his eyes, but he smiled at her. Then she squeezed the trigger and set him free.

That wasn't the only plague haunting her dreams. She was still coming to terms with the way her powers had been shifting, changing, since Nadine infected her with a succubus's kiss. Transforming, slowly, into a gift she couldn't recognize.

She remembered clamping her hand over the face of one of Hausler's half-demon thugs. And *pulling*. The cambion screeched as she drank his infernal energy, the fabric of his very soul; she unleashed it from her other hand, turning it into a torrent of blue flame.

When she was finished, the cambion was nothing but a shriveled husk. Mummified and bone-dry.

She still didn't know how she did it, only that something was growing inside of her, Nadine's curse of endless hunger melding with her natural talent for conjuring and commanding the elements. Her magic had always been a strange alchemy, a strain of witchcraft unlike anything else they'd ever encountered in the field. Now it was getting stranger.

At least her secret was out. No more dragging that weight around, and despite her worst fears, her family had her back. Now she had to protect theirs. While burdened with exhaustion and a half-useless foot.

I'll make it work, she decided. She was a damaged machine, not a broken one. Not yet.

The steel deck of the *Imperator* bounced under Harmony's feet, jolting its way through a patch of rough air. The former military cargo plane, converted to Vigilant's flying base of operations, had been packed and fueled in haste. Heavy supply crates, fixed to the plane's inner belly with ratchets and nylon straps, surrounded the tarp-draped body of a muscle car. Even hidden under green oilcloth, it cut a mean silhouette.

Dr. Cassidy steered her wheelchair with a shove, coasting over to Harmony. April had steel hair and steel eyes, taking in everything behind the sharp frames of her bifocals. Her voice, tinged with an Irish brogue, was pitched lower than usual.

"Harmony. There's something we need to talk about."

"Should I call everyone over?"

April shook her head. "Just you and me. I came upon some...information. Something you need to know."

A sharp whistle turned their heads.

"Eyes up front," Jessie called out. Her inhumanly turquoise eyes glittered with eager anticipation. "One hour to touchdown. Let's do this thing."

She stood by the command center, a long console topped by a wall of flickering, blinking screens. Monitors tracked mission plans and movement, bringing in real-time updates from their teams in the field, painting it all in blue neon. Kevin hunched over the console, typing with furious speed; occasionally he paused, listened to something in his headphones, then jotted down notes on a crumpled scrap of paper before updating the overhead displays.

"We've got to clear this storm," he muttered. "Our comms are hanging on by a thread and I'm trying to coordinate three teams at once. On that note, Bravo just breached their target. Reporting heavy resistance, multiple casualties. I'm waiting for hard intel."

"Let me know," Jessie told him, "and give me one ear in the meantime. Ladies, gentleman, let's get reacquainted with tonight's mission objective. You know her, you strongly dislike her—"

April took her station at the console and rapped a button. One long screen went blank, a wireframe map of the nation going dark, quickly replaced by a file photograph. The woman in the photo had olive skin and big, bright eyes, wearing a look of perpetual curious innocence.

"—it's Dima Chakroun, Nadine's personal accountant. We've never gone up against her in the field, but we did go *around* her when we jacked Nadine's financials from her personal laptop."

"She never knew we were there," April said, looking up over her glasses at the screen. "A textbook operation, complications notwithstanding."

"Tonight, she's going to get to know us," Jessie said. "Here's the situation: Nadine knows that the Basilisk is missing, and so is five million dollars of her money."

"Any chance she knows he's dead?" Kevin asked.

Harmony shook her head. "Not likely. I left his body in a burning building, minus its head. She'll figure it out eventually, but right now she's flying blind. For once, we've got the informational edge."

"An edge, and eyes on our next target," Jessie said. "Dima was enjoying a lavish dinner at a Michelin-starred restaurant when she got a call from Nadine. Couldn't get ears on the line, but it's not hard to guess what they talked about. Reportedly, Dima got up mid-meal and left in a panic. April?"

"We still have all the data we mined when she first came to our attention," April said.

A few quick key-clicks, and another monitor bristled with expense reports, checking ledgers, a live feed from a database at Chase Bank.

"You'd think someone working for Nadine would practice better operational security," April said, "but she hasn't changed her passwords in months. We're tracking every payment she makes with her credit cards, when she makes them, and where. Not only can I follow her every move — until she wises up or disappears — but I can build a fairly reliable profile of her immediate plans."

"Leading us straight to Nadine's hiding spot?" Harmony asked.

"No such fortune. It looks more like she's cutting and running. She's been racing all over LA, draining her personal accounts, tapping her emergency caches, and she's lined up a red-eye flight to Paris."

"Mama is *angry*," Kevin said, sliding his chair down the row of keyboards and adjusting his headset.

"Nadine goes into murder-mode if she has to pay for parking," Jessie said, "and I'm just barely exaggerating. Five million dollars and her best assassin go missing on the same night? She's got to be losing her goddamn mind right now. Dima's the caretaker of the cash. If Nadine can't skin the Basilisk alive, she's the next best target, and Dima is smart enough to grasp that. She's loyal, not suicidal; she's deep enough in the organization to know exactly what kind of sick, nasty shit Nadine does for kicks."

"So we intercept her before she can board that flight?" Harmony asked.

"A very tight window—" Jessie wobbled on her feet as the plane carved through another patch of turbulence. "—getting tighter by the minute, thanks to this weather. But if we can snatch her, there's a good chance we can flip her. Let's just remember one thing. April?"

An old and faded crime-scene photograph filled the screen right next to the accountant's innocent, sweetly smiling face. A tangle of limbs in a blood-drenched bedsheet, wet crimson against starched white, the edge of a mutilated torso with the hint of an exposed broken rib.

"Dima Chakroun is a true believer," Jessie said, "and she sacrificed her first boyfriend to the infernal powers when she was fourteen years old. We can tie six former paramours, all currently missing or dead, to her trail after that. Don't let her looks fool you: she's sociopathic, dedicated to her cause, and should be considered armed and dangerous at all times."

Jessie drew her weapon, a Sig Sauer P320. She kept the barrel pointed to the deck as she squinted down the sturdy pistol's sights, checked the load in the magazine, and slid it back into the holster under her blazer.

"She's our best living link to Nadine's operations," Jessie said. "We're taking her down tonight, and we're bringing her back alive."

CHAPTER TWO

Dima knew this day would come eventually.

She couldn't claim that Nadine hadn't held up her end of their devil's bargain. Years of faithful service had brought wealth, luxury, pleasures of every kind, and a special phone number to call when she needed little problems — like a parking ticket, or a corpse — to disappear. Good times.

All the same, she'd seen other members of Nadine's inner circle fall out of favor, be it from making a fatal mistake or just getting on the demoness's cruel side. And when they fell, they fell hard. And kept falling. Forever. Unlike them, Dima kept her eyes clear and her options open. She made a contingency plan.

Dima considered herself a bit of a renaissance woman. Her first loyalty was to hell, but Los Angeles had no shortage of strange lodges, gurus, and cults, all bobbing and slipping along the oil-black waters of the occult underground. In her spare time she had earned the grade of Adeptus Minor in the Temple of Amber Twilight, a reserved table at the Hollywood Dinner Club, and the Grace of Sparks from the Church of the Last Configuration, among other honors. And they all owed her favors. Now she raced against the clock, aiming to collect on every single debt before she skipped town and burned her passport behind her. A new, bulletproof identity, one she'd lovingly curated and hidden away years ago, was waiting for her in Paris.

This was her last stop before LAX. A library — well, more of a book cathedral, with a domed ivory ceiling and towering shelves lining every wall. It was closing time. The lights in the reading galleries went off one by one, the acoustics turning each click of the switch into a cannon-shot.

"I need—" Dima started to say, then caught herself, "—*Nadine* needs to borrow *The Wise Sailor's Almanac*. She's asked me to deliver it to her directly."

The reference librarian was a punk rocker by way of Mister Rogers, with a lime-green undercut, pierced nose and lip, and a conservative sweater-vest. He raised one hand above the counter between them, fingers curling and uncurling in a certain order, like stroking secret keys on an invisible typewriter. Biting back her frustration, Dima responded with her opposite hand, offering up the pass-symbol for his sign of testing.

"One of the centerpieces of our collection. Irreplaceable."

Dima's eyes narrowed. "Is that a refusal?"

"Not at all." He took a slight step back, cowed. If not by her, then by the three men with prison-yard stares and bulging jackets standing at her back. "You've more than earned the right to request books from the invisible archive. I would never challenge my superiors—"

Another gallery went dark. Another coffin-lid *click* echoed through the library.

"The book, please," Dima said. She fought the urge to look at her phone.

"And she'll return it...when?"

Dima gritted her teeth. "Three days. At most."

He inclined his head. "I'll be right back. If security comes around, don't worry, he's one of ours. Just give the sign and he'll leave you be."

The Wise Sailor's Almanac was the testimony and personal journal of a particular British seaman, one who had seen certain terrible things in the South Pacific and, subsequently marooned, utterly lost his mind. Dima had read it before, along with almost every volume of note in the Devourers of the Word's "invisible archive."

It wasn't entirely uninteresting: mad ramblings mixed with fragments of potent spells and experiments in cannibalism, some of which she'd marked to try for herself someday. Far more important, right now, was the rare book dealer in Marseille who was desperate to find a copy of his own. He was offering six figures for the book, which in addition to all the other treasures she'd "borrowed" tonight would provide Dima's new identity with a nicely feathered nest.

The overhead lights went out. Dima was blind for a moment, her eyes struggling to adjust to the muted streetlights glowing through the windows, the only thing she could see by. The library stacks and rows of study-tables became inky blobs in the dark.

"Excuse me," she called out. "Patrons, still here. Could you turn on the lights, please?"

No answer. Not even from the resident security guard. Not a peep.

Dima's breath went tight as her chest clenched. Couldn't be her. Nadine would have announced herself. After all, Dima's three bodyguards were loyal members of the House of Dead Roses.

She was planning to kill them in the airport parking lot. She'd known them for years, so she felt a twinge of regret about that, but not much.

She tried again. "Hello?"

Her voice echoed back at her, bouncing until it died away. She tapped her closest bodyguard on the shoulder, pointed, and sent him off with a firm nod. He drew his pistol. So did the other two, staying close, turning to cover every angle.

"If he's not back with that book in thirty seconds," Dima said under her breath, "we're leaving. Something is very wrong here."

The man on the move was Kohler, a demonic half-blood who had offered up his tongue, one toe and three fingers to prove his loyalty to the House of Dead Roses. Nadine rewarded him for his self-inflicted suffering with a kiss. And gold, and pride, and a cause to fight for, but Nadine's love was worth more than that. Nadine's love was pure and all-consuming, a fire he dreamed of burning in.

The cambion inched his way down the stacks, penned in by walls of books, his sharp ears perked. His enhanced eyes quickly adjusted to the dark, the world turning black and white.

A sudden *slam* turned his head just in time to see a trio of hardcover books launch off the shelf and pelt him in the face.

One cracked against the bridge of his nose, hot and salty blood streaming down his upper lip. On the other side of the shelf he glimpsed a clenched fist, the turn of a shoulder, then nothing, as his attacker silently sprinted toward the end of the stacks.

Kohler cursed under his breath and launched into pursuit, gun held high, his finger on the trigger. He heard more books falling on the other side, a hailstorm of paper and plastic-wrapped covers, as the entire shelving unit shuddered.

Trying to push it over on me, he thought, sprinting toward the gap at the end of the aisle. *We'll see about—*

Jessie plunged down from the top of the shelves. She hit him boots-first, one heel driving into his shoulder, the other cracking against the back of his skull. He crumpled to his knees and her weight drove him down the rest of the way, mashing his face into the carpet. She kicked the revolver out of his hand, sending it bouncing up the aisle, and her other foot stamped down on his throat. She leaned in, putting all her weight on that leg, feeling the cambion's trachea start to buckle as he wheezed and flopped on the floor.

The second bodyguard rounded the far end of the aisle and opened fire, flooding Jessie's vision with white-hot muzzle flare as a stray bullet tore along a row of paperbacks. Jessie threw herself backward, pulling the trigger twice as she fell, landing on her ass and rolling for cover. The bodyguard let out a canine yelp of pain; at least one of her bullets found the mark, but no telling how badly she'd tagged him or if he was still in the fight.

She scrambled to her feet. Mobility was the cardinal rule of any gunfight; you stop moving and you're dead. She adjusted her grip on her gun and went hunting. She swept a book off the floor with her other hand as she rose, plucking the closest one from the fallen clutter.

Her second target stumbled into sight with one hand pressed to his forearm, blood guttering through his fingers. She threw the book at his face. Instinct made him bat it away, ruining his aim, and she fired for center mass. One bullet impaled his heart, the second ripped through his stomach and out the small of his back, and he dropped with a wet, rattling wheeze.

• • • ● ● • ● ● • •

Dima heard the swiftly escalating sounds of violence twenty feet from where she stood, a brawl becoming a shootout. Flashes of fire lit the darkened gallery, leaving nuclear blossoms on her retinas. Tommaso — her third loyal drone, a gift from Nadine — tugged at the sleeve of her designer blazer and she fixed him with a lethal glare until he let go.

"Ma'am—" He turned his back on her, aiming into the dark, toward the trouble. "—we have to get you to safety."

Safety. As if safety could exist in a world with Nadine in it. She needed that damned *book*. He wasn't wrong, though: Dima hadn't survived this long by taking stupid chances, and she'd prefer being poor but alive to wealthy and dead. Straight to the airport then. In the meantime, she still had to deal with the last man standing.

"Go," she said, pointing toward the fight. "Cover my back, buy me half a minute's head start, and I'll meet you at the car."

She almost hoped he survived. The mental image of Tommaso charging down the library steps only to find her and the car long gone, off to the airport without him, was too scrumptious not to enjoy.

She had her own methods of self-defense. As she scurried through the darkness, trying not to run face-first into a shelf or clip her heel on a chair while she hunted for the exit, Dima hooked and curled her fingers. Ten fingertips squirmed in ten different directions, joints creaking and cracking, hunting the points of a forgotten constellation. One by one they captured a current of power that made her hands tremble and sent tingling waves of heat up her arms, like old antennae tuning into a hard-to-find channel.

This conjure-sign, harvested from the pages of the Six Contemptible Sacraments, had no formal name. But it was, she knew from experience, *highly* effective.

CHAPTER THREE

Tommaso met Jessie in the dark, barreling toward her in a full-on charge. She broke his stride with a knuckle-punch to the throat. Then she batted away his gun hand and hammered his chest, three quick strikes to drive the air from his lungs and leave him reeling.

A crushing weight hit her from behind, arms latching onto her, one curling around her neck and squeezing while a voice screeched in her ear. In the corner of her vision she made out bulging veins, an eye like a runny egg yolk. The reference-desk librarian was back, wearing his true face now. She tried to shake him loose while Tomasso rallied, blinked away the pain, and came at her.

Tomasso used her for a punching bag while the librarian dug his knees into her back and hauled with both arms, intent on choking her out. As her vision blurred and the blood roared like thunder in her ears, an old familiar presence fluffed its tail and whispered in her ear.

Let me out.

Jessie broke into a run, carrying the screeching demon-librarian on her shoulders. Then she spun, gritting her teeth, and threw herself backwards. They hit a study table together, the librarian sandwiched between Jessie's muscle and the cold, hard wood. The wood snapped under their combined weight, buckling down the middle, dropping them to the library floor in a shower of sawdust and splinters. The arm around Jessie's neck dropped loose as the creature flopped in the wreckage, stunned. She wasn't doing much better, her body a battlefield erupting with tiny explosions from her spine to her knees, but she pushed through the pain.

Let me OUT, the wolf growled in her ear.

Tommaso was framing her in his sights. Jessie shot first. Three times, drawing a jagged line from his abdomen to his heart, and he stared blankly at his cratered body while his jaw went slack. Then the rest of him shut down all at once, his body crumpling to the bloodstained carpet.

She forced herself up, groaning, one of her legs wobbly and threatening to turn traitor. No time for that. She put her full weight on it. The pain would keep her awake, focused. Up ahead was a solitary patch of light, the overheads in the library's white-tiled foyer. Dima was struggling with a locked door, trying to get it open.

Jessie raised her weapon with one exhausted hand, trudging toward her.

"Dima. Give it up. We're not here to hurt you. Back away from the door, put your hands behind your head—"

Dima twirled on her heel. Jessie had just enough time to recognize that one of her hands was *wrong*, fingers bent into bone-breaking contortions, the air around them shimmering like a heat mirage, before she let her curse fly.

The wave of toxic magic slammed into Jessie and knocked her off her feet, her vision flooding with stars, like a sea of cameras all popping flashbulbs in her eyes. Electricity coursed through her muscles, making them jerk and convulse, blue lightning crackling along her outstretched arms.

Dima sniffed. Then she turned her back.

"Don't know who you are, but at least you took care of Nadine's minders for me." She twisted the lock on the library door. "Thanks for that."

Dima's heels clicked as she gingerly walked down the library's sweeping granite steps. Her escape plan, a polished black Escalade, waited at the curb. Harmony watched from the shadows, her lips a thin and bloodless line. Dima never should have made it out of the building. Something was wrong.

She tapped her earpiece. "Jessie? I can't see you. Report."

"Hey," came the strained reply. "I aced her guards, but she put some kind of whammy on me. Think I'll be okay but my body's made of jelly right now."

Dima approached the Escalade. It squawked in response to her key fob, doors unlocking.

"Need you to finish this one without me," Jessie said.

Without her. And with a bum leg she could barely walk on.

"You have to take her alive," Jessie added. "If we blow this—"

"I know," Harmony said. "I'll get it done."

Harmony turned a key and fired up the Hemi Cuda. The muscle car gave a throaty growl as its headlights sliced through the dark. She only needed one foot to drive, and she was parked half a block behind Dima's getaway ride.

Even if you had more markers to call in, Harmony reasoned, *now you're good and shaken and all out of cannon fodder. There's only one place left for you to go.*

Dima drove north through the city and Harmony followed, tailing her from a distance. They cruised up South Sepulveda Boulevard. Just as expected: Dima was heading for the airport, ready to leave her old life behind.

Can't let her get into the terminal. If she makes it past airport security, she's as good as gone.

Lamplight broke the road into bubbles of asphalt and darkness as the two drivers dodged and wove through the late-night traffic, a whale with a shark on its heels. Harmony saw beyond the horizon; the city resolved into a wireframe map, a grid of shimmering sapphire light, expressed in distances, angles, raw data.

She considered overtaking her, going aggressive right here and now. She could surge up, execute a PIT maneuver, and knock Dima's ride out of action. But that still left the problem of subduing her and getting away with a struggling hostage. There would be witnesses, maybe recordings, cops if she didn't move fast enough. Her FBI cover could excuse a host of minor crimes, but kidnapping wasn't one of them.

The data didn't lie. There was only one place Harmony could take her with maximum cover and escape potential. Right at the edge of freedom.

"Kevin? Coming up on LAX. I'm going to need a few select security cameras to go to sleep for a while."

"Define 'a while?'" his voice crackled in her ear.

"Ten, fifteen minutes tops."

"I can get away with that, I think. Already have a backdoor into their security network, but I haven't used it in a while, might have to finesse it some."

A plane rumbled overhead, a low and vast-winged shadow blotting out the clouds, turning as it rose for takeoff.

Dima was headed for terminal parking, the garages closest to the airport. Convenient but pricey at fifty dollars a day. *Doesn't matter*, Harmony thought, *she's not planning on ever coming back*. Harmony slid up closer behind her, carefully narrowing the distance.

A ticket machine popped and whirred and spat out a rectangle of cardstock. Harmony plucked it, tucking it into the Hemi Cuda's sun visor, and a gate swung high to let her through.

"I'll scrub the record of your license plate when you leave," Kevin said. "That'll take me a little more time, but it shouldn't be an issue if you don't draw too much attention."

Remains to be seen, she thought.

She prowled behind the Escalade, following Dima's lead up a tight, winding ramp boxed in by naked concrete. The first floor was closed off, filled to capacity. So was the second floor. The third offered the promise of a few open spaces, with an open gate next to an electronic sign on wheels. The sign blinked out a message, amber letters on black, advising drivers that there was more space open on the rooftop level.

This was good enough for Dima. The Escalade thumped as it leveled out and squeezed through the open gate. Harmony followed, stopping just a few feet ahead. She kept the car running. Every move she made from this moment on was a gamble, and now she was leveraging time versus risk.

She bit back a groan as she stepped out of the car, her broken toes igniting with volcanic pain. She put one hand on the sleek black hood to steady herself and hobbled as fast as she could manage. A triangular rubber block held the electronic sign in place. She kicked it aside with her good foot and hauled it backward, using it as a makeshift blockade across the entrance. Any more travelers who came this way would just keep going, circling around on their way to the upper deck. Passengers leaving the airport on this level would still be a problem, but at least she'd cut down the number of potential witnesses.

A sharp stab of panic hit her as she got back in the Hemi and slithered around the next bend. All she saw was a dusty car graveyard, row after row of sleeping cars under dimly flickering lights, no sign of the Escalade.

There. There it was, tinted cockpit looming above its low-slung neighbors, the back door hissing open. Harmony kept things slow, headlights off; she wanted to get close before she made her move, but the acoustics in the garage turned whispers into roars. Thankfully, Dima wasn't on high alert; she was more focused on wrestling a pair of enormous, overstuffed suitcases from the back of her ride. She wasn't leaving anything behind, at least not anything valuable.

Harmony lined up the Hemi and stared. Her fingers drummed the steering wheel.

A psychic ripple flitted through the air. Mind to mind, the slightest touch of gossamer. Dima turned. She froze in the open aisle, a suitcase in each hand, and locked eyes with Harmony.

Harmony stomped on the gas, and the Hemi Cuda's engine roared like a panther.

CHAPTER FOUR

Harmony did the math. Speed. Angle. Distance. It was an equation. Most things were. She could have bounced Dima off the Hemi Cuda's hood, sent her flying, put the muscle car in reverse and finished her off for good. Thinking about the role Dima had played in Nadine's operations, not to mention her track record of unsolved murders, stoked a small fire of temptation.

But that wasn't the job. So as the Hemi turned into a missile on wheels, blazing down the aisle between the rows of tight-packed cars, she kept her hands on the wheel and watched Dima's moves. The accountant started to double back, to throw herself clear. She wouldn't make it. So Harmony nudged the wheel just slightly off-course, making sure to miss.

The Hemi slammed into one of Dima's suitcases, blasting it open, littering the oil-stained floor with fluttering papers and clothes and broken antiques. Dima lunged out of the way and hit the ground on her elbow, rolling out of sight between a pair of cars, while Harmony stomped on the brakes. The Hemi squealed, swerving and drawing twin jagged lines of tire rubber, throwing her against the seatbelt. She held the wheel with one hand and kept it under control until the ride shook to a dead stop. She shoved the door open, pulling her Sig, nearly buckling to one knee when her broken foot touched down on the dirty concrete. It felt like her toes were crawling with fire ants, biting with razor teeth and pumping her full of poison.

She poked her head up — then dropped when Dima opened fire, a pair of bullets smashing into the Hemi Cuda's armor-plated hull. The crumpled shells left dimples in the jet-black steel. Harmony popped up, aiming for a sprinting shadow. Her retort blasted out the back window of a minivan, shredding the stick-outline stickers of a happy family.

She held her next shot. The shadow was gone. The garage acoustics bounced Dima's fluttering footsteps off the concrete pillars, making them sound like they were coming from five directions at once.

She's running. Dima could take the stairs or the elevators to reach the airport terminals. Once she did, safely surrounded by federal security and crowds of witnesses, she'd be out of Harmony's reach for good. Harmony risked raising her head out of cover, eyes hard, scanning fast for the closest way out. She found it to her right, lights softly glowing above the doors of an elevator bank. Two hundred feet away, give or take, with no trace of Dima but the echoes of her soft-soled shoes.

Harmony took the gamble. She limped toward the elevators, aiming to cut her quarry off at the pass. She had a perfect line of fire. She just needed Dima to show herself.

The footsteps faded, echoing into silence.

Flesh prickled along the back of Harmony's neck.

She has to run if she wants to live. Only one reason she'd change course.

Harmony froze, her nerves on edge, ears perked. Now she focused on everything *but* the elevators, her gaze slowly sweeping across the lanes of parked cars and the narrow gaps and pockets of shadow in-between. The moment of hesitation saved her life. Her only warning was a sudden scrambling sound and the rumble of knuckles against metal as Dima came at her, launching herself over the hood of a pickup truck and throwing herself down on the crouching agent. They hit the concrete together, grappling for Harmony's gun while she fought for leverage. Dima's hand clamped around her throat and squeezed hard, fingers digging in tight.

She spat a single spiraling word, something blasphemous that speared into Harmony's ear like a corkscrew. Harmony's mind exploded. The world turned into a wash of static and hornet-stings.

"You hear that sizzling sound?" Dima hissed. "That's your synapses burning out. I'm sending you straight to hell in a cardboard box, bitch."

Harmony couldn't breathe. Wasn't sure if it was from the spell or the slender hand still squeezing her throat, crushing her windpipe. She felt fingers pulling at her gun but that was the least of her worries right now. She couldn't do anything about the curse as it carved through her defenses and into the meat of her brain, not with Dima on top of her.

First things first, then. Fear would kill her faster than anything, and pain was only pain. She pushed past them both, searching for some untouched and tiny spot deep inside of herself. Her situation was a puzzle. Puzzles had solutions.

Opening move, she thought. *Positional advantage*.

Harmony shifted her weight, sliding along on one hip, getting gravity on her side. She rolled up while Dima flipped over and down.

Now, the gambit.

She let go of her gun. Dima wanted it. She could have it; it would steal her focus for a few precious seconds. Harmony stayed close, using her weight to stop Dima from turning the weapon around.

Retaliation, she thought.

Harmony broke the clinch just long enough to rise off the garage floor. Dima, holding the Sig by the barrel, quickly turned it around in her grip. She almost had a shot. Harmony's elbow dropped down hard and slammed into Dima's teeth. Dima squealed, fumbling the gun as she rolled and spat broken porcelain and blood onto the concrete.

And alchemy.

She'd stolen time, and she put it to work conjuring her power. The old familiar mantra echoed in her ears: *earth, air, fire, water, garb me in your raiment—*

But there is so much more, answered a voice that wasn't entirely hers, echoing from the cave of her heart. It was the voice of her hunger, her constant companion since the day Nadine forced it upon her. Companion and partner, now. She used it, sucking in Dima's curse and drinking it down, spinning it in her stomach. She rewrote it by instinct like a composer with a quill, jotting down a note here, crossing one out there, changing its tone and key while keeping the spirit of the original piece. Making it her own.

Dima sat up, sputtering, blood drooling from one corner of her twisted mouth. She raised the stolen gun.

Harmony flicked out her fingertips. The curse boiled forth, a swarm of seething, burning gnats, and smashed into Dima with crushing force. She flopped onto her back and seized up, her limbs spasming, scarlet froth spilling from her gaping mouth. Then she fell still.

Harmony sat motionless, empty now, watching her. Dima's chest slowly rose and fell. Just unconscious, not dead. *Mission accomplished*, she thought.

Then the backlash hit. Harmony listed to one side and threw up on the garage floor while her stomach twisted itself into knots. She waited for the worst of it to pass, then tapped her earpiece with a trembling finger.

"Harmony here," she rasped. "Dima's down. Could use some help bringing her in."

"En route, be there in five," Jessie said in her ear. "You okay, partner?"

My powers are changing. Evolving. And I have no idea why, and no idea what I'm turning into.

"I'm fine," Harmony said. "Flight crew, get the *Imperator* ready for takeoff. Very special package inbound."

The trunk of the Hemi Cuda whistled open. Dima — gagged, with zip ties binding her wrists and ankles — squealed furiously at her captors. Harmony and Jessie stood side by side, looking down at her.

"I'm going to take that gag out of your mouth," Jessie said, "so that we can have a reasonable conversation like mature adults. If I even hear the hint of the first syllable of a spell out of you, I'm going to finish what my partner started and knock out the rest of your teeth. We understand each other? We good?"

Dima nodded, sullen. Jessie bent her head forward, untied the cloth, and let her spit it out.

"Who *are* you people?" Dima demanded. "You're not with Nadine."

"No, we aren't." Harmony snipped the ties binding her ankles. "What we are, to you, is a badly needed lifeline. In fact, we're your best chance of survival."

Jessie lifted Dima out of the trunk as easily as a sack of groceries and set her feet down on the steel deck. Dima turned slowly, wide-eyed, taking in the belly of the converted plane and the banks of screens along the hull.

"And...where am I?"

"This is a little like *Cash Cab*," Jessie said. "Except instead of a taxi, it's a plane. And instead of answering trivia questions, you're going to help us take down your boss. Oh, and if you get the answers wrong, I'm throwing you out the door at thirty-six thousand feet. Without a parachute."

"She's not bluffing," Harmony added.

Dima gave them a derisive snort, her pert nose crinkling.

"Of course she is. I'm no good to you dead."

"You're no good to us alive-but-uncooperative, either," Jessie told her. "And considering the body count you've racked up, not to mention all the shady shit you've done for Nadine and her people, you probably want to avoid giving me any more reasons to imagine your head on a plate. So. Ready to play?"

CHAPTER FIVE

As a gesture of goodwill, Harmony cut Dima's wrists loose. Dima promptly crossed her arms tight across her chest, glaring daggers.

"Why would I turn against my mistress? Even if I had the desire to, which I do not, the worst you can do is kill me. Nadine's vengeance stretches far beyond the grave and her reach is infinite."

Harmony had learned that every interrogation was different. Sometimes you could offer a suspect some slack and plenty of line, hoping they twisted themselves up in it and gave something away. Other times called for shock treatment: lay all the cards out on the table, let them know what *you* know, and let the truth — just how deeply they're screwed — sink in.

"Nadine is rolling up her operations and going to ground," Harmony said. "She thinks she's under attack, possibly by people within her own organization, and paranoia has her clawing at shadows. Her favorite assassin has gone missing, along with five million dollars of Nadine's money."

Dima's almond eyes widened. "How do you—"

Harmony cut her off with a snap of her fingers and nodded to Kevin, seated over at the command console. He brought up a spreadsheet on the biggest monitor, magnified so Dima could read the first lines from a distance. Her jaw slowly fell.

"These are Nadine's personal financial records," Harmony said, "which you, and you alone, were entrusted with protecting."

"Remember that office party when you got a bout of sudden food poisoning?" Jessie asked her. "We robbed you blind and you never even knew we were there."

"You—" Dima shook her head for a moment, reeling at the implications. "You still haven't told me who you are."

Harmony gestured to the screen. "But I did. We're your lifeline. Nadine doesn't know that her accountant got sloppy. And as long as you cooperate, she never has to find out."

"Alternatively," Jessie said, "we can drop you right on her doorstep and let her know how you sold those records to us behind her back."

Dima's face went pale. One corner of her mouth twitched. She still couldn't take her horrified eyes off the screen.

"I...I have never, ever betrayed—"

Jessie put a hand on her shoulder. "The truth isn't important. What matters is what Nadine believes. And right now she's hunting for a fox in the henhouse."

"You know that," Harmony added. "That's why you were running. Because five million dollars is missing and Nadine's out for blood. She's either going to blame you or the Basilisk."

Jessie's hand tightened on Dima's shoulder.

"Erich Hausler was practically a son to her," Jessie said. "You? You're the hired help. Trusted, valued, sure. But expendable. She'll blame you. She'll capture you. Then she'll torture you until you tell her where her money is. And since you have no idea...well, she's going to torture you a *lot*. Unfair, but it's not like you don't have it coming."

Dima tried to regain a tiny bit of composure, just a scrap. She wrenched her gaze away from the screen and shrugged Jessie's hand from her shoulder, turning to face Harmony.

"Your partner doesn't seem to like me very much."

"I like you even less," Harmony said. "She's just more expressive. You have a choice to make: we can save your life tonight and put you back in Nadine's good graces, or we can nail your coffin shut. Completely up to you."

Dima's eyes narrowed.

"Let's say I take your offer."

"Wise choice."

"Assuming you can hold up your end of the bargain — and to be clear, I don't believe that for a second until you show me some proof — what do you want in return? If you're looking for Nadine, I can't help you. She contacts me when she wants something, not vice versa, and on the rare occasions we meet in person I don't get much in the way of advance warning."

"She's just taken a massive financial hit. We both know it." Harmony nodded up at the spreadsheet on the screen. "But even before the escrow money disappeared, along with her favorite killer, she was directing you to sell off assets. A business here, a piece of artwork there. Your boss needs liquid capital."

Dima sighed. "I told Nadine not to take risks right now. She insisted it wasn't a risk at all, that Hausler would just use the five million to get access to the auction, and he'd come home with the cash and with the prize. Is he dead, by the way?"

"Very," Harmony said. "And if she hasn't found what's left of his body yet, she's not going to."

"I'm more concerned about his soul."

"If you found yourself in hell after bitterly disappointing Nadine," Jessie said, "how would you react?"

"I'd run and never stop running," Dima said.

Jessie waved her hand, a *well, then* gesture. Dima nodded in silent understanding.

"Do you have the money?"

Harmony countered her question with a question. "What is Nadine saving up for?"

"Just because I guard her bankbook doesn't mean I guard her secrets. All I know is she's planning some large-scale operation involving the House of Dead Roses, and it's going to be expensive. Very expensive. Given the Basilisk's failure, it's probably off the table now."

"Or she'll go after what she wants twice as hard," Harmony said. "If so, she's going to need you to find more sources of revenue, fast."

"And?"

Jessie moved to stand behind Dima. Looming, quiet, standing inside her personal space and her shadow, close enough for Dima to feel the hot breath on the back of her neck. Harmony closed in from the other side, holding her gaze.

"From this day forward," Harmony told her, "you work for us. You'll report every contact you have with Nadine. Every call, every email, every request she makes of you."

"You want me to be your double agent."

"And in return, we'll keep you safe from her."

Dima answered her with a bitter little laugh.

"Nobody is *safe*. Not in this world or any other. Not from a monster like her."

"You can take your chances on your own," Harmony replied, "but we already discussed how that's going to end for you. You know I'm right."

Dima was silent for a moment. Her gaze fell, darting down and to the left, as she contemplated her choice of fates.

"And no more recreational murders," Jessie said. "Consider yourself officially de-fanged."

"You ask a great deal of me."

"Considering what you're getting in return, you should be thanking us for the great bargain."

Dima's eyes flashed. She looked to Harmony.

"Let's talk about that. What I get in return. You're certain you can shield me from Nadine's wrath?"

"Ms. Chakroun," Harmony said, "we're about to put you solidly in her good graces. This is a win-win scenario."

The *Imperator* touched down in Nevada, boiling down from the desert sky. Harmony didn't leave the plane. She didn't want to be back here. Not this soon. Maybe not ever, though she knew she'd go where the job took her. Cold night wind billowed into the belly of the plane, prickling her skin and making her toes ache.

They left Dima on the tarmac, armed with a plan and a warning.

"So what's stopping me from taking these lovely gifts and walking away?" Dima had asked during the choppy descent, working every angle.

"We still have Nadine's financial records," Harmony told her. "The ones you were supposed to guard with your life, remember? And as long as we do, we can destroy you with a single phone call. You play fair with us, we'll play fair with you."

"Playing fair" wasn't part of Dima's vocabulary. But blackmail she understood.

Damn it, why didn't I cut and run sooner? I should be on a jet bound for Paris right now, drinking wine in first class and celebrating my good fortunes. But no, I had to be greedy. I suppose these are those "wages of sin" I keep hearing about.

No putting this off any longer. And if she played her cards right, pleasant days might come again. She clung to what little hope she had left as she dialed her phone.

"Dima," Nadine's voice seethed in her ear. "Where the hell have you *been?* I have been calling you and calling you—"

Moment of truth. She could either side with Vigilant, turning traitor, or tell the truth and throw herself on Nadine's mercy.

Easy choice. Nadine didn't have any mercy in her. Dima would take the option that let her survive the night and worry about tomorrow when it came. Just like always.

"Following a lead on Hausler's location," she said. "It was a trap. Enemy operatives were waiting for us."

"Your bodyguards?"

"Terminated. They gave their lives to cover my escape."

"They did their jobs, then," Nadine said. "I'll get you new ones. Nature of the enemy?"

"Human."

Nadine fell silent for a moment while Dima held her breath. She thought she was on safe ground a second ago, but she felt the demoness's mercurial mood shifting on a single word.

"*Harmony,*" she purred. "She's just aching for a rematch. One last dance. I'm almost inclined to oblige her."

"I...don't know who that is," Dima said.

"Not your business to know. Don't ask questions, just obey me. You're in Nevada?"

"Yes, ma'am."

"The Roses safehouse in Reno. Go there. Stay put and wait for further instructions. In the meantime, leave darling Erich to me. Your job is simple: *find my fucking money.*"

CHAPTER SIX

Part of a video wall in Vigilant's conference room kept track of Nadine's known investments, cross-checking them against the stolen financials. They began, on the night the Basilisk died, as a constellation of stars shimmering across American soil. One by one, night after night, they winked out until only darkness remained.

Nothing they could do now but wait for Dima's call. Nothing Harmony could do but train. Her wounds kept her off her feet — the only cure for broken toes was time — and Jessie made it clear that she wasn't leaving the building again until she was mission-ready.

Sitting on her hands was a crueler form of torture than what she'd suffered from the Basilisk's hammer. After all, Nadine was hardly the only threat burrowing up from the pits of hell. A cemetery had been unearthed in the Midwest, every coffin opened, every corpse taken. A serial killer on the East Coast was leaving sigils carved into his victims' flesh, occult markings linked to the Manson Family and the Zodiac murders. Residents of a tiny nowhere town in California had been plagued by obscene, threatening phone calls, and the callers spoke with pitch-perfect copies of the victims' own voices.

And she couldn't help.

She watched as teams rolled out, then came back again, sometimes bloodied, sometimes with trophies, while she sat on the sidelines. So she trained. Body and mind, rising at dawn and ending long after midnight. She did pull-ups while listening to lectures on criminology and forensic chemistry, anything to push the boundaries of what she already knew. On the firing range, leaning on a crutch and sighting down her weapon with one hand, she wore earbuds under her hearing protection and audited a class on crime scene analysis. By night she studied cold cases and filled her sleep with unanswered questions.

"You know this isn't sustainable."

Harmony was huddled over a microscope, listening to a forensics seminar while she studied a trace sample of dirt, scribbling in a notebook at her side. She hadn't heard the door open. April sat in her chair, in the doorway, and Harmony greeted her with a blank look.

"Driving yourself into the ground won't heal your foot any faster," April said.

"I'm a damaged machine. Not a broken one. I can fix myself."

"You're not a machine."

"Agree to disagree." Harmony made a note on her pad, squinting into the microscope. "Neurons, gray matter, moving parts of muscle and bone fueled by protein. By definition, a machine is—"

"You know perfectly well that isn't the point. Dehumanizing yourself isn't going to make you stronger."

Harmony looked up from the microscope. She fixed her bloodshot eyes on April.

"My human parts," she said, "are the parts that keep failing."

April watched Harmony work for a while in silence. Her aged hands rested upon a folder in her lap.

"And hurting yourself is going to fix that, is it?" she asked, her voice softer now.

"I'm *training*."

"You're punishing yourself for being injured in the line of duty."

"No, I'm punishing myself for—" Harmony paused. "I mean, no. I'm not."

The corner of her mouth twitched. She looked over at April, then at the folder on her lap.

"Did you need something?"

April took hold of one of her chair's wheels. Her other hand stayed firmly in place, holding the folder shut.

"A conversation you're not ready to have yet," April replied. "Tell me, have you ever heard of *kintsugi*?"

Harmony shook her head.

"It's a Japanese art form. You should look into it. It might be...enlightening."

She turned her chair around and rolled out, leaving Harmony to her work.

Days became weeks, passing in a glaze of sweat and exhaustion. Harmony lost the crutch, walking on tender toes as her body knit itself back together. Then she ran. Every day, on the treadmill in Vigilant's basement gym, pushing her muscles and her mind harder than she ever had before.

In her mind's eye she shot Geordie Tynes a hundred times. When she wasn't thinking about him, she was thinking about Nadine.

Harmony's hunger was coming back. She'd have to feed soon if she didn't want it to shatter her from inside and make it impossible to tap into her magic. She could call Romeo; it wasn't like anyone would bat an eye, now that the whole team knew her dirty secret.

Or maybe I could just let it burn, she thought, her running shoes thumping as she tapped a button and kicked the treadmill's speed up another notch. Her arms pumped, lungs searing, her gaze fixed on something a thousand miles away.

Jessie was over on the weight bench, pumping iron, wearing a t-shirt with the sleeves cut off. Her dark skin glistened, muscles taut as iron, as she lifted a barbell laden with heavy plates.

"I'm ready," Harmony said. "Give me a mission."

"You're not," Jessie grunted, pushing the weights in the air. "You need a full medical screening before I let you go back in the field."

Harmony powered down the treadmill. She leaned against it, gasping for breath.

"Look at me," she said. "I'm *ready*."

"You're ready when some doctors — who know a lot more than me — get a look at you and *say* you're ready. I'm not bringing you back in the field just to get you hurt all over again.

Just keep it chill for a few more days, a week tops. Can you do that for me?"

Harmony's shoulders sagged. She mopped her face with a hand towel.

"Yeah," she said.

"Good. I like when we're in agreement." Jessie took a deep breath, straining. "Now do me a favor: put another couple of plates on this bar for me."

Harmony could wait if she had to. She had more training to do anyway. She threw herself back into endless study, endless work, pushing herself to the limit until she fell asleep exhausted, then got up to do it all over again.

Then she got the phone call.

It came in through an old, forgotten relay and landed in a shuttered office somewhere in the bowels of Washington, DC. On paper, Harmony and Jessie had FBI credentials, thanks to Vigilant's original incarnation as a shadow counterpart to the Bureau. They didn't use them much anymore, but the old backdoors and cover identities still held solid. Someone out there wanted to talk to Agent Black, someone with the juice to leave a robotic voicemail on a dusty phone in a silent room.

It felt strange. Harmony saw her life as a before and after split: *before* was the time when she and Jessie were Vigilant Lock's lapdogs, unwittingly working for the very demonic forces they'd sworn to fight against, and *after* was when they brought the entire sham crashing down and took over Vigilant, turning it into the covert operations group it was always supposed to be. Cryptic messages and veiled phone calls to unlisted numbers in DC felt like before-time business. A ghost from the past.

Alone in her office, in the light of a green-shaded desk lamp, Harmony dialed the number and waited. It rang three times, then clicked.

"Hello, Harmony," Nadine said. "I'm glad you got my message. You're very hard to find."

"So are you," Harmony replied. Her stomach was tight as a funeral drum, her mouth dry.

Nadine giggled.

"Was that you and your little friends, playing games out in the desert? You know, for a moment I almost thought *you* stole my money. My accountant reassured me that you don't have that kind of skill."

Harmony bit back a sigh of relief. Dima was holding up her end of the bargain, running interference.

"We were hunting bigger game than you."

"As if such a thing could even exist," Nadine purred into Harmony's ear. "How many times a day do you think about me?"

"As little as possible."

"You are a *terrible* liar."

A cold fury grew in the pit of Harmony's stomach, a swirling miasma of dark clouds preparing to become a storm. She took deep breaths.

"What do you want, Nadine?"

"What I've always wanted. The House of Dead Roses is expanding its reach, Harmony. Opportunities are everywhere. I want you on board."

Harmony barked out an incredulous laugh. "Excuse me?"

"I. Want. You." Nadine let the words hang in the air for a moment. "Darling, I put my hunger inside of you. I carved my initials into your heart. That's a forever thing. Stop fighting it. Come and surrender yourself to me. I can feed you. I can teach you. I'll make you strong."

"You oppose everything that I stand for. Literally everything."

"Not true. Do you think I want to destroy your world, Harmony? I'm a daughter of the Choir of Lust. I need humanity. I want to cultivate it."

"You want to conquer it."

"Six of one, half a dozen of the other. Look at the way your leaders have been running this planet. Can you honestly tell me I'd do a worse job?"

"You're a fucking rapist," Harmony snapped.

The line went silent.

"Don't you *ever*," Nadine growled, her voice soft and lethal, "judge me by human standards. I am not a talking monkey. I am a being so far evolved beyond your blinkered, parochial perspective that your limited human ethics are meaningless to me."

"I'll judge you by any standard I damn well please."

"Think on this. I'm winning, Harmony. I don't do anything *but* win. Every single time we dance, I come out on top."

Harmony thought grimly of the headless Basilisk and his dead henchmen, left to burn. *Not every time*, she thought.

"I can either find your little social club and wipe you out," Nadine continued, "down to the last of you, but only once I have the time to get around to it. Because you're not a threat to me. You're a mosquito, and mosquitoes eventually get swatted. Or you can join the winning team and get right with me. Leave the old woman and the computer geek behind, but you can bring the bitch with you."

"Watch it."

"What?" Nadine chuckled. "She's the spawn of the King of Wolves. Literally a bitch. It wasn't a pejorative. You know what your problem is, dear? You take everything so seriously."

"You know what your problem is?" Harmony countered.

"Do tell."

"Me. Because I'm going to *end* you."

"You're adorable. Give me a call when you're ready to put your foolish pride on the shelf and learn your proper place. Come to me, Harmony. Come to Mommy."

Harmony spent the rest of the night alone on the firing range, feeding rounds into a Benelli tactical shotgun, tearing paper silhouettes into ragged shreds as the weapon kicked against her shoulder. By the end she had a splotchy, purple bruise and every pull of the trigger sparked a starburst of pain, but she didn't mind. It gave her something to focus on.

The next morning, another unexpected call came in. This time straight to Harmony's personal cell. She didn't recognize the number. The voice on the other end was young, breathless, and scared.

"Miss Black? Um, we don't know each other, my name's Melanie and I'm Daniel Faust's apprentice."

Faust. Her self-proclaimed nemesis and all-around pain in the butt. Harmony closed her eyes and pinched the bridge of her nose.

"Daniel's hurt," Melanie said, "really...*really* bad. He said if I was ever in serious danger and he couldn't help, that I should call you."

Harmony opened her eyes. *Unexpected*, she thought. She held her silence and let Melanie fill in the gaps.

"We're stuck in this little hospital out in Phoenix, and some really bad guys are looking for us. I know I'm asking a lot, but—"

"I'll be on the next flight out."

If Jessie wouldn't give her a mission, she'd make her own.

CHAPTER SEVEN

Harmony flew to Phoenix alone, leaving a note behind. It was a quick mission, in and out of the fire; she shot a tiger-spirit, exorcised a medieval knight, saved her former enemy's life, and came back home again. She felt her heart pumping for the first time in months. She felt like she mattered for a little while. The next morning, she had to face the music.

"When, exactly," Jessie asked, her turquoise eyes blazing, "did you decide to start acting like me?"

She sat across from Harmony in Vigilant's conference room, with its U-shaped table of smoked glass and a video wall streaming constant updates from their teams in the field.

"Meaning?"

"Going rogue, taking on a solo op without telling anyone, vanishing for a day and a half and coming back like nothing happened. There is exactly one person allowed to pull that bullshit around here, and you're looking at her. She's me."

"Someone needed help," Harmony said. "That's what I do. I help. If I'm not out in the field, making a difference, I am *nothing.*"

Jessie held her gaze for a long moment, contemplative.

"I really wish you didn't believe that," Jessie said.

The conference room door slid open and Kevin poked his head in. He was out of breath, chestnut hair mussed like he'd just run all the way across the building.

"Dima Chakroun's calling in on a burner," he gasped. "She's holding on line two."

Jessie's hand slapped the phone on the conference table. Clinking glasses and the din of low conversation washed through the room.

"Speak," she said.

"Can't talk long," Dima whispered over the speaker, "but I've got something for you. Nadine's making a move. She thinks she's figured out a way to address her shortfall of cash."

"What's the plan?" Harmony asked.

"A heist. I don't know what she's after — not yet — but she's talking about it like it's the solution to all her problems. I assume you don't want those problems solved."

"Indeed we do not," Jessie concurred.

"Well, you're in luck. I've managed to worm my way into her good graces to the point that she's giving me a little more responsibility. I'm in charge of financing this operation. I'll be in the loop from start to finish."

"Which means," Harmony said, "you can get us inside."

"If I do this, will you let me off the hook?"

Jessie and Harmony shared a look across the table. Not a chance. They'd use Dima until she was used up, and if she was lucky they'd retire her with a bullet instead of tossing her back to Nadine. Still, hope was a powerful motivator.

"We'll talk about it," Harmony said, "after you deliver on your end of the deal. Where is this 'heist' supposed to be happening?"

"Chicago, and the timeline is razor-tight. How fast can you get here?"

"How fast do you need us?" Jessie asked.

"I propose we discuss the details over dinner. Say, nine?"

Jessie shot a questioning look at Harmony. Harmony gave a firm nod in response.

"We'll be there," Jessie said.

"Splendid. I'll make reservations and send you the details. I only eat at Michelin-starred restaurants, so please make an attempt to dress appropriately."

Jessie broke the connection, then looked to Harmony and Kevin.

"I'll go and tell April," she said. "Kevin, pack an overnight bag. We're going wheels-up in one hour."

Harmony swallowed around a lump in her throat. She held her silence until Kevin disappeared from the doorway.

"Me too?" she asked.

Jessie let out a heavy sigh. She walked over and put a firm hand on Harmony's shoulder.

"You know that scene in every cop show where the chief is all, 'You're too close to this case! You're in too deep! Now hand over your badge and your gun?'"

"Yeah...?" Harmony said.

"See, I hate that. It never made any sense to me. I get the best results when I take shit *incredibly* personally, and I think my sheer petty vindictiveness should be a shining example for the rest of you."

She pulled out a chair next to Harmony and sat down, swiveling to face her. Jessie's smile faded along with her usual casual snark. There was something deeper in her expression now, her eyes like radioactive oceans as she leaned close and lowered her voice.

"There's a chance, not a guarantee but a pretty good chance, that this gig could point us right toward Nadine's hiding place."

"Agreed," Harmony whispered.

"I know, after all the crap she's put you through...I know you need this. So yeah, I'm declaring you officially back on duty, effective five minutes ago."

She nodded to the conference room door.

"C'mon, bestie," Jessie said, "let's go ruin a heist."

The *Imperator* shuddered down through smoke and storm, the steel deck rattling under Harmony's feet. She'd spent most of the flight in a fold-down jump seat, clinging to a can of ginger ale and feeling green around the gills. Aselia, their Cajun pilot, sounded like was talking through a tin can as her voice crackled over the speakers.

"Sorry for the rough ride, y'all. Mother Nature ain't too happy today. Good news is, we're getting ready for our final descent, and we should be touchin' down at O'Hare in twenty. I do suggest buckling up. That means you too, Jessie."

Harmony's stomach lurched as the cargo plane shook and then dropped, plummeting like the first dive of a roller coaster before leveling out with a whine from the overtaxed engines.

The cloud cover broke, roiling, spreading wide to reveal the gray, cold, wet city below.

Chicago shivered in the icy rain. It clung to the curling ribbon of Lake Michigan's shoreline for comfort, bunched up tight and tall and then sprawling, spilling to the west, a frozen flood of black asphalt, tomb-gray granite, and strobing red lights that swayed in the stormy wind. Harmony had the sense of vast engines in motion, invisible webs moving people and money in an intricate dance like the lines of a summoning sigil.

The city became a tapestry of blue neon light in her mind's eye. Now she saw engines inside of engines. Hierarchies of dominance and instruments of social control, gears churning to drive productivity, to drive profits, with human lives just one tiny column on a vast spreadsheet of costs and returns.

So inject some chaos. Change it up and see what happens.

Harmony blinked. The thought slipped into her head unbidden, and it wasn't hers. She didn't think like that. Bringing order to chaos was her job and her calling.

But she couldn't deny, as the *Imperator* descended like a steel raptor from the storm-cast sky, that she really, truly, wanted to break something.

Dima asked to meet at a place called Sepia, over on North Jefferson Street. Harmony and Jessie took a cab over from the airport. The restaurant lived up to its name, with exposed brick walls, deep wooden details, and swirling slabs of tan marble with chocolate streaks. The restaurant had been built from the husk of a nineteenth-century print shop, and it kept the old, sturdy bones of the place intact.

The accountant met them just inside the door. She wore a glittery scarlet cocktail dress that hugged her curves like a second skin, and she gave them a dour look as she approached.

"Really?" Dima said. "I said to dress appropriately."

Jessie was wearing a trendy blazer with jeans and an aquamarine top that matched her eyes, along with her ubiquitous dark glasses. Harmony had opted for her usual, a tailored men's suit with a salmon necktie. She glanced down at herself.

"What's wrong with my—"

"She's underdressed and you look like a fed. You know what? Never mind." She hailed a passing hostess. "Chakroun, party of three? We have a reservation for private dining."

The hostess led them to an alcove in the back of the restaurant where a chandelier draped in chaotic, ornate wickerwork dangled above a table for eight. The wall curled to embrace the table, appointed in a sprawling sepia-tone design that made Harmony think of the runes around a magician's circle. Dima casually flipped a hand toward the far side of the table while she pulled back a chair.

"I bought the room out," she explained. "No sense having anyone listen in on our discussion. Or being seen with the two of you."

"We could have met somewhere more private," Jessie pointed out.

Dima unfurled her cloth napkin and draped it across her lap. "Nonsense. For one, I've had a very long day and I need to eat. For another, if I told you I wanted to meet behind closed doors, you'd anticipate an ambush. I don't need that kind of stress in my life, so I figured this would put you more at ease."

Harmony believed her, but she saw the third, unspoken reason.

"And this is for your own protection."

Dima glanced at her, raising one perfectly sculpted eyebrow. "Hm?"

"Unlike you," Harmony said, "you know we won't put civilians in danger. Meeting us in public keeps you safe, too."

"The thought did occur."

"Tell us about this heist," Jessie said.

"Hold," Dima said, raising a finger. A waiter swooped in, and she tilted the wine menu, tapping a line midway down the page. "We'll start with a bottle of the 2019 Ridge Monte Bello. Thank you."

Once he left, she stared at his back for a long moment, until she was sure he was out of earshot.

"Nadine's been in an absolute lather over that missing five million."

"She'd be in a lather over a missing five dollars," Jessie said.

"True enough. And she knows you were in Las Vegas the night everything went down. But don't worry. I threw her off the scent."

Harmony thought back to the phone call and Nadine purring in her ear. Her stomach clenched.

"Thanks for that," she said.

"It wasn't hard. Once she looked at the evidence, she knew it couldn't have been you. I just had to nod and smile a lot."

Harmony squinted at her. "Evidence? And what do you mean, *couldn't* have been us?"

"She found the remains of her beloved Erich Hausler," Dima said, "minus one head, and with extensive burn scars. I guess there was just enough left of his fingerprints to identify him."

In a heartbeat, Harmony was back there again. Her toes reduced to bloody pulp under Hausler's hammer, her wrists sliced up from her desperate attempt to cut herself free. She baited him into unleashing his power and then redirected his gaze...straight toward the onyx wall of glass, and his own reflection.

His head erupted. Chunks of shattered skull and torn chest hit Harmony's chest with the force of a heavyweight punch. A tidal wave of hot, steaming blood and gray jelly splashed across her face, flecks of gristle catching in her hair.

She snapped back to the present. Blinking, her heart racing. She remembered now how she felt in the moment, when she looked at her own reflection. She was a gore-drenched, wild-eyed nightmare, a harbinger of death, all civilization and pretense stripped away.

She had never felt so alive.

"It wasn't Hausler's corpse that clued her in," Dima continued. "It was the others, his little hench-pals. That's how Nadine figured out she's under attack by a rival from down under. She thinks it's some up-and-comer from the Court of Jade Tears, trying to make a name by knocking her down a few pegs."

That wasn't right. At all. Harmony tilted her head at Dima. "Explain."

Dima slipped an elegant hand into her purse, coming up with a cell phone.

"Apologies for bringing up crime-scene photos before dinner," she said. "It doesn't bother me, but I assume you ladies have more delicate constitutions than I do."

Jessie tugged down her dark glasses. Her eyes glowed in the soft light.

"You have no idea what I eat," Jessie told her. "And you don't want to find out."

Dima swallowed, hard, and flipped through her gallery of photographs. She showed them a corpse. Harmony recognized it instantly.

She was broken, bleeding, running on fumes, but she forced herself to fight with nothing but sheer willpower, taking on the rest of the Basilisk's half-demon thugs. One brought his pistol up. Her training told her to go for the gun, but her heart had a different idea.

She clamped her hand over his face and pulled. A torrent of thick, hot energy, a seething and crackling rope of black light, tore from his veins and turned Harmony's heart into a burning machine. Overclocked, all pistons pounding at a fever tempo.

Dima tapped the picture on the phone. The body was horrifically shriveled, like a human raisin. Empty of blood, empty of soul.

"What you're looking at," Dima said, "is the aftermath of a succubus attack."

Harmony curled her arms across her stomach.

"You don't see this sort of thing often, because, well...to be honest, most members of the Choir of Lust are dumb as doorknobs and they're kept down in hell for a reason. Bimbos and himbos galore, if you're into that sort of thing. The smart ones, like Nadine — or, if I absolutely must, Caitlin — know how to cover their tracks. This is the work of a powerhouse fledgling, a demon with raw power and no training."

"There could be another explanation," Harmony said. She didn't even believe herself.

Dima shook her head. "Trust me. Nadine knows the handiwork of her own kind. Also, there's this."

She scrolled to another photograph, another dead man. This one looked like a charcoal briquette in the vague shape of a human, petrified and splattered against a flame-charred wall.

Harmony remembered. She felt it all over again. The magic she pulled from the first cambion washed through her, hand to hand, veins to veins, her heart as the conduit. She unleashed a dark blue inferno, boiling from her skin like a living weapon.

"That's pure hellfire," Dima said. "It has a signature. An aftertaste, if you like. And humans can't wield pure hellfire, not without being consumed by it. This massacre was the work of a demon. One of Nadine's own."

CHAPTER EIGHT

The first course was served. Harmony chose the heirloom tomato panzanella, a lively Tuscan salad with chunks of dried bread, soft Italian mozzarella, and ripe, tangy tomatoes. Jessie opted for the steak tartare.

Harmony barely touched her plate. The thought of eating made her sick right now. She had wondered what she was mutating into, what her powers were becoming. And now she knew.

No, we don't, she corrected herself. *That's not how any of this WORKS. If Nadine spread her powers to everyone she kissed, there would be a legion of people like me out there. Infernal magic isn't contagious.*

Her scientific observations said one thing. Cold logic said the opposite. Objective truth, the one thing Harmony needed and craved, danced just out of her grasp.

Her phone vibrated against her hip. It was a text from Jessie, sitting right next to her. She clearly didn't want to air this in front of Dima. *U ok?*

Will be, Harmony texted back. She needed to focus on the mission.

Nothing mattered but the mission.

"What do you know about Ardentis Solutions?" Dima asked.

Harmony racked her brain. The name was vaguely familiar.

"Tech company, right? I read something about them winning a big Department of Defense contract last month."

"And the month before, and the month before that." Dima had also ordered the steak tartare. She lifted a glistening chunk of raw meat, laden with a glob of beef-fat jam, to her gently curling lips. "They've made a name for themselves providing low-cost, effective body armor for the military. They also produce armor packages for civilian vehicles, riot shields, less-than-lethal munitions..."

"Sounds like you don't approve," Jessie said.

"One of the first things Nadine taught me," Dima said, "is that foot soldiers are expendable. It's their job to die for their mistress, and they should be happy to do it."

"That include you?"

"*I* am not a foot-soldier. I'm the money."

"And what does Nadine want to steal from a defense factory?" Harmony asked. "Doesn't sound like she has much use for anything they make."

Dima's gaze dropped to the table. She sipped her glass of red wine, a frown playing on her dark lips.

"I don't actually know."

"The money," Jessie says, "doesn't know what she's been assigned to steal."

"It's not like that," Dima said, flustered. "I'm in charge of financing the operation, handling logistics, and hiring a crew. I'm not the only member of the Roses on board. She has Josh Orville heading up the actual heist plan, and...well, Nadine's being even more paranoid than usual, under the circumstances. Everyone is on a strict need-to-know basis. My part of the job doesn't require me to know what the target is, so...none of my business, as Nadine made perfectly clear when we last spoke. She had her claws around my neck at the time."

Harmony couldn't place the name, but Jessie looked surprised. "*The* Josh Orville?"

"The same," Dima replied.

Catching her partner's blank expression, Jessie explained. "Youngest player to ever win the World Series of Poker. Then he went and grabbed three more bracelets, just for good measure. Kid's incredible at the table; they call him the Mastermind."

"So does Nadine," Dima said, her voice dry. "But for quite different reasons. She met him at some tournament a few years back, at the Bast Club, and took a liking to him. He's been working under Nadine's...tutelage ever since, and he's got a rare gift for strategy. Every major Roses operation, at least for the past couple of years, has Josh Orville's fingerprints all over it."

Jessie and Harmony shared a glance. They didn't need to say a word, because they were thinking the same three words:

high-value target. If they wanted to force Nadine to come out and play, taking her "mastermind" off the table could do the trick.

"There's one other Rose in the mix," Dima continued, her nose wrinkling in distaste. "Ricky Corbin. He's Josh's self-appointed bodyguard and right-hand man."

"You don't like him," Harmony said. A statement, not a question.

"His own mother wouldn't like him. Ricky has two addictions: Nadine's kiss and crystal meth. Hard to say which one he's more loyal to. He's a cheap thug, but don't underestimate him: he lives on a hair trigger. I once watched him beat a man to death in a bar, a man twice his size, because Ricky didn't like the look on his face. Zero filter, zero restraint or compunction: he's an animal with a bit of crude cunning, which is just how Nadine likes her enforcers."

"What about the rest of the crew?" Jessie asked.

"That's my bailiwick. I'm supposed to hire all the assets we need from the local underworld, with a tiny upfront token payment and the rest of the share to be paid out upon completion of the job." Dima paused. "I have been clear about this, yes? Nobody is actually getting paid. Cleaning up the loose ends will be Ricky's job."

At first, the reasoning seemed obvious: Nadine was legendarily cheap, and if she could save money by recruiting local thugs and killing them off once the work was finished, she would. No question.

Except.

She also had a ferocious sense of pride, and she had built her own order in hell, the House of Dead Roses, with her own two hands. And while a valued specialist like Dima would be amply rewarded for her skills, Harmony couldn't imagine the rank-and-file members, psychotic devotees of Nadine's "love," were getting paid anything beyond survival wages in the first place.

It's not about minimal cost, Harmony deduced. *It's about minimal witnesses. Whatever she's after, it's something so hot she can't even risk her own people talking about it.*

If Josh Orville is her number one schemer right now, and the only one who knows exactly what we're stealing, he's probably the key player in her design. Ricky could go either way; like Dima said, foot soldiers are expendable. Nadine might be planning to kill him as soon as he mops up the hired help.

And then there was Dima herself.

"So Nadine just…decided you were due for more responsibility and a field promotion? Gave you this task out of nowhere?" Harmony asked.

Dima preened. "It was touch and go. For a while I was sure she suspected I was behind her missing money, but apparently I never left her good graces."

Sometimes Harmony marveled at how easily people who lied for a living could be taken in by another, better liar. She kept her thoughts to herself.

"Got two more spaces on your hiring list?" Jessie asked.

"I assumed as much," Dima said. "Just tell me who you want to be and where I'm supposed to know you from, and I'll get you into a meeting with Josh Orville. Just so we're clear, that is the *end* of my involvement. I'm already sticking my neck out for you people. If you're caught or exposed, I'll kill you myself just to prove my loyalty to Nadine."

Harmony contemplated her untouched glass of wine. She raised it slowly, staring at Dima over the crystal rim.

"Just so *we're* clear," Harmony countered, "you're going to do what we tell you, when we tell you to do it. And if you even think of betraying us, I will personally make sure Nadine learns about every single screw-up and every tiny bit of treachery that happened on your watch. We might roast in hell side by side, but your pit is going to be a lot hotter than mine."

Dima's cheeks paled. She looked from one woman to the other and back again.

"I never did get your names."

"No. You didn't."

"But you're Harmony Black."

Harmony stared at her from across the table, silent. Her lips tightened.

"She talks about you all the time," Dima said. "She's obsessed with you. Says she knows you better than you know yourself."

"Wrong," Harmony said.

"She says, deep down inside, you're just like her." Dima looked her up and down. "You know, up close, I can really see the resemblance."

Kevin had booked them a two-queen suite at the Fairmont Chicago, overlooking Millennium Park in the heart of the Loop. The halls were cold and clean, their room door opening onto an expanse of cool blue carpet shot through with black, jagged cracks like a bed of winter ice. From their window, Harmony gazed out into the urban night. People strolled along the side-walks, milling along the open paths of the park, and the cen-terpiece — an elephantine chrome sculpture that locals called "the Bean" — caught the reflection of a bone-shard moon along its curving metal skin.

Jessie swept the room for listening devices while Harmony used her phone to check for infrared emitters. It was standard tradecraft, a ritual they both knew by heart, and neither one said a word until they'd marked the room clear.

"Okay," Jessie said. "You want to talk about that?"

"Dima Chakroun is a dead woman walking and she doesn't even realize it."

"More likely than not, but I think you know that's not what I meant."

Harmony sat down on one of the beds. The ivory bedspread sank under her weight.

"The things she says I did, I can't do." Harmony frowned. She stared at her ghostly reflection in the silent television screen. "Or I can't do...the things that I remember doing that night. I've been over it again and again and there's no explanation that makes sense. I'm not a monster—"

"Hey, hey, whoa." Jessie sat down beside her. She reached out and took both of Harmony's hands in hers. "First of all, leave the value judgments at the door. Nobody's calling you a monster."

Harmony had been handling that job on her own. Her gaze fell to the ice-field carpet.

"Look at me," Jessie said. "Eyes up here. Hon.../ am a monster."

"You're not—"

"Uh-uh." Jessie pressed a fingertip against Harmony's lips. "Mouth closed, ears open. You're getting unusually-empathetic-Jessie tonight and this takes a lot of effort on my part. I was born a monster, thanks to my fucked-up serial killer parents and their equally fucked-up god. I am a monster, and I'll always be a monster. And I'm good with that. I *like* being who I am, what I am. And that is why I can speak to this point with a bit of hard-earned authority, all right?"

She lowered her hand, placing it back over Harmony's.

"You're going through some scary changes right now, and we don't have it all figured out. But we will. The important part is, you're still the same Harmony I've known for years. Still my partner, still my best friend." She looked her in the eye. "And if you turn evil, I'll put you down myself before you can hurt anybody. That help?"

Harmony blinked.

"Weirdly, it does."

"Yeah, I figured. I know how you think." Jessie gave a mock shudder. "Just what I need, your weird nerdiness rubbing off on me. C'mon, let's get some sleep. Tomorrow morning, we're going undercover."

CHAPTER NINE

Kevin was at their door at eight a.m. sharp, with a battered military surplus backpack over one shoulder and a metal-hulled briefcase in each hand. Harmony waved him in, shutting the door behind him and drawing the deadbolt.

"Jessie's finishing up in the shower," she said.

"No problem, I just need a second to set up."

He laid his cases on the closest rumpled bedspread and put his backpack on the credenza, pulling out a heavy-duty laptop. In a minute he had a secure connection open to the *Imperator*. April sat at the console, her grave expression filling the screen as she slipped her steel-rimmed bifocals on.

"Ladies," she said, "you have your work cut out for you this time."

Jessie emerged from the bathroom trailed by wisps of hot steam with a towel wrapped around her hair like a turban.

"Stopping a heist but we don't even know what the bad guys are trying to steal," she said. "Sounds like a usual workweek for us."

"Don't take the opposition lightly. Meet Joshua Orville, the current apple of Nadine's eye and the chief strategist for the House of Dead Roses."

Video clips blossomed on the screen. Josh wore dark glasses to the poker table and a perpetual sneer. In one clip, he responded to a losing hand by hurling a fistful of chips in his opponents' faces. In another, he celebrated victory by shaking up a bottle of champagne, popping the cork and making it rain foam all over the poker table. Rival players dove for cover as the shot froze mid-frame.

"Mister Orville is the *enfant terrible* of the gambling world. He's the John McEnroe of poker, with a bit less class and grace."

Harmony noted a zoom on one of the still images, the camera fixed on his curled fingers. What was left of them. He was missing two joints of the ring finger on his left hand, one joint of the middle finger on his right.

Jessie saw it too. "Nadine really loves that Yakuza shit, doesn't she?"

"Looks like he's failed her a few times," Harmony mused. "And she still made him her top strategist. Suggests his win rate is...higher than average."

"Don't take him lightly," April cautioned. "He's a born tactician and a keen student of human psychology. There's no indication that he's much of a physical threat, but then again, he doesn't need to be."

New images washed over the old ones, blossoming on the screen. First was a mugshot, though it could have been a mortuary photo for all the life in the subject's dull, blown-out pupils. He was so wasted he looked like a skeleton under a thin, stretched out canvas of tattooed and leathery flesh, all weird lumps and hard angles. Half of his front teeth were missing, the rest coated in caps of stainless steel.

"This is Richard Corbin," April said. "Goes by Ricky. Ricky is a very violent man. As far as we can tell, he started his career fresh out of juvenile hall, feeding his habit by robbing and killing drug dealers."

"That's a high-stakes game," Jessie mused.

"And he rarely lost. We're not sure exactly when Nadine brought him into the fold, but his last three arrests — two for aggravated assault, one for manslaughter — were derailed by some extremely well-paid lawyers."

Harmony frowned. "Why?"

"Guessing she wants to keep him around," Kevin said.

She shook her head and murmured, "But foot soldiers are expendable."

"Huh?" he said.

"Never mind. Sorry. Please, continue."

"We've only had time to do a few hours of opposition research," April said, "but there are enough bodies strewn in Ricky

Corbin's wake to fill a small graveyard. He kills for pleasure. By all accounts, he's quite good at it."

"And considering it's already his job to take us out once the heist is done..." Jessie said, her voice trailing off.

April nodded, her image in one small corner of the laptop screen. "Conduct yourselves accordingly."

"I was up all night putting your cover identities together," Kevin said, popping the hasps of one of his two briefcases. He paused. "...you're welcome. Anyway, it was a rush job. I'll do what I can to shore things up once I get back to the plane, but tread lightly. These personas are good, but they aren't bullet-proof."

He took out a pair of black leather folios, like the envelopes for the check at a fancy restaurant, and handed one to each of them. Harmony opened hers to find a row of credit cards, a Social Security card, and a driver's license, all carefully faded with artificial wear and tear. The opposite side of the folio held pocket litter: receipts from an out-of-state diner, scribbled notes, a faded page from a doctor's prescription pad, all to back up her story.

"Harmony, you're Julie Law, a professional shooter with a track record."

Harmony tugged out her new license and pursed her lips. "Reno?"

"Hey, the Vegas mob is still in all kinds of disarray," he said, "and Reno's their kissing cousin. I picked it because it'll be that much harder to check up on your story. Nobody knows anything in Nevada right now."

April chimed in. "That said, we've seeded a few stories and made them easy to find, like connecting you to a few unsolved missing persons cases. Anyone who digs into your background will find the telltale signs of a careful, methodical assassin."

"And since you're there as extra muscle," Kevin continued, "you can work your way into any part of the heist. You'll be right there when it goes down. Jessie, Dima's bringing you in as the wheelman."

"I can deal with that," she said.

"You're Ace Ridley, a local freelancer who hires out to Chicago's street gangs when they need a professional getaway driver.

Nothing fancy, not an underworld superstar, just a reliable operator with reliable wheels."

Kevin reached into the briefcase and handed her a pair of license plates. They were crusted with dirt, faded with wear; Harmony would swear they had been on the road for years, if she didn't know they'd been printed late last night. Kevin was good at his job.

"Pop these onto the Hemi," he said. "If anyone runs the plates, they'll lead to a flimsy cover identity. If they dig into that, they'll find your *real* cover identity."

"Like I'm a small-time player who didn't quite know how to cover her tracks," Jessie said, following.

"And if I'm guessing right, that's where they'll stop digging. You're both expendable, so it's not like they're going to vet you for a long-term career with the House of Dead Roses. All you need to do is convince these people that you're on the level and you can handle the job."

Oh, that's all, Harmony thought. Ricky's skeletal mugshot was still on the screen. Droplets of dried blood flecked the shoulder of his faded white tank top.

Kevin popped the hasps on the second briefcase.

"Just in case," he said, taking a pair of sleek pistols from the precision-cut foam inside the case. He spun them around, offering them grip first.

Harmony took hers, turned her hip, aimed at the floor on the other side of the room and stared down the sights. The weapon was a Sig Sauer P238, cast in shades of storm gray and black, compact enough to disappear in the palm of a hand.

"Nice thing about going undercover as criminals," Kevin said, "is that everyone's going to expect you to be strapped. Ammunition is hollow-point, and you've got two magazines each."

Jessie raised an eyebrow. "What, no radical-invasive-bone-shredding bullets, or whatever you usually send us out with?"

"Nope. Neither of you — neither of the people you're pretending to be, I mean — would be walking around with military-grade tech or dropping three figures on a single box of ammo. The better you fit in, the fewer questions they'll ask. The fewer questions they ask...well, you know."

He had more gifts. The first was an old favorite — an old favorite of Kevin's, at least: the latest version of the ballistic pen from Vigilant's skunkworks department.

"Same as before, but streamlined and a little more powerful," he explained, holding up the innocuous-looking fountain pen. "Cock the pocket clip back to ready it, press down to fire. The bottom of the pen is a spike made from aircraft-grade aluminum, propelled by a one-shot cartridge of CO_2."

Harmony took the pen. Jessie didn't argue: Harmony knew she had spent a frustrating afternoon practicing with the thing on the firing range before returning it to the skunkworks with a one-word report: "*Finicky.*"

Next he brought out a pair of sleek running shoes in sea-foam green. Jessie leaned closer.

"Just my size," she said. "Are these knife shoes? Tell me you finally made me a pair of knife shoes."

"Knife...shoes?" Kevin said, edging away from her.

"Yeah, you know. You click your heels together and knives stick out the front and you kick-stab people to death."

"I'll, uh, see if that's on the production schedule. But no. This is our new escape and evasion kit. Based it on an old OSS design from World War Two, actually. The classics never go out of style."

He peeled back one of the insoles to reveal a treasure trove. A variety of lockpicks and tension rods, cast in high-impact white plastic, lined the belly of the shoe. Everything was laid horizontally and carefully spaced to ensure the shoe would bend and move naturally with the wearer's foot.

"You've got picks in the left shoe and some small survival goodies — fishing line, a hook, a serrated blade, that kind of thing — in the right. Remember, this is all plastic, so you can walk right through a metal detector: nobody should catch you with anything short of a full-body search, but the picks *will* break if you put too much stress on 'em, so be gentle."

"Gentle is my middle name," Jessie said.

Nobody had a response to that.

"Harmony, you get the last goodie in the prize box." Kevin held up a wristwatch. It was a Michael Kors design in austere platinum with a minimalist face, silver on midnight black, and it looked like it was made for Harmony's wrist. She took it, curious, looking for the hidden trick.

"We wanted you to have a bit of added firepower in the field," April explained, "seeing as they're hiring muscle, *not* a magician."

'She's right on that," Jessie said. "You start slinging magic around, they're going to have a whole bunch of questions."

Harmony slipped the watch onto her wrist. It was snug. Comfortable. Kevin brought her attention to a pair of nearly imperceptible needle holes on its outward-facing side.

"Your watch is loaded with a Taser. Turn the face counterclockwise until it clicks to arm, press the crown to fire." Kevin tapped the ridged nub on the side of the watch. "Once the barbs lodge in your target, press the crown a second time to discharge the current. Should drop anybody on the spot, assuming they're not tweaking on PCP or, you know, a demon or something."

Harmony thought about Nadine. If they played their cards right, this mission would pave a path right to her doorstep, but that was secondary to thwarting the heist and capturing her pawns. For once, she didn't anticipate facing demons or monsters in the field. Just men. Men who had a choice between good and evil, and willingly embraced the darkness.

The thought left the taste of bile in her mouth. As much as she hated Nadine, her archenemy was born of hellfire. She was only what she was created to be, and never had a chance to choose another path. People like Dima Chakroun, like Josh Orville...they *wanted* this life.

Fine. If they could take the ride, they could take the consequences.

"Effective range?" she asked.

"Seven feet, but closer is better," Kevin said. "Hold your shot until you're point-blank from the target, if you can manage it."

She gave the watch a grim nod, letting her jacket sleeve fall over it as she lowered her arm.

"Let's move on," April said, sitting in the corner window of Kevin's laptop screen. "We've been trying to identify exactly what Nadine's target is. We're still in the dark but...there are troubling patterns on display. Something is afoot at Ardentis Solutions, and it may need our intervention."

CHAPTER TEN

A new window opened on the laptop screen. The man in the photograph made Harmony think of Andy Warhol, with his stern glasses and his messy shock of stark white mad-scientist hair. His hair fell over one side of his face in a cascade, an ivory curtain, while the other side was horribly pockmarked with old acne scars. His skin was a canvas of faded sores and craters. He was older, maybe in his late seventies, but his one visible eye burned with the determination and focus of a man a quarter of his age.

"This is Lorne Murrough," April said, "the founder and CEO of Ardentis Solutions. He holds dual degrees from Stanford in electrical and chemical engineering and a net worth somewhere in the range of two hundred million dollars. He founded Ardentis seven years ago, after a long run at Lockheed Martin, and immediately started racking up lucrative government contracts. Nothing suspicious there: by all accounts, Ardentis makes superior body armor for a competitive price. I found a bit of hanky-panky, some undeclared gifts to a few key senators, but..."

"But everybody does that." Jessie leaned closer to the screen. "Poor guy must have had some devastating acne as a kid."

"Not as a child," April said. "In 1969, Mister Murrough was drafted into the Vietnam war. He registered as a conscientious objector, due to his beliefs as a Seventh-day Adventist, and was enrolled into Operation Whitecoat."

That rang a bell somewhere in the back of Harmony's memory.

"That was an Army project," she said. "Some kind of medical testing program?"

April nodded. "Exactly. The objective of Operation White-coat was to create antibiotics and counteragents to protect against biological warfare. All of the volunteers were pacifists like Murrough. They were injected with various forms of bac-teria — *Coxiella burnetii*, rabbit fever, yellow fever, hepatitis, anything the program's leaders thought might be weaponized against American troops — and then treated with experimental cures to determine their effectiveness and proper dosage."

April brought another picture up on the laptop screen. A black-and-white photo, taken from a high school yearbook. In this one Lorne looked like a beefy all-American high school linebacker with a big grin, dark hair, and a perfect complexion.

"This is what he looked like before he entered the program. He was in Whitecoat until 1973."

"Doesn't add up," Harmony mused. "Draftees only had to serve for two years."

"He volunteered for more. Mister Murrough has some very strong views about the sanctity of life. Ardentis creates body armor, vehicle defenses, less-than-lethal munitions...I'm still working on a profile, but so far, it's all consistent."

"And yet," Jessie said.

"And yet, over the course of the last year, they've made some troubling hires."

A spread of employee photographs, all smiling and crisp and taken in front of the same stainless-steel corporate sign, blos-somed on the screen.

"Biomedical experts. Immunologists. Virologists. Specialists in epidemic research."

April lowered her head, staring over the rims of her steel bifocals.

"Ardentis Solutions," she added, "doesn't *have* a medical di-vision."

"Or they don't have one on the record," Jessie mused. "Not one they want anybody knowing about."

Harmony saw the world like a jigsaw puzzle sometimes. There were a handful of pieces, all meant to snap together and draw a complete picture. You just had to put them in the right order and draw the connections. This one fell together in her mind's eye, pieces falling like a perfect line of dominoes as they clicked.

"He has a bioweapon. Nadine wants it."

Everyone turned to stare at her.

"It's simple," she said. "He's following his nature. Whoever Murrough was before he joined the Army doesn't matter. Operation Whitecoat is where he was born. He gave them his health, his looks, everything he had, and then came back and volunteered for two more years because he believed in the work that deeply."

"You think he's trying to start up his own private CDC?" Jessie asked.

"That's exactly what I think. It's not like the threat of germ warfare ever went away. But you can't develop a cure for a plague without having samples of that plague on hand to study. And since he doesn't have the legal authority for that kind of operation, he's keeping it under wraps. He doesn't want accolades or awards, he just wants results."

"So he's on the side of the angels," Kevin said, "but he doesn't know a hardcore devil's out to jack his stuff. What would Nadine even do with a bioweapon?"

Harmony heard Nadine's voice in her ear. *Do you think I want to destroy your world, Harmony?*

"Not for personal use," she said. "Nadine is desperate for money and she's still missing five million dollars. She'll sell it to the highest bidder."

Jessie rubbed the back of her neck, wincing.

"Christ, that's even worse. She's probably got North Korea and ISIS on speed dial. Okay, change of plans. I thought we'd show up to the meeting, capture Orville and shut this whole operation down tonight—"

"But we can't," Harmony said. "Not until we know what Murrough is keeping in his lab and decide how to deal with it. Not really part of our mandate — I mean, we're supposed to be hunting *supernatural* threats, but as long as we're here..."

Jessie flashed a smile and reached for her dark glasses.

"You know the best thing about running an independent espionage bureau beholden to nothing and nobody but a few big-ticket donors? Donors who are all terrified of us?" she asked. "It means we can do whatever we want."

"They're terrified of *you*," Kevin said.

"And they damn well should be." She put her sunglasses on and reached out to Harmony. "C'mon. Let's go pretend to be bad guys."

They swapped out the plates on the Hemi Cuda down in the hotel garage. Then they rolled out, Jessie behind the wheel, into a gray and cold afternoon. Dirty rain drizzled down from the sky, smearing the muscle car's windshield as they merged into heavy, sluggish traffic on I-90 East. Dima had sent them an address for the meet. It was down in Joliet, about an hour southwest of the city.

Joliet was born as the City of Steel and Stone. Steel mills boomed in its heyday, and a vast quarry provided a rugged foundation to build upon. Now it was a town in transition, looking for new ways to grow, but the past was on display everywhere Harmony looked. They rolled past the shadow of the old Joliet Prison, now a tourist attraction, looking like a Gothic castle with crenelated towers and sturdy fortress walls. Century-old houses built to outlive their architects lined narrow, broken streets.

Warning chimes sounded up ahead and a drawbridge slowly lifted, making way for a tugboat and a barge laden with shipping containers. Jessie drummed her fingers on the steering wheel, staring at the black line of a storm on the distant horizon.

"Honestly," she said unbidden, "I really wanted to just walk into this meeting, kneecap Josh, toss him in the trunk, shoot everybody else in the face, and call it a day."

"I know," Harmony said.

"And I *like* undercover work. It'd just be great if we could have a mission where the bad guys weren't hatching some nefarious scheme. Just once in a while. As a treat."

"If they weren't hatching a nefarious scheme, they wouldn't be bad guys."

The bells continued to chime, traffic stalled out in front of the drawbridge. Jessie turned and stared at her.

"I'm gonna need you to stop being logical. You know it pisses me off."

Harmony shrugged.

"On that note, though," Jessie added. "There's a chance — a slim one, but a chance — that Dima's going to try and make her own play tonight. If she can come up with some bogus reason for Orville and his psycho buddy to take us out, her hands stay clean and Nadine might never find out that we flipped her."

Harmony thought it through. Jessie was right. On one hand, it would be a huge risk for Dima, maybe one with eternal consequences if Nadine smelled a whiff of treachery. On the other hand, frightened people make stupid decisions. And Dima was frightened. She glanced at the Hemi Cuda's dashboard.

"If things are sliding out of control," she said, "I'll ask if we have enough fuel for the trip back to Chicago. That'll be the sign to go weapons hot."

Jessie took that in. She moved her jaw like she was tasting the idea.

"And then we kill everyone in the room. Take the 'mastermind' alive if we can, but everyone else is expendable. I can work with that as a backup plan."

"Nadine wants this," Harmony cautioned, "and when there's something she wants, she never gives up. If we take out her entire crew, she'll just send another one — and next time, we won't have an inside edge."

"So we try to make this work, at least until we know exactly what they're aiming to steal and what to do about it."

"Until," Harmony agreed.

The address at the end of the line was an auto body shop with a tiny parking strip out front and a big plastic sign that had caved in from the elements long ago. Now it was just a rusted frame and a few chunks of jagged plastic, colors faded, depicting half of a car with a smile-shaped grille and headlight eyes. The sign in the window said *Out of business* but there were lights on inside. Jessie parked up front.

Dima met them at the door. She looked like she stepped out of a spy movie, in a glamorous black trench coat and a wide-brimmed hat. She barely looked at Jessie, focusing her ire on her partner.

"You still look like a goddamn fed. They're going to make you. They're going to make you in a second and then they're going to kill all of us. I don't know how I let you talk me into this insane idea—"

Harmony cut her off, her voice low and calm.

"The only thing that's going to get us killed," she said, "is panic. Trust us to do our jobs, and focus on doing yours."

"And we're not talking you into anything," Jessie added. "We're *blackmailing* your evil ass. I know it's a fine distinction but you should probably keep it in mind. Now can you pull your big girl pants on and introduce us, or do you need some time to hyperventilate first?"

She walked them inside. Dima took the lead, bringing them through a dusty, desolate office that had been stripped for anything worth selling, and into the garage.

As Harmony stepped through the open doorway, the muzzle of a gun brushed against her hair. The hammer went *click*.

CHAPTER ELEVEN

The three women froze in their tracks. Harmony smelled fetid breath as it washed over her cheek, the skeletal man with the gun leaning close enough to murmur in her ear.

"Now what do we have here?" Ricky Corbin drawled. He nuzzled her hair with the fat barrel of his revolver, finger firmly on the trigger. "I didn't think we were hiring entertainment 'til after the job was done."

"Ricky," Dima said.

"Girl, if I want you to open your whore mouth, I'll unzip my fly. The man told you to recruit some serious muscle and you came back with a couple of Girl Scouts."

Turn. Grapple. Wrist lock. Disarm. The moves rode in on a flood of adrenalin, straight from Harmony's mind to her body, but she forced herself to keep perfectly still. Ricky's profile pointed to a rage addict who didn't know how to back down and would never let a perceived insult slide. She could take his gun away, but then she'd have to kill him and this whole mission could implode on the spot.

She felt Jessie behind her, ready to start blasting if Harmony dropped their code-phrase. Instead, Harmony wriggled her fingers gently, silently easing her back.

Then she turned to face Ricky, standing with his gun pointed right between her eyes. She didn't blink.

"The last man who pointed a gun at me," she said, "is in twenty-seven pieces, buried in a landfill outside of Reno. And I liked him."

He gave her a lopsided, curious smile, showing off steel-jacketed teeth in a bed of rotten gums.

"That so?" he asked.

"Name's Julie Law," Harmony said, then nodded back at Jessie. "You can call her Ace."

"Never heard of you," Ricky said.

"I'd be a pretty lousy hitwoman if you had. Getting away with murder is half the job."

His smile grew, cocky now.

"You?" he snorted. "You're a professional killer. Seriously."

"Miss Chakroun's verified my bona fides. Believe her. Or I can take you out to Reno and show you that landfill, but it's a thirty-hour drive and I was told this job is on a tight schedule."

"You were told correctly," said a new voice. "Ricky? I appreciate your zeal for operational security, but get your gun out of our new friend's face. *Please.*"

As he reluctantly lowered his weapon, grumbling, Harmony turned. She recognized Josh Orville from the mission briefing. He looked like he was around Kevin's age, a lanky college student with a know-it-all smirk. Diamonds glittered on his wrist, encrusting a white gold victory bracelet from the World Series of Poker.

He stood at a folding table, the empty body shop converted to a mission control room. Diagrams and floor plans were propped up on easels, and his knuckles rapped a thick binder stuffed with loose pages. Mismatched folding chairs sat scattered around the oil-stained concrete floor. Another member of the crew was already here, this one a stranger. He was dapper, lean, with a black mustache and a tailored tan suit.

"Come on in, grab a chair and take a load off," Josh called out. "Dima told me all about you two. Have to say, impressive resumes. We'll see if you're as good as your reputations. You've met Ricky. Guy on my left, call him Houston."

The man with the mustache raised a casual hand in greeting. He didn't seem inclined to speak.

"Dima, sweetie," Josh said. "I see our safecracker, our shooter, and our driver. Know what I *don't* see? The other three people you hired for this gig."

Dima took out her phone, scrolling through a string of texts.

"They should be here any second. I can make some phone calls—"

"Do that."

As Dima slipped outside, Jessie dragged a folding chair across the floor, closer to the table.

"Never thought I'd be driving for Josh Orville," she said. "I'm kind of a fan."

His eyebrows went up. "Yeah?"

"Yeah. That last tournament? I've never seen anyone dominate their opponents like that. It was like you could read their minds."

"I'm just that good," he said with a smile. "You play at all?"

"Oh, no," Jessie lied with a wave of her hand. "I'm terrible at gambling. I just like to watch a pro at work."

"You came to the right place, then. I'm going to show you a whole new set of skills."

Harmony stifled the urge to smile. She wasn't good at the touchy-feely stuff, working her way into a target's confidence, but Jessie could charm anyone. *Or she finds their weak spots*, Harmony reflected, *and gets them to charm themselves*. Josh was in love with his own ego, and she was playing right along.

Dima returned, and they heard shuffling footsteps at her back. Ricky brandished his revolver and started striding toward the door.

"Ricky," Josh said, "please do not shoot my new employees."

"Just bein' security-conscious, boss-man."

One of the new arrivals would stand out in any crowd, with a rooster-comb mohawk the color of a desert sunrise and a battle-jacket covered in patches for death metal bands. He stood out even stronger in Harmony's second sight, his soul a twisted mass of barbed wire around a beating, bloody heart. *Cambion*, she thought. Half-demon, half-human, a foot in both worlds but belonging to neither. Not the first time they'd found a cambion resorting to a life of crime.

The other man was more conventionally dressed — so conventional, in a turtleneck sweater and neatly pressed slacks, that he could vanish in a crowd — but he had Harmony's full attention. There was something...wrong with him, on a magical level. Not demonic, just *different*, his energies seething and twisted like a knotted-up garden hose. His face was severe, eyes keen behind thick black-rimmed glasses. Harmony thought his cheeks were unusually ruddy at first, then she realized he was wearing stage makeup. His skin was just shy of albino, devoid of natural pigment, like a bloodless corpse.

Dima gestured to the cambion. "This is Dart, our second shooter—"

"Least this one looks like he can throw down," Ricky grunted.

"—and this is Doctor West, the sensitive materials handling specialist you requested."

Harmony felt certain they were on the right track now. There were only so many reasons to bring a doctor on an industrial heist, and they already had a pretty good idea of what Nadine was after.

"Welcome, gentlemen," Josh said. "And then there was one."

"I just spoke to our final recruit. She ran into traffic but she'll be here in five minutes."

"Excuse me," West said in a reedy voice, raising his pale hand. He kept flicking baleful glances at Harmony and Jessie, mostly at Jessie. "I wasn't told about the...composition of this team."

Josh did a double take. "No reason you would, Doc. See, this is my crew. I hire you, you do a job, I pay you, and then you go home. It's very simple. Why, is there a problem?"

"Not a problem as such, per se, no. It's just that I prefer not to work with females, if at all possible. I find them...unsanitary."

"*Wow*," Jessie said.

"And that one in particular," he said, pointing a timid finger at Jessie. "She's a bit, um, how do I word this...dark-complexioned, by which I mean..."

"Josh?" she said. "Put your boy on a leash before he says something he'll *wish* he could take back."

Josh leaned back against the folding table, tilted his head and let out a sigh.

"Doc, your job is to keep any unfortunate accidents from happening during the heist." He gestured at Jessie. "It's Ace's job to get us out and bring us home, alive, in one piece, and five steps ahead of the Chicago PD. If you're wondering who I consider more important to the team right now...stop wondering."

"Well," West said, miffed. "So much for valuing intellectual expertise."

"Not gonna lie, I do have a thing for a hot chick with a hotter set of wheels. But I value you enough to pay you ten thousand dollars, cash, for that 'intellectual expertise' of yours. Ten grand for one night's work should be enough validation for anybody."

"Suits me fine," Houston said, speaking up for the first time.

"And that goes for all of you," Josh said. "You follow my orders to the letter, you hold it together for five, maybe six hours, and you go home flush. Ten grand, each. That's American dinero, understand, don't ask me for payment in gold Krugerrands or any of that goofy underworld shit."

He lied so smoothly Harmony would almost have believed him, if she didn't know they were all slated for death at the end of the job. Dart, the rooster-haired cambion, raised a hand.

"What about crypto?" he asked, hopeful.

Josh rolled his eyes. "Sure, just let me make a Bitcoin transfer from my public, openly viewable crypto wallet to you, a known felon. That'd be great for my reputation. Really. No problems for me at all. I'm paying you in clean, laundered cash, period. Once you've got your money, do whatever you want with it."

"It is curious," West said.

Josh stared at him, expressionless.

"Gonna finish that thought, Doc?"

"Well, you're quite the high-profile individual, at least for aficionados of games of chance. An odd choice to be leading a heist. And then there's the considerable reach your...associate Dima has shown. Signs of backing from a larger organization." He sat back in his folding chair, his gaze intent, and steepled his fingers. "I'm just wondering who we're really working for."

Ricky swaggered up behind him, his gun in one hand and a fresh bottle of Corona in the other. He took a swig, guzzling the cheap beer down, and crouched behind him. The barrel of Ricky's gun stroked softly against West's cheek. The doctor froze, petrified.

"You're a real clever one, aintcha?"

"I...do my best to excel at my professional disciplines," he stammered.

"Maybe you should be a little less *clever*," Ricky murmured in his ear, "and a little more *smart*. You get my meaning, son?"

"I think we understand each other," West said, swallowing hard.

"Yeah, see," Ricky said, rising to his full height and strolling away. "Now you're thinkin' the right way. Try to keep that up."

Footsteps echoed from the empty office. Dima held up a hand, stopping Ricky before he could terrorize another new arrival.

"It's all right. Everyone, this is the last member of our crew. She goes by Cherry, and she'll be our electronics expert."

That wasn't her name, or at least not the name she'd used in the past. Harmony knew the slight young blonde woman — with a demeanor and haircut that made Harmony think of Tinkerbell — by a different one.

She usually called herself Bette Novak, and the last time they crossed paths, she'd tried to arrest Harmony's entire team.

CHAPTER TWELVE

Harmony and Bette locked eyes from across the room. Bette was a pro; her flicker of surprise was instantly buried under a shroud of calculated apathy. Josh waved her in and she grabbed an empty folding chair. Not the closest one, but the only one that would let her sit directly behind Harmony and Jessie.

Jessie pretended to stretch, leaning her head back, shoulders straining. In the moment, she looked back at Bette and murmured, "Let's not be stupid."

"Wouldn't dream of it," Bette whispered back.

Ricky held up his phone and looked to Josh. "I gotta take this. It's that guy with the thing."

Josh gave him a gesture of benediction and turned to the rest of the crew as Ricky stalked out of the garage.

"All right, time is money and Ricky's already been briefed, so let's get this party started." Josh stood at the folding table, his splayed fingertips resting on the stuffed file in front of him. "First up: everyone in this room is a professional, and you were picked because you're damn good at your jobs. Act like it. Second up: some of you might be used to knowing every little detail about a score before you go in. That's not how I operate. You're going to have to take some things on trust."

Dart, the cambion hitman, gave a careless shrug. "Don't need to know nothin' about nothin', long as I get paid."

"That's the spirit I'd like you all to embrace," Josh said. "Here's what I can tell you: our target is Ardentis Solutions' Chicago R&D labs. Our timetable is tight because my employer believes they're planning to relocate the package to a much more secure facility."

Houston, the dapper safecracker, raised a finger. "Package. That what we're calling it?"

"That's what we're calling it. A nice shiny box that must not, and I cannot possibly stress this enough, be opened under any circumstances."

"What's in the box?" Dr. West asked.

"Your ass, if you get curious. The package will be locked down in a BSL-4 laboratory, under heavy anti-contamination seals and a string of electronic locks. You'll verify that the seals are intact before you move the package, while Cherry—" He gestured at Bette. "—will confirm that the electronics haven't been tampered with."

West's eyebrows lifted. So did Harmony's. BSL-4 was the highest level of biosafety protocols. Infectious diseases and airborne toxins could be studied in a BSL-3 lab; BSL-4 was reserved for the worst of the worst. Viruses that could ravage entire cities if they slipped out. Infections with no cure.

Josh walked to one of the standing easels and flipped a stiff poster board around to face the mismatched crew. It bore what looked like a security-camera photo, washed out but still capturing enough detail to make Harmony's pulse beat faster.

"This is the package," he said.

It was a coffin.

Not literally — maybe — but Harmony couldn't look at the ivory box and see anything else. Six feet long, two feet deep, a flat-bottomed capsule of pristine white plastic. A string of five wheel-locks the size of hockey pucks lined one side of the box, while the seams were completely sealed in what looked like strips of black rubber under transparent, hardened glossy foam. A black screen set into the top of the casket provided a constant status feed; most of it was too faint to make out, but Harmony noticed internal and external temperature readings.

"How heavy is that thing?" Dart asked.

Josh's reply was interrupted by the return of his henchman Ricky, off his phone and onto a fresh bottle of beer. He tossed back a swig as he walked over to where West and Dart were sitting side by side.

"So. Just talked to my boy. Had him doing some unofficial background checks. You know, just making sure everybody's who they say they are."

He kept circling the room, a shark on the move, his gaze drifting past Harmony and falling on Jessie. Harmony's stomach tensed. Her Sig Sauer was riding in a concealed holster on her right ankle. She didn't reach for it, but she kept her hand empty and limber.

"A ten-year-old could've followed the paper trail on your car registration," Ricky said. "You're lucky I liked what I saw. As for you..."

He fixed his gaze on Harmony.

"Jury's out on you, but you're cool. For now." Bette was his next target. "Your story is perfect. So perfect it smells like bullshit, but my boy got one of your past clients on the phone and he backed up every last detail."

He turned back to Dart and Dr. West.

"Not everybody came out looking so clean. So, Doc, anything you want to tell the class? Anything you've been hiding?"

As Ricky prowled toward him, looking equal parts drunk and mean, the fastidious doctor squirmed in his chair.

"I...I'm not sure what you could possibly be referring to."

"Ooh, I think you do. See, somebody in this room is here with ulterior motives. And that just pisses me off, abusing our hospitality like that. Makes me feel downright murderous."

West tugged at his turtleneck, utterly flustered.

"Let's not...lose our heads," he stammered.

With all eyes on them, nobody noticed Bette leaning forward and putting her lips to Harmony's ear.

"I know you're inclined to heroics," Bette breathed. "But if you blow our covers to save this jerk, I'll kill you myself."

Ricky threw back the bottle again, drinking deep, belching before he grinned down at the terrified doctor.

"Last chance, Doc. Tell 'em the truth, or it's gonna go real bad for you."

"Please," West said, "I...I implore you to listen. I have no idea what you're talking about. Whatever you've been told, it's a lie, I swear. Just give me a chance to prove it!"

Ricky stared him dead in the eye, silent as the grave.

Then he burst into laughter, doubling over, tears welling in his eyes.

"I'm *fucking* with you, Doc! Goddamn, you brainiacs have no sense of humor. Loosen up a little, huh?"

West blinked, stunned, and slowly forced a terrified smile.

"Oh," he said, "a ruse. That was...quite amusing."

"Yeah," Ricky said, contemplating his bottle. "I like to keep the mood light. You know, I'm really a friendly guy when you get to know me. Except when I have to do something like this."

He whipped the bottle of beer across Dart's forehead, tearing his scalp open and sending him to the floor in a shower of broken glass. Gripping the neck of the bottle, Ricky kicked Dart onto his back before dropping one knee on his chest and bringing the jagged stump of the bottle down, jamming it into the cambion's throat. An artery ripped, sending a hot jet of blood spraying across the dirty concrete floor. Dart's feet hammered the garage floor in a death-spasm as Ricky stabbed him again and again, carving his face and neck into mutilated trenches of gore.

Dart's feet gave one last kick and fell still. His one remaining eye stared blankly at the ceiling as a trickle of blood washed over it, burying it in scarlet. Ricky clambered off him, contemplated the wet hunk of green glass, and tossed it onto the corpse's lap.

Josh stared at him, expectant.

"Sorry, boss-man. Had ourselves a ringer in the mix. The *real* Dart turned up dead in a dumpster last night. This boy's from..." He hesitated, choosing his words carefully in front of the hired help. "...out of state."

A spy from another court, one of Nadine's rivals? Harmony had her suspicions, and Josh's flash of sudden panic — masked just as quickly behind his practiced poker face — made her even more certain.

"All right," he said, collecting himself. "This is not a problem. Game hasn't even started yet. Just need to make some small adjustments in strategy. For the rest of you...take this on board as a life lesson. You be straight with me, I'll be straight with you. You mess around, you'll be talking to Ricky instead. Any questions?"

There were no questions. Dr. West, his cheeks and eyeglasses flecked with the cambion's blood, stared in horror at the cooling corpse beside him.

"Then let's move on," Josh said. "Ardentis Solutions uses Gold Star Security for on-site protection. We'll be going in at shift change, disguised as security officers. Ace, I need you to source a vehicle for this job. It needs to be clean as a whistle, with room for the whole crew plus the package."

"Can do," Jessie said.

"Good. As soon as you have our wheels, notify Dima. She's working with a print shop to fabricate a vinyl kit, so we can roll in looking like we belong there."

"We'll need uniforms," Harmony said.

"Houston's sourcing those," Josh said with a nod to the safe-cracker. "We'll be picking them up right before the heist, to make sure that it won't gum us up if they're reported stolen. There's one more wrinkle in the mix, and his name is Nicolas Castillo."

Josh turned another poster board around, showing a candid black-and-white photograph of a man sitting at a sidewalk cafe. He was small, dark, with a peppery beard that looked too big for his face.

"Doctor Castillo is Ardentis's R&D golden boy. A certified genius, and he built the containment unit for the package. We need him. Problem is, he always had an inclination toward paranoia, and whatever he's been up to these past few months, it's only getting worse. He doesn't go into the office anymore, not unless the boss makes him. He lives in a house in the middle of nowhere—"

"So we go grab his ass, easy," Ricky said.

"—a house in the middle of nowhere, defended by heavily armed private security. These aren't Gold Star flunkies: Castillo has a lot of money, and he's spending every nickel on keeping himself in lockdown."

"So we go grab his ass," Ricky repeated, "and anybody standing in our way gets dropped."

"That's more like it. Okay, folks, especially considering our uninvited guest, time's tighter than ever. Tomorrow is Friday. I want that vehicle sourced and ready by tomorrow afternoon. Tomorrow night, we're all going to take a ride out to Castillo's place and make the snatch. By the next morning, I'll have all the answers I need out of him. Houston will have a source for our uniforms by then, and Dima will have the wrap to disguise our wheels. We spend Saturday afternoon going over the details of the plan, everyone learns their parts, and we execute that night. We deliver the package, and come sunrise on Sunday, each and every one of you is five figures richer. We go our separate ways and this all fades into a happy memory. We good?"

"We're good," Bette murmured, her voice soft behind Harmony's back.

CHAPTER THIRTEEN

The Joliet Route 66 Diner was frozen somewhere in a dream of the Fifties, with a neon sign out front and vintage Americana on the walls, along with a tribute to the Blues Brothers, Joliet's claim to fame. Jessie ordered the breaded pork tenderloin, swimming in brown gravy. Harmony had a Greek salad with feta cheese.

Bette ordered a small fruit bowl and a glass of ice water.

"So," she said, casting a gimlet eye at the diner door and making sure no one from the meet was on their tail.

"So," Jessie replied.

"No hard feelings about Vegas, I hope."

"You busted into the auction posing as an FBI agent," Jessie said, "which, for the record, is *our* scam, and then you tried to capture my team."

"You undermined my operation," Bette fired back. "I was there first."

"Like hell you were—"

"Please," Harmony said. She laid her palms flat on the table. "We won't get anywhere like this. To that end, let's establish some agreed-upon facts so we can stop dancing around."

She looked to Bette.

"Your Bureau credentials were cheap fakes that would never have stood up to serious scrutiny. You have no inside connections at the FBI, because if you did you'd have done a better job. On the other hand, your Air Force credentials are rock-solid. Bette Novak, Master Sergeant — at an age where most enlistees are nowhere near that rank — and attached to the National Air and Space Intelligence Center."

"You've been doing your homework," Bette said.

"I had a lot of time to study recovering from that mission in Vegas. Now, you're clearly an op for a shadow agency, just like we are." Harmony's eyes flashed a warning as Bette's lips parted. "If you're going to deny something that basic, we've got nothing more to talk about."

"Fair," Bette said. "And I've studied you, too. Vigilant Lock. We're building quite a file, though I'm not sure how much of it is accurate."

"We deal with demons and supernatural threats," Harmony continued, "but those are never the missions we cross paths on. You're a magician — I've seen you channel lightning — but you don't hunt the same monsters we hunt. You're also not associated with the infernal courts."

"We would know," Jessie added.

"Conclusion?" Bette asked.

"You belong to a special military unit," Harmony said, "strictly black-book and off the record, with funding directly from the Air Force budget. Authority probably goes up the chain to somebody in the DoD. I couldn't guess if the president knows you exist."

"I have Yankee White clearance," Bette said. "Well, one of my identities does."

"You aren't interested in demonic incursions. You only step in when the threat is extra-dimensional, and you've got a keen focus on world-jump technology. Finding it, securing it, and making sure nobody else has access to it."

"Good guesses. Pretty accurate."

"Deductions," Harmony said.

"As a gesture of inter-agency goodwill, I'll give you a name," Bette said. "You can call us Majestic."

"Is that your actual name," Jessie asked, "or are you just fishing for compliments?"

Harmony's mind was a steel trap, snatching facts like books from a library shelf. She frowned slightly.

"As in 'Majestic-12.' An organization founded in the nineteen-forties to investigate appearances of alien spacecraft."

"That's right," Bette said.

"That's wrong," Harmony countered, "because Majestic-12 is a hoax. The Bureau examined the alleged MJ-12 documents ages ago and proved they were bogus. I've studied them myself."

Bette smiled for the first time all night. Her fork speared her small bowl of fruit salad, impaling a chunk of cantaloupe before raising it to her pink lips.

"Of course it was debunked," Bette said. "We — and by 'we' I mean our founders, obviously I'm not that old — made absolutely certain of it. Let me lay some facts out for you: Majestic was formed in 1947 at the direct order of President Truman. There weren't twelve of us; the actual headcount was more like twenty-three, give or take a few hangers-on. And yes, we were supposed to hunt for aliens. We found out, just as quickly, that the threat isn't from outer space."

"It's from the worlds next door," Jessie said.

"Exactly. We have ample reason to believe that every verified case of alien contact is actually a cross-world incursion. They do not come from the stars, and they do not come in peace."

"And the hoax part?" Harmony asked.

"My predecessors got sloppy, and word leaked," Bette said. "Just as we were realizing the true nature of the threat, a whole community of self-proclaimed UFO hunters and conspiracy nuts jumped in on our act. We realized we had a chance for a misdirect, so we used the *National Enquirer* to 'expose' our own agency."

"Knowing the exposure itself would be debunked later," Harmony said, "you kill two birds with one stone: first, anyone who might poke into portal tech gets bamboozled into hunting for Martians instead. Second, it looks like you never existed in the first place. Conspiracy theorists will still believe, but get the facts all wrong, and everybody else won't believe in the first place."

"Nailed it."

"That's...elegant," Harmony confessed.

Her thoughts were clockwork, gear-teeth sliding together, clicking as they turned in a spiraling mosaic. The size of the 'package' belied her earlier assumption that they were stealing some kind of traditional bioweapon. Virus samples were nowhere near that big, even in secure storage. Knowing Bette's mandate drew a new picture, and Harmony tested it with a pointed question.

"You don't know who Josh Orville works for, do you?"

Bette recovered fast, but the irritated flash in her eyes gave her away.

"You came at this from the opposite direction," Harmony continued. "Majestic is keeping an eye on Ardentis Solutions. You found out about the 'package,' then you learned there was already a crew being assembled to steal it. You put yourself in the mix, just like we did, and here you are."

"Considering the dearly departed Dart, or the infiltrator who was pretending to be him," Bette said, "let's say Josh has some serious information-security problems. How'd you two get onto the guest list, anyway?"

"Trade secrets," Jessie said. There was no reason to think Bette would rat out Dima for her betrayal, but leverage was leverage.

"Now let me try the Sherlock Holmes stuff," Bette said, eyeing Harmony across the table. "You have no idea what the package is. You want Josh... No. You want his employer. You know, I'm giving you a lot here, and you're giving me nothing. A little back-scratch would be nice."

Harmony shared a glance with Jessie, who gave a subtle nod in response.

"Josh belongs to an infernal faction called the House of Dead Roses. The Roses are under the command of a succubus who goes by Nadine, though she's churned through half a dozen other aliases in the time we've been hunting her. They're...well, they're like us. An independent bureau, but straight out of hell. They provide intelligence and counter-intelligence services for the demonic princes, the deniable and nasty kind. No flag, no ideology, just profit."

"I'm aware of her," Bette mused, sipping her ice water through a straw. "Vaguely. Does she still look like Taylor Swift?"

"Regrettably," Harmony said.

"You going to tell us what's in the package?" Jessie asked.

"Probably wouldn't even if I could," Bette said, "but to be honest, I have no idea. Above my pay grade. I just know that Ardentis has been a body of interest for Majestic for quite some time, and whatever's in that casket is something they shouldn't have."

"I assume you don't want it landing in Nadine's clutches either," Harmony said.

"It belongs to Uncle Sam, because we say it does, and Uncle Sam is always right. I've been ordered to facilitate the heist, safely remove the package from the Ardentis labs, learn who the buyer behind Josh Orville is — which you've just handled for me, thank you kindly — and liberate the package at the end of the ride. Due to...certain political reasons, it'll look better if the heist is blamed on petty criminals. A direct raid on the lab would be exceptionally more dangerous and step on too many toes."

"Ardentis has military contracts," Harmony observed.

"In spades, and his contact list is filled with more golden stars than an observatory. Also, we don't believe Ardentis is a bad actor; they're in possession of dangerous materials that aren't theirs to play with, but their intentions are good. I'd rather not get into a shootout with these people."

Harmony thought about their own briefing that morning, and her conclusion that Lorne Murrough was trying to revive his own, covert version of Operation Whitecoat.

"I'm inclined to agree," she said. "One problem with your plan. Nadine wants all loose ends snipped at the end of this job, and she doesn't intend to pay any of us."

"Murder on delivery," Bette mused. "You just can't trust anyone anymore. And that's assuming Ricky doesn't go off with that hair trigger of his and gun us all down the second we open the laboratory doors. Can we work together on this?"

Jessie's lips pursed, tight. Harmony found her hand under the table, giving it a light squeeze. Jessie made eye contact, read the question in her eyes, and grudgingly nodded.

"I think we can at least agree to watch each other's backs," Harmony said. "And the package?"

"Coming home with me," Bette said. "Which shouldn't be a problem, because the package isn't the reason you're here."

"We don't know that until we know what's in it," Jessie said.

"You know that it's being kept in a biolab with level-four security protocols and it's more locked down than Fort Knox. Here's the real question: do *you* have access to a BSL-4 facility? Because we do, and there's a sterilized bay already prepped for containment along with a highly trained research team."

Harmony couldn't muster an argument for that. They had a tech and research support group, but nobody on their roster had the kind of expertise needed to safely study and contain something that hot. Pretending otherwise would just put innocent people in danger. Jessie wasn't so keen on the idea.

"And we just have to trust that you're not planning something nefarious, right?" Jessie said. "We know you're not working for the courts of hell, but there are other players out there. Nastier ones."

"Oh, you're talking about the Network and the Kings of Man?" Bette's smile was cherubic. "We identified them as an existential threat and started racking up dead operatives while you people were still chasing demonic half-bloods around the woods, doing your cute little X-Files thing. It is Uncle Sam's belief — and it is my belief, because Uncle Sam is always right — that the future of warfare isn't nuclear. It's interdimensional. We won't be fighting over territory on this world, not when we can strip-mine resources from the planets next door. Meanwhile, moving troops, munitions, even a single well-placed assassin into the very halls of power will become child's play."

Harmony thought about their run-in with the Overlord's agents, and their veiled threat of war. The casual mention of how they could teleport a warrior in advanced power armor straight into the halls of Congress, unleash a mechanized massacre, and warp out again before the last body hit the floor.

"Borders will disappear," Bette said, "along with the concept of security as we know it. Flexible, agile covert agencies like yours and mine will thrive, while entrenched social structures collapse."

"Sounds like you're looking forward to it," Jessie muttered.

"To the contrary, it's the future I've sworn an oath to fight against. But I'm a patriot and a realist. We can't prevent the inevitable, not with this many sharks in the water. All we can do is delay it, to our dying breath if necessary. You and I are after the same goal here: keeping that package, whatever it is, out of enemy hands. I can keep it safe. Can you look me in the eye and say the same?"

Jessie's gaze narrowed to turquoise slits.

"Fair."

"Let me sweeten the pot as a show of mutual cooperation," Bette offered. "You help me secure the package, I'll help you grab Josh Orville. I'm assuming you want him alive so you can make him squeal."

"Best lead we've got for tracking down his boss," Jessie said. "I'm going to squeeze him until he pops."

"We'll work together, then. We'll see the job through, cover our tracks, neutralize the rest of the heist crew, and capture Orville along with the package. We both take our prizes, go our separate ways, and hope that all of our future meetings can run this smoothly."

They couldn't trust Bette. Then again, they couldn't *not* trust her, and they were going to need one another to pull this off. All they could do for now, Harmony reflected, was keep their cards close to their chests and watch for any sign of betrayal.

"Just so we're on the same page," Bette added, "any preferences regarding the rest of this motley crew?"

"Dima's useful," Jessie said. "Houston and Doctor West look like local talent, and I don't much care about either of 'em. Whatever happens to them, happens."

"And Ricky?"

Jessie's lips pursed in a thin, tight line.

"I've got this rule," she said. "Somebody points a gun at my best friend, I kill them. Maybe not right then and there. But I do kill them."

"Noted," Bette said, holding her gaze.

CHAPTER FOURTEEN

They drove back to the city, merging into downtown traffic as a beaten-copper sun boiled down and coated the cold waters of Lake Michigan with a glittering coat of fool's gold. While Jessie drove, Harmony sent all the details from their meeting ahead to the *Imperator* so April and Kevin could start digging.

There was a message waiting in their hotel room. Harmony connected her secure laptop and sat on the edge of a queen bed. Kevin's image blossomed in a video feed, and he didn't look happy.

"We got something," he said. "Something Bette or her handlers already knew, I'm guessing."

He slid his chair aside, making room for the ruddy hair and wild beard of Bran MacDermott. Formerly a senior executive at Talon Worldwide in charge of the company's secret portal-research program, he became a pawn in the wake of Talon's downfall. Their pawn, now, after they saved him from an attack by the Sisterhood of the Noose.

"Nicolas Castillo," Bran said. "I knew the bloke. Before he signed up with Ardentis, he was one of mine."

"In research and development?" Harmony asked. Jessie sat beside her on the edge of the mattress, and it sank under their shared weight.

"Specializing in biotech security. We had some...dodgy materials, passing in and out of that shop, and he kept everything on triple lockdown."

That was consistent. If he designed the protocols for that containment unit, it was natural that Josh Orville would factor him into the plan. Far easier — and safer — to make him handle the casket than to trust it to amateurs.

"What's your take on his character?" Jessie asked.

"A bit over-cautious for my liking," Bran mused. "Stomped the brakes any time the ride got nice and fast, you know? Not how I prefer to do science, but a solid professional through and through."

"We did some quick background on the rest of your crew," Kevin said. "Well, on the ones that survived the interview, anyway."

"Hit me," Jessie said.

"The guy calling himself Houston is linked to a good twenty different aliases, and there's no evidence he's ever actually set foot in Houston. Changes IDs with every job, but his rep does precede him. He's cracked every lock under the sun, up to and including at least half a dozen bank vaults. Only thing that stands out, beyond an obsession with protecting his real name, is that none of his crimes involved any violence. As far as I can tell, he doesn't even carry a gun."

"A robber and a gentleman," Jessie said.

"As for Doctor West, he's currently gainfully employed as a coroner for Cook County. Lots of spotty attendance, and his spending is out of line with his reported income. Typical markers for a crook with a day job. What has me concerned is what I'm hearing from the grapevine: West is a known fixture at the Bast Club."

Most big cities had a hangout catering to the denizens of the occult underground. The Bast Club was Chicago's trendiest nightspot for magicians, demon-bloods, and supernatural weirdos, and pretenders were not invited.

"I knew I sensed something odd about him," Harmony said.

"Yeah," Kevin said, "so watch your backs until you figure out what his deal is."

"Now we just need wheels," Jessie said. "I can grab something off the street — been a while since I've had to hotwire a car but it's not like I forgot how. We'll be running a pretty big risk, though."

Harmony saw the problem. The second their ride got reported stolen, a single squad car rolling up behind them at the wrong moment could derail the entire heist. Even the best-case scenario would end with a bunch of dead cops. Josh was planning to execute his own team at the end of this job; he wouldn't blink an eyelid at collateral damage.

"We've got an idea there." Kevin turned in his chair and called out, "Hey, April? You want to get in on the call?"

Another window popped open. April sat back in her chair, her eyes cold as steel behind her bifocals.

"Your vehicle will be ready in the morning," she said.

Jessie raised an eyebrow. "Just like that?"

"You'll still have to pick it up. I suggest getting a good night's rest. Tomorrow will be a long day for all of us. Jessie? Could you call me, please? I need a word."

Jessie gave Harmony an uncertain look, then nodded. "Sure."

"How is she holding up?"

Harmony was in the hotel room. Jessie stepped out into the hall, pacing the pale carpet, phone to her ear.

"Fine," Jessie said. "Like always, why?"

"She's not fine."

Jessie leaned back against the wall and closed her eyes.

"You're still pissed that I cleared her for duty."

"Literally minutes after chiding her for not taking her rehabilitation seriously. Did you think about the message you're sending?"

"She's not a kid, Aunt April. She's a grown-ass woman and she can make her own choices. Her foot's fine, I watched her run on it."

"This is about more than her *foot*. She was tortured. Then she was forced into a position where she felt she had to kill an unarmed man."

"Yeah, and it all happened because of Nadine," Jessie shot back. "So how am I going to tell her to stay home while we're in the field, taking care of business? She doesn't need more therapy to feel better. She needs action."

"She isn't you."

"She's my best friend," Jessie said. "I know what she needs better than anybody. And right now, we've got Nadine's master

strategist square in our sights. Worst-case scenario, we disman-
tle more of her organization and leave her with empty pockets.
Best case, we track her ass down and *end* this, once and for all."

April was silent for a long moment.

"We'll discuss this later," she said.

The next morning, their ride was waiting as promised. Harmony
and Jessie rode back to the airport, the overcast sky streaked
with a skewed crosshatch grid of vapor trails. A jetliner thundered up into the clouds, a steel raptor glistening under cold
rain.

The Hertz rental lot was open for business. A couple of security cameras mounted on concrete poles swept across the
parking bay.

"Okay," Kevin's voice said in Harmony's ear. "You're looking
for a cargo van, the kind people rent when they're moving
house. All the cargo vehicles should be clustered together near
the back. Look for license plate K as in king, L as in legal..."

They found it, and Jessie pulled up snug beside it. She left
the Hemi Cuda idling as both women got out. Harmony marked
the security cameras and moved to cover Jessie with her body,
standing in the line of sight while she pretended to look at her
phone.

Behind her, she heard the whispery metal sound of a lockpick
and a tension rake. Then the door of the van — a long white
hauler with the Hertz logo emblazoned on both sides — popped
open for her. Harmony held her breath, bracing for an alarm,
but all she got was silence as Jessie slipped into the driver's seat
and ducked down low.

A minute later, the van revved to life.

Jessie pulled out, driving the stolen van. Harmony hopped
behind the Hemi Cuda's wheel and followed her close, using
the muscle car to block any cops from running the van's plates.
A few minutes later, Kevin spoke up again over the earpiece.

"And you're both golden. Updated the Hertz database, and
that van has officially been rented for the next week, by...a name

I made up on the spot and already forgot. Doesn't matter. The point is, nobody's going to miss it."

"Cool," Jessie said on the shared line. "Harmony, let's take the van over to the meet-up. We've got a scientist to kidnap."

The whole crew was waiting in Joliet. All except for Dart, whose corpse was probably rotting in a dumpster out back. A curling smear of dried blood encrusted the garage floor, a lingering reminder of yesterday's violence.

Not that they needed one, with Ricky swaggering up next to Josh, his oversized revolver jammed into the waistband of his jeans. Jessie led them out into the parking lot, the rest of the gang in tow.

"You stole a cargo van?" Josh asked.

"You needed something big enough to hold all of us, plus the package," Jessie said, "and I covered my tracks. This is what I do for a living, feel me?"

"Hey, no complaints here. I was just hoping for an Escalade or something cool. You know, leather seats, sport package—"

"We need to turn this ride into a Gold Star security vehicle," Jessie countered. "Gold Star doesn't drive SUVs, they drive vans."

He acceded to her wisdom as he climbed into the passenger seat up front. Jessie drove. Harmony got in back with Ricky, Houston, and Dr. West.

"Where are Dima and...Cherry?" she asked, using Bette's new alias. She settled down on the bare, ribbed metal floor as the van began to move.

"They ain't up for this kind of party," Ricky said. "Afraid they might break a nail. You know how *ladies* are."

Harmony wanted, very badly, to shoot him right in his smug face. Instead she forced herself to take a breath and reply, "Sure."

She understood Dima not coming: she was the financier, not the muscle. Bette's absence was more worrying.

"Y'all are strapped, I assume," Ricky said.

West opened his lab coat, flashing a shoulder holster. The pistol inside had a textured chestnut grip and a distinctively long, thin barrel.

"Is that a *Luger*?" Ricky laughed.

"It's a reliable weapon," the coroner said. "I've owned it for years."

"Since when, the end of the Third Reich? Okay, okay." He turned to Houston. "Let's see what you brought to the party."

"I didn't," he said. His groomed mustache twitched.

Ricky's smile faded. "Say that again?"

"I don't carry weapons on a job. They're a liability and a distraction."

Careful, Harmony thought. Ricky had two modes, gregarious and murderous. He was all steel-toothed smiles and jokes when he came aboard, but that mask was slipping fast and Houston didn't seem to realize it.

CHAPTER FIFTEEN

"Let me get this straight," Ricky said. "See, I know I'm not the swiftest bee in the hive, so maybe I just misunderstood. Are you telling me that you came along on this job without a gun?"

"Without a weapon," Houston said. The clarification didn't help Ricky's increasingly dark mood.

"Castillo's gonna be surrounded by shooters. What the hell did you think we were gonna use on 'em, harsh language?"

"I *thought*," Houston said, his voice growing tight, "that I was hired for a burglary. No one told me until yesterday that we'd have to abduct someone."

"We need the professor to get at the package. It's all the same job, dipshit. Besides, I didn't hear you whining yesterday."

"Oh, I'm sorry, I had just finished watching you murder a man with a bottle of beer. I was a little distracted."

Black storms roiled behind Ricky's eyes.

"So what you're saying is," he replied, his voice dangerously soft now, "I got your attention."

Houston's dander was up and he had no idea how much danger he was in. Harmony thought about the Sig Sauer strapped to her ankle. One bullet at point blank range and their Ricky problem would be over.

And so would the mission. He wasn't a new hire, he was a key man, Josh's bodyguard and high enough in the Roses' twisted hierarchy to be a rare exemption to their usual "everyone is expendable" policy.

Houston wasn't. They needed his skills, but safecrackers could be replaced.

The world slid into slow motion as she did the math. If she did nothing, Ricky was going to either beat Houston to a pulp or murder him on a whim. And if she did nothing, her cover would stay intact, the mission would go on, and she'd get what she wanted. What she needed.

Can you sacrifice this man, she asked herself, *to get closer to Nadine?*

Can you save his life, if it means never finding her?

"See, if I got your attention," Ricky was saying, "maybe I just need to do that again—"

"I'll watch him," Harmony blurted, grabbing the psycho's attention.

"Does he need a babysitter now? I want him to pull his damn weight."

"And he will," she said. "I'll make sure of that. We're going to need someone to tackle Professor Castillo and sit on him, and that someone is going to need two hands. Let him handle that, and you and me can handle the guards."

Like a toddler, Ricky was easily distracted. He forgot all about his beef with Houston, focusing on her now.

"Show me what you got, Hit-girl."

Harmony pulled up the leg of her slacks, showing him her ankle holster. Ricky snorted.

"Aw, that's a cute little purse gun. Real intimidating."

She stared him dead in the eyes.

"I don't draw my weapon to intimidate people," she replied. "I draw my weapon to kill them. By the time someone lands in my sights, there's nothing left to talk about."

"Huh," Ricky said, his expression unreadable. "You never draw it out, though? Make 'em piss their pants, or fool 'em into thinking they've got a fighting chance? You're missing half the fun."

"My targets don't see me coming, as a rule."

"Just...lights out, just like that?" Ricky rubbed the sunburn on the back of his emaciated neck. "You don't even talk to 'em first?"

"A predator," Harmony said, "doesn't need to explain anything to prey."

A cold shiver ran down her spine. She was staying in character, talking the way she thought a contract killer from Reno would talk. But those last words...weren't hers. They were alien, washing in on a whisper and a fresh current of magical hunger. All the same, Ricky nodded, impressed.

"Shit, okay. Not the way I do things, but I can respect the attitude."

The cargo van crossed the Illinois border at sunset, rolling through Indiana, curling around the south side of the lake on I-90 until they reached Michigan. Jessie took an off-ramp outside New Buffalo. The going turned rough, broken asphalt rumbling under the van's wheels, while dark forests closed in on both sides of the road. Mossy trunks and grasping boughs blotted out the bone-white moon, casting skeletal shadows in the headlights.

"Here's good," Josh finally said.

Jessie pulled over to the side of the road. The engine fell silent, and the sounds of crickets and night-birds flooded in.

"House is a quarter-mile northeast through the woods," Josh said. "We know Professor Castillo is home, because, well, he never leaves. May I remind you that we need him *alive*. If he dies, we're screwed."

"And the opposition?" Harmony asked.

"We don't have exact numbers, but expect five to ten hostiles, all armed, all with military training. Castillo wanted the best and he didn't skimp on the hiring budget. Hope you're ready to exercise that trigger finger, because we're not leaving any witnesses behind."

The crew moved through the forest on foot, spreading out and keeping low. Their footfalls rustled in the underbrush. A spiderweb, glistening wet, clung to Harmony's face as she walked between a pair of leaning oaks. She brushed it away with one hand, holding her pistol in the other with a ready grip.

She didn't like anything about this. Castillo wasn't the problem; Josh wanted him alive and intact, and she and Jessie would make sure he stayed that way until they could spring him loose. The problem was a houseful of security guards who hadn't done anything to deserve the storm that was headed their way. They were prepared to die for their boss, but that didn't mean they should have to.

A distraction. She could pull that off. Something noisy to drag all the guards to one spot, away from the real fight. Josh's comment about not leaving witnesses aside, they were here for Castillo. Once they grabbed him, especially if bullets were flying, Josh would have a real incentive to get the crew out of there.

"We should split up," she whispered to Josh. "If the professor tries to run for it, we want every door and window covered."

The poker player had come for a fight, cradling a machine pistol in a shoulder sling. He threaded the barrel of a sound suppressor onto the weapon's muzzle while he walked, sure-footed in the tangled grass.

"Read my mind," he said.

He held up a curled fist, gesturing for everyone to stop in their tracks, and waved the crew into a close huddle.

"We're about thirty seconds out," he breathed. "Hit-girl, Doc, Houston, you circle around the house and make your way in through the back. Me, Ricky, and Ace have the front."

Harmony and Jessie shared a silent glance. Jessie didn't look enthused about following Josh and his pet psychopath into battle. On the other hand, if anyone could keep them reined in, it was her. Harmony would have to handle the rest of the job.

Castillo's house was a modern split-level, with a wrap-around deck and walls of smoked glass between artificially weathered slabs of knotty gray wood. A string of black SUVs sat parked out front, their engines cold. Up on the deck, a man in a black suit with a rifle in his hands walked a lonely patrol.

"All right, kids, let's make this happen," Josh said. "On my command, execute."

A pebbled path circled the house in a lazy, lopsided way, bending to curl around a leaf-littered patio pad and a barbecue grill that was collecting cobwebs in the dark. One of Castillo's men walked the path, stones crunching under his leather shoes, heavy iron riding under his black jacket.

He didn't expect to need it. They'd been sitting on the professor for over a month now and the one thing they all agreed on was that the man was clinically paranoid. He needed a therapist, not a team of professional bodyguards. That said, they weren't in the therapy business and the money was good, so they'd stay as long as the checks kept coming.

His radio crackled. "Unit three, check in. Over."

He plucked it from his belt and raised it to his lips. "Nothing to report, control, same as the last time you asked and the time before that. Is there going to be a shift change soon? My feet are killing me. Over."

No answer. Typical. He was thinking of snarky to say, hopefully the kind of snark that wouldn't get him fired, when a shadow fell over his back, standing in his moonlight.

He turned just as Ricky brought up his survival knife in both hands. It punched through the bodyguard's chin, through the upper palate of his mouth, and straight into his brain. The guard shook, electrified, as blood guttered down onto the blade and baptized Ricky's hands.

His killer ripped the blade free and sent him falling, dead as a stone, onto the pebbled path.

The sight of a side door, a curtain drawn across its tiny window, gave Harmony a burst of hope.

"Okay," she whispered to Houston and West, "more exits to cover than we thought. You two are going to hunker down here, get behind some bushes, and watch for anyone trying to run. I'll go in through the back and flush them out. If you see Castillo, grab him."

"Why us?" the doctor asked, eyes suspicious behind his severe glasses.

"Because he's not armed and you are, and I want you to guard each other's backs. I don't need backup inside the house; I do this for a living. This way we cover more ground and cut off more avenues of escape. Any other questions?"

"Not at this moment in time."

She left them covering the side door and slipped around the back.

Josh stood in view of the second-floor deck, gazing up at a patrolling, rifle-toting guard. And past him, a glass door looking in on a brightly lit study, the door cracked to let the cool night wind inside.

Jessie followed his line of sight. "I can climb that, no sweat," she whispered.

"A driver and a gymnast?"

"I'm multitalented," she said.

"Works for me," Ricky grunted. "You go high, we'll go low, we flush the place out and meet in the middle."

Jessie was already planning on how she'd take the rifleman out. She had a dozen ways of disabling a man without killing him, she just had to decide how realistic she wanted to make this look. Josh was a step ahead of her.

"I'll clear you a path," he said.

Then he raised his machine pistol and fired off a three-round burst.

The pistol clacked like a mechanical typewriter. All three shots found their mark, stitching up the rifleman's chest, blowing two craters in his heart and neck while the third bullet ripped through his jaw and left it dangling by a thread of wet sinew as he pitched forward, collapsing to the deck.

Four of Castillo's men were in the kitchen, slapping greasy cards down on a folding table, plastic chips rattling as they slid from pile to pile.

Then they heard the gunshots.

The suppressor dulled the noise, but there was still no mistaking that sound, not for men who lived and breathed for the battlefield. They kicked back chairs, scrambling, two of them

racing for the front door while the other two ran upstairs, shouting for the professor.

The front door of the house thundered inward under Ricky's
steel-toed boot. The bodyguard closest to the door brought his
automatic up but Ricky had the drop on him, his fat revolver
booming like a cannon as he opened fire. Josh was right behind
him, cradling the machine pistol in both hands and aiming from
the hip as he went full auto. Steel-jacketed hornets flooded the
narrow hallway and dropped two men in a storm of screams and
bloody mist.

Chapter Sixteen

Harmony heard the gunfire. Too late for a distraction, now: all she and Jessie could do was minimize the casualties. A window looked in on the kitchen, chairs fallen, a poker game abandoned, and she smashed the glass with the butt of her gun before clambering inside. In her mind she was back at Quantico's infamous kill house, clearing rooms made of plywood, facing down actors with paintball guns.

Here, only survivors would get a passing grade. She let her training take over, her stance controlled but fluid, her gaze carving the house into pie slices as she marked blind spots and potential threats.

She rounded a corner, and came face to face with one of the professor's men. They stared at each other over the barrels of their weapons, aiming point blank at each other.

"Drop it," he barked. "I *will* shoot you."

"Listen to me," Harmony hissed in a low voice. "I'm an FBI agent, and I'm undercover. I'm here to protect Professor Castillo. Those men rampaging through the other side of the house are terrorists, and they're out to kill every single person on this property."

It wasn't entirely true, but close enough. The guard scrunched up his face. His aim wavered, just a little bit.

"Bull," he said.

Harmony was fast. Faster on the draw than most people gave her credit for, at least until they saw her in a fight. She was pretty sure she could drop him. Instead, she tilted her pistol, pointing it toward the ceiling.

Down the hall, Ricky's hand-cannon boomed two more times. A man screeched in agony until a third bullet silenced him.

"Would I do this if I was on their side?" Harmony asked. "Now listen. If you want to save Castillo's life, I'm his best hope. Where is he?"

He weighed his odds, looked her in the eye, and decided what to believe.

"Upstairs. Study. There's a panic room built into the back of the closet."

"Good," Harmony said. "Now go out through the kitchen. Climb out the window, run and *keep* running. If those men spot you, I can't protect you, understand? Don't stop for anything."

Jessie found Castillo first. The professor was in his second-floor study, hunched over a desk and burning the midnight oil. His computer screen was a river of eye-watering calculus and chemical analysis.

He looked just like his picture: short, dark, and terrified. He fell out of his chair as Jessie slipped through the sliding glass door, her gun in hand. At the same moment, his office door burst open on the other side of the room and two of his men stormed in.

A pistol cracked. The bullet whined past Jessie's shoulder, blasting the patio door into a waterfall of broken glass. Instead of returning fire Jessie tossed her gun to the carpet and launched straight at them, crossing the room in the blink of an eye.

She grabbed one guard by the wrist and twisted it until she heard a pop, swinging a leg up and driving her knee into the other man's gut at the same time. The first man jabbed for her eyes, and she chopped the flat of her hand against his throat. He fell in a heap, choking, while the other managed to bring up his pistol. She grabbed it by the muzzle, ripped it from his grip, and whacked him across the head with the butt of the gun, splitting his scalp open. He hit the floor, out cold and bleeding, a scarlet stain like a glass of spilled wine spreading across the plush white carpet.

Castillo almost had Jessie's fallen gun. He was fumbling with it when she grabbed him by the scruff of the neck, hoisted him up like a mother cat with a naughty kitten, and snatched her weapon out of his trembling hands. Her dark glasses had come off during the fray and her eyes blazed like radioactive sapphires.

"They'll live," she told him. "And so will you, but only if you do *exactly* what I tell you."

Jessie dragged Castillo out through the patio door, shouting that she had their target. The heist crew boiled out in all directions, leaving the house a kicked-up hornet's nest. There were at least three bodyguards still on their feet, and they popped up behind broken windows, opening fire in the dark.

Harmony heard gunshots whine through the trees. She ran through the tangled forest, a mad dash for survival as Josh sounded the call to retreat. Jessie took the lead with the professor tossed over her shoulder like a sack of potatoes and his wrists zip-tied behind his back, and Josh stuck close to her side. Ricky laid down wild, blistering cover fire. Not even aiming, just blazing away and peppering the house with bullets as fast as his skeletal finger could squeeze the trigger.

Once the house faded from view, swallowed by the forest, the last few crackles of gunfire faded into echoes. Harmony forced herself to walk, to catch her breath, to focus. She checked the load in her Sig Sauer, making sure she wasn't running on empty.

Someone loomed at her side in the shadows. It was West, the coroner looking twitchier than usual. His lips twisted into a grimace as he leaned close to her.

"I know a secret," he murmured in a sing-song voice.

She gave him a blank look. He tapped his nose, winked, and slipped away through the underbrush.

They loaded Castillo into the van and laid him down on his belly, trussed up like a prize hog.

"Relax," Josh told him. He switched places with Ricky, sending the killer up front to ride with Jessie while he spent some quality time with their captive. "You're among friends. You saw what we did to your men: if we wanted you dead, you'd be dead."

"Because you want something," the professor shot back, his eyes bulging with fear. "And once you get it, I'm finished. None of you are wearing masks. I've seen your faces. You *have* to kill me."

"I can understand how you might think that, sure," Josh said, utterly reasonable. "The truth of the matter is, I'm showing you my face because I'm planning on getting to know you a whole lot better. You see, I've got this aunt. And her name is Nadine. Aunt Nadine has a lot of money and she loves sharing it with her good, special friends. She's got a job offer for you. One that requires your special skills. Trust me, pal: I realize this is a big shock and probably pretty scary, but one day, I promise you're going to look back on this moment and thank me."

It was a testament to Josh's gift of the bluff, Harmony realized, that she honestly wasn't sure if he was telling the truth or not. She knew for a fact that once the heist went down, he was under orders to terminate the crew and tie up any loose ends. But considering they didn't know what was in that containment unit, she couldn't say with any authority that Nadine *wouldn't* need to keep Castillo alive for the long haul.

Of course, that didn't matter much. She knew from experience that after a few days in Nadine's hands, the professor was going to wish he'd died back in his own house.

It was one in the morning by the time they pulled into the garage in Joliet. They hustled the professor inside under a cloak of darkness. Josh came back out again, walking with Harmony and Jessie.

"Dima says she's gonna have the disguise for our ride ready tomorrow by noon at the latest, so I need that van back here pronto. Houston did his part and found us a source for uniforms.

Tomorrow we hit the place, costume up, go over last-minute planning, and raid the lab."

"All in one day?" Harmony asked.

He tapped a finger against his temple. She couldn't help but stare at the missing nubs, his punishment for failures past.

"I've got it all worked out. Trust the man with the plan. Now if you ladies will excuse me, I need to have a long heart-to-heart with Professor Castillo."

Harmony's eyes darkened. She knew they needed Castillo alive and breathing for the heist. That didn't mean they wouldn't hurt him first.

"What are you going to do to him?"

Reading her expression like a book, Josh snickered.

"Nothing rough, if that's what you're thinking. I wouldn't say this where Ricky can hear it, but torturing somebody for information is strictly amateur hour." He held up the poker bracelet on his wrist. Its diamonds glittered in the pale moonlight. "This is what *I* do for a living. Trust me, come morning he'll be eating out of my hand. He'll tell me his whole life story and he won't even realize he's doing it."

Alone in the van, Jessie drove while Harmony swept for bugs. She didn't trust anyone on the heist crew, and Dr. West's leering sing-song patter about knowing a secret had stuck with her.

"Creepy incel being a creepy incel," Jessie said. "News at eleven. He was probably just trying to intimidate you. You know, you being a *feeemale* and all."

A faint thrumming sound drew Harmony's gaze skyward. A traffic helicopter swept over the nearly empty highway.

"I'd like to believe that. Meanwhile, I want to know where—" Harmony paused as her phone began to buzz against her hip. She took it out and checked the screen, a lozenge of glowing light in the darkness. "And speak of the devil."

She recognized the number. They had traded contact information back at the Joliet Diner. She put it on speaker so Jessie could join in the conversation.

"Where were you?" Harmony demanded.

"I gave Josh a cheap excuse to let me sit it out," Bette said. "I'm the team's electronics pro. He needs me tomorrow."

"Considering we just survived a shootout," Harmony said, "your help would have been appreciated out there."

"And you had it," Bette replied.

"Excuse me?"

"Look up."

You couldn't see the stars out here, this close to Chicago. The light pollution turned the sky into a canopy of solid black. All she could see was the traffic copter in the distance.

"No," Jessie said.

"You can't see me," Bette said, "but I'm waving down at you right now. I had some major misgivings about this op, so I figured I could smooth the road with a little bit of overwatch. Turned out I was right, too: the second the shooting started, a silent alarm fired straight to the New Buffalo PD and the Michigan State Police. I pulled a lot of strings, called in some favors, and stalled the response. If not, you would have been up to your ears in state troopers before you reached the border."

"Well...thanks for that," Jessie said. "And you are going to be with us in the trenches tomorrow, right?"

"All the way to the bitter end," she promised.

After she hung up, the distant chopper veering off, Harmony sat back and frowned. Jessie gave her a sidelong glance.

"Whatcha thinking?"

"It was a foolish mistake."

"I don't think we need to blame ourselves for that one, hon. I mean, we're not planning the mission this time: we're here to screw up somebody *else's* mission, and all we can work with is what Josh gives us."

"Not our mistake," Harmony said. "His. And that's the entire problem."

Chapter Seventeen

Jessie drove the van, cruising down an empty ribbon of highway and hugging the slow curve of the road.

"His mistake," she echoed.

"Josh is Nadine's 'mastermind,' or so Dima tells us."

"He's not perfect," Jessie pointed out. "I counted four missing finger joints. That's four times he let Nadine down. Or maybe just one if she was in a really bad mood that day."

"That makes him more dangerous, not less," Harmony countered. "She wouldn't keep giving him chances unless he had a lot more wins than losses. But this was...sloppy. He planned the abduction of a key figure in this heist, a man we supposedly need in order to get at the target, and Josh didn't bother checking to see if he had a silent alarm in place? It's like he didn't care about getting caught."

Jessie frowned into the distance as she drove, her eyes glittering in the dark.

"When I was with him and psycho-boy out front, I was getting ready to climb the trellis and take out the sentry up on the second-floor deck. Had it covered, no sweat, and Josh just...blew him away, and kicked up the whole hornet's nest. I mean, sure, he doesn't know how good I am in a fight and maybe he thought he was being a gentleman by clearing my path..."

Her voice trailed off. She didn't believe that any more than Harmony did.

"His behavior makes no sense," Harmony reasoned, "unless he already knew. He already knew he had a guardian angel watching from on high, and that alarm wasn't going to slow us down."

"You think Bette is compromised?"

"Either she and Josh made a deal under the table and she's lying to us," Harmony said, "or her cover is *blown*."

"We have to warn her," Jessie said.

Harmony flicked a glance at her phone. "When it's safe. He won't hurt her before the job is done. If he knows who she really is, he knows she wants the package — meaning, just like tonight, he can trust her to do her job until the heist is over and done. Ironically, Bette's the most loyal member of this entire crew, because they're both waiting until the curtain drops to stab each other in the back."

"If he's got ears on her," Jessie said, "there's a non-zero chance that we're blown, too."

"Same deal. He could know every last detail about us down to our shoe sizes, and he'd still play dumb until we've got the package in hand. It's all the same to him: if he believes our cover stories, he's under orders to execute us when the job's done so Nadine doesn't have to pay up. If he knows who we really are...same outcome."

"That's the kind of deviousness I'd expect from one of Nadine's golden boys."

"It's what I'd expect from a poker player," Harmony replied.

They drove in silence for a bit after that, an evening DJ keeping up a smooth stream of patter on the cargo van's tinny radio.

"Forecast says we're looking at the storms clearing up and blue skies into the weekend," he said over the tail of a classic rock song. "Don't forget to come down to Navy Pier for Live on the Lake, one of the biggest events of the season. We'll have bands from rock to reggae playing up in the Navy Pier beer garden, a fireworks show at sunset, and of course yours truly as the master of ceremonies. Area parking will be limited so plan ahead—"

Harmony clicked the radio dial. She picked up her phone and turned to Jessie.

"When did he say Dima would have the van wrap ready tomorrow? Noon?"

"Noonish," Jessie said.

"So we have a few hours in the morning before the main event."

"Penny for your thoughts?"

Harmony brandished her phone.

"I don't like going through doors without knowing what's on the other side," she said, "and I'm not trusting our lives to a man who we know — whether he's blown our covers or not — is planning on murdering us. We need to plan ahead, and Josh Orville just handed us the perfect angle."

She called the corporate offices of Ardentis Solutions. She had expected to leave a voicemail message, and was surprised to get a live body on the line.

"Thank you for calling Ardentis Solutions," the woman said. "How may I direct your call?"

"This is Special Agent Harmony Black with the Federal Bureau of Investigation. We're investigating the abduction of one of your employees, one Doctor Nicolas Castillo."

"We just heard," the woman said. "Everyone's broken up over it. Have you found any leads?"

"Nothing we can discuss at this time. However, my partner and I would like to tour your offices and examine his workspace in case there's something relevant to the case. Tomorrow morning perhaps, at nine?"

"Um...please hold," she replied.

As hold music warbled over the phone's speaker, Jessie gave her a sidelong smile.

"'Investigating' the abduction that we committed. Using Josh's own plan against him? Slick."

"I've been known to play cards myself, every once in a while," Harmony said.

The operator came back on the line.

"I just spoke to Mister Murrough," she said, "and he'd be very pleased to meet with you and answer any questions you might have. Would tonight work?"

"Tonight?" Harmony said.

"He works evenings. You'd be welcome to visit any time before five. That's a.m., of course. I'll put your names on the visitor list and tell security to expect you."

· • ● ● ● • ● ● • ·

The Ardentis plant was down on Chicago's southwest side, in a rugged industrial corridor that lived in the winged shadow of Midway Airport. Motels on the main drag offered rooms by the hour and dented, broken police cameras dangled from lamp-poles.

Jessie took a right, angling down a rough road built for cargo hauling, passing a pair of late-night semi trucks as they trundled toward the freeway. Ardentis was just ahead, looking like a prison behind a tall ring of razor-wire fencing. A security hut squatted next to the parking lot entrance, barring the way through with the swing arm of a steel gate painted hazard yellow.

Jessie put her dark glasses on.

She pulled up to a stop, and a young man in a Gold Star Security uniform came out with a clipboard. He wore a pistol on his hip, a bulky police special in a rawhide holster.

"Special Agents Temple and Black," she said. "We have an appointment with Lorne Murrough."

He looked at her, looked at their Hertz cargo van, then back at her.

"Bureau's making budget cuts," Jessie said.

That was good enough for him. The gate swung up and they rolled through, into a parking lot that was still half-full long after dark. The plant itself was a cluster of stark steel-walled cubes reinforced with a lattice of riveted steel beams, all painted a rusty orange. A maze of glass-walled walkways, lit up from within like neon tubes in hues of stark white and cool, icy blue, stretched from building to building high above the ground floor.

Harmony held her silence as they parked and walked, following signs and a yellow striped path on the ground to the front office. More security guards, two behind the curved arc of a white plastic desk and a third stationed by a bank of elevators, fixed them with raptor stares as the automatic doors hissed shut behind them.

They had to check in a second time on a second list, showing their badges before one of the guards tapped a button. The farthest elevator door whispered open, opening onto the empty cylinder of a cage.

"Mister Murrough's expecting you," the guard said. "That elevator will take you straight to his office. It's already keyed; don't press any buttons."

There wouldn't have been any to press, Harmony noted as they walked into the cage. The brass panel to one side of the doors only had three buttons: the penthouse, the lobby, and an emergency stop. As the doors glided shut, Jessie leaned close.

"I thought Gold Star didn't carry guns," she murmured.

"Apparently they do if you pay for the premium package. Also clocked four cameras in the lot, two in the lobby. Front desk has a silent alarm button, just like a bank teller's."

"Taking care of those is Bette's job," Jessie said.

If they could trust her to hold up her part of the plan. If she wasn't working a side angle with Josh. Too many *ifs*. They danced around Harmony's head, frustrating her, taunting her like a swarm of gnats.

The elevator glided to a smooth stop and the doors rumbled wide, opening onto a long and narrow hallway appointed in rich, dark wood. Electric light sconces, shaped like Victorian candelabras, curled from the walls on either side and cast the corridor in spheres of light and shadow.

The double doors at the end of the hall opened onto a cavernous penthouse. A wall of glass looked out over the rambling streets of the South Side and the industrial corridor, crimson lights gleaming from the soot-stained mouths of towering smokestacks. The penthouse was a span of ivory marble, track lighting here and there illuminating the room like a string of spotlights surrounded by darkness. Modern furniture, all chrome and black leather, sat clustered in conversation nooks around pristine ivory rugs.

A kidney-shaped glass desk commanded the center of the room, cluttered with books and files and open laptops, as well as a full spread of covered dishes and a bottle of wine in a stainless-steel bucket. The man seated behind the desk was just as commanding. As Jessie and Harmony crossed the threshold, Lorne Murrough rose to his full height, a shaggy giant in his early seventies with a cascade of white hair falling over one half of his pockmarked and acne-scarred face. The half of his mouth they could see curled into a nervous, almost boyish smile.

"Agents! Special agents? I'm sorry, I'm not sure what the proper nomenclature is. No disrespect intended. I'm Lorne Murrough, and this is my company. Please, won't you join me for dinner?"

Chapter Eighteen

As Lorne removed the bell-shaped covers from the serving plates, curlicues of steam kissed the penthouse air with the rich aroma of garlic and butter. It was a seafood feast, with scallops and shrimp on skewers dusted with rich herbs, alongside the pink glistening meat of a Maine lobster tail. A steak medallion, bloody rare and topped with a perfect sprig of parsley, finished the banquet.

They sat down at his desk and Lorne reached for a cloth napkin, unfurling it and tucking one end into his collar like a bib.

"I hope you don't mind," he said, "but I always enjoy a late supper while I'm working. Helps me keep the wheels turning. Help yourself if you're hungry, there's more than enough. And please, tell me you've got some good news for me. The New Buffalo police have been less than forthcoming. Is it true that someone *died* out there?"

"There were casualties," Harmony said, "but we feel confident that Doctor Castillo was abducted. You haven't received any ransom demands, or anything of that nature?"

"No, but I'm willing to pay, obviously. I'm not hanging one of my employees out to dry; that's not how we do things at Ardentis. Is that what you think this is about? Money?"

Harmony and Jessie shared a glance.

"We're not ruling anything out until we know the motive." Harmony brandished her card, sliding it across the glass desk. "If you are contacted by the kidnappers, I want you to notify us right away. In the meantime, would you be willing to let us inspect his workspace, in case he left something behind that might help us find him?"

"We could come back with a search warrant," Jessie added, "but that's inconvenient and embarrassing for everyone involved. Nobody at Ardentis is under any suspicion and we know you're a good citizen, so we wanted to give you the opportunity to clear things up, quick and easy. No fuss, we'll take a quick look around and be out of your hair."

Lorne plucked the bottle of wine from the ice bucket. Pale Chardonnay splashed into his waiting glass. He gave both women a questioning look, holding up the bottle.

"Not on duty," Harmony said, "but thank you for offering."

He put the bottle back and lifted his glass, swirling the wine under the cold track lighting. Then he tossed back a generous swallow.

"More for me, which I'll need before this is all over," he said. "My lawyer's going to be furious at me tomorrow, but then again, that's what I pay her for. C'mon. I'll give you the two-dollar tour myself."

Lorne ran the tour. Harmony ran a security audit.

The plant was a maze, but colored lines on the white tiled floors steered visitors from the central offices to production and processing to the R&D facility at the far end of the property. They crossed from cube to riveted cube by the skyway, a glass tunnel bathed in icy blue light. Lorne towered over both women. He walked with a certain awkward gait, like he'd broken a leg once and it never quite healed.

"We're very proud of our work here," he was saying. "It's not enough to deliver front-line protection to our nation's troops, we also have to deliver innovation at an affordable price."

"From what I hear about the DoD bidding process," Jessie said, probing lightly, "the Pentagon is more concerned with cost than quality."

Lorne's half-visible smile fell. He walked up to the door at the end of the hall, a slab of reinforced steel, and held the card on his lanyard up to a scanner. The panel beeped and the door slowly slid open on silent runners. He stepped over the threshold and waved Harmony and Jessie inside.

"Their priorities," he said, "are not my priorities. An unfortunate reality of government contract work. My bottom line is that Ardentis Solutions is in the business of saving lives. Complications or not, that's the only business I want to be in."

He wasn't the only one who worked late at Ardentis. The R&D labs were still bustling well after midnight, with a skeleton crew of white-jacketed researchers carrying out experiments in a hamster maze of curling glass corridors and white-walled labs. Exposed ducts ran along the unpainted girders overhead, and the constant grinding hum of the air conditioning system kept the galleries museum-cold.

Harmony drew a map in her mind. Their lives might depend on it if things went wrong tomorrow. As they walked past gyroscopes and heavy machine presses and bays where scientists worked with their gloved arms buried in glass-walled isolation chambers, she realized this was only part of the floor plan. Red-jacketed doors barred the way here and there, the color popping out in the sea of antiseptic white and stainless steel, and if she understood the layout correctly, over half of the laboratory was on the other side of those doors.

"What's through there?" she asked innocently as they walked together.

"That, I'm afraid, you *will* need a warrant for," Lorne said, his tone light. "But you don't need to. Doctor Castillo only works in this part of the lab; I don't think he's ever even set foot in there. Come to think of it, I don't believe he even has access."

Lorne Murrough might have been on the side of the angels — he hadn't given them a reason to think otherwise, not yet — but he was a terrible liar.

Harmony tensed at the sound of muffled gunshots up ahead. Lorne caught her look and chuckled.

"No worries, Agent. It's just our test range. Here, let me show you something. Give a proud father a chance to brag, would you?"

He passed out safety-yellow earmuffs, pulling a pair over his wildly unkempt waterfall of hair before using his card to unlock another security door. The room beyond was a private shooting range, five lanes with paper targets dangling from mechanical clamps on a rolling track. The last lane was occupied by a life-sized target dummy, its body made of shimmering ballistic gel.

A lone researcher was threading shells into a sleek pump shotgun. He turned to see the new arrivals and quickly inclined his head.

"Mister Murrough, sir. I didn't know you were coming down."

"Just keeping you on your toes, Jack. Giving these ladies an unofficial tour. Trying out the new DOVE rounds?"

"Yes, sir, um..." He fell silent, giving the women an uncertain glance.

"It's fine, they're public servants, just like us. Give us a demonstration!" Lorne beamed like a kid on Christmas morning and lowered his voice. "My pride and joy. These aren't for sale yet, they need a lot more testing before I'm ready to let 'em leave the nest, but we're about to revolutionize the less-than-lethal munitions market."

The scientist obliged him, taking a shell from an unlabeled cardboard box and holding it up for inspection. It didn't look like anything Harmony had ever seen before: a shotgun slug with a recessed, spiral channel along its length, strung with coppery-red wire. The base clicked softly as he rotated it on a concealed screw, then loaded it into his weapon.

"Directed Overload Voltage Emitter. DOVE," Lorne explained. Then he paused. "We're workshopping the name. It's a step up from 'Secure Pulse Activated Round for Knockdowns,' but just barely."

"We're better at science than we are at acronyms," the researcher conceded, shouldering the shotgun.

"That's marketing's job anyway," Lorne said. "Let 'em earn their paychecks."

The researcher took aim downrange, focusing his sights on the ballistic-gel dummy, and squeezed the trigger.

Once, when Harmony was a kid, a transformer outside their house got hit by a bolt of lightning. She didn't remember the explosion, just that she had been sitting in a chair in her room, studying, and suddenly she was dazed and down on the carpet with blood roaring in her ears. The memory rushed back as the slug hit the target and erupted with the force of a stun grenade.

Her entire body tingled, heart thumping, from an impact twenty feet away.

"Feel that?" Lorne said, his one visible eye manic. "Look at the dummy's chest. Minimal penetration, minimal physical injury. Just a less-than-lethal round with a payload designed for maximum incapacitation. You can even adjust the discharge. Setting one, the default, hits about as hard as an electric cattle prod. Setting five...well, show 'em, Jack."

The researcher gave his boss an uncertain look, but decided not to argue. He took another shell from the box, twisted the screw on its base until it clicked five times, and loaded his shotgun.

Harmony threw a hand over her eyes as the slug connected and then burst into a helix of blue lightning that ripped the ballistic-gel dummy clear off its moorings, scorching it black as the torso went tumbling, rolling up the lane until it thumped against the back wall of the firing range. Crackles of diamond light clung to its skin for a moment before fading, like the last dying sparks of a campfire.

"You said *less* than lethal?" Jessie asked.

"Level one is the default for a reason, obviously," Lorne said. "But if you need to make a rampaging rhino take a nap — or take down a heavily armed tweaker high on PCP — our DOVE rounds will get the job done."

"And you're just trusting that people won't jack those babies up to level five as a matter of course, without even thinking about it?"

"I trust," Lorne said, "that the people who have the great responsibility of guarding this nation will use wise and rational judgment. Walk with me."

He led them out of the firing range, collecting their earmuffs and hanging them on a peg on the other side of the door.

"This nation's problem has never been our warriors in uniform," Lorne said. "The problem is a crisis of cowardice from the ones in command. We keep our warriors in shackles, while the paper-pushers give orders concerning battlefields they'll never set foot on or even see. The closest they'll ever get to seeing the blood and the loss and the grief is scribbling their signatures on a stack of condolence letters."

Harmony saw a gap in his armor, an opportunity to press.

"You were a conscientious objector back in Vietnam, weren't you?" she asked.

"Seventh-day Adventist," he said. "We believed in supporting the country, just not carrying a gun to do it. Lost my faith around the same time we lost the war, but I was proud to do my part. I served in the medical corps. Of course, that's where I lost my illusions, too. Saw the grim irony of the whole thing."

"Meaning?" Harmony asked.

He stopped mid-stride, turning to look down at her with his one visible eye. His face was a cratered moon, a ravaged, arid waste pockmarked with pink sores and old scar tissue.

"I spent years...sick. Sick every waking hour of the day. Dosed up with the nastiest germs you've ever heard of and a few you probably haven't, so they could devise antibodies and cures. It was good work. Necessary work, to save lives. But then I realized something: isn't it funny that they'd infect me with these horrors, a loyal citizen who willingly embraced my civic duty and volunteered to serve my country...but not the enemy? Of course, no, we could never use such weapons on the enemy." He flashed a wan smile. "That would be *barbaric*."

He started walking again, leading them to a circular cluster of desks divided by low gray fabric walls, an open-plan office where geometric screensavers rippled across dark workstation monitors.

"Administration after administration, I hoped things would change. Never have. We sell our warriors out, in this country. Wring them dry, break them like toys, and toss them away. Doesn't matter who's in charge: the cowards at the top never change."

He paused, catching himself.

"Sorry. I shouldn't have had that wine, clearly." He gestured to one of the desks. "This is Nicholas's desk, though to be honest he mostly works from home these days. He's more of a big-ideas guy than a hands-on researcher, so telecommuting works fine for both of us. Go ahead, please, do whatever you need to."

Harmony carried out a half-hearted search, going through the desk drawers under Lorne's watchful eye, but she knew it was a waste of time.

This wasn't Dr. Castillo's desk.

Chapter Nineteen

As the cargo van slowly backed out of the parking spot down in the plant's parking lot, Harmony glanced at a security camera on a post near the razor-wire fencing. The gray eye of the camera smoothly tracked them as the car rumbled toward the gate.

"He's lying," Harmony said.

Jessie took off her dark glasses. Her eyes glowed, soft, in the shadows.

"Tell me more."

"Not only is he lying," Harmony said, "as soon as he found out we were coming, he got a dog and pony show all ready for us. Those desks in the lab all had nameplates, except for the one he said belonged to Castillo. That's because it wasn't his. I picked through the clutter and spotted a couple of vape pens in the top drawer."

Harmony glanced sidelong at her partner.

"Check the dossier. Castillo doesn't smoke."

"He just picked some random employee's desk, stashed the nameplate and lied to our faces," Jessie said.

"Correct. I suspect that was the reason for the whole gun show on the target range."

"He stalled us for a couple of minutes so one of his flunkies could run ahead and set things up."

Harmony nodded. "Whatever's on the other side of that lab, behind those red doors, is where we'll find the package. That's where Castillo *really* works. No chance Murrough was going to let us take even a tiny peek. There's a reason he shut us down with a smile. Ardentis Solutions is a government contractor with five-star brass on speed dial; he knows perfectly well that we'd never get a search warrant for his high-security labs, not in a million years."

"So much for the 'that's not how we do things at Ardentis' spiel. He'd rather protect his secrets than protect Castillo's life."

"Not terribly surprising. Depending on what the 'package' really is, Murrough and everyone who works with him could be looking at hardcore prison time. We'll relieve them of that burden tomorrow."

"Today," Jessie said.

Harmony squinted at her. Jessie pointed to the clock on the dashboard.

"It's way past midnight," she said. "We should get back to the hotel and grab a few hours of shuteye while we still can."

"I'm not tired."

Jessie's hands tightened on the steering wheel.

"Are you legitimately not tired," she asked, "or are you in one of your 'sleep is a luxury I can't afford because I'm on a *mission*' moods?"

"I don't sound like that," Harmony said.

"Uh-huh. Answer the question."

She didn't know how.

She was tired. She knew that. But she'd felt that way for a very long time. Exhaustion dogged her footsteps, but sheer willpower kept her moving. One foot in front of the other. And again. And again.

Harmony didn't enlist in this war. She was drafted when she was six years old, the night a monster came to her house. Sometimes, when she closed her eyes, she still felt her father's big, strong hand squeeze her arm. Then he smiled at her, one last time. And then he died.

She remembered the reflections of the squad car lights outside the kitchen window, strobing in cherry red and deep winter ice. Too late to help anyone, too late to save anyone. Barry was one of her father's deputies. Harmony tried to tell him that she saw the killer. That it was the Bogeyman.

Just a bad man, Barry told her, tapping the star on his chest. *This badge means it's my job to find bad people and make them go away so they can't hurt anybody else. And that's exactly what I'm going to do.*

But he never did.

This was Harmony's crusade. Her purpose. Her motive to keep breathing when she really couldn't find any other reasons. And if she was killing herself by inches, that was just the price of the ticket. Years of battling madmen and monsters had left her a patchwork quilt of scars, inside and out; there was a reason she never wore short sleeves, even in the summer heat. She didn't quit. Then Nadine, desperate and cornered, burned her kiss into Harmony's soul along with a hunger that couldn't be sated by any mortal food. She still didn't quit. Just kept moving. One foot, then the other.

She hated her body. Hated everything about it. It didn't seem fond of her either, waking her every morning with a chorus of old aches, old injuries, old memories of every time she was too slow or too late to save the day. She couldn't even use magic without fighting through debilitating cramps, and now that her power was mutating in strange and alien ways, she couldn't trust it.

She was going to die in the field someday. She knew this. She was at peace with it. Until the day the monsters got lucky, she'd take as many of them down as she could. Harmony's mind was a fine-tuned engine, eager for the fight; she just needed her traitorous flesh to cooperate a little bit longer.

The cargo van dipped into the Fairmont's hotel parking garage.

"April called me the other day, after the briefing." Jessie's voice was unusually hesitant. "She wanted to talk to me about your medical evaluation."

Harmony glanced to her right, down the line of rental cars and out-of-state license plates. Her lips went tight.

"Don't park by the Hemi," she said. "Take the next turn, dip down and park on the lower level."

There was plenty of open space up top, and Jessie gave her a sidelong glance as she rolled right past the sleeping muscle car. She asked a question with her eyes.

"Hopefully I'm wrong," Harmony said.

The engine rattled as Jessie killed the ignition. They got out and backtracked on foot. Harmony paused near the bend in the sloped drive lane, nodding up toward the bubble of a safety mirror mounted high in one corner. Now Jessie could see what Harmony had spotted on their way in: a dark figure, squatting near the Hemi Cuda's front bumper, now rising to its full height and making a quiet getaway in the opposite direction. He was six feet tall plus a few inches, broad shoulders draped in a cheap, shabby trench coat, and he wore a fedora with the brim pulled low over his shadowed features. He had an awkward, limping gait, at odds with the uncanny silence of his footsteps.

Harmony and Jessie locked eyes for a fleeting second. Jessie nodded. While her partner approached the limping man from behind, Jessie broke into a sprint, ducking behind concrete pillars and circling around to emerge and stand square in his path.

"Boy did you pick the wrong night to break into people's cars," she said, hands on her hips. "Don't worry about it. We're not going to call the cops, and if you need money for food or something, we can help you. But if you took anything from that sweet ride over there, I'm going to need you to give it back. Now."

The man turned, wheeling around on his one good leg, only to find Harmony standing behind him. In the dim garage lighting, with his hat pulled low, the man's face was a lumpy blur. His hands, though, gave Harmony a queasy feeling deep in her gut. The texture was all wrong, like cheesecloth dipped in wax.

He froze. Then he turned back to face Jessie and froze again, like a broken computer program still trying to carry out its instructions.

"Not gonna hurt you, dude," Jessie sighed. "We've just had a really long night, we're about to have an even longer day, and I don't have the time or the patience for this right now."

"Hurt," the man echoed, with a voice that sounded like he was gargling motor oil.

Harmony crouched and drew her pistol from its ankle holster. Jessie saw the warning in her eyes and slowly lowered her hands. Then she curled them into fists.

"*Hurt,*" the man roared, and he bent forward as he barreled at Jessie, his bad leg kicking out behind him with every lurching step. She was ready for him. The second he came within reach she leaped up and spun on her heel, snapping out with a jaw-shattering kick to his face. Harmony heard bones snap. He didn't even feel it. He lashed out and backhanded Jessie hard enough to knock her off her feet and launch her into the hood of a parked car. The hood dented under her weight as she hit it and rolled off, falling, tumbling to the concrete floor in a stunned daze. The car's alarm shrieked and its headlights began to flash, painting the shadowy garage in flickering metronome strobes of hard white light.

Harmony already had her weapon up and she fired for center mass. Two rounds punched through the back of his trench coat, one a perfect kill-shot, straight to the heart. He just stood there, his hat fallen off in the fight, and slowly turned to face her. The aftermath of the gunshots roared and echoed through the concrete cavern of the parking garage.

She amended her assessment. It would have been a perfect kill-shot, if the man wasn't already dead.

Sparse black hair clung to his waxy scalp as he greeted her with empty, milky eyes. His belt had come undone and his coat hung open. He was naked underneath, his hairy skin fish-belly white, his chest bearing the long Y-shaped stitches of a fresh autopsy.

Harmony shot him between the eyes. His head snapped back, the bullet tearing a bloodless crater in his forehead, splintering bone and pulping brain. He still didn't go down. He staggered backwards, almost falling, but stayed on his feet. Then he turned and broke into a lumbering run.

She ran over and put an arm around Jessie's shoulders, helping her back to her feet. Jessie winced and rubbed the back of her neck.

"Shit. Zombie. Apparently not the kind that goes down when you shoot 'em in the head, either."

They'd encountered the risen dead before. Mostly courtesy of their old nemesis Bobby Diehl, who infused his 'quiet ones' with titanium endoskeletons and remote-control technology. But Diehl was in hiding, probably in another country by now, and this wasn't one of his creations. This was something different, something lonely, ragged, a creature that stank of fear and formaldehyde.

Harmony checked Jessie over. She was afraid, too. "Are you all right?"

"Nice thing about having the blood of an alien god," she grunted over the blaring car alarm, "is that I can take a beating like a champ. Let's get after that thing. It's probably trying to run back to whoever reanimated it, and I *really* want a word with that person."

That wasn't the real problem, Harmony knew. Neither was the idea of a dead man with a hole in his skull stumbling around downtown Chicago, though that needed fixing. The real problem was the dead man was *scared*, like an animal recoiling from a burning flame, and he was strong enough that his backhand would have snapped any normal person's neck.

If Jessie was right and he was fleeing to whatever charnel house he called home, he'd kill anyone standing in his path.

Chapter Twenty

The Chicago Loop was a graveyard by night, at least compared to the hustle and bustle of broad daylight. Come five o'clock, commuters fled the city in droves. This late at night even the bars were closed, last call a fading memory, and only a few stray taxi cabs cruised through the quiet dark.

The dead man wasn't hard to spot. He was running as fast as his twisted leg would let him, heading down a long straight sidewalk on a sharp hill, straight for the outskirts of Millennium Park. Jessie had her phone out, talking breathlessly as she and Harmony sprinted side by side, chasing their quarry down.

"Kevin, need you to scramble a cleanup team, pronto. Right about now there's going to be reports of multiple gunshots in the Fairmont's parking garage. I need every security recording within a hundred yards wiped, and I need it done now."

Kevin stifled a yawn. "On it, boss."

"We're also going to need a body retrieval."

"At the garage?"

"No," Jessie said. "I'll call back and tell you where. We haven't killed it yet. Just have the team on standby."

The side of the park facing South Michigan Avenue was under heavy construction, sidewalks blocked off and building supplies tarped down in the shadows of tall scaffolding. The park closed at eleven and the only people in sight were a couple of distant security guards, their flashlight beams bobbing across the lush, sculpted green.

They had no idea what was coming their way. If they saw the dead man, they'd try to stop him. If they tried to stop him, they'd die. Harmony's lungs were burning but she dug deep and found a fresh burst of strength, just enough to keep her going.

He broke west, crossing the edge of the grassy park on a diagonal, heading for the boulevard. He ran into the construction work, nearly colliding with a plywood wall, and froze for a minute. Recalculating, consulting some arcane GPS in his broken undead brain, before lurching south.

"This way," Harmony gasped, pointing up ahead. "He's trying to get around the construction work. We can cut him off."

Up ahead, an elephantine sculpture slumbered in the dark. Its artist dubbed it the Cloud Gate, but everyone just called it the Bean, for obvious reasons: it was a giant curved kidney of stainless steel, thirty feet tall and twice as long, with skin like liquid mercury. It caught their reflections, turning them into funhouse-mirror wraiths, while the trapped streetlights in its belly took on a mad carnival glow.

Jessie leaped over a park bench, her gait so low she looked like she was loping instead of running, almost on all fours as she blazed a trail. Her eyes were a pair of burning sapphires. While Harmony circled around to cut off the creature's escape, Jessie threw herself onto his back and got an arm around his throat, intent on twisting his head clean off. He bucked wildly and threw her over his shoulder, sending her hurtling to the pavement. She hit the ground and rolled, tumbling to a stop under the shadow of the Bean.

"Burn it," Jessie hissed. Harmony was already in motion, meeting the dead man in mid-stride, reaching deep into her aching stomach and searing lungs to call to her magic. *Earth, air, fire, water—* she started to recite in her mind, the invocation she'd learned at her mother's knee as a child.

Except she didn't need the words tonight. Her hand clamped down on his face, a move born of pure instinct, and she did the same thing she did to the Basilisk's henchman back in Vegas. She *pulled*.

Her arm went cold, then numb, as death flooded her body. She found the core of this twisted creature and she leeched it out, swallowing death and pain and rot and fear. It was infecting her, drowning her. She felt her heart stop beating.

Harmony slammed her opposite hand against the Bean. The perfectly smooth steel was cool to the touch. She had a bellyful of death and needed somewhere to put it, so she made herself a channel, pulling from the animated corpse, pushing toward the sculpture, her arms like electrical lines as the last twitching, serpentine trace of power slipped from the corpse, wormed through her veins and slipped out the other side with a faint, venomous rattle.

The dead man collapsed like a puppet with its strings cut.

She had left her mark. Where she had pressed her palm to the stainless steel, the sculpture now bore the outline of a hand, seared jet-black.

The blowback hit. She doubled over, then fell to her knees, crawling to the edge of the pavement before throwing up in the grass. It felt like her guts were trying to turn themselves inside out. Worse than it had ever been, but she'd never taken energy like that inside her body before, and from the way her stomach was heaving it was like her body was trying to cast out every last trace.

"Yeah, Kevin," she heard Jessie say behind her. "That body's ready for pickup. Tell the boys to put it in secure containment. It's dead, but...well, it was dead when we found it too, and it damn near kicked our asses. Better safe than sorry."

She hung up and knelt, gently pulling Harmony's hair back as she retched up the last of her dinner.

"Hey, hey," Jessie said, her voice soft now. "I got you. You're okay."

Harmony spat bile into the grass and wiped the back of her hand across her mouth.

"I know who sent it," she said.

Jessie helped her to her feet, and she walked over to the corpse on shaky legs. The dead man's coat hung open, his autopsy stitches popping at the edges. A strange fluid, such a bright shade of green it seemed to glow in the dark, leaked in dribbles from his nose and one ear.

"You were right," Harmony said. "He was trying to run home."

She drew a line with her pointing finger, from the north side of the park, to the wall of construction along South Michigan, to the opposite side. She took out her phone, tapping fast to confirm a hunch.

"He was trying to go west. And do you know what's almost perfectly west of here, give or take a block?"

Harmony showed Jessie her phone.

"The Cook County Morgue. And we know someone who works there."

"Our 'special materials handling expert,'" Jessie said. "That motherfucking weasel."

"Really wanted to brag that he knew a secret about me," Harmony said.

"Leaving aside the 'how,' I want to know how many of these things he has. Actually, scratch that. What I really want to know is, is he spying on everybody on this crew...or just us?"

She didn't need to explain the distinction. There was no honor among thieves; if West was spying on everyone, it was just criminal self-preservation. If he was only spying on *them*, maybe even at Josh Orville's behest...that pointed to a thornier problem. A problem they didn't have time to solve, considering it was almost three in the morning.

They had a heist in a few hours, and they still needed a plan to deal with the double-cross they knew was waiting in the wings. And considering Bette's questionable loyalties and West's snooping, now they had to brace for the double-crosses they hadn't even spotted yet.

False dawn glinted on the horizon as they stumbled into their hotel room, dead on their feet. Harmony pitched onto her bed face-first, collapsing on top of the covers, not bothering to take her clothes off.

"We should stay up," she mumbled. "Need a better plan."

Jessie clicked off the lights. With a tired smile, she got onto the same bed, snuggling up against Harmony.

"We have a plan," she said. "First thing when we get there, I'm gonna take the wayward doctor aside and I'm going to put the fear of Jessie into him. It's like the fear of God, but a lot scarier."

"That's not—" Harmony said, half asleep already. "We need contingency plans. A strategy for handling Bette, whether she's—"

"Shh."

As Harmony rolled onto her side, Jessie moved up behind her. Their bodies pressed together, warm in the dark. Jessie's breathing slowed until it matched Harmony's, their chests rising and falling in unison.

"What we need," Jessie said, gently stroking Harmony's hair, "is a few hours of rest. Go to sleep, hon. You'll feel better, I promise."

"But what if..." Her voice trailed off.

"Shh. I'm officially pulling rank as team leader and changing your job title tonight. You're the little spoon. Rest now."

"But—"

"Whatever you're about to say is the big spoon's problem. Let the big spoon handle it, and *go to sleep.*"

Neither of them said anything after that, slipping away into troubled dreams, stealing a few hours to rest and heal before facing the fight of their lives.

CHAPTER TWENTY-ONE

On the drive to Joliet early Saturday morning with the sunlight pushing down through broken rainclouds, they decided to divide and conquer. Jessie would corner West, get the truth out of him, and ensure he played ball, at least until the end of the job.

"What galls me," she said, drumming her fingers on the steering wheel, "is that we can't risk scaring him off. We might *need* his ass, or at least Josh thinks we will."

"So much for putting the fear of Jessie into him."

"Oh, no," she said. "I'm gonna make him piss his pants. I just have to use a little finesse to make sure he falls in line and acts like a good little necromancer."

"Finesse," Harmony echoed.

"What?" Jessie lifted an eyebrow. "Bitch, I'm *great* at finesse. Meanwhile, I need you working Bette. We agreed on the situation here?"

"She went rogue yesterday and ended up saving us from a silent alarm that Josh didn't seem to factor into his plans. He doesn't have a reputation for being sloppy, and as far as I can tell he doesn't have a death wish. So either they're working together and he told her to cover our tracks when we snatched Castillo, or Bette's cover is blown and he knew she'd pull strings to protect the operation."

Harmony fixed her gaze on the highway ahead. Blades of golden light slipped between the dark clouds, stretching down to brush against the wet, cold earth.

"Of course," she reflected, "if she's a traitor, then she would have told him all about us. *Our* covers were blown before we walked in the door and Josh is just playing us, because he knows

— exactly like Bette — we want the 'package' and we'll ride this out to the end."

"On the other hand..." Jessie said.

"On the other hand, if she's compromised and doesn't know it, a word of warning might save her life. On the *other* other hand, if she's a traitor, telling her what we know could push her to escalate matters."

"Josh still needs bodies for this heist. Even if he knows everything, he'll play dumb until the job's over. That's when they'll make a move." Jessie paused. "Damn."

Harmony glanced over at her. "What?"

"Just wish we knew his exit strategy. Stealing the package from Ardentis is only half the job tonight. We need to steal it *twice*, first from the lab and then from Josh and his pet psycho. I'd really like to save the rest of the crew if we can, too. Well, maybe not West, screw him, but Houston seems like a decent guy. And getting on good terms with Bette and her people might lead to collaborations down the road. At the very least we could work out some kind of intel-sharing deal, assuming she's not already planning to murder us."

"Assuming," Harmony said.

They pulled up outside the shuttered garage in Joliet. Dima came out to meet them along with West and Houston, the three of them lugging long cardboard boxes over to the cargo van.

West looked...troubled. Harmony noticed, as she got out of the van, that he didn't make eye contact.

Your monster never came home last night, she thought. *You sent a dead man to spy on us, and he vanished off the face of the earth. I'd be worried, too.*

"Josh and Ricky are on their way with the doctor," Dima said. "By all accounts things went swimmingly."

"You weren't there?" Harmony asked.

Dima gave a petulant sniff.

"No. Apparently there is a fine art to gentle interrogations, a fine art that I clearly know nothing about. I was not invited to participate."

Harmony almost felt sorry for her, until she remembered how many mutilated bodies Dima had left in her wake over the years. All signs suggested that Dima had a tragic, ego-fueled misunderstanding of her role here. She thought she was running the show, when she was just another expendable, marked for death at the closing curtain. Someone had to pay for losing Nadine's money.

"Is Cherry here?" she asked, invoking Bette's alias.

Dima rolled her eyes and jerked a thumb over her shoulder. "Inside. Little Miss Perfect is going over her electronics kit, which is why she can't help disguise this van with the rest of us."

"I'm not afraid of a little hard work," Jessie said, circling the van and taking the other end of Dima's cardboard box. She looked over at Harmony. "Hey, why don't you go ask Cherry about that problem you were having? We'll probably be too busy to get a chance later."

"Problem?" Houston asked. He glanced between the two women. "Anything I can help with?"

"Nah," Jessie said as Harmony walked to the garage door alone. "A target up in Reno disappeared on her last month and it sounded like some kind of hacker business. I said she should have a word with our resident expert. I mean, hey, free advice."

"Can't argue with that," Houston said.

West still hadn't spoken a single word.

Bette was sitting in a folding chair in the empty garage, a laptop propped on her knees. A backpack, hot pink with blue piping, sagged in the chair next to her with its top flap half-unzipped. She glanced up as Harmony walked in but didn't stop typing.

"Already told Dima I'll be out in ten minutes. Making sure my gear is ready for tonight is a *little* more important than pasting some decals on a stolen van."

"We need to talk."

Bette stopped typing. She eyed Harmony, then nodded to a nearby chair.

"Come over here," she said in a low voice, reaching into her backpack. She took out a gadget, some kind of card reader with a canary-yellow shell, tethered to a ribbon cable, and handed it to her. "Pretend you're helping me calibrate this."

Harmony dragged over the chair and sat facing her, close enough for their knees to touch. She leaned in and dropped her voice to a whisper.

"That silent alarm at Castillo's place. You're absolutely certain it triggered? Nothing interfered with it?"

"Like I said, straight to the cops and to the nearest sheriff's station. You don't even want to know the work I had to do to quash an armed response."

"That's the problem," Harmony started to say. "Josh is—"

She bit her words short as the garage door rattled, then swung wide. Josh walked in with Doctor Castillo in tow, the two of them looking like old college buddies instead of a kidnapper and his victim. Ricky followed a few feet behind, his eyes heavy-lidded, lazy and mean.

"Whoa, thought we had the room to ourselves," Josh said. "Sorry. Interrupting some juicy girl talk?"

Harmony glanced over at him. "I'm helping Cherry double-check her tools. Wouldn't be much fun if something broke in the middle of the heist."

"Really?"

Josh meandered toward them, walking in a slow, spiraling arc.

"That's interesting," he said. "Dima told me you're some badass gun for hire, but she didn't say you knew anything about electronic security."

"I don't." Harmony held up the canary-yellow box before passing it back to Bette. "But I can follow basic directions and change a pair of batteries. They've even got little plus and minus signs showing which way they go."

He looked like he was about to say something, then reconsidered, pursing his lips. He flicked his fingers at the garage door.

"Cute. We do need the room for a few minutes, though. Out, both of you. Do me a favor? Help Dima with the van. Between you and me, I don't think she knows what the hell she's doing."

"Ain't that a first," Ricky drawled.

• • • ● ● • ● ● • •

While Harmony was inside, Jessie went to work on Dr. West. He held his silence and so did she. She just *stared* at him, fixing him in the smoky lenses of her dark sunglasses, as the crew worked to apply unwieldy sheets of vinyl to the stolen cargo van. He worked on one side of the hood and she moved to the opposite side, making sure he found her looking right at him every time he shot a furtive glance in Jessie's direction. He moved to the back of the van. So did she. Standing closer this time, invading his personal space.

"I...need something from my car," he stammered to the others, curling a finger around his shirt's collar and tugging it awkwardly. "I'll be right back."

He had parked around back. Jessie gave him a five-second head start. Then she followed him, silent as a cat.

To her absolute lack of surprise, West drove a hearse. It was dusty, painted a blueish black, with the Cook County seal emblazoned on the doors and a placard reading *Official Business* propped up behind the front windshield. He was opening the passenger-side door when Jessie strolled up behind him.

"Do you like zombie movies?" she asked.

He spun around and she punched him in the gut.

West dropped to the dirty pavement, sputtering, gasping for air and turning green. Jessie casually stood over him, leaning in and tilting her head.

"Just for the record," she said, "that was a love-tap. Like, I hit my girlfriend *twice* as hard as that. She's half-demon and a serious sadomasochist, so she gets off on that shit, but the point is..."

She leaned closer, her shadow falling over his terrified, up-turned face.

"The point is," she continued, "that if you try anything stupid, I am going to *fuck you up*. So don't be stupid right now, okay?"

"I'll...I'll scream for help," he said in a tiny voice.

"And I'll beat you to death with a tire iron before anyone even comes looking for you. Listen, asshole: what I'm going to tell you right now, against my better judgment, might actually save your life. But first, let's start with last night. Tell me about the zombie."

"I do not employ *zombies*," West hissed, his professional pride rising above his fear. "Zombies are the product of primitive and savage mysticism—"

"You want to be real careful throwing around words like that right now."

"What? 'Mysticism?'"

She stared at him.

"I am a scientist and a medical professional." He put a finger to his temple, glaring up at her. "My work is just like my mind. Superior."

"You are truly not helping me to help you right now. Why were you spying on us?"

"I wasn't. Spying on you, that is. You are of no interest to me. Your friend, on the other hand? She's not what she's pretending to be."

"Keep talking."

"I knew she was trying to keep us outside, at Doctor Castillo's residence. So I followed her. She had one of the doctor's men at gunpoint. Instead of pulling the trigger, she talked to him. Convinced him to leave, alive, even after he saw her face."

West craned his neck and grew a sickly smile.

"She's not one of us," he said. "She's a federal agent."

"Who have you told?"

"No one, yet. I wanted to learn more before I brought my findings to Joshua. Where is my reanimated cadaver, by the way? I would like it back."

Jessie took a deep breath. She wasn't a religious woman — she'd faced a few creatures that could legitimately be called gods over the years, including the bastard whose own blood ran in her corrupted veins, and not one of them was worthy of worship — but sometimes she really wanted to pray for fortitude in the face of stupidity.

"Here's where I do you a solid, and trust me, you don't deserve it. Remember how you asked Josh who he really works for? You wanted to know who's behind this whole shindig."

"I do," West said, miffed at the memory. "And then his...gorilla intervened."

"Well, here's the fun part," she said. "I'm going to tell you exactly who we're working for. And then I'm going to tell you what Josh has planned for all of us at the end of this ride."

Harmony was out front, carefully lining up a vinyl sheet across the cargo van's side door with obsessive millimeter-tight precision, when Jessie and West walked back up the alley side by side. West's face was stark, eyes fixed in the distance, like he'd just seen a ghost. Jessie drifted past Harmony, lingering just long enough to whisper two words in her ear.

"He'll cooperate."

The cargo van's transformation was half complete, with a bold Gold Star Security logo and badge covering the old Hertz rent-a-car logo, when Ricky ambled outside.

"The man wants you all in the garage," he called out. "Time to get this show underway."

Chapter Twenty-Two

They filed into the garage where Josh held court at the folding table. Castillo — looking remarkably unharmed and content — stood at his side.

"The good doctor will be joining us this evening," Josh said.

Houston's hand went up.

"Yes?" Josh asked.

"More people means less profit. How will this affect the split?"

"It won't," Josh said. "A deal is a deal. I'm paying Doctor Castillo out of my cut. You will receive your full compensation, as agreed, once our business is done."

West made a disgruntled throat-noise. Jessie shot him a look of warning and he shrank in his chair.

Cooperative or not, the mad mortician was still a dangerous liability. His mouth could get them all killed, and Harmony had no doubt that if he was backed into a corner he'd offer up anyone and anything — her and Jessie, in particular — to save his own skin. She had to trust Jessie to handle that. She was focused entirely on Castillo.

He was perfectly at ease, standing next to Josh like they were old friends. Just yesterday they invaded his home, gunned down half of his bodyguards and took him hostage, and he was...fine. Harmony knew that Josh was slick; he bluffed for a living, earning diamond bracelets by manipulating his opponents into making fatal mistakes. But was he *that* good?

Maybe, she decided. But she knew one other way to change a man's mind overnight. A succubus could do it.

Nadine could do it.

The more she speculated, the more Harmony realized she was playing mind games with herself. She wanted it to be Nadine, because that meant she was close. Close enough to touch. Close enough to hurt. She had to accept that there were other explanations, and not of the supernatural kind. Castillo might have debts, or some other leverage Josh would have used against him. Maybe he was just greedy and Josh convinced him that a massive payday was waiting for him at the end of this ride. People turned traitor all the time. Some needed less of a nudge than others.

And that brought her back to the way they'd found him. Lorne Murrough had shown her a workstation that wasn't Castillo's, and they knew he was a recluse who avoided going into the office at all costs. He also surrounded himself with private security, like some kind of A-list celebrity.

He either feared being attacked, or he expected to be attacked, long before the House of Dead Roses and Josh's heist scheme came into the picture.

So what are you really afraid of? she thought, staring at the slight, twitchy man behind the card table. *And what did Josh offer you? How did he take your fears away?*

"I know where the package is being held," Castillo said, no more forthcoming about the "package" and its contents than Josh himself, "and I can lead you straight to it."

"You have full access?" Bette asked. "Can you walk us through security?"

He shook his head. "Unfortunately, as of this morning, all of my laboratory permissions have been suspended. My remote login credentials have been deactivated, and I have no doubt that my keycard is useless. I assume it's a precautionary measure, given my present circumstances."

Harmony saw a chance to gently press, and she went for it.

"I'm sure everyone at Ardentis is worried about you," she said.

A flicker of distaste crossed the doctor's face.

"If they cared about me," he said, "they would have listened to me. Everything that happens to them now, they brought upon themselves. I'm done playing Cassandra."

Josh looked smug as a cat with a saucer of milk as he reached over and rubbed Castillo's shoulder.

"I can safely move the package and maintain the integrity seals," Castillo added. "After all, I designed them."

Ricky had been leaning against the cinderblock wall, watching the proceedings with his usual air of lazy contempt. At that, though, he pushed himself away from the wall and walked slowly around the room.

"So what you're sayin' is," Ricky drawled with a pointed look at West, "now we got two hazardous material specialists on this crew. Seems to me like we only need the one."

West, flustered, looked between him and Josh with a protest on his lips. Castillo saved him.

"Actually," he said, "I'll be grateful for the assistance. It's a two-person job."

West pursed his lips, looking like he was torn between gratitude and his wounded pride.

"Yes," he said, forcing the words out. "I will be most pleased to...*assist* you, Doctor Castillo. You should take the lead. Of course. That's...simply rational."

Josh clapped his hands. "Okay. Settled. We're one big happy family. Now before the main event, we've got one last bit of business to handle. Houston?"

"I found a source for uniforms," the mustachioed safecracker said. "Gold Star operates an office in Skokie. That's a suburb, about an hour north of here if the traffic is good. It's mostly an administrative office where they process new hires and handle human resources. Meaning they not only have a selection of official uniforms, all crisp and shiny-new, that's also where they print employee ID cards. We'll look just like the real thing, because we'll be wearing the real thing."

"What kind of security are we looking at?" Bette asked.

"I cased the place early this morning. Hoped they'd be all locked up for the weekend, but no such luck. They've got a fenced-in parking lot, but the gate is left wide open whenever people are working in the office and nobody mans it. Camera in the lot, another in the lobby, and I'd bet cash money nobody's watching 'em. They're feeding straight to a recorder. Wipe the recording on our way out, we're free and clear."

Jessie furrowed her brow. "What about guards?"

"That's the beauty of it," Houston said. "There aren't any. This is administration. Paper-pushers and desk-jockeys. They don't keep any cash on site and there's nothing to steal, so nobody over there is expecting to get hit. We wait until they close, cut through the fence, we're in and out in fifteen minutes. By the time anyone realizes a robbery went down, we'll already be finished at Ardentis and long gone."

"Yeah," Josh said, "that's not going to work for me. Strict timetable, remember? We hit 'em this afternoon."

Houston stared at him. "In broad daylight? Maybe I wasn't clear: they're *open* on Saturdays. Skeleton crew compared to the usual staff, but there'll be plenty of civvies around."

"Too hot to handle?" Ricky asked, a cruel smile on his lips. "Oh, right. You're such a pussy you don't even carry a gun."

Houston shot to his feet. His folding chair kicked back, clattering on the oil-stained concrete floor.

"I'm a goddamn professional," he fired back. "I didn't sign up for any of this cowboy shit."

Ricky's smile faded and his eyes went beady and hard. He slowly closed the distance between them.

"Well, you're in with a cowboy-shit crew now, muchacho. So are you gonna lace your boots up and get with the program, or do we need to make some last-minute staff cuts?"

Harmony knew, in a quiet moment of clarity, that someone was about to die. Ricky was loyal to his master, but Josh couldn't control him: he was an attack dog, off his leash and eager to bite. And if Houston didn't back down Ricky was going to beat him to death, right here, right now. She and Jessie could intervene, make a show of force and save Houston...but then they'd have to kill Ricky. *He'd be embarrassed*, she thought. *He's a hopped-up rage addict with an ego made of paper-thin glass. You don't humiliate a man like that unless you're ready and able to kill him, because he's sure as hell going to kill you.*

She saw the light. A third option.

"We can optimize the timetable," she said.

Now she had Josh's full attention. Houston and Ricky were still squaring off, giving each other murder-eyes, but they held their ground for the moment.

"We're not done putting the vinyls on the van," she explained. "We could be looking at a time crunch, unless we divide the work. Dima, Houston, and the two doctors can apply the finishing touches and make sure the disguise is perfect, while the rest of us raid the Gold Star office."

"Now that's the kind of proactive problem-solving I like to see," Josh said.

Ricky squinted, nodding slowly, and took a step back.

"Yeah, sure." He locked eyes with Houston. "You can have a little sewing-circle with the rest of the ladies, while we take care of business."

He turned his back on the man. Houston's hand clenched into a fist. *Don't do it*, Harmony thought.

Houston took a deep breath and relaxed his grip. He picked up his fallen chair and sat back down.

"Okay," Josh said. "Team Gold Star, you're with me. Team Vinyl, I want that van looking pristine, perfect, and ready to roll the second we get back."

Harmony saw an opportunity. This was her chance to finish her interrupted conversation and warn Bette that her cover might have been blown.

"We're going to need a ride, since we came in the van." She turned to Bette. "Can we go with you?"

Before she could answer, Josh cut her off. "Not a problem. We'll all fit in my truck. Yes indeed, one big happy family."

Josh's truck was a platinum beast, a heavy-duty Ford pickup with dual back wheels and a covered cargo bed. Harmony, Jessie, and Bette slid into the long backseat bench while Josh got behind the wheel and Ricky climbed in on the passenger side.

"We got the fun job," Ricky said as Josh pulled out onto the street and pointed the truck north.

"Tonight's the fun," Josh replied. "This is just housekeeping. Ricky, gloves please."

He leaned over, scooped up a cardboard box of disposable latex gloves from the passenger-side floor, and yanked out a pair for himself before passing the box to the back seat.

"Ladies, glove up if you'd be so kind," Josh said.

Bette's eyes narrowed. "We won't be there for an hour yet."

"Which gives us plenty of time to go over the plan. Trust me, you'll want gloves for this."

The tight, sticky gloves snapped tight against Harmony's wrists. She tilted her head, curious, as Ricky bent forward again. This time he came up with a burlap sack that rattled, something metallic inside, as he handed it over to Jessie. She opened the sack and the other women leaned in to take a look.

It was a bag of guns, more or less. A mismatched collection of cheap, janky pistols, some tinged with rust or sporting cracked grips, each one wearing the dull gray tube of a sound suppressor.

"Ladies' choice," Josh said. "Take your pick."

"We already have weapons," Harmony said.

"You don't have these. Thanks to a friend of mine in the Chicago PD, each of these lovely pieces got up and walked out of an evidence locker last week. And each one of them has..." He glanced up, meeting Harmony's eyes in the rearview mirror. "Hey, Hit-girl. What do you call a weapon that can be tied to an active murder case?"

"In Reno," she said, her voice carefully neutral, "we call that 'weight.'"

"The Latin Kings got shit taste in guns, but they sure go through a lot of 'em," Ricky said.

"Hence the gloves," Josh added. "We'll be abandoning these weapons at the scene of the crime. Just a little extra obfuscation to confuse the boys in blue, assuming they find them once the fires are out."

"Excuse me," Jessie said. "Fires?"

"Didn't we mention?" Ricky said, turning in his seat and flashing a hungry grin.

"Must have slipped my mind," Josh said.

"Yeah, so," Ricky drawled, "we need these disguises for the job. Can't have word getting around that a bunch of Gold Star uniforms got jacked the same night a crew of badass hombres *in* said uniforms show up at the Ardentis plant. Naw, that's just sloppy. So we're going scorched-earth on this place. We rock in, take what we need, and toss a Molotov on our way out."

"It's the middle of the day," Harmony said. She felt a cold, crawling sensation on the back of her neck. "The office is open. It's going to be filled with people."

Ricky snorted at her.

"You know better, girl. Wage slaves, working for the man day in and day out, going home to their empty beds and TV dinners.

They ain't real *people*, not like you and me. Shit, they oughta thank us for this."

Bette's hands clenched on her knees until her knuckles turned white.

"Joshua?" she said. "I need you to clarify our instructions, because I do not want to misunderstand what we're doing here. It sounds like Ricky is saying—"

"We're going to kill them all," Josh said. "No witnesses. No survivors."

Casual. Just like that. The words hung in a sudden silence as he pulled the truck onto an on-ramp and merged into highway traffic.

CHAPTER TWENTY-THREE

Ricky's beady-eyed gaze swept across the back seat until he locked eyes with Harmony. She felt like she was in some twisted nature documentary. She just wasn't sure if this was a mating display, a threat, or both.

"Ain't gonna be a problem for you, right, killer?"

She couldn't let this happen. She wasn't going to sacrifice an office filled with innocent people for the sake of the mission, and she knew Jessie wouldn't either. They'd find another way. They always did somehow. For now she had to thread the needle, pretending to be on board with the plan while — hopefully — steering Josh toward a less murderous solution.

"Of course it isn't a problem," she said. "But it is sloppy. We don't want to draw attention, so we're going to commit a massacre and then burn the building down? Admittedly I don't have Mister Orville's keen strategic mind..."

"Thanks for that," Josh said.

"...but this is going to be front-page news for a week. How does that help us?"

"Two ways. First of all, the sheer level of overkill will have the cops looking for a motive in all the wrong places. Nobody is going to believe this was about a box of uniforms and some ID cards. The abandoned guns will help with that."

"Everybody knows the street gangs in Chicago are out of control," Ricky said with a chuckle. "Those boys love to wild out and get trigger-happy."

Josh nodded. "We're weaving a narrative. Telling a story, and nobody is going to question it because it slots neatly into a whole set of preexisting beliefs. Which brings us to the number two reason: I *want* the press to scream about it. If we do this right, at least until the next shiny distraction comes along, it'll be wall-to-wall coverage."

Harmony sat back, her eyes distant, following his logic.

"Gun violence, gang violence," she mused. "You're cooking up a banquet for pundits and op-ed writers."

"With everyone looking for the wrong culprits in the wrong direction. And in all that noise and fuss, a tiny little break-in at Ardentis is back page news. Just a blip, off the radar and soon forgotten."

"Ardentis won't forget," Jessie pointed out.

"They won't be in a position to complain. Oh, they'll report some kind of burglary, for sure, but they won't be able to tell the cops what we really stole."

Because they shouldn't have it either, Harmony thought. She had suspected all along that Lorne Murrough and his lab rats were looking at prison time if anyone found out what they were really studying — the whole reason for last night's dog and pony show — and Josh had just confirmed it for her.

"When do we find out what's in the package?" she asked.

"You don't," Ricky said. "You do your job, you get paid, you go home and forget this ever happened. Gets no simpler than that. The package ain't nothing you need to worry about."

They would have to agree to disagree on that one. Harmony held her tongue after that. She wasn't going to get either of them to let something slip, not here and now, and as they rolled across the town border into Skokie, she had a much more pressing problem to solve: how she was going to stop an impending massacre.

The Gold Star office looked like Houston described it: chain link fencing encircled the building and a small parking lot, but the gate out front was unmanned and wide open. A single lonely camera was mounted high on a lamppost, angled to keep an eye on the employees' cars.

"Make sure we wipe any security recordings on our way out," Josh said. "And when I say 'make sure,' I mean triple-check and then triple-check twice."

The building wasn't that big. One story, red brick walls and a flat roof, treated windows catching the parking lot and reflecting it back like a mirror. Harmony was counting cars. The lot was only a quarter full, the Saturday skeleton crew that Houston had warned them about.

Assuming most employees drove themselves, factor in public transportation considering there's a bus stop one block over...minimum of eight civilians inside, she reasoned.

None of them were going to die here. Not today. Not on her watch.

Josh drove past the office building. He found a lonely strip mall just down the road, half the stores shuttered and out of business, and parked at the edge of the lot.

"We walk from here," he said, turning in his seat. "Here's how this is going to go down. Speed is an absolute priority: we get in, we grab what we need, and we get out fast. Cherry, you grab anything we need for cranking out a set of ID badges. Blanks, printers—"

"On it," Bette said.

"This is your area of expertise, so get it right and get it done." He turned to Jessie. "You're hunting for uniforms. They buy 'em in bulk, so look for cardboard boxes, probably in a storage closet somewhere."

"Did we get a list of sizes?" she asked.

"Just take everything. We'll make it work. Hit-girl, make a beeline for the security room. Your job is to cover our tracks. No recordings, no evidence, nada."

"What will you two be doing?" Harmony asked.

She already knew the answer. She needed to hear it from his lips.

"Handing out job termination notices," Josh said. He ran his fingers through his hair and flashed a boyish smile. "Not the severance package anyone was hoping for, but that's life, isn't it? Some people get lucky. Some people don't."

Harmony had a plan. Risky, rash, but good options were in short supply right now. First, she had to bait a bull and get away with it. As they all got out of the pickup truck, she walked alongside Ricky.

"You ready for this?" she asked.

He hit her with a cocky grin. "Kinda question is that? This'll be shooting fish in a barrel."

"You wouldn't mind making it more interesting, then."

He gave her a longer, more appraising look now, as he rubbed one hand against the sweaty bristle on his emaciated chin.

"Talking my language now. What do you have in mind?"

"A little competition," Harmony said. She pitched her voice lower. "You and me, we're the only real shooters on this crew. A lot of people can't kill in cold blood. They freeze up. But you and me...we won't."

"Hell, that's how I knew you were legit on day one. It wasn't how you kept your cool with a gun to your head. It was the *look*."

She arched an eyebrow, curious. Ricky pointed to his eyes with two fingers.

"Anybody can shoot back when the lead starts flying," he says. "That ain't no great feat of courage. But the first time you stand in front of an unarmed man and you both know it's over, and he's got nowhere to run, nothing to fight back with, no power left and you just..."

He slowly raised his latex-gloved hand, squinting as he squeezed an imaginary trigger.

"...bang," he said. "It's that split-second before you pull the trigger. That's the moment when you know what real power feels like. You're not just judge, jury, and executioner. You're fuckin' God almighty."

He flashed his rotten gums and chrome-sheathed teeth.

"That's the high that changes you forever. All I gotta do is look in your eyes, and I can always tell if somebody's been there or not. You? You been there."

For a moment Harmony was standing on the tarmac in the cold desert night, the lights of the Vegas strip in the distance and a jetliner roaring into the darkened sky. She was facing down Geordie Tynes with a gun in her hand. His hands were empty.

"*Thank you*," he whispered, with tears in his eyes and a quavering smile on his lips.

Then she shot him dead.

"You were saying something about a competition?" Ricky asked.

She snapped back to reality. She chewed the corner of her bottom lip until she tasted copper on her tongue. The wolf-pack strode through the open gate and into the office parking lot, the glass doors of the lobby dead ahead.

"Let's see who can take the most heads," she said. "Loser owes the winner a drink."

"Make it a six-pack and you got a deal. After all this hard work I'm gonna want to get good and lit."

He started to speed up as they neared the lobby doors. She fixed him with an expectant glare, feeling her heart slam against her ribcage. This was Harmony's gambit, and if it didn't work she'd have nothing left up her sleeve.

"What?" he said, catching the look.

"Chivalry really is dead, huh?"

Ricky cocked his head to one side, like a confused dog. Then he got it, and let out a snort of derision as he slapped Josh's arm.

"You see this? Chicks are all the same. Pretend they can hang with the big boys, but the second you let 'em, they want special privileges and shit."

Harmony tasted bile in the back of her throat. She swallowed it down and held her tongue while Josh gently chuckled.

"C'mon, man, nothing wrong with a little sportsmanship."

"Yeah, yeah." Ricky pulled open the door, stood aside and bowed with a mocking flourish and a twirl of his hand. "Ladies first, of course. I'll even give ya a three-second head start. You just make sure that six-pack is nice and frosty for me."

Exactly what she needed.

The lobby, a tiny waiting room with a reception desk, was empty. Small favors. The office floor was on the other side, through an open arch, and Harmony broke into a sprint as she charged across the floor. She raised her janky, stolen gun, sweeping the room with the tube of her sound suppressor. The world lurched, time slowing down, Harmony's stomach plummeting like the first drop of a rollercoaster ride while her vision painted the world in imaginary lines of blue light, angles, measurements, distances, targets. The office had an open floor plan, gray felt cubicles swimming on a sea of baby-blue carpet, the room ringed with smaller private offices with doors and glass window-walls. Most were dark, locked for the weekend. A pair of broad hallways ran east and west at either side of the open floor, curling toward the back of the building, and a wall of tinted glass looked out onto the parking lot.

A young man in a cheap shirt and cheaper tie was working the skeleton shift, typing away at a lonely keyboard in the middle of the cubicle farm. He looked up, head popping over the gray felt wall like a curious gopher, and he looked straight at Harmony.

She raised her gun and opened fire.

CHAPTER TWENTY-FOUR

"*Run*," Harmony mouthed. Then she squeezed the trigger three times, the suppressor turning her bullets into hoarse coughs, slamming into cubicle walls to the left of the hapless file clerk. The third shot hit an office window, blasting it out, filling the room with the crash of breaking glass. The office worker ran for it, ducking low and charging toward the eastern hallway.

"*Got one*," Harmony shouted.

"Where?" Ricky demanded, rushing up alongside her, a split second too late to see the action.

"He went down somewhere over there," she said, gesturing with her gun toward the middle of the cubicle farm.

"Focus up," Josh snapped. "You've all got jobs to do. Get to it."

That's my girl, Jessie thought. She didn't see the clerk either, but she knew her partner well enough to pick up on Harmony's play. She ran ahead of the pack, picking the western hallway. The door to the men's room slammed open under the heel of her boot as she gave it a vicious kick. Just like Harmony, she was going loud on purpose, sending out a warning to anyone in earshot. The message was simple: *Get out. Now.*

She walked down the line of toilet stalls, each door meeting her boot one after the other. Empty. She repeated the routine in the women's room next door, but this time she wasn't alone.

There was a woman in the far stall. She was trying to hide, pulling her legs up as she squatted on the toilet, but Jessie could hear her quivering breath and taste her fear-sweat on the stale air. It smelled like a rare porterhouse steak, and her mouth started to water while the beast inside, her constant companion, wagged an eager, fluffy tail.

You can have this one, the Wolf whispered. *No one will ever know. You've been so unnaturally restrained lately. No pleasure. No fun. Take this one, as a treat.*

I bet her blood tastes like candy.

Jessie took a deep breath, squeezed her eyes shut and pinched the bridge of her nose.

"Okay, first of all," she breathed, "shut the fuck up."

She followed the aroma and tried to ignore her growling stomach. There was a quarter-inch gap between the door and the wall of the toilet stall, wide enough to see the woman inside, huddled and shaking like a baby doe.

"Listen to me," Jessie hissed. "Stay here. Stay quiet. Do not leave this room under any circumstances, or you will die. Do you understand?"

The woman just stared at her, shell-shocked, unblinking.

"Nod your head if you understand me."

Her head bobbed a little.

"Very good. Now cover your ears."

Jessie turned to the back corner of the bathroom, raised her gun and shot twice. Her first bullet drove a moon-crater in the stainless-steel paper towel dispenser. The second hit the corner of a sink, breaking off a fist-sized chunk of dirty porcelain and sending it to shatter against the tile floor.

As she headed out the door, Ricky tried to barge in. Jessie put her fingers on his chest, gently steering him back.

"Just one," she said. "I took care of her."

His face reddened. Now he'd lost two targets, and his blood was up.

"Idiot, you're on uniform duty! You think you're gonna find 'em in the shitter?"

"I saw her run in there and try to hide," Jessie countered. "What was I supposed to do, ignore it? She could have called 911."

"You're supposed to follow orders, do your damn job and let me do mine." Ricky gritted his chromed teeth. "Forget it, just...just do your job!"

Flustered, he charged off in the opposite direction. Jessie moved fast, smooth and silent, every footstep charged with intent.

As Harmony pretended to scour the floor for victims, she spotted two: a man and a woman, huddled together and holding on for dear life as they crouched behind a desk in a darkened office. She put her finger to her lips, staring at them from the other side of the window, and made a *shh* gesture.

Josh was on the other side of the cubicle farm, going over the floor plan with Bette. He pointed, starting to turn in Harmony's direction. If he came this way, he'd be on her in seconds — and on the civilians, too.

Her free hand dipped into her pocket, coming out cradling her tactical pen. She flicked the pocket-clip back with the tip of her thumbnail. The firing lever clicked into place. She turned to the wall of tinted glass that looked out onto the parking lot, on the far side of the cubes. She took aim, working math like a billiards champ, and squeezed the clip.

The spike on the tip of her pen, a tiny scalloped spear of airplane-grade aluminum, fired on a puff of compressed air. It hit the window and blew it out on a spray of jagged chunks, harsh sunlight washing in through the smoke-tinted glass. Harmony slipped the spent pen back into her pocket and pointed with her gun, all in one smooth motion.

"Over there," she shouted. "One of the employees broke the window and crawled out into the parking lot!"

Josh whirled around, facing the broken glass.

"God*damn* it," he shouted, a cry of mingled fury and fear. He sprinted through the lobby and threw his shoulder into the door, bursting out into the parking lot. Harmony looked to the two huddled clerks, put her finger to her lips again for emphasis, then pointed up the hallway. They leaped from their hiding spot and ran for safety, still squeezing each other's hands.

Jessie had to be careful.

She'd been caught out of bounds once already. Ricky was on a hair trigger, wanting to get his murder-boner on, and she couldn't risk looking suspicious a second time. She decided that getting the job done and getting out was the fastest way to save anyone else who was still in hiding.

She found her prize in an unlocked utility closet across the hall from the Human Resources office. Three big cardboard boxes, festooned with Chinese shipping labels and plastic packets holding papers from customs, each stacked with crisp uniform shirts and black trousers in individually wrapped bundles. She scooped a crate up in her arms — light as a feather, for her. Her footsteps faltered as she heard the cough of a suppressed gunshot from HR.

Bette came out holding a pair of shoebox-sized containers under one arm, her stolen pistol dangling limp in her other hand. Behind her, on the floor, Jessie saw the body. Part of it, anyway: a pair of legs, one high-heel shoe dangling loose at the end of a motionless foot, the carpet dark with a port-wine stain. Bette's face was a mask of grim determination.

"She had a gun," Bette said in a low voice. "I tried to talk her down. She didn't give me a choice."

Jessie didn't see a gun. She also knew that if she checked, whether she found a piece or not, Bette would know she didn't trust her. Couldn't risk it. She swallowed her suspicions.

"Did you get what you needed?" Jessie asked.

Bette hoisted the two shoeboxes. "Oh, yeah. I'm done here." She nodded to the lobby doors. "Let's go then."

Harmony found what she needed in the IT department. Their server room was the size of a broom closet, with old machines gathering dust as their LEDs flickered in silence, and she found the security console — an old oblong black plastic pizza box, probably bought off the rack in some big-box store and set up by an amateur with a half-read instruction manual. She cut the connection to the cameras, ending the feed. She started to wipe the hard drive, then paused. On an impulse, she yanked the cables and took the box with her.

The far corridor ended in a storage room. Accounting file boxes filled skeletal metal shelves, months and years and client names scribbled on their sides in fat black marker. A loading dock offered a way out.

On the far side of the room, a lone cowering survivor couldn't bring herself to take the chance. She was an elderly woman, pressed into the corner with her back to the wall, petrified.

Harmony glanced up the hall, back over her shoulder. Clear. For now.

"*Go*," she hissed, pointing to the back door.

She didn't move. A gunshot echoed in the distance, down on the far side of the building.

"Deep breath," Harmony whispered, locking eyes with the woman. "Left foot forward. Right foot forward. I know you're scared but if you want to live through this, all you need to do is *start walking*."

Something registered behind the woman's panicked stare. She took a step forward. Then another. Then she ran. She sprinted toward the back door of the storage room, safety and freedom dead ahead. Harmony raised her pistol, aiming just to the woman's left, intending to fire a harmless shot and claim another "kill" as soon as she was outside and safe.

She had her hand on the push bar, two steps to freedom, when a gun went off just behind Harmony's left shoulder. A bullet tore through the elderly woman's dress and shattered her spine. She slumped to the concrete floor, feet kicking, body convulsing as she spat up a gout of hot blood.

"That's more like it," Ricky said, stepping up alongside Harmony and licking his lips. He held his gun high like a victorious cowboy. "Too slow, sugar-tits. This point goes to *me*."

He strode past Harmony and stood over the dying woman. He studied her, savoring the moment, then put a second bullet in the back of her head. She fell still.

Harmony was frozen. Her mouth bone-dry, her head throbbing. Ricky had his back to her. The pistol in her hand felt like it weighed a million pounds, but she knew it would be the easiest thing in the world to raise it, take aim, and blow this bastard away. He would never even see it coming. Lights out, just like that.

She told herself, a moment later when they were both sprinting to the lobby to meet up with the rest of the crew, that she spared him for the sake of the mission. Even if she found an excuse to cover up the killing, Josh was already looking at his brilliant plan going sideways thanks to an "escapee" who didn't actually exist. In his mind he'd be worried about discovery, ruin — and even worse, pissing off Nadine. Losing a key member of the crew right now might push him into doing something crazy, and Harmony needed him to stay predictable.

That was only half of the truth, though. In that brief moment, when she had Ricky dead to rights and knew she could snuff him out with a curl of her finger, Harmony had made a quiet decision.

Ricky Corbin was going to die at her hands. But before she killed him, she was going to make damn sure he understood *why*. She wanted to see the look in his eyes right before she sent him to hell.

CHAPTER TWENTY-FIVE

Harmony and Ricky met up with Jessie and Bette in the lobby. Josh stormed in from outside, breathless and drenched in sweat.

"He got away," he panted. "Couldn't find him. Cops are probably inbound, we need to leave *now*. Everybody do their part?"

Jessie hoisted the big cardboard shipping box in both arms.

"Not lugging this around for my health," she said.

Bette slapped the shoeboxes she took from HR. "We're good for IDs."

Josh shot a glance at the oblong black box cradled under Harmony's arm. "What's that?"

"Security recorder."

"I told you to wipe the damn thing, not swipe it!"

"I *did*," Harmony lied. "That's not good enough. In case you haven't noticed, we just committed a mass murder. This will go federal, and the feds are going to bring in their forensic boys. You know, the kind of experts who can reconstruct data from an 'erased' hard drive. All of our faces were recorded on the way in here. Do you really want to take any unnecessary risks right now?"

Bette stepped alongside her, backing her up before Josh could reply.

"She's right. Once we bring the unit back to the garage, I've got a neodymium magnet that can scramble its insides for good. That plus a power drill should do the trick properly. Trust me, I do this all the time."

Josh tugged at his hair, pacing for a second before he suddenly turned.

"Okay, okay, screw it, fine. Toss the stolen guns. Throw 'em anywhere, doesn't matter."

"I'll grab the Molotov from the truck," Ricky grunted.

"No time. Everybody still gloved up? Nobody left anything behind? That's the best we can do. Toss the guns and let's go."

"Point is," Ricky groused on the drive back to Joliet, "it seems to me I'm the clear winner of this contest. We both saw the bitch I dropped. I didn't see any of yours."

"You don't believe me?" Harmony asked. She had been riding along in the back seat, sitting in icy silence.

"Didn't say that. I'm saying, fair's fair." He turned in the passenger seat, shooting a withering look at Jessie. "Woulda had two kills if *somebody* didn't step on my toes back there."

"I told you already: I saw her run into the restroom to hide. If I didn't take her when I did, she probably would have called the cops. We almost got caught as it is."

They had cruised across the Skokie border to the tune of sirens in the distance, the banshee wail of ambulances and squad cars rolling in like a storm front made of steel.

"Messy," Josh muttered under his breath. He had the steering wheel in a white-knuckle grip. "Too messy by far."

Messier than he knew. Harmony managed to save three of the office workers, and every one of them got a perfect look at her face. She hadn't been able to catch up with Jessie — no privacy to speak of, not yet — but she gathered from the talk about the woman in the bathroom that Jessie was in the same boat.

At least she had the camera footage, but the real problem right now wasn't the survivors giving an accurate sketch of Harmony and Jessie to the cops. That they could find a way to deal with. A bulletproof alibi was as close as Kevin's hacking expertise and Vigilant's in-house print shop.

But what happens when those survivors tell the police that a pair of women matching our descriptions hid them from the other shooters and helped them to escape? she thought. *If that hits the news before tonight, our cover is blown and we're as good as dead.*

Out of her control. Harmony wasn't good at handling things outside of her control. Her anxious fingers drummed softly on the pizza-box square of the security recorder, resting warm against her lap.

"You just don't step on a man's toes like that," Ricky said. "That's all I'm trying to get across here. You don't do it."

Josh dug in his pocket as he drove, taking out his phone. He saw the screen and turned two shades of pale. From her seat in back, Harmony caught a glimpse of the caller ID. A single word: *Boss*.

"I have to take this. Shut up for a minute. All of you. I'm serious, don't say a goddamn word." Josh put the phone to his ear. "Yes, ma'am."

Cold fingers of wraith-mist clenched around Harmony's spine.

"Yes, that was us—" Josh stumbled in mid-sentence, wincing. "No, ma'am, that wasn't exactly the idea."

The phone wobbled in his hand, as he clenched it with half-severed fingers.

"Yes, ma'am. We have everything we need for tonight. No problems on this end. We'll meet Nyx with the package at the agreed-upon — oh. Oh, well...sure. Of course, please give her our regards, and I'm looking forward to seeing you. Thank you, ma'am."

He hung up the phone and spat a curse under his breath.

"Trouble?" Ricky asked. He looked nervous. Harmony had never seen him look nervous before. Until now, she wasn't sure he even felt that emotion.

"Slight change of plans. You know how the boss was sending her daughter to meet us at the drop?"

Ricky groaned and slumped in his seat. "God, I hate that creepy bitch. She's worse than her mom, and that's saying something."

"She's busy, so the boss is coming to collect. Personally." Josh glanced to the rearview mirror, his gaze sweeping across the three women in the back seat. "No worries. This is good for you three; she's also the paymaster, so she'll make sure you all get what you have coming to you."

"I thought Dima was in charge of the money," Jessie said.

"Dima's in charge of jack and shit," Ricky snorted. "And I am all out of Jack."

Back at the garage, the rest of the crew had already put the finishing touches on the getaway ride. The decals and a bit of polish transformed their wheels into a pristine, freshly washed Gold Star security van, identical to the rest of the fleet.

Inside the garage, Bette set up at the card table, breaking out boxes of ID blanks and connecting a small printer, along with a thermal laminator, to her laptop.

"Everybody take twenty," Josh called out. "Last chance for a full stomach before we get this show underway, so I suggest you take it."

Houston nodded back over his shoulder. "Saw a Culver's down the street a ways. Want me to run down there and pick up some grub for everybody?"

Josh rummaged in his pocket, dug out a wad of folded bills and handed it over.

"Good man. Get me one of those...butter-burger things. A double. With cheese."

He was hungry. As far as he knew, he had just overseen a mass murder. A massacre, carried out at his command, and he was hungry.

Harmony needed air.

The derelict garage backed up against a vacant lot, and beyond the lot stood an embankment overlooking the Des Plaines River. She sat down on the grimy white stone and dangled her legs over the side, staring down at the dark, rippling waters. A chemical tang clung to the dirty air, and a hot breeze ruffled her hair.

Familiar footsteps crunched on gravel at her back.

"Room for two?" Jessie asked.

Harmony patted the wall at her side. Jessie sat down next to her. For a minute or two, they shared a companionable silence and watched the river flow.

"Could have gone a lot worse," Jessie said.

"Could have gone a lot better."

"We can't save everybody," Jessie said. "You know that. It's part of the job, goes with the territory. We save as many as we can, and when we lose we take the pain, we suck it up, and we keep fighting."

Harmony didn't answer her.

"Bette shot one of the employees," Jessie said.

Harmony turned and stared at her.

"She said the woman had a gun, that she had to draw down or get shot herself."

"Did she?" Harmony asked.

"Possibly. Don't know. Couldn't verify without losing Bette's trust. Something interesting, though. You know how good my sniffer is." She tapped the side of her nose. "Terror, arousal, the rush of adrenalin — they've all got a unique scent."

"Sure."

"Know what I didn't smell on her? Any of that. Cool as a cucumber from start to finish. I don't think her heartbeat even sped up."

"I've been trying to take Bette aside and feel her out," Harmony said, "in the hopes of figuring out if she's a traitor or — if Josh discovered who she really works for — send her a warning. I got her alone and he swooped in like a hawk."

"I'll take a stab at it."

Jessie leaned back, pressing her palms to the rough, broken stone at her back, scraggly weeds poking through cracks along the edge of the embankment.

"Once upon a time," Jessie said, "I asked you to be my conscience. You remember that?"

Harmony nodded, with a question in her eyes.

"I needed that, because...you know I don't see things, feel things, the way most people do. Thank my fucked-up parents and my fucked-up childhood. I'll be honest, that body on the office floor? I didn't care, hon. She wasn't anything to me. I look at a dead stranger and I feel...nothing. I never will. It's not how I'm wired."

Jessie gazed out across the river, took a breath, and continued.

"What I feel, so deeply, all the time, is rage. Not rage for the victims. Rage against the victimizers. People like Josh Orville, the wealthy, the well-connected. They get away with murder and they *keep* getting away with it until someone forces them to stop. And that pisses me off like nothing you can imagine."

"I get it," Harmony said, her voice soft.

"I think you're starting to," Jessie said. "But will you let me do something for you right now?"

She turned her hips a little, sitting closer to Harmony at the river's edge, and took both of her partner's hands.

"Let me be *your* conscience today," Jessie said. "Because I see you, and I know you. I know you're tearing into yourself right now, telling yourself you're not allowed to rage, not allowed to grieve. Like you have to be some kind of mystery-solving robot. You're on this tight leash, all the time, digging into your neck and strangling you, and you know what the funny thing about that is?"

"What's that?" Harmony asked.

"You're the one holding the leash, hon." She leaned close, her breath a hot puff of air against Harmony's ear. "Let it go. Because tonight, we are going to *end* these fuckers. I want you to know that you have permission to enjoy it. I *want* you to enjoy it. And when the right moment comes...you're allowed to lose control."

She squeezed Harmony's hand and rose to her feet, brushing off her jeans.

"I'm going to head back inside. You should too. Just...take a second, all right?"

Harmony stood up but she lingered behind, watching the river roll, breathing the industrial air.

Nothing comes before the mission. That was her motto and her maxim, had been for years. It was the vow that kept her going through the hardest and most brutal nights of her life. She wore her professional detachment like a shield, a wall between her and the pain. She didn't take things personally.

Maybe the strange force causing her powers to mutate was messing with her head. Or maybe she was just opening her eyes for the first time. Either way, she was starting to think she was looking at this all wrong.

Josh Orville had made a fortune playing poker, but he wasn't her opponent in this game. His mistress was. Josh and Ricky and Dima were nothing but chips to be wagered and sacrificed. If she wanted to win this fight, and take Nadine down once and for all, her old ways weren't going to cut it anymore.

To beat Nadine, Harmony would have to be craftier than Nadine. More ruthless than Nadine. More vicious than Nadine, if she had to be. She couldn't do all that and stifle her emotions at the same time. Something would have to go. Something had to break.

Harmony's body was a patchwork of scars, and the agents of the House of Dead Roses had inflicted more than their fair share. Her worst scars of all, the ones on the inside, had been carved by Nadine's own hand.

They owed Harmony. They owed her in blood and they owed her in pain. She decided, as she turned and set her sights on the garage, that their payment was long overdue.

CHAPTER TWENTY-SIX

A pressed uniform shirt sheathed in a plastic baggie sailed through the air. Houston snatched it in one hand. Ricky, walking the opposite way, snagged the second one as Josh threw it underhand.

"Everybody," Josh called out, "suit up. Cherry's on ID duty. Get a uniform, get a card, get ready to kick some ass because we're rolling out in one hour."

While Harmony joined Josh in digging through the box, looking for a uniform her size, she saw Jessie approach Bette by her laptop and printer rig. She couldn't miss how Josh seemed to tense up.

You don't want either of us talking to her alone, she realized.

Sure enough, he lingered just close enough to stay in earshot while Bette took a photo of Jessie, printed and laminated it, and handed her a perfect copy of a Gold Star employee badge.

"I need to go get changed," Harmony said.

Ricky flashed a chrome-toothed grin, his top off, showing off his physique — all skeleton and gristle — as he unwrapped his new uniform shirt.

"We're all friends here," he said.

"Not like that," she replied, and walked into the dusty side office. Once the door was closed, she moved fast, unwrapping her uniform and quickly changing — but not before grabbing the silky cleaning instructions tag at the neck of her new blouse and ripping it from the fabric.

Her ballistic pen had spent its one shot, but it could write just fine. She pressed the ripped garment tag to the wall for support and scribbled *COVER BLOWN* in the tiny margin. She kept it hidden in her right hand, pressed to her palm with the curl of her thumb, as she returned to the garage and walked up to Bette's table.

"My turn," she said.

She sat down across from Bette and held still for a photograph. In her peripheral vision, Josh was watching them both like a hawk. Under the table she shifted the garment tag from her right to her left hand. Then she waited for the perfect moment.

As Bette's printer began to hum, spitting out the ID card, Harmony pretended to reach for it. As she did, she uncupped her hand and let the garment tag fall onto the table on the far side of the laptop, where Josh couldn't see it.

Bette caught her move and her vibe, falling into rhythm on the spot. She made a show of slapping Harmony's hand.

"*After* I laminate it," Bette said. "No touching."

When her hand dropped to the table, her fingers passed over the tag. Then it was gone.

"Sorry," Harmony said. "Guess I just got over-excited."

Bette glanced down. Just a flick of a gaze, as she looked from the laptop screen to the purloined tag and back again. Harmony had to give her credit: she wouldn't have caught the flicker of distress in Bette's eyes if she hadn't been watching for it. Message delivered. Stoic once more, Bette laminated Harmony's fake ID and passed it across the table to her.

"We're all excited," she said. "Whatever happens, we'll just have to play it by ear and watch each other's backs, won't we?"

Bette could send a message too. Harmony met her eyes and nodded, an unspoken promise. She got up and drifted across the garage, sidling up next to Jessie.

"She knows Josh is onto her," she murmured.

"Assuming she's not a traitor, and playing us."

"Fair," Harmony conceded. "Either way, she's not quitting. She wants to let it play and she's trusting us to keep her covered."

"Then we do that." Jessie nodded up toward the front of the room, where Bette was packing up her gear.

Josh held up his hands, stepping behind the card table. The rest of the crew stood scattered around the garage, loosely united stragglers, all eyes on the man with the plan.

"Ladies and gentlemen. Welcome to the big show."

He walked to the two easels that flanked the card table and flipped a pair of poster boards around. They bore blueprints, stark maps of the Ardentis Solutions plant. The floor plan lined up with what Harmony remembered from their late-night visit, but anything past the red security doors was a deep blue void.

"Come sunrise," Josh said, "each and every one of you is going to be ten thousand dollars richer. Just like that. All you have to do is earn it. We infiltrate Ardentis, we secure the package, we bring it to the rendezvous point, we get paid and go home happy."

Harmony raised her hand. "And where is the rendezvous point?"

Josh put a finger to his temple. "Right up here, Hit-girl. Because I'm the only person who needs to know. You do your job, I'll do mine."

Harmony thought of a counterargument, but Jessie was a step ahead of her. "And what if something happens to you out there? We'll be stuck with this mystery package, no one to sell it to and nowhere to take it."

Heads nodded around the room, muffled grumbles rising; everyone but Ricky agreed, and even Dima — the only member of the crew not wearing a security uniform — looked uncomfortable as she glanced down at the oil-stained concrete.

"Okay, first of all," Josh said, "nothing's going to 'happen' out there because we are going to be in and out like ghosts. By the time anyone at Ardentis even realizes they've been hit, we'll be long gone."

"I believe you," Harmony said. "I'm also a realist, and I've been on too many 'easy' jobs that went south with no warning. There's no such thing as a sure bet."

Josh's voice was tighter now. "*Second* of all, I'm the only genuine gambler in this room, so don't talk to me about sure bets. I've laid the groundwork, I've checked all the angles, *I am in control.*"

Barely, Harmony thought. The "mastermind" had been agitated ever since the operation in Skokie nearly blew up in his face, and now he was clinging to this runaway horse for dear life. He knew the danger here, and so did she: if Josh let Nadine down this time, he could lose a lot more than a finger.

Josh's hand slapped one of the blueprints, his finger landing on the long, fenced-in rectangle of the parking lot.

"We load up the van and ride right up to the front gate. Gold Star vans go in and out three times a day, nothing unusual to see. We're going to time it so we arrive exactly ten minutes before the shift change."

Houston shook his head. "Guard at the lot gate's gotta know who all the regulars are. He'd buy *one* new face, but not a whole vanload."

"Which is why we need to make sure he doesn't radio back."

Josh turned, locking eyes with Harmony.

"You'll distract him when we roll up. Then you'll kill him before he can make a fuss. Easy, right?"

The sun had already set by the time the crew piled aboard the disguised cargo van. Harmony drove. She kept one eye on the rearview mirror, her gaze sweeping across the crew's grim and silent faces. She took inventory.

Bette was a wild card. Either she was in mortal danger, or she was working for Josh and playing double agent. They wouldn't know until she let something slip or the guns came out.

Josh and Ricky were a double threat, and Harmony appreciated Nadine's sense of balance. Josh was smart, maybe even the genius he claimed to be, but she was pretty sure she could take him if it came down to a fight. Ricky was book-dumb but cunning like a fox, and he thrived on raw brutality. They both needed to go, but not yet. Not until they'd snatched the "package" out from under Ardentis's thumb, in case Josh was hiding yet another secret or two.

Josh's words, from after the Gold Star raid, came back to her unbidden: *She's busy, so the boss is coming to collect. Personally.*

Harmony wanted to know where. She'd protect Josh's life if she had to, right until the second she got what she needed from him.

Dima was trickier to figure. Harmony was almost certain that Dima had been marked for death, slated to earn a ten-thousand-dollar bullet at the end of the night just like everyone else on the crew. She thought she was leading pigs to the slaughter, too conceited to realize she was one of the livestock. Nadine was cutting loose ends. Warning her might do more harm than good, though: Dima was a schemer to the core, not to mention a murderous psychopath, and Harmony could see her try to recoup some status by turning on her and Jessie.

Castillo she couldn't read at all. The man designed the package's containment and security protocols, then promptly decided he wanted nothing to do with Ardentis, working from home and hiring a security team for his personal protection. Now he was all aboard with trying to steal the thing, right alongside the crew who'd kidnapped him. She'd have to keep a close eye on him.

Houston was the only member of this crew she *didn't* feel like she had to watch. The genial safecracker was just as he appeared: quiet, competent, and entirely in over his head. He had no idea who he was really working for, the danger he was in, or what was waiting for him at the end of the road. They'd have to keep him safe if they could.

Then, finally, there was the neurotic Doctor West. The coroner — and, apparently, part-time necromancer — was a walking ball of intellectual arrogance and conceit. A dangerous combination, considering he could cause real problems with a single stray word. They'd just have to hope Jessie had scared him silent.

The Ardentis plant was just ahead, the windowless rust-colored walls and girders rising up in the shadow of industrial smokestacks. The parking lot was half empty. Harmony eased her foot down on the brake as she drove up to the gatehouse, then put it in park. Another guard in a Gold Star uniform — thankfully, not the same one from the other night — came out from the hut with a clipboard.

"Hey, a new face," he said to Harmony though the driver-side window. "You just transfer over?"

"Brand new," she said, holding up her fake ID.

"Oh, you're gonna love it, night shift at Ardentis is the easiest job in the world." His smile faded as he ran his finger down his clipboard. "Huh. I...don't see you on the access list."

Harmony made a show of rolling her eyes. "Typical. My manager told me this might happen, I guess it was a last-minute schedule change and they don't always get 'em updated after usual business hours. Can I use the phone in your hut? I'm sure they'll clear everything right up. It's my first day and I really don't want to be late."

"Yeah," he said with a shrug, "sure thing."

She hopped down from the driver's seat, leaving the van idling as she joined him in the gatehouse. He turned his back to her, reaching for the phone at the end of a narrow desk.

Harmony snared one arm around his neck, trapping his throat in the crook of her arm, and squeezed. She drove a heel into the back of his knee, forcing him to drop to the ground, wheezing as she grappled him from behind.

She held on tight as his strength slowly ebbed. He slumped in her arms, sagging to the floor of the hut. From outside the open doorway, all they'd be able to see from the van were his limp and motionless feet. She checked his pulse. Still breathing.

She rose and drew her gun.

She flipped it around in her hand, knowing she'd be visible in the gatehouse window from the waist up. She raised the gun in her hand and brought it slamming down, butt-first — onto a folder stuffed with papers on the guard's tiny desk. The metal impacted with a muffled *crack*. Not quite the sound of a man's skull breaking, but close enough. She hit the desk a second time, holstered her weapon, and got back in the van.

Ricky let out a long, low whistle. "Damn, girl. That man even have a face left?"

"Wasn't going to waste a bullet," Harmony said, throwing the van into gear. "If you wanted him to have an open-casket funeral, you should have told me so."

CHAPTER TWENTY-SEVEN

Back at the garage, Josh had continued the briefing, moving his pointing finger to the front lobby and the nighttime security desk. He looked pointedly at Bette.

"Tell 'em about the cameras."

"There's a camera overlooking the lot," she said, "southeast corner. It's imperative that we park as close to the lobby as possible, in the first row. Shouldn't be hard after hours."

"More cameras inside," Jessie ventured.

"And we'll handle those."

"*I'll* handle those," Dima said, shooting a look of distaste at Bette.

"Sure, hon. You'll handle it with my software and my expertise."

"Ladies," Josh said. "But yes. The rest of us will wait in the van while Dima neutralizes the security in the lobby."

The infernal accountant was the only member of the crew not dressed as a security guard. She'd changed her look in a different direction, shimmying into a tight flame-red dress with a halter neck, the fabric hugging her curves and leaving little to the imagination. Her stiletto heels clicked rhythmically as she approached the sliding glass doors. They whistled wide and she emerged from the darkness, stepping into the sterile electric glow of the lobby.

The two men working at the security desk tonight both looked up, gazes fixed on Dima with obvious desire. She flashed a dark-lipped smile, unzipping her tiny envelope of a purse as she strutted up to them.

"Evening, boys. I'm with the *Sun-Times*, here to interview Lorne Murrough. He's expecting me."

One guard tapped his keyboard, pulling up an appointment list. The other just stared, fixated on her cleavage. She leaned forward, putting her elbows on the security desk and pushing her shoulders back, commanding his full attention.

"I'm sorry," the first one said, "are you sure you've got the right day? Mr. Murrough doesn't have anything on his schedule tonight."

"That's odd," Dima said with an exaggerated pout. "Here, let me show you my identification. That might clarify things."

Her hand slid from her purse, clutching a thin black plastic handle. The switchblade snapped open mid-swing. She ripped it across the first guard's neck, tearing his throat open and showering the ivory tile floor in crimson mist as his jugular sprayed like a fire hose.

He clawed at the gash, choking on his own blood and convulsing in his chair while the second guard stumbled back, shocked, and reached for the gun on his hip. Dima flipped the blade in her hand, reared her arm back and threw it like a dart. It drove straight into the guard's left eye, burst it like a grape, and impaled his brain.

He gurgled once, spat a mouthful of blood, and crashed to the lobby floor.

All business now, Dima circled the desk with three efficient steps, drawing a USB stick from her purse. She slotted it into the computer, waited for windows of neon code to blossom like a mushroom patch on the blood-spattered monitor, and sent a quick text to Bette.

"Once Dima has the lobby under control," Josh had told the gathered heisters, "we move in and do our thing."

Bette held up a finger. "Real important. The patch I'm giving Dima will muddle their security systems long enough for me to get in there and lock it all down, but there's still a chance of trouble. If anyone's actively watching the lobby camera—"

"Doubtful, considering I chose this exact time to guarantee minimum levels of staff on site," Josh said.

"—or if Dima just screws it up," Bette continued, ignoring the death glare from across the garage, "there's the risk of a silent alarm going out. We enter the lobby and *wait* until I check things out and give the all-clear. No cowboy nonsense, no craziness. You follow my lead and do not proceed until I say so."

Ricky stared at her, unblinking, over the neck of a fresh bottle of beer.

"Some reason you were eyeballin' me in particular just now when you said that?" he asked.

Instead of answering him, Bette turned to his master instead.

"If they get an alarm out and I can't run interference, we'll be up to our armpits in cops before we get anywhere near the package. This is the most critical part of the entire job. I need everyone to stay cool."

"And cool we will stay," Josh had agreed, firing a warning glance at Ricky.

"She took the lobby," Bette hissed as the text came in. "Go, go, go."

The cargo van's side door rattled open and the crew boiled out, staying low and moving fast, swarming the lobby doors like commandos. Bette was first through, yanking her laptop from her backpack as she ran to the security desk, powering it up and reaching for an octopus nest of cables.

Harmony's blood went cold at the sight of the two corpses, the Jackson Pollack spatter of scarlet on white slowly congealing on the pristine tile floor. And Dima, practically preening.

"Nobody takes another step," Bette snarled, typing furiously. "I mean it."

"We are on a tight schedule," Josh said.

"Don't push me." She gritted her teeth. "I'm wiping the footage of Dima's little rampage and putting every security camera in the building on a twenty-second loop."

Dima drifted past Harmony. She leaned close, close enough for Harmony to catch the trail of her musk perfume, and whispered in her ear.

"Don't stare at me like that. You're pretending to be a killer just like me, remember? Act like one."

"We told you not to hurt anyone else. We had an *agreement*."

"You want the package? Then these men had to die." Dima gave her a cruel smile before moving on. "Anything for the mission. Isn't that your motto or something? So that's exactly what I did. You can thank me later."

"C'mon," Ricky said, shooting a pointed look at Bette. "We gotta *go* already."

"Interrupt me one more time and see what happens."

Ricky glared and took a step toward her. "Maybe once your part's done we don't even *need* no fancy computer whiz—"

Josh got between them, quick, and put a hand to Ricky's chest.

"C'mon, man. The plan. Stick to the plan. Help Houston with the cleanup."

Josh had pointed to another spot Harmony recognized from their late-night visit to Lorne Murrough. It was the skybridge, the elevated walk linking the main building to the opaque rust-colored cube of the R&D facility.

"Once security's down, we take this route straight from the lobby to the labs. Now remember: the skyway's totally open, lit inside, dark outside, glass walls all around. We'll be visible for a good twenty seconds. If we look our part, keep our uniforms crisp and our chins up, nobody will even think twice. Move with purpose and if you see any employees on the way, for the love of God, don't make eye contact."

"What about me?" Dima asked, the only one of them without a disguise.

Josh reached into the half-empty cardboard shipping crate, pulled out another shrink-wrapped uniform, and tossed it over to her.

"You're hanging back and holding the lobby down. Change clothes, clean things up, and man the desk until we're finished. If anyone comes in, play dumb and act like it's your first day on the job. If anyone gets suspicious, make sure they never leave."

"'Play,'" Ricky echoed, snickering.

"Meanwhile, the rest of us take the skybridge to R&D, get through the security door on the far end, and we should be golden from there. No exterior windows in the labs, only a skeleton crew on site, and the cameras won't be a problem. As long as we stop anyone from triggering an alarm, we're golden. On that note, *everyone* is on crowd control duty. I want to hit that lab like a swarm of locusts. You see somebody, you take 'em down hard and fast, period. Your eighty-year-old grandmother with osteoporosis is in there? Sucks to be her tonight. You take her down."

"Dead or alive?" Ricky drawled.

Castillo answered for him, clearing his throat and speaking up for the first time since the briefing started.

"Alive, if at all possible," he said. "We may need them, in case any of the lab protocols have been changed without my knowledge. Also, whoever's in charge tonight should know this week's punch-code for the restricted wing."

Bette nodded. "I can crack the door without it, but that'd save us a lot of time. Once we're inside, every second matters."

"All right," Josh told the rest of the room, "you all heard the score. If you grab a hostage, truss 'em up like a Thanksgiving turkey, but minimal damage otherwise."

He rested his fingertips on the card table.

"We get that far, we keep things cool, and the rest of this job will be nothing but wine and roses. Trust me."

While Dima stripped off her little red dress right there in the lobby, utterly uninhibited, Ricky and Houston grabbed the dead security guards by the arms and hauled them into a broom closet. There wasn't much they could do about the blood, though most of it was on the tile behind the front desk, invisible to anyone from the other side. Harmony and Jessie grabbed a stack of newspapers from the chairs in the corner of the lobby and spread them in a heavy, thick layer, covering the fast-drying stains. Houston found a hazard-yellow *CAUTION Wet Floor* sign in the closet and set it out in front of the chaotic mess.

"That's it," Bette said, swinging down her laptop's lid. She yanked out a couple of cables and cradled its rugged clamshell under one arm. "Cameras are blind, nobody in the security office noticed a thing, and we're good to go."

Dima strode up to the desk, dressed in her new uniform, and gracefully slid into the chair of the man she'd just murdered as if it belonged to her.

"I'll keep watch," Dima said. "Good luck."

"Don't need luck when you've got skill," Josh said. "Okay, boy scouts and brownies, let's move."

The wolfpack ascended a long, straight staircase, passing through a push-bar door and emerging onto the skywalk. The glass tunnel was lit from above in cool blue light, casting the night-world beyond the glass in murky darkness. Harmony's skin crawled. Anyone outside could see them, but not the other way around. All they could do was march, trying to look like they belonged here.

Up ahead, at the far end of the suspended tunnel, the laboratory door hissed open and a pair of Gold Star guards — real ones — came out, heading in the opposite direction.

"Stay frosty," Josh hissed through gritted teeth.

The two groups met halfway down the tunnel, taking each other's measure in a silent flickering glance, a faint and professional nod, before going their separate ways.

Then one of the guards stopped in his tracks.

"Excuse me," he said, turning. "Who are you people? Can I see those ID badges? Because I know the entire night shift and none of you are on it."

Harmony was reaching for her lanyard and polishing a cover story when Ricky drew his gun.

He shot the guard point-blank in the chest. Even with a sound suppressor, the bullet clapped like thunder in the glass hallway, the aftermath roaring in Harmony's ears. The second guard went for his gun and had just cleared his holster when Ricky rammed into him, slammed him against the wall hard enough to leave spiderweb fractures in the glass, put his weapon's muzzle under the young man's chin and blasted the top of his head off in a spray of matted hair and splintered bone. As the second body fell to the carpet, bathed in icy blue light, a wet dark mass clung to the fractured glass behind him.

"You fucking *asshole*," Bette roared. "You stupid, impulsive *amateur*—"

Ricky spun, pointing his gun in her face. "Say that again, bitch. Look me in the eye and say that again."

Houston almost grabbed for Ricky's arm on impulse. He caught himself, yanking back at the last second and flailing his empty hands. "You didn't have to do that, man! We could have bluffed our way past, easy."

"Time is of the essence," Ricky growled, firing a look at Josh. "Ain't that right, boss-man?"

"Christ, it is now!" Josh broke into a run, waving for everyone to follow him. "They would have heard that in the lab. Let's *move*!"

CHAPTER TWENTY-EIGHT

Jessie crouched and snatched a keycard from one of the fallen guards. Bette was prepared to crack the lock, but this would be faster. She pressed the blood-smeared lozenge of plastic to the reader beside the laboratory entrance and the door swung wide with a hiss.

The lab was in chaos. As the crew stormed in, papers were flying, doors slamming, researchers in fluttering white coats running in three directions at once. They'd heard the shots from the skybridge, and they didn't need to see invaders with guns to know they were in danger.

Houston broke into a charge, throwing himself onto one of the fleeing scientists and bringing him down in a rough tackle. They hit the floor, rolled, and the safecracker yanked his hostage's hands behind his back. Another escapee fled through the firing range, the door whisking shut behind him.

Ricky ran after that one. Harmony drew breath to shout a warning, but it was too late. He slapped the panel beside the door and it whistled open again.

The researcher on the other side shouldered his shotgun and opened fire.

The slug hit Ricky square in the chest and launched him off his feet, wreathed in a crackling, eye-searing flash of blue lightning. He hit the floor, shaking and twitching like he was having a seizure. Josh marched toward the doorway with his gun high, firing again and again, drawing a line of bloody craters from the scientist's guts to his forehead.

Bette ignored the fray, commandeering the closest desk and slapping her laptop down. She bared her gritted teeth as she leaned into the screen, her face bathed in violet light.

"Problem?" Harmony asked.

"Understatement of the year, but I'm on it."

West and Castillo found another researcher, this one a young woman, cowering behind a refrigeration unit. They dragged her from her hiding spot, hauled her out front, and threw her to the floor next to her fellow hostage, covering them both at gunpoint.

"Tie 'em up," Josh snapped, racing over to crouch at Ricky's side. Harmony took care of that, brandishing a handful of zip ties and binding the captives' wrists. A moment later Jessie emerged from the cubicles in back with a third researcher, an older man, and knelt him down with the other two.

Ricky stirred, groaned, and pushed himself to his feet on trembling arms.

"Holy..." He patted his chest and winced. "Goddamn, didn't even break skin. Gonna have one hell of a bruise, though. Anyone get the number of the truck that hit me?"

Now that she'd seen Ardentis's electrified DOVE munitions in action — first against a ballistic-gel dummy, then against a real threat — Harmony knew one thing for certain. She could put those to good use.

"That all of 'em?" Josh asked, looking over at the three hostages.

"Looks like," Houston said.

"'Looks like' doesn't mean shit," Josh snapped, flustered. "Fan out, search this place from top to bottom and *make sure!* Hit-girl, find out which of these eggheads has the code for the high-security lab. Break some fingers if you have to. Cherry, talk to me."

Bette didn't look up from her screen. "Someone hit the silent alarm just before we came in."

"Can you handle it?"

"Trying to focus here. Go away and let me cook."

Harmony crouched down eye-to-eye with the three captured researchers. She pointed to the red-tinged steel door at the other end of the lab.

"We need to get in there. At least one of you knows how. You can avoid a lot of trouble and a lot of pain by telling us."

"Screw that," the older scientist said. "Once you've got the code, there's no reason to keep us alive. In fact..."

His voice trailed off as he saw Castillo standing at Harmony's shoulder.

"Oh, you bastard. You're behind this whole thing."

"Not even close." Castillo tapped Harmony on the shoulder. "The gentleman in the middle is Deacon, the overnight lab supervisor. I should know. I promoted him. He's got the code, I guarantee it."

"Forget it," Deacon stammered. "You're not getting it out of me."

"Folks?" Bette's voice rose above the rest. "Got a problem over here."

Harmony didn't have time for this. She aimed her pistol. Not at Deacon, but at the young man to his left. Then the woman on his right.

"Pick one," she said.

Deacon blinked. "Excuse me?"

"We need you," Harmony bluffed. "We don't need them. So pick which one I kill first. Their blood is on your hands. Or you can give us the code. Your choice."

The color drained from Deacon's face.

"That's...monstrous," he whispered.

"Just your bad luck that you ran into some hardcore fuckin' monsters tonight," Ricky said as he swaggered up, dropping an appreciative hand on Harmony's shoulder. "What's it gonna be, egghead? Five seconds before my girl here paints the walls. Four...three..."

"Two-eight-one-seven!" Deacon blurted out. "Two-eight-one-seven. That's the code. Please. Don't hurt any-one else."

"*Seriously*, guys," Bette called out.

Harmony ran over to see what the problem was. Josh was right behind her.

"Silent alarm went out," she said, her eyes burning as she glared up at Josh. "It was over and done before we even breached the lab, thanks to your rabid-ass dog over there."

Josh cursed under his breath and tugged at his shirt collar.

"Okay, okay," he said. "We can still pull this off. What's the standard police response time in this part of town? Twenty minutes? Thirty? We'll be long gone by then."

"That's the problem."

Bette turned her laptop screen. Most of it was gibberish to Harmony, machine-talk and code, but a single phone number strobed in an amber window.

"That's *not* the police. All of the alarms in this plant are wired to ping 911 and the alarm company if they're triggered, except for the ones in the lab building."

Josh leaned in and squinted at the screen. "So...who is that?"

"The alarm called out to a private number. The cops aren't coming."

"Because they don't *want* the cops coming," Harmony breathed. "Whose number is that?"

The HVAC system had been constant background noise over the shouts and chaos of the laboratory raid. It chugged and whirred, gusts of cold air flooding the exposed industrial piping that ran up the walls and squeezed between bare ceiling girders.

With a final grinding wheeze, it died. Silence, pin-drop silence, fell over the lab. All Harmony could hear was strained breath, the faint whimpers of their hostages...and the overhead crackle of a PA system turning on.

"Hello, there." Lorne Murrough's curious voice filled the room, seeming to drift from the walls all around them.

No one moved. No one said anything.

"Well, this is awkward," Lorne said. "The whole situation, I mean, but also, you've really done a number on my security cameras. I can't see you, but I know you're in there, so...could the leader — I'm assuming you have a leader — of this band of merry men please pick up the interoffice phone? I'd like to speak with you."

Everyone looked at Josh. He grimaced, shook his head and mouthed a silent protest. He and Ricky had an eloquent conversation with their hands while Harmony scanned the lab, spotting a black desk phone with a steadily blinking light over by a centrifuge. She was tempted to answer it herself, but Lorne knew her voice — and worse, he knew her under her guise as a federal agent. One wrong word and he could kill her without even trying.

"Listen," Josh hissed at Ricky, "we're free and clear right now. Security is down, the cameras are blind, and the only people who can identify us are dead. Right now, we are *safe*."

Jessie nodded her head across the room, pointedly glancing at the hostages. Josh rolled his eyes.

"The dead and the not-dead-yet, is that better?" he said under his breath. "If I get on the horn with this guy, I'm one voice-print away from an arrest warrant."

"I am not quite so public a figure," Dr. West said, taking charge and striding over to the desk phone. He pulled back a swivel chair and dropped into it before tapping the intercom button.

"Yes," he said, "I am...the boss."

"Thanks for picking up," Lorne said, his voice still projecting over the PA system for all to hear. "I'm showing there should be four scientists working in the outer lab right now. Are they safe?"

West turned in his chair. The fastidious mortician stared at the bullet-riddled corpse in the door of the firing range.

"A statistical majority of them are," he said.

"Let's keep it that way. Please understand that those people are everything to me. This isn't just a company. It's a family. My family."

"Then you'll be willing to cooperate, to keep them safe," West suggested.

"Just tell me what you want."

West turned to Josh with a question in his eyes. Josh mouthed the words *safe passage*.

"We'll be leaving shortly," West said, leaning close to the desk phone. "We expect no interference, no tricks, no police."

"Of course," Lorne said. "You won't be surprised to learn I have a fair amount of pull with the Chicago PD. I'll keep them back. Say, two blocks away from the plant? More than adequate for you to slip away."

Harmony narrowed her eyes. She leaned close to Jessie.

"He's lying. The alarm didn't notify the police."

"He could have called them himself."

"Why?" Harmony whispered. "You heard Bette: every other alarm in this facility is normal. The ones in the lab were designed *not* to call the cops. Why give himself extra work if that's what he was going to do anyway?"

"Of course," Lorne added, "nothing is given for nothing. I'll need you to release my employees first."

"Poppycock," West scoffed. "And how would we expect you to hold up your end of the bargain after we hand over our only leverage? Do not toy with us, sir, and do not prevaricate. We are dangerous men."

Lorne sat in the dark, cavernous comfort of his penthouse of-fice, a four-course feast laid out before him on silver platters amid endless stacks of paperwork and reports. All of it forgot-ten now, as he juggled windows on his monitor and typed out commands while "negotiating" with the invaders in his lab.

He scrolled along a wireframe map of the lab building, study-ing access and control points, while his chief of security sent a steady stream of text messages straight to his desktop.

Sir, cameras are still in lockdown. Full power cycle might reboot them and let us back in, but we're seeing a lot of bizarre network activity and we don't know what else the intruder did to our systems here.

He typed back quickly: *Don't care what it takes, I want eyes on that lab.*

"I wouldn't dream of anything less than full transparency," he said, humoring the reedy-sounding man on the other end of the phone line.

Move to Contingency Red, Lorne typed in the message box. *And as soon as you get control of the cameras, notify me at once.*

There was a delay, a lonely cursor strobing on a blank line while his head of security mulled over his response.

Sir, the response read, *you realize that could require a full sterilization of the facility?*

Lorne reclined in his tall-backed leather chair. He picked up his glass of white wine, contemplating it in the dim electric light.

Whatever it requires, Lorne typed back. *No one leaves that laboratory alive.*

CHAPTER TWENTY-NINE

"I don't see how we can possibly trust you," Dr. West said, staring imperiously at the desk phone.

"Considering I'm the founder and president of an anti-war organization that creates life-saving devices and inventions to protect innocent people," Lorne's voice echoed over the PA system, "and you're the leader of a gang of thieves who invaded my workplace...I hope you can imagine what that sounds like from my perspective."

"Oh," West said, deflated.

"Mm-hmm. A little silly, right? I'm not the one who needs to prove his trustworthiness here. But if you could, say, set *one* of my employees free, it'd go a long way to demonstrate your good faith."

"Well, that...that does sound quite reasonable."

Castillo had been listening, staring, glowering at the desk phone as his hands clenched at his sides. He couldn't take any more of this. He marched over and snapped, "You're playing right into his hands, idiot!"

Josh made a frantic slashing motion across his throat, shaking his head wildly, but it was too late. A soft, curious chuckle washed over the PA system.

"Oh, there's a familiar voice. Nicolas, Nicolas, Nicolas, what am I ever going to do with you? And here I thought you'd been kidnapped."

"And a fat lot you did about it, *old friend*. I'm sure you celebrated when you found out."

"You wound me," Lorne said. He glanced at his dishes, untouched since the silent alert came in. He did have another sip of wine. He was going to need a second bottle by the end of this.

Satisfying, though. Ever since Castillo turned hermit, invoking an archaic work-from-home clause and surrounding himself with armed men, Lorne considered him a minor but annoying loose end. Castillo was convinced Lorne wanted him dead, hence the bodyguards. Which he did, to be perfectly fair, but in more of a "it'd be nice if that guy keeled over one morning due to natural causes" sort of way. He wasn't actually going to *do* anything to him.

Now here he was, part of a gang of thieves...which meant Lorne knew exactly what they were here to steal.

And now he had a perfect excuse to snip that dangling loose end.

"I wound *you?*" Castillo's voice barked over the intercom.

Lorne got up, strolled across the penthouse office, and tugged on the frame of an oil painting, a faded but lush pastoral. It swung on a concealed hinge, exposing a safe beneath. He keyed in the access code and the stainless-steel door popped open with a metallic clank.

The interior of the safe, stuffed with papers, banded bills, and stacks of gold coins, smelled like gun oil. He reached in, his weathered hand closing around the textured walnut grip of a service pistol.

"I've never been anything but a friend to you, Nicholas. I'm sorry you chose to repay my kindness like this. Hurt, to be honest."

• • • ● • ● ● • •

"Hurt? You're hurt? You hypocritical, self-righteous—"

Josh grabbed Castillo's shoulder as the small man raged at the desk phone, forcibly dragging him back.

"He is *playing* with you," Josh hissed, spinning him around and staring him dead in the eye. "You're giving him intel and he's giving you nothing. Use your damn head."

Castillo took a deep breath, steadied himself, and nodded.

"No, no, you're right," he said. "I'm sorry. I didn't realize...how it would feel, being back here."

"You're fine." Josh snapped his fingers to get West's attention. "Hang up. He's stalling. Wasting our time."

Harmony had been watching the hostages.

They were cowed, for the most part, but the younger man was squirming like an eel. He was working his legs back and his arms forward, trying to get his zip-tied wrists under his feet so he could bring his hands in front of him.

When he made his move, it happened in a heartbeat.

His wrists slipped around his shoes and he leaned back, swinging his hands up. Then he jumped to his feet and ran. Not for the exit, but for the red-jacketed security door on the other side of the lab. He hit the keypad and punched in the access code.

The red door let out a puff of compressed air and ground open like a bank vault, swinging slow. He barreled across the threshold just in time for Ricky to gun him down, two shots to the middle of his back, shredding his spine and impaling his heart on shards of shattered bone. His corpse hit the floor and slid on a rough metal grating, leaving a smear of blood across the grid of dark steel.

"What was that?" Lorne's voice demanded, rising an octave.

"An unwise decision," West told him, "on the part of one of your employees. If you have any hold over your people, Mister Murrough, I suggest you tell them to obey us."

"Listen to him," Lorne started to say.

"*Hang up*," Josh mouthed at West, incensed now.

West broke the connection, cutting Lorne off in the middle of a word.

"He is right, though," Josh said to the two remaining hostages, motioning to the open door with his gun. "You should really listen to us. Gents, get 'em on their feet. We're all taking a little walk together."

The young woman lurched forward, her tied hands clenching behind her so tightly that her knuckles turned white.

"You can't," she stammered. "You can't go in there. You can't make me go in there—"

Ricky put the fat barrel of his revolver to the back of her head.

"You will find," he said, "that I can make you do anything I goddamn please. Now *up*."

Harmony helped her to her feet, while Jessie hauled her boss, Deacon, up alongside her.

"Listen," Harmony said, her voice soothing. "You're thinking about running. You just saw what will happen if you do. You need to be calm right now. What's your name?"

The young woman swallowed hard. She searched, desperate, for some kind of life-preserver in Harmony's eyes.

"Franza," she said.

"Franza, listen carefully. Do what you're told, cooperate with us, and you'll be fine. I'm going to get you through this."

That wasn't a bluff, she quietly resolved. That was a promise. No one else was dying here today. Nobody but the people who needed killing.

Ricky threw a too-familiar arm around Franza's shoulder, scratching his head with the muzzle of his gun as he steered her toward the open doorway.

"C'mon," he said, "let's see what kinda goodies await beyond the mystery door."

The crew gathered at the open doorway. They stepped across the threshold, and over the body of the dead scientist, footfalls clanking on the dark steel grid lining the floor. Then they stopped.

"What," Josh breathed, "the actual *fuck* is going on in here?"

"We didn't have a choice," Franza whispered, her face pale. "He didn't give us a choice."

The hallway was about fifty feet long, a narrow mantrap with a security door at each end. It was lined with prison cells. Each cell had a transparent wall and door, made from some kind of reinforced heavy-duty plastic, and stainless-steel fixtures. Each cell had an occupant.

The one closest to Harmony stared, gap-mouthed and empty-eyed, at nothing. He wore a soiled and tattered hospital gown, the ratty fabric caked with a dark rainbow of bodily fluids, and a smeared ring of cracked dried blood painted his lips. His veins bulged like black worms, bubbling under the skin as if his blood had been replaced with boiling tar. Across the hall, just five feet away, his counterpart in the opposite cell was a tangle of skin and bones and long, knotted hair, huddled in the far corner with her head bowed. Her flesh was covered in weeping sores, oozing watery pus, and her broken toenails were jet-black.

"Oh, no," Houston murmured, walking from cell to cell. "This is not what I signed up for."

Ricky kept his hostage moving, marching Franza down the corridor toward the sealed door at the end. West and Bette took up the rear, bringing Deacon along as their unwilling escort.

"What is this?" Ricky asked, flashing a cocky grin at the listless, twisted prisoners in their plastic cages. "Some zombie shit? Y'all doin' zombie shit down here? Pretty sure that's not allowed."

"That's not it, not in the slightest," West marveled. The coroner made a beeline to a cell whose occupant, his hospital gown torn to reveal more wormy veins pulsing around an emaciated, half-broken ribcage, stared vacantly into space. He fished in his pocket and produced a penlight, shining it into the prisoner's eyes. "I need a subject for hands-on study but...I'm seeing a visible pulse, no pattern of lividity, I have limited but demonstrable pupil response..."

"English, Doc."

West looked up the hall and beamed.

"These people aren't dead. Or undead. They're something...else."

"Look what he did with my miracle," Castillo muttered, pushing past him. He turned to Josh. "May we? Please?"

Josh nodded and pointed at Franza. "You. Get the inner door open."

Ricky walked her up to the access panel, but it wasn't like the one in the outer lab. No keypad this time, just some wall-mounted goggles and a dull, square pad underneath.

"It's a biometric scanner," Franza said. "I need to look into it and touch my thumb against the pad at the same time."

"So?" Ricky asked.

She arched an eyebrow. "So my hands are tied behind my back."

He sighed, tugged a hunting knife from his boot, and gave her a good long look at the blade. Then he turned her around and chopped at the zip ties, freeing her wrists. She rubbed them, wincing, and leaned into the panel.

West was supposed to have been watching Deacon, her boss. Too enraptured by the world of scientific possibilities unfolding before his very eyes, he didn't notice his captive slowly inching away, easing toward the door they'd entered from. Or how he turned his back — and his bound hands — toward a small glass-fronted box that jutted from the wall between a pair of cells.

On the other end of the cell block, the reader responded to Franza with a beep and a merry little chime. The inner door slowly hissed open and everyone turned, eager to see what lay ahead.

That was Deacon's cue. He curled a fist and punched through the thin panel of glass, lacerating his knuckles, and yanked the emergency handle beneath.

The overhead light shifted from stark white to amber as a klaxon split the air. Both of the doors on either side of the mantrap made a hard grinding sound as they slowly began to swing shut. Meanwhile, locks all along the corridor popped with a pneumatic rush of air.

The cells were opening.

Deacon sprinted, making a mad dash for the way out. West and Bette both shot at him, but their bullets went wide, tearing into lab equipment and shattering monitors as he ducked out of sight.

"No, no, *no*," squealed Franza, struggling in Ricky's grip. "We have to go, we have to go *now!*"

"You heard the lady," Josh said, shooting a nervous look over his shoulder as he led the charge. The crew stormed the inner door, slipping through the increasingly narrow gap as the heavy slab of reinforced steel drew itself shut on a slow, crushing mechanical arm.

Harmony was the last through the door, covering their escape and making sure everyone else made it. Jessie grabbed her wrist and yanked her over the threshold. She spun, looking back through the fast-closing doorway, while Franza, in a blind panic at her side, hammered a *Close* button with the heel of her hand.

One of the prisoners stumbled out into the hall, sniffing the air like a feral dog. He turned toward Harmony and spotted her through the gap.

He dropped to a crouch. His jaw fell, bones crackling, muscles tearing as his mouth stretched impossibly wide. His lips tore and black blood guttered down his sore-encrusted chin like an oil spill.

Then he screeched, a sound like nails on a chalkboard pumped through a rock-concert amp, and charged straight at her.

CHAPTER THIRTY

The screeching prisoner careered up the corridor while Franza helplessly pounded the *Close* button and the mantrap door continued its slow, grinding arc shut. More prisoners were turning now, filling the halls, bursting into frenzied animal squeals as they broke into a mad run. Harmony leveled her gun and held her breath, sighting through the gap, finger brushing the trigger as the creature in the lead narrowed the gap between them with long, loping strides. Ten feet, eight, six, four—

—the security blockade wedged into place with a final hiss of compressed air. Jolts rocked the thick slab of metal from the other side as the captives, their howls muffled, slammed their bodies against the door in a desperate frenzy.

Harmony took a step back, lowering her gun, studying the inner lab. This was an octagonal chamber, the metal walls washed in slow strobes of amber from the emergency lighting, another two security doors offering ways out on opposite walls. She didn't see anything matching the package's description. The centerpiece of this room was an operating table. Empty, sterile, but she couldn't miss the drains set into the tile floor. The equipment here was for morticians, not surgeons.

Josh was about to say something, ready to take charge, when a pistol's hammer cocked just behind his left ear.

Houston pressed the muzzle of his pistol against the back of Josh's head. Josh slowly raised his hands, one clutching his own gun — its barrel carefully pointed to the ceiling — and the other wide open. Ricky turned, scowled, and braced his revolver in both hands before taking aim squarely between Houston's eyes.

"What do ya know," Ricky said. "Thought you were too much of a pussy to carry a gun."

Houston threw his words from the other day back at him. "Figured I needed one, being part of a cowboy-shit crew and all."

"Ricky," Josh said, "please do not escalate things right now. Thank you."

"I want answers," Houston snarled.

"And you'll receive them," Josh said.

Ricky held his aim steady, slowly side-stepping to get a better angle.

"Just so you know," he told Houston, "I'm gonna take that piece away from you. Then I'm gonna stick it up your ass, just about as far as it'll fit and then some, before I pull the trigger."

"*Not helping*," Josh said.

Deacon burst onto the skybridge. The inner lab door had sealed itself off, locked down thanks to the failsafe he triggered, but he still ran like the devil was on his heels. At least until he saw the corpses of the two dead guards out on the bridge, one slumped like a lifeless doll against a web of fractured glass. He pressed his back to the opposite wall, mouth bone-dry and pulse racing, and inched past the corpses. Then he sprinted all the way down to the lobby.

"Call Mr. Murrough," he gasped, racing up to the security desk. "Then call 911!"

Dima rose from the desk, prim in her stolen uniform, and put on a face of pure concern as she circled around.

"Don't worry, sir, whatever it is, we'll take care of it. You're in good hands." Dima reached out and gave his arm a reassuring squeeze. "I'll protect you. What happened?"

"It's...I can't even talk to you about it, it's...I need Lorne. Please. Just get Lorne on the phone."

"Of course, come here. Come with me. You're all right now. You're safe."

Still holding his arm, she eased him around to the back of the desk. He snatched up the phone, trying to punch in an extension with helplessly trembling fingers.

He saw Dima's shadow fall over him and felt something cold, like a sliver of ice, pressed against his throat from behind. Then Dima's blade whipped across his jugular. She gave him a rough shove, sending him sprawling to the floor, wide-eyed and gasping as his lifeblood guttered onto the tile.

"Seriously?" she growled. She snatched up her cell phone. "Oh, hey, 'boss-man.' I don't know if you knew you had a missing hostage, but I just took care of him for you. What the hell are you *doing* up there?"

• • • ● ● • ● ● • • •

"Well," Josh said, remarkably calm under the circumstances, "right now I've got a gun pointed at the back of my head. Oh, and do you hear that alarm in the background? That's because we're trapped and the only way out is a sealed-off corridor filled with bloodthirsty psychopathic zombies."

"They're not zombies," West said.

"So here's the thing," Josh said, "I need you — and by 'I' I mean all of us — to hit up the building blueprints, contractor payments, alteration requests, literally anything you can find out about this lab. And most importantly, find us another way out. Because if you don't, we're all going to die in here."

Dima's voice purred over his cell phone. "You're not selling me on this idea."

"Normally I love our playful banter, but this is a really bad time for it."

Ricky had Houston framed in his sights. Houston's hand didn't waver, keeping his gun's muzzle pressed to the back of Josh's skull.

"Put it down," Ricky snarled.

"Second I do, I'm dead," Houston countered.

"You're a dead man either way. Only question is how slow you're gonna go out."

"We don't have time for this," Jessie said. "I don't know what those things are, but if we don't work together, we won't make it out of here."

"Somebody knows," West said in a sing-song voice, gazing at Castillo.

"I didn't know he had gone this far. Not this fast." Castillo flung an accusing finger at Franza, the researcher. "Ask her."

Franza squeezed her eyes shut, as if this was a nightmare she could will away.

"He didn't give me a choice," she said.

"Dima, sweetheart?" Josh said, squeezing his phone. "I don't know if you can hear the peanut gallery on your end, but things are a little tense and I'm gonna have to let you go. Find us an exit route, ideally by the time we secure the package. We can still salvage this."

"Are you insane?" Houston tilted his head. "We're screwed. We're trapped. There are at least a dozen maniacs between us and the only way out, and you want to *finish the heist?*"

"Correction." Josh hung up and pocketed his phone. "There are a dozen maniacs between us and the one way out *that we know of.* We'll find another."

The thumping from the sealed door, and the frenzied animal yowls of the prisoners on the other side, only grew louder. Jessie looked at the terrified researcher.

"Can they get through that thing?"

Franza didn't open her eyes. She sank to the floor, curling her knees up and wrapping her arms around them, borderline fetal as she gave into her fear.

"Let's not stick around and find out," Bette said. She brushed past Franza, heading for the closest other door, digging in her backpack and coming up with a brushed-steel box connected to a fat ribbon cable. She brandished an automatic screwdriver in her other hand. It whirred softly as she attacked the bolts holding a keypad to the wall.

"Nobody's going anywhere until we get some answers." Houston stared, intent, at the back of Josh's head.

"Ricky, listen to me," Josh said. "Houston is going to put his weapon down. You're going to do the same. You are not going to shoot him."

"The hell I ain't."

"*Ricky.*" Josh inhaled through gritted teeth. "He's our box-man, and we don't know what kind of obstacles are waiting for us up ahead. It's a little too late to go shopping for a replacement now, you get me? We need him. Now both of you, kindly lower your guns so we can have an adult conversation."

Houston and Ricky locked eyes. Slowly, as one, they both pointed their weapons to the sky. Then they lowered them. For one tense heartbeat Harmony was sure Ricky would change his mind and gun him down on the spot, but the man wasn't entirely immune to reason. Houston was a veteran safecracker with a knapsack full of tools and goodies, and there was a very real chance they'd need every last one of his tricks to get out of here.

The PA system crackled, and Lorne Murrough spoke from the walls.

"Hm. Unfortunate. I still don't have camera access but judging from the failsafe going off, I must assume you've done...well, just what I expected you to."

Harmony had an idea. She hunted for a phone and found one mounted over a cluttered workstation. She snatched up the receiver and gestured to Jessie, who scooped Franza up and ushered the terrified young woman over. Harmony put the phone to her ear.

"M-mister Murrough," Franza stammered. "I'm...I'm alive. I'm in here. With them. They made me, I mean, I didn't...I didn't mean to..."

Lorne leaned back, resting his hands on the smooth glass curve of his desk, and closed his eyes. Not what he wanted to hear.

"Franza, my dear. Don't tell me anything about the thieves. I'm afraid they might hurt you if you do. Are you alone in there, though? Did any of your colleagues make it?"

"N-no." Her voice trembled over the phone's speaker. "Mister Deacon got away, he's the one who triggered the failsafe. Every-one else is..."

Her voice trailed off, answering the question. Lorne steepled his fingers in contemplation.

Everyone looked skyward when Lorne answered, after a long and thoughtful pause.

"Your service has meant more to me than I can say. You have... a child, yes? And an elderly mother in Seattle? I will personally ensure that they want for nothing. You have my promise on that."

Franza slowly turned, staring at the phone receiver in her hand with a look of dawning horror.

"Obviously," Lorne said, "and sadly, sacrifices must sometimes be made for the greater good. You will not be forgotten, Franza. Never forgotten. Not by me."

There was an audible *click* as he hung up the phone.

Franza's lips parted but nothing came out beyond a tormented, breathless squeak. Harmony put an arm around her, gently easing her away from the phone. Franza dropped the receiver and it dangled, swinging, at the end of a curling black cord.

Josh puffed out his cheeks and looked over at Castillo.

"I thought *I* was a cold-hearted son of a bitch," he said. "You actually worked for that asshole?"

"For far too long," Castillo said.

"No wonder you were looking for a new job."

"Excuse me," Houston said. "I believe you were going to give us some answers?"

"Sure, but seeing is believing. Cherry, baby, how are we doing on that door?"

Bette flashed a thumbs-up just before her control box, tethered to the exposed guts of the keypad, let out an electronic blip. The door ahead whistled open, another slab of steel to put between them and the twisted captives in the outer hallway.

"All the answers you want are just up ahead," Josh said. "Along with the package...so, by default, your money is just up ahead too. Shall we?"

"You first," Houston said.

Josh flashed a salesman's smile.

"Now where is your sense of adventure?"

CHAPTER THIRTY-ONE

The high-security labs, Harmony realized, were built like a string of honeycombs. While the outer shell of the facility was a giant windowless cube, the interior was a set of individual octagonal labs joined by diagonal corridors, and each corridor served as a defensive mantrap with solid security doors at each end. Thankfully, this one was flanked with dull metal walls instead of more prison cells. Bette held up a hand at the end of the hall, pausing to unscrew another access panel and go to work with her customized tools.

That's a lot of empty space, so what's between the walls? Harmony wondered, gently easing the terrified Franza along with one hand and cradling the compact grip of her Sig Sauer with the other. *Just an open cavity, with the individual rooms held up on support beams?*

They might be able to use that.

It was getting hotter in here. Sweat pooled on the small of Harmony's back, her starchy uniform blouse sticking to her prickly skin.

While Bette worked, Ricky cast a gimlet eye at Houston.

"Tell me something," he muttered in Josh's ear. "If she can get us through these doors, why exactly do we need to keep our 'box-man' around?"

Houston heard him. Without turning back, he gave his answer to the wall.

"In this knapsack," he said, giving the heavy army surplus bag over his shoulder a rattle, "I've got — among other tools of the trade — a couple of jam shots, a diamond drill, and a borescope, any and all of which we might need to get out of this hellhole alive. A situation we're only in, if I could be so bold as to remind everyone, because of your complete lack of professionalism."

Ricky stared daggers at the back of his head.

"Oh, and if you're thinking of jumping me and taking the bag," Houston said, "ask yourself: do you even know how to *use* any of this stuff? Because I don't think you do."

"Wanna gamble your life on that?" Ricky asked.

"I'm pretty sure that's exactly what I'm doing."

Behind him, Josh put a light hand on Ricky's arm. He shook his head. Ricky grumbled, taking a shuffling step back.

LEDs strobed along the base of Bette's codebreaker and the little box chimed just before the next door popped its seal with a pneumatic hiss.

"Assuming they haven't completely rearranged the place since my last visit," Castillo said, "the package should be just up ahead."

Four doors in four corners ringed the surgical theater at the very heart of the maze. Angled lights on swing arms cast the chamber in bands of stark white light and harder shadows, while clusters of engines, like hospital life-support machines, beeped and clacked and stood sentry over a singular patient. Graphing pens shook across a scrolling reel of paper, charting arcane readings from a cluster of glossy black cables.

Those cables ran across the surgery floor to an operating table at the heart of the room. Upon it wasn't a person, but a thing. Harmony instantly recognized the "package" from Josh's first briefing. Up close, it looked even more like a coffin.

The casket was ivory and pristine, a long flat-bottomed capsule ringed with a set of wheel-locks, its seams caulked with tight black rubber. A black screen set into the top of the casket strobed with constant updates, tracking the temperature inside and outside of the containment unit.

The temperature in the room, according to the screen, was eighty-two degrees. As Harmony watched, it kicked up to eighty-three. The coffin's interior held frosty. Probes and cables snaked from the machinery all around the operating table, vanishing into gasket-sealed tubes all around the base of the casket.

"This is it," Josh breathed, approaching the package with quiet reverence.

Harmony wore a coin under her blouse, drilled with a tiny hole and suspended on a delicate silver chain. It was faded, tarnished, the outer rim ringed in faded Greek words. Legend attributed it to her great-great-grandmother, the first witch in the Black family bloodline, who herself claimed it had once belonged to the Oracle of Delphi. Harmony didn't believe that; her great-great-grandmother, as her own mother often confided, was a bit of a huckster.

Wherever the coin really came from, though, it reacted like a tuning-fork in places where reality had gone thin. It would flutter against her breastbone in the presence of strong magic, like a canary in a coal mine offering early warning of danger.

Now it bounced on its chain, hammering her skin like a moth trying to escape through a closed window. And the closer she neared the containment unit, the more agitated it became. The coin had never reacted like this before.

Franza cringed away from the casket, leaning into Harmony.

"Please," she whispered. "Just...leave it alone. Don't open it. Whatever you do, don't open it."

Josh ran his fingers along the smooth white plastic, staring at the casket like a long-lost lover.

"Wouldn't dream of cracking this beauty open," he said. "That honor goes to someone much more deserving, though I do hope I'll be there to witness it."

"Answers," Houston said. "*Now.*"

"Like I said, seeing is believing. Gather around, kids. C'mon, closer. It won't bite."

The crew edged closer to the containment unit, clustering around it. Josh tapped the display, the screen responding to his touch as he tapped his way through a string of menus.

"I wasn't going to show you this," Josh said, "but considering the circumstances, I think you should all know what kind of stakes we're playing for tonight."

"Don't," Franza whimpered. She turned and buried her face into Harmony's shoulder.

Two more taps, and the display seemed to go translucent. From the angle, Harmony thought, it was broadcasting a live feed from a camera inside the coffin's lid.

There was a body inside. Just not a human body.

She recognized the creature in a heartbeat. Not anything she'd ever seen in real life, though. She'd seen it on movie screens, on TV shows, a dozen iterations of the same nightmare. "That's..." Houston's soft voice trailed off into silence. He shook his head in disbelief. "That's a fucking alien."

The hairless body was small, maybe four feet tall, and spindly, with matchstick arms ending in three-fingered claws. It had rubbery gray skin and an oversized bald head with a single open eye. The eye was a sphere of solid jet, so black it seemed to swallow the light. The other eye had been extracted, leaving a scarred cavity behind. One leg had been cleanly amputated below the knee, and a half-dozen of the tubes and hoses snaking across the surgery floor ended here, piercing the creature's flesh.

"It is indeed a creature from another world," Josh agreed. "Probably not quite the way you're thinking, but close enough. This is what we've been hired to steal."

"The miracle I found," Castillo said. "The miracle I entrusted to my old 'partner.' And look what Murrough did. I had no idea he'd taken his obsessions this far. He's *harvesting* it. Chopping it up for parts like a goddamn stolen car."

"Got ourselves a dead spaceman," Ricky said.

"No," Dr. West said, standing over the casket with a look of absolute triumph. "Look around. These machines, the data recorders...this entity is quite alive."

Josh nodded, firm, pointing to him and Bette. "And we need to keep it that way, at least if any of you want to get paid tonight. You two check the seals and locks. We need a way to disconnect all those tubes — safely — and get this thing moving without breaching the casket's integrity and *without* waking up the occupant. Can you handle that?"

"On it," Bette said, her steely gaze fixed on the creature inside.

Josh turned his attention toward their sole surviving hostage. "Listen. You want to get out of here alive, same as us, right?"

Franza's head gave a jittery nod.

"Tell us what your boss triggered on his way out. The lockdown. How do we lift it?"

"Forget that," Ricky said. "Tell us about the damn zombies."

"They're not zombies," West sang out, huddled over the casket.

Franza took a shuddering breath and wiped the back of her hand across her eyes, getting a grip on herself.

"The failsafe seals all the doors and shifts the lab to emergency power. It can only be lifted by Mr.— by Lorne's direct authorization, from a console in his office. God, I can't believe he...abandoned me like that. Years of loyalty, and he left me to die."

"It's what he does," Castillo said in a bitter voice, joining Bette and West in inspecting the casket seals. "You're not the first and you won't be the last. Don't blame yourself: he's very good at convincing people they're fighting the good fight. I speak from experience."

"Those bodyguards at your house," Harmony said. "They weren't there to protect you from people like us. They were there to protect you from *him*."

"Figured it was only a matter of time," Castillo grunted, kneeling down to study the wheel-locks on the side of the casket. "Murrough is a monster. Even I underestimated just how monstrous, considering the gauntlet we just ran through."

"Yeah," Ricky said, his reptile gaze fixed on Franza. "Tell us about the zombies already."

Behind him, West looked up and raised one finger in the air. Then he paused, closed his mouth, waved a dismissive hand and went back to work.

"The creature," Franza said, nodding at the containment unit, "doesn't look like us, but its DNA is ninety-eight percent human. Lorne wanted to know how it would...interact with human beings."

"Interact," Jessie echoed, her voice flat.

"With injections of blood and alien tissue. We made a mistake, though. At first we thought it was just a catastrophic reaction, the way our subjects transformed into...well, you saw them. But that wasn't the whole story. I discovered the truth."

Franza tilted her head, raising her chin toward the casket.

"That thing in there. It's *sick*. It has a disease, and we inadvertently passed it to our entire panel of test subjects."

"I knew it," West chirped. Harmony wasn't sure if she believed him.

"It's not like any pathogen I've studied on Earth," Franza went on, "but it shares trace elements with both rabies and Crimean-Congo hemorrhagic fever."

"Airborne?" Harmony asked.

Franza shook her head. "No. It spreads by fluids. And unfortunately, as you've seen, victims become wildly irrational, gripped by fury. Mentally, they've been reduced to wild animals. The disease eventually kills them as their organs shut down, but until their final breath they want to spread it. Something about the virus compels them to attack and infect as many people as they can."

Her gaze sank to the surgery room floor.

"They weren't trying to kill us back there," she said. "They were trying to make us just like *them*."

"This virus. How infectious is it?" Harmony asked.

"In tests? One hundred percent. Whatever this is, our immune systems have no defense against it. And worse, the incubation period is...a matter of minutes. At best. Just a drop of blood or saliva in your mouth — or in your wounds, if they manage to bite you — is all it takes."

Jessie frowned. She contemplated the gun in her hand.

"Help me out here," she said. "Lorne Murrough, the guy who spent his entire career engineering new ways to protect and preserve life, the guy who started out testing cures for plagues...is cooking up one of his own? Make it make sense."

The intercom system squealed as it crackled to life.

"Considering you've come this far," Lorne's voice calmly echoed through the walls, "I would be happy to shed some light on that for you. I wouldn't want you to think badly of me."

CHAPTER THIRTY-TWO

A screen on one wall — before now keeping track of the temperature and heartbeat readings from the casket — became a window into Lorne Murrough's penthouse office. He sat behind his desk, staring into his webcam, cradling a nearly empty glass of wine in his pale, weathered hand.

"Little late to the party, pal," Ricky said to the screen. "I already think you're a piece of shit."

"Well, you would know," Lorne replied. "I want to be very clear on something. You people broke into my home, murdered my employees, and now you're threatening my life's work. You're the villains of this story. I'm the hero. I will triumph over you, and I will move on, just as I have done with every adversity I've ever faced. You will not stop me."

A flash of anger clenched Harmony's stomach into a knot. She gestured at Franza.

"I think your former lab assistant might have some thoughts on what kind of a 'hero' you are."

"I do what is necessary for the greater good. I always have, and I've never spared myself from the cost. I sacrificed my youth, my health, my looks, all on the altar of medicine. Not for any financial reward but because it *needed to be done*. By the way...I got control of my cameras back. You can see me, and I can see you, too. Hello, everyone. Such an interesting looking ensemble you are. Some very surprising faces."

Harmony and Jessie shared a quick glance. One word about their late-night visit to interview Murrough and this whole masquerade would be over and done. Harmony kept a limber grip on her compact pistol, checking targets and sightlines, while Jessie casually moved to the other side of the room, circling behind Ricky and Josh.

"When my former partner brought me the...'miracle,' you called it, Nicolas? Not the word I would have chosen. I knew, in that very moment, that we were looking at nothing less than an existential threat to the survival of the human race. I believe the creature before you is an advance scout, sent to test and probe our world's defenses."

"You're paranoid," Castillo scoffed.

"The poor wretches behind and below you would beg to differ."

Josh shot an alarmed look at Franza. "*Below* us?" he whispered.

She gave a helpless nod, teetering on the verge of panic.

"I tried to tell him, the creature is just sick. Probably no more than a common cold on its own world; it might not have even realized what it had before it came here. It's like...you ever read *War of the Worlds*? It's just like that, except instead of the aliens accidentally being defeated by human diseases, it's humans—"

"It's nonsense," Lorne said, cutting her off. "I've spent my entire life studying the art of war. I know an attack when I see one. The *thing* in that containment unit is nothing less than the vanguard of a full-scale alien invasion. I tried to bring my concerns to the government — keeping the alien a secret, of course, because I knew they'd take it from me. Or try to. They laughed in my face. All my decades of service, all my sacrifices, and they laughed in my face. That was when I knew the burden of saving the Earth fell on one man's shoulders alone: mine."

Jessie pretended to scratch the back of her neck, making eye contact with Harmony while she twirled a finger around one ear.

"You were trying to find a cure," Harmony said. "Just like your work with Operation Whitecoat."

"At first, yes. That was the plan. Learn all the creature's secrets, plunder its blood and bones, and prepare for if — and when — its comrades attacked. But then I realized how short-sighted I was being. What use is a cure for a single virus, when they might have hundreds, even thousands of variations stockpiled as weapons? And what use is anything I do when the men in power are too weak and cowardly to step up and do their jobs?"

Castillo pointed to the hoses that ran from the casket —
and from the creature's pierced flesh — to snake across the
operating theater floor and vanish into the steel walls.

"He's not trying to cure the virus," Castillo said. "He's synthe-
sizing it."

"I am."

Jessie's brow furrowed. "I don't get it. So you're going
to...what, juggle some molecules around and try to infect them
with their own bug?"

"The time for action is now," Lorne said. "Once the invasion
begins, it will be far too late. To survive, we need leaders who are
capable of stepping up and making hard decisions. The current
crop, sadly — just like every administration in my entire lifetime
— falls far short of the mark. But we can fix that."

He finished his wine, reached for a half-empty bottle, and
filled his glass almost to the brim.

"Next week, I have an appointment with the Joint Chiefs of
Staff to discuss a purchase order for my new DOVE munitions.
I've been an honored guest at the Pentagon more than once in
the past, but...this time around, I'll be bringing a little something
special along with me. That same afternoon, I have a meeting
scheduled with a senator I own. He's expecting his usual bribe,
which he'll get, along with a surprise. Oh, and by lucky tim-
ing...the President is going to be addressing Congress that very
day."

Houston stared at the video screen in growing disbelief.
"You're gonna turn them into more of those...*things?* That's
insane!"

"I have never been more rational in my life, nor has my
purpose ever been more clear. The only way to fix the system
is to destroy it. The outbreak won't just remove the old chaff to
make way for new leadership, it'll be global news. No one will be
able to connect me to it. There will be terror, confusion, mass
panic. And that very night, I'll reveal the alien to the world and
open their eyes to the real threat."

Harmony's blood ran cold as she saw his plan play out in her
mind's eye.

"You're going to make them all believe," she said. "You're
going to stage an alien attack."

"And then, in the anarchy, I will volunteer to serve, as I've done my entire life. The workers, the soldiers, the people will finally have control...with me as their gracious shepherd. And when the invasion finally comes, we will be ready. I will make them ready."

Dr. West scoffed at the screen.

"Who would believe a pizza-faced clone of Andy Warhol? Get a job teaching art school."

"Now hold on just a second here," Ricky said. "I don't know how any of this science stuff works, but I've seen plenty of zombie movies."

"They're not—" West paused, reconsidering. "To be perfectly fair, the difference is academic at this point. Please, continue."

"You got any idea what happens if this shit spreads?" Ricky demanded.

Lorne sipped his wine, unconcerned.

"Of course I do. Why do you think I chose two of the most heavily guarded and heavily monitored places in the country to strike? There will, unfortunately, be some level of contagion. Staffers, visitors, anyone unlucky enough to show up for work that day — acceptable losses all — but the Pentagon and the Capitol Building are hardened against terrorist threats. The second an alarm goes up, armed response will be swift and crushing. The infected will be killed off before they can escape. The disease will not spread, at least not beyond where I will it to spread. The men who stand in the way of our world's survival will die. Only the fear will remain."

"Hell of a gamble," Jessie said. "All it would take is one. One single stray getting away, reaching a street crowded with civilians and going to chomp-town...are you really ready to take that kind of a risk? You could *cause* the apocalypse you're trying to stop."

"I am a man of vision," Lorne said. His one visible eye, the other buried under his mop of snow-white hair, glared from the screen. "And this...this is what I've been training for my entire life. Everything I've done was just preparation for this monstrous burden. This is what I am *for*. This is the only reason I was even born. This plan. This cure for the coming darkness."

In Harmony's mind's eye, his words became concrete things, etched around the screen in blue neon light as he spoke. Certain phrases and words popped out, brighter than the others. *My purpose. What I am for.* He spoke with the zeal of a religious convert, but nothing in April's profile had even hinted at any signs of delusion or narcissism. Either he'd spent over seventy years secretly nurturing and concealing a savior complex, or he wasn't the same man — a selfless philanthropist, by all accounts — he used to be.

"Mr. Murrough," Harmony said, "please. Hear me out. This isn't you. You've spent your entire life trying to help people. To protect people. Now you're talking about 'acceptable losses.' When did you start believing *any* life was an acceptable loss?"

He froze, his glass of wine halfway to his lips. Then he set his glass down on the desk.

"When I understood the enormity of the threat, and the fact that I am the only man alive who can do anything about it. Do you think I enjoy this? My heart is in bleeding tatters and the things I'm going to do, the things I *must* do, will damn me straight to hell. Deservedly. And yet I have no choice. Not if I hope for even the slightest chance of saving the human race. You must understand: these aliens are, and I do not use the word lightly, evil. Pure, ontological evil."

"How can you possibly know that?" Harmony asked.

Lorne reached up, took hold of his wild hair, and pulled the curtain aside.

"Aw, fuck me sideways," Ricky muttered, staring up at the screen. "That ain't right."

Now Harmony knew what had happened to the creature's missing eye. Lorne had one of his own plucked out, the replacement — an orb of jet black so deep it seemed to consume and drain the very colors around it — bulging from his skull. It had grown to the size of a billiard ball, cracking and twisting the bones of his face around it, one of his cheeks jutting out at a broken angle and one temple, normally concealed under his thick, shaggy white hair, bubbling under the skin like a head of cauliflower. A web of veins stood out like worms under his skin all around the alien implant, black as tar and pulsing with strange energy.

"I know," Lorne explained, "because I am, as I said, a man of vision."

Chapter Thirty-Three

"The next time someone calls me a mad scientist," West murmured, staring up at Lorne's mutilated face, "I believe I have the perfect counterargument."

Lorne held one hand over his human eye. Only the inky void remained.

"I see as they see, like this," he said. "And do you know what I see? *Prey.* I have...urges. Urges I have to fight with every waking breath, but that's why I was chosen. I have a will of iron. It wants to dominate me, like it wants to dominate every living thing on this planet, but I won't let it."

"Why?" Castillo demanded. "Why did you do this to yourself?"

"I needed to know. I needed to understand. I performed the procedure myself. It wasn't hard, I knew how to do it. I..." Lorne trailed off. He lowered his hand, revealing his human eye again, and frowned. "Sometimes I think I was hearing the voices before I underwent the transplant. But that can't be right."

"Listen to me," Harmony said. "You've been tricked. You're not fighting it. You're giving it exactly what it wants."

"Lies."

"Look at your principles," she said. "Now look at your actions. They don't match. Can't you see that? Lorne Murrough doesn't condemn innocent people to die. Lorne Murrough doesn't believe in acceptable losses. You're a *hero*. This isn't what a hero does."

For a moment, she thought he might be hearing her. Then his lips twisted in distaste. He grabbed his glass from the desk, slammed back a swig of wine, and shook his head at the camera.

"I am doing what must be done. No more and no less. History will remember me as the greatest man who ever lived. It won't remember you at all."

He tapped a key and killed the feed. The screen went dark.

• • • ● • ● ● • • •

Lorne pushed back his chair. He rose and paced, walking the sanctum of his penthouse office from end to end, leaning forward and muttering with his hands clasped behind his back.

"Eve of victory, eve of everything that matters, and now this happens. No. No. Keep it together. You have a purpose."

They're here to kill you, whispered a voice. It sounded almost like his. It came from the mirror in his executive bathroom, a span of beige marble and chrome on the other side of an open doorway.

Lorne stepped into the bathroom and faced himself in the mirror. He pulled back his hair, exposing both eyes. He saw his own reflection again in the jet-black sphere, twisted and strange and floating in a pool of ink.

You know who they are, his reflection said.

He knew. The second he got control of the security cameras, he knew. Those two women, Temple and Black, had come to him with false smiles, false concern...and real badges.

In a trance, Lorne put his hand over his human eye. His lips moved, but he heard the voice coming from the mirror.

And what does that mean, Lorne?

His hand swayed, exposing the human eye and blotting out the alien orb.

"The government is onto me," he said. "They're not thieves. They're feds. They're all feds. Castillo must have turned state's evidence against me."

His hand drifted back to the other side of his face.

Your plan is in ruins. They'll never let you into the Pentagon now. Oh, they'll pretend to, but you'll be arrested the second you walk through the door. They're going to disappear you, Lorne. Then they'll take your company. Destroy everything you built. You know what you have to do.

Lorne's head drooped. He put his free hand on the edge of the marble sink, squeezing it until his knuckles turned white.

"I don't want to do that."

You have to. You knew there was a threat of discovery, or that something might go wrong. That's why you came up with the contingency plan in the first place, remember?

He remembered. He thought he did, at least. His memories had been fuzzy of late. Sometimes he remembered the same event two different ways, or woke with vague recollections of a conversation he never had.

It's the stress, soothed the man in the mirror. *Have another glass of wine and relax. But you know what you have to do, Lorne. To save the world, sacrifices must be made.*

Lorne drifted away from the mirror, back across his office. Standing beside his desk, he picked up his glass of wine with one hand and the office phone with the other.

"Patch me through to the head of security," he said, and waited while hold music softly played at the far edges of his troubled thoughts.

"It's Lorne," he said. "I'm carrying out the Pyrrhus Contingency. Have the men meet me downstairs."

He checked the load in his pistol. Then he concealed it under his lab coat and strode to the penthouse door.

"Okay," Josh said, staring up at the black and silent screen. "I'd like to say something."

All eyes turned his way. It was definitely hotter in here now. Harmony felt sweat beading along her back and brow, matting her hair in the stagnant, stale air.

"This job did not go according to anyone's plan, including mine," he said. "I can say it, I'm a big enough man to own up to my mistakes. But here we are. This is the situation. A few of you don't like me very much. I get it."

Josh pointed up at the screen.

"But *that* motherfucker is batshit crazy. We can agree on that, yeah?"

No dissent. Even Jessie caught herself nodding in agreement. Josh's hand rested on the white plastic casket. The creature within was motionless, lost in a frozen slumber. Harmony wondered if it dreamed.

"I suggest," he said, "that we put our issues aside, find a way out of this shitshow, and take the alien with us. We all get paid and, hey, bonus, that lunatic doesn't get to make any more zombie juice."

"I'm down," Houston said. "On one condition. Let's burn this whole place to the ground on our way out."

"Finally speakin' my language," Ricky grunted.

Josh snapped his fingers at Franza. "You. Science girl. How would you like to make ten thousand dollars?"

She blinked at him.

"I'll take that as a yes. Cool. Welcome to the crew. The cash is already earmarked and waiting for you, and all you've gotta do to collect is get us out of here alive. Now tell me something good."

Franza swallowed hard and nodded, looking up at him with puppy-dog eyes. Harmony didn't have the heart to tell her it was nothing but false hope: the best thing she had to look forward to, even if she could get them out, was a single breath of fresh air and a bullet to the back of the head.

Unless I stop him.

The Sig Sauer was heavy in her hand. She could wrap this up right now. Kill Josh, kill Ricky, and the others would probably fall in line. She could count on Bette and Houston. West was a coward, easily intimidated, and while Castillo seemed loyal to his new masters, it felt like he was mostly driven to get back at Lorne Murrough. A sudden change in employment wouldn't affect that one bit.

Harmony wasn't impulsive. She thought, planned, always tried to be three moves ahead. But now a compulsion grabbed her so hard her gun arm went taut, muscles clenching like someone was clinging to her back and working her body like a puppet. It took everything she had to keep her weapon at her side, pointed to the floor.

We need them, she told herself. *Until we get out of here, until we secure the casket, we need them.* At first, she needed them to lead her and Jessie to the package. Now it was a simple matter of survival.

"The lockdown switches everything to emergency power," Franza started to say. "Necessary functions only, no air conditioning—"

"He won't even have to lift a finger to kill us, come sunrise," Bette muttered. She wiped her hand across her forehead and flicked away a bead of sweat. "We'll bake in here."

"At the far end of the secure lab wing, there's a service elevator that goes all the way down to the basement. But the elevator is locked down too, we can't use it."

"Let me figure that out," Josh told her. "Let's hear more about that basement."

Franza nodded, biting her bottom lip.

"It's all maintenance down there. HVAC, conduits, fuseboxes. There's an emergency exit. A tunnel that leads to the surface. I've never even seen it, but it was part of my safety training. If we can get that elevator running somehow, I think I can open the exit for us. That's not the real problem, though."

"You mentioned other 'test subjects' earlier," Harmony said.

"There's a secondary pen. We...ran out of room upstairs."

"How many?" Bette asked.

"Two...dozen? Give or take a couple?"

"Let me guess," Jessie said, slumping against the operating-theater wall. "The doors are open and the monsters are loose."

Franza replied with a timid nod.

"Screw that," Ricky said. "Let's just go back the way we came."

Josh thought it over, his fingertips drumming against the casket.

"No good. There's a dozen of those freaks all jammed into one tiny hallway, barely five feet across. They might not be smart, but they're fast. The second we get that door open, they'll swarm us." He looked back at Franza. "How big is the basement?"

"P-pretty big, I guess?" she stammered. "I've only been down there once, during my orientation, but I remember a lot of twisty hallways and side passages. There are storage rooms, a backup generator..."

"Meaning the freaks are probably spread out. Good chance we can face them one at a time instead of fighting the whole herd. With a little luck, we might even slip on by."

His fingers stopped drumming.

"So the basement it is. We're heading down, kids. All the way down." Josh flashed a cocky smile. "We're all going to hell eventually, so we might as well get an early taste."

CHAPTER THIRTY-FOUR

Bette, Castillo, and Dr. West set to working on the casket, decoupling hoses and preparing it for transport. Harmony pulled Franza aside, tugging her sleeve until they were just out of earshot.

"What else can you tell me about this facility?" she asked. "The outside looks like a solid windowless cube, but the inner floor plan doesn't seem to line up."

"It doesn't. All three of the buildings at this plant were built the same way: inner rooms wrapped up inside a big outer shell. The shell is for added security. That's what they told me, anyway. The rooms are all held up with struts and support beams. They kind of...float in a big empty space."

"If we could reach the shell, any chance we can cut through it?"

Franza shook her head. "It's half a foot thick. They're intentionally designed so that if something catastrophic happens — a fire, an explosion, a viral outbreak — nothing gets in and nothing gets out. We're buried alive in here."

On the casket's status display, the air temperature kicked up another notch.

"What if the outer shell needs maintenance? Are there any access hatches, anything like that?"

The researcher thought about it, glancing to one side and combing her memories.

"I think so? I mean, I've never seen anyone actually use it, but I'm pretty sure I've spotted one or two. What difference does it make? Even if we could reach the shell, we couldn't break it open."

Harmony was thinking ahead.

Jessie swung by and caught her eye. "So Josh is convinced we can fight our way through the basement."

"You disagree?" Harmony asked.

"In theory, no. These zombies — and I'm gonna keep calling 'em zombies, just to piss West off — are fast and feral, but we've taken on a hell of a lot worse together. If I let the Wolf out, I could probably take them on all by myself. Fighting isn't the problem. What'll happen when we start ripping into these things?"

"Blood," Harmony said, "everywhere."

"And how much of that blood does it take to turn a person into one of *them*?"

"One drop," she said.

"Mm-hm." Eyes shrouded behind her ubiquitous sunglasses, Jessie slowly scanned the operating room. "We need to be smart about this."

They drafted Franza to help and searched the lab, rummaging through drawers and cabinets. Jessie snapped open a lock with the butt of her gun. The noise turned Ricky's head. He was on the other side of the lab, conversing in low tones with his master.

"What're you doing?" he drawled, suspicious.

"I'm thinking about bloodshed," Jessie told him. "Also thinking about facial protection. Hit those cabinets behind you, see if you can find anything."

A box of latex gloves was better than nothing. Harmony tugged a pair on, the tight rubber snapping against her wrists, while Franza went around handing them out to the rest of the crew.

"Got some of those heavy-duty surgical masks," Ricky called out.

Good, Harmony thought, *but still not good enough*. That still left their eyes exposed, a major conduit into the body. Jessie found the solution: a sheaf of translucent, flexible plastic sheets, used for protecting important papers and X-ray photos. Harmony stripped off her tie, twisting it in her grip and giving it new life as a headband, tying it tightly behind her hair to hold the plastic sheet firmly over her face.

The rest of the crew followed suit, using belts and purloined cables to make their improvised face-shields. Slightly more equipped for the journey down, they finished preparing the casket for transport. One by one, hoses hissed and decoupled from the containment unit, slithering free as glistening probes and wet black valves clanked onto the tile floor at their feet.

"Check your exposed skin," Harmony cautioned. "Watch out for cuts, sores, any opening that could let the contagion in. There's no cure for this illness, or at least none that we're going to find tonight. You get infected, you're good as dead."

Bette ran ahead to open the next security door with her bypass device, while the others gathered around the casket and took up pallbearer positions.

"On three," Josh said. "And please remember: our paycheck depends on bringing this package back in pristine condition. The occupant — so long as he stays sleeping, safe and sound — is worth more than all of us put together."

"To put it another way," Ricky chimed in, "you break it, you *buy* it. Get my meaning?"

"Wordplay," West said. "Clever."

Ricky shot a glare at him.

"No," West quickly added, "I mean it was genuinely clever. Kudos."

The casket, Harmony discovered as they hoisted it together, was surprisingly easy to move. The containment unit itself had been built with durable but ultralight materials, and its alien occupant looked like he barely weighed fifty pounds soaking wet. Still nothing she'd want to haul around all by herself, but a team of hands made light work.

Halfway up the next corridor, another antiseptic stretch of barren, steel-floored hallway between honeycomb-shaped laboratories, a cherry-red emergency box hung on one wall with an ax and a firehose pinned down behind glass. Castillo broke the protective shroud with his elbow and grabbed the weapon.

"Don't want to tell you how to do your business," Jessie said, balancing the back corner of the casket on her shoulder, "but you probably want to stick to your gun. Getting up close and personal with these things is a bad idea."

"It's not for the infected," he replied.

The final door whistled open onto a small antechamber shaped like a wedge of pie, with a single elevator standing at the triangle's apex. The panel above it was dark, the keypad lifeless. They set the casket on the tile floor to rest their backs, and Bette unscrewed the access panel for the elevator's keys. A minute later she shook her head.

"No good. Controls have been completely severed. Like Franza said: the only person who can get this box moving is sitting in a penthouse over in the next building, and I don't think he's going to help."

"Hence the ax," Castillo said, stepping up. "Gentlemen, if I could get a little extra muscle, please?"

He used the ax's head like a crowbar, grunting as he wedged it between the elevator doors, driving it a few centimeters deeper by pounding the heel of his hand against the back of the blade. Then he leaned into the handle, twisting it to one side. The elevator doors opened just a crack, fighting him. Ricky and Houston flanked him, digging their fingers in and hauling back on the heavy steel panels. They inched back, the tension like a rubber band stretched to the breaking point — and then surrendered, rattling open the rest of the way.

Beyond was nothing but an empty shaft. Harmony approached the edge, holding her breath as she looked down. The elevator cab was parked down at the bottom of the shaft, twenty or thirty feet below.

Houston leaned in beside her and shook his head. "Access ladder on the side of the shaft. We can climb down easy enough, but I don't see how we're gonna get the package down there."

"I do," Josh said. "With great care and impeccable skill."

At his direction they ransacked the machines in the surgical suite and the rest of the inner workrooms, harvesting electrical cords and stout computer cables, anything they could twist and knot. They wove the casket in a cradle of improvised ropes, binding cords to cords to create the longest tether they could.

"Double-check those knots," he said. "If they come undone halfway down, we might as well open the doors wide and give those freaks a big kiss. Better way to die than what we'll have coming, trust me on that."

His brow was slick with sweat, a wet smear under the curve of his improvised face shield.

They carried the casket up to the edge of the elevator shaft. Then, with the entire crew working together and taking up the knotted cable tether, they eased it over the edge of the chasm.

"Hold *tight*," Josh grunted, leaning back on his heels with his knees bent. "Now lower it, slowly. One hand over the other, nice and easy."

The casket swayed and turned in lazy circles as it began to descend, a few jolting inches at a time. The knotted cables strained and the vestibule went silent save for rasping, strained breaths and the sounds of creaking, crackling rubber. Harmony fed the rope forward, one hand then the other, falling into a steady and determined rhythm with the rest of the crew. The air was sweltering, her muscles straining and hands aching as she grappled with the cord.

Then, with a faint, gentle thump, the casket touched down on the roof of the elevator cab. Josh rushed to the edge of the open shaft, leaning down to squint at the device's display panel.

"Can't read it from up here," he mused, "but it looks okay. Hell, I think we might actually pull this off. Everybody, follow me. We go down the ladder, pop that hatch, *carefully* lower the casket down into the elevator car, and it's a smooth ride to the exit."

"Smooth," Houston echoed. "You remember there's a whole pen of those things down there and they're out for blood, right?"

"Sure, but we've got three things that they don't."

Josh touched the muzzle of his gun to his temple, sheathed in translucent plastic, in a wry salute.

"Guns, brains, and ample motivation to succeed," he said. "They're hungry. I'm betting that we're even hungrier."

CHAPTER THIRTY-FIVE

Dima had been engrossed in a terminal behind the security desk, down in the main lobby where they'd stationed her. She was hunting for building plans, contractor emails, anything they could use to find a way out of the secure labs. It wasn't looking good. She was an accountant, not a hacker like Bette; she could find a missing penny in a mile-long spreadsheet, but when it came to cracking secure accounts she was useless. Besides, it wouldn't help even if she struck gold: her calls to Josh were being shunted to voicemail, and considering the crew's total silence she suspected they were deep enough in the labs, buried under slabs of concrete and steel, to lose their phone signals.

Or there's a cell jammer in play, she thought, eyes darkening. Would Lorne Murrough arrange something like that? No reason to think he wouldn't.

"And speak of the devil," she murmured, staring out through the glass wall of the lobby. She watched Lorne stride across the parking lot alone, moving like a man on a mission.

She was supposed to guard the lobby. She was *supposed* to do a lot of things, but Dima hadn't come this far in life by following the rules. She waited until he passed, then slipped out into the dark to tail him. The lobby door whispered shut at her back and a brisk night wind ruffled her hair, smelling of smoke and chemicals.

Stray gravel crunched under her shoes as she padded past the shadows of girders and slumbering parked trucks, then followed Lorne up an alley between the towering rust-colored cubes of the two production buildings. The thoroughfare was littered with pallets, construction supplies, and stout bags of concrete mix. Dima ducked behind the barrel-shaped shadow of a cement mixer, hiding as Lorne turned to check behind him. He waited, lingering at the far mouth of the alley, until a short-bodied truck with the Ardentis Solutions logo on its side rolled up and grumbled to an idling stop.

Lorne and the driver exchanged words Dima couldn't hear from her hiding spot. He pointed up ahead and jogged alongside the truck as it rolled off, heading where he had pointed.

Dima followed, staying low, pressing herself to the rust-colored steel wall at the next corner and taking a peek. Further back, down an unmarked driveway at the edge of the plant's barbed-wire fence, was a drainage ditch jacketed in water-stained concrete. Dima was no architect, but she knew the ditch was deeper than it needed to be, and it had been built at an angle that concealed the inner walls from casual passers-by.

The truck — about the size of a package delivery van, with a rolling door on the back — beeped as it backed up toward a hatch concealed in the bottom rear of the ditch. Two men got out, both of them wearing neon green clean-room biohazard suits, pulling on masks and affixing containment seals as they rendezvoused with Lorne.

"Sir," one said, "you should really be wearing protection. We can run back to the auxiliary lab and get you another suit."

"I'm immune," Lorne snapped. He cast a dour stare at the hatch, a rounded slab of steel next to a retinal and fingerprint scanner. "Get ready, I'll open it up."

The back door of the truck rattled open, and the men in the clean suits grabbed their gear: shotguns mounted on nylon shoulder straps and a pair of long catchpoles ending in wire nooses. One offered a third shotgun to Lorne, who slung it over his shoulder before leaning into the panel beside the door. A thin ribbon of blue light washed over his one exposed eye, chiming softly as the fingerprint pad strobed.

The door jolted open, just a crack, then let out a mechanical garbage-disposal grinding whine as it slowly yawned wide. With the men's backs turned Dima decided to chance it: she slipped closer, staying low and moving from cover to cover, to get a better look. Beyond the hatch was a wide corridor walled in gray concrete, directions marked on the floor in thick stripes of yellow paint. The paint faded into the shadows, paling until it vanished out of sight.

"The Pyrrhus Contingency," Lorne breathed, his human eye fixed upon the darkness. "I hoped it wouldn't come to this, but here we are. You gentlemen are going to help me make history today."

"Sir." One of the men spoke, his voice muffled through the mask of his clean suit. "We've been briefed on our part, but we don't really understand what the purpose of—"

"As you said," Lorne replied, cutting him off. "You've been briefed on your part. Do that. Let me worry about everything else. I think our first lucky contestant is about to arrive."

An infected researcher, still wearing the tattered, blood-soaked remnants of his old lab coat, came barreling out of the darkness. He fired up the tunnel with a cat-like shriek, black teeth and rotten gums bared, hands clutching eagerly for Lorne's throat.

Lorne casually leveled his shotgun and pulled the trigger. A DOVE slug slammed into his former employee's chest, sheathing him in a cocoon of blue lightning as he stumbled, still moving but dazed. One of the catchpole nooses whipped over his head and drew tight around his neck. The technician with the pole swung him around, using the long, sturdy pole as leverage, and threw him into the back of the delivery truck like a sack of potatoes. The second technician hit their catch with another electrified round, putting him down for the count.

The next two infected came as a pair, screaming up the tunnel side by side as they launched themselves down the killing funnel like cannonballs. Shotguns erupted, muzzle-flash lighting up the dark in short, brutal flashes. A tech swung his catchpole, missed, stumbling back and almost falling under one of the infected victims before Lorne blasted his attacker from the side and sent him rolling across the dirty asphalt, convulsing wildly. The second infected, stunned and lassoed, was hurled into the back of the van.

While they grappled with the other one, trying to get its head in the wire noose and pull it onto its feet, a tech backed up and pumped two more rounds into the belly of the truck.

"They're getting up again," he gasped. "They're shaking it off too fast!"

Animal howls drifted from the tunnel beyond the open hatch, a hive slowly rousing to the smell of fresh meat.

"One more," Lorne said. "I want at least one more. Two would be better, but—"

The third infected victim went stumbling into the open truck door. Another slug drove him back, the three flailing bodies falling on top of each other, shuddering with epileptic spasms.

"Sir, we can't keep them docile!"

"*One more, goddamn it*," Lorne roared.

A fourth infected boiled from the dark, her bloody mouth stretched so wide it tore open at the corners, her jaw dangling unhinged like a snake. Lorne rushed to the control panel as the two technicians stunned, lassoed, and corralled it, pumping two more rounds into the belly of the truck before jumping up to haul the rolling door down and trap the victims inside.

One of the techs swung a heavy lock down, sealing their captives in the back of the delivery truck. The captured infected hurled themselves at the rolling door, bodies slamming against metal, broken fingernails scrabbling.

The tunnel hatch slowly grumbled shut. In the distance, blood-washed eyes flicked open and pale, torn faces looming, a gathering swarm of tangled, swaying limbs and ragged clothes. The air filled with low feral whines.

"Here they come," one of the techs breathed, taking aim through the closing gap.

The pack surged, a dozen broken bodies with a single hungry mind, intent on escape. Lorne and his men opened fire through the gap. One infected fell, then another, the rest stampeding over their comrades' bodies like a swarm of enraged fire ants.

They were ten feet from the exit, bounding across the painted yellow safety lines, when the hatch ground shut and locked with a solid *clang* of steel on steel. Lorne quickly pressed his thumb against the fingerprint reader, then keyed in a string of numbers.

"Final override," he said to the two technicians waiting uncertainly behind him. "We have some uninvited guests in the facility, and I suspect they're going to try to get out this way. Unfortunately for them, I just turned this hatch into a wall. Sealed for good. Even *I* can't open it now. Honestly wish I could see the surprise on their faces, assuming they even make it this far."

"Sir?" one of the techs said. "This is as far as our briefing went. What do you want us to do now?"

"Yes. Right." Lorne bowed his head for a moment, his curled hand to his chin, searching for the perfect words. "Gentlemen, you've done honorable and valiant work. You deserve a much greater reward than I can possibly grant you. And I assure you, that in the new world to come, your names and your sacrifice will be remembered by all."

"Sacrifice?" one said. "Wait—"

Lorne drew the handgun from under his lab coat, raised it in one swift motion, and shot him between the eyes. The other tech scrambled back in shock, reaching for his shotgun, and Lorne drilled him twice in the chest. Both men dropped to the concrete, eyes wide, stone dead.

Dima had seen the whole thing, crouching low in the shadows behind a pallet of concrete mix. She watched as Lorne turned toward the truck and holstered his pistol. He ran one hand through his ragged ivory mane, pulling it aside to expose the inky black orb of his alien eye.

This was *not* going according to plan. Not Josh's, not Nadine's, and certainly not Dima's.

Then again... she thought.

She had no idea what Lorne Murrough was up to, or for that matter why he looked like a mad scientist from a 1950s sci-fi movie, but Dima was a canny operator and she knew an opportunity in the air when she smelled one. Some of her least favorite people in the world were trapped in that laboratory. For a moment she considered cutting bait and walking away. The first glimmer of dawn was on the horizon, casting the sky in shifting shades of cold violet, and she could be gone before the sunrise.

But where would she go? Harmony and Jessie — *meddling bitches*, she thought with a bitter taste in her mouth — had thwarted her first attempt to flee to Paris. She could make another go, with the two of them buried alive in that steel-cube tomb, but they'd confiscated her luggage, her books, her relics and contraband, all the occult sundries that were supposed to feather her retirement nest. Even if she escaped across the pond, she wouldn't have a pot to piss in once she landed. That wouldn't do. Dima was a woman of expensive tastes.

Stay the course a little longer, then? That idea had potential. If the crew escaped from the lab, if they'd taken any casualties in the process, she could work with that. If Harmony and Jessie died in there, the links between them and Dima would be effectively severed; she could go back to work for Nadine with a smile, no fear, no blackmail, and take her time coming up with a new exit strategy. If Josh and Ricky died, she'd still be in the agents' clutches, but she'd also still be alive and — hopefully — protected from Nadine's suspicions. If none of them made it out alive...well, she'd go where the wind took her.

And if a few people needed help dying to set up the perfect outcome for herself, she could handle that too. It wouldn't be the first time or the last.

CHAPTER THIRTY-SIX

Josh's sneakers landed on the roof of the elevator cab with a hollow thud. Houston and Castillo were the next ones down, the rest of the crew still descending the narrow, hard rungs of the emergency access ladder.

"Cover me," Houston said, crouching low to pull back the elevator's roof hatch. It swung up and over, open to the cab below.

The cab's doors were shut, just like the ones far above at the top of the shaft. No one was inside. Emergency lighting flooded the elevator's cage in deep, shimmering amber.

Houston dropped down first, his heavy knapsack jangling at his side. He stayed in a crouch, head cocked, holding up a finger as his keen ears listened for any trace of the infected. He looked up at the open hatch and flashed a quick thumbs-up. Castillo dropped down, then Josh, the rest of the crew touching down on the roof of the cab behind them. Ricky slithered down, joining the other three men in the cage below and training his gun on the elevator door.

"Okay," Josh whispered, looking up. "We're going to wedge these doors open. Then you are going to *very* carefully slide the casket through the hatch, down to us. Like I said: we already did the hard part. Keep sharp, don't do anything stupid, and it should all be smooth sailing from here."

Castillo repeated his method from up above, gently working the blade of his fire ax into the crack between the elevator doors, wriggling the weapon to one side and forcing a gap wide enough for fingers to slip through. Josh and Ricky flanked him while Houston guarded the rear. Everyone else, giving them room to work, waited on top of the elevator cage.

The ax blade twisted, forcing the elevator doors to part, just a crack. Amber emergency lights gleamed beyond, casting puddles of light along a shadowy concrete tunnel.

Grey-skinned hands with broken, blackened fingernails rammed into the gap from the other side and hauled the door open. The infected researcher — mouth encrusted with rusty smears, his veins writhing under his skin like black worms — fell through the doorway and onto Castillo, dragging him to the floor of the cage under his dead weight. A flailing arm knocked Castillo's improvised mask off, sending it skittering into the corner before his attacker leaned over, almost nose to nose, and vomited up a gout of blood. The obscene baptism flooded Castillo's open mouth, his nose, his eyes, and then the infected psychopath went in for a kiss. His teeth closed over Castillo's bottom lip, pulled, and *tore*.

"*Shoot the fucking thing*," Josh screeched. He was pinned so tightly in the cramped elevator car, trapped between one wall and the mutant and Castillo's screaming, flailing body, that he couldn't get a clear shot. Ricky's gun roared like a cannon, the echo booming up the elevator shaft and leaving Harmony's ears ringing. The infected researcher's head snapped back and he collapsed on top of Castillo, pinning him down with dead weight.

Castillo writhed, howled, trying to wipe the gore from his face as his lip dangled, ripped half open. Houston took one sharp step and got into Josh's face.

"'Smooth sailing,' huh? Real smooth. We haven't taken one goddamn step and we just—"

"Time and place," Josh snapped over Castillo's hoarse, anguished shrieks. "This isn't the time and this isn't the place. If you've got an issue with my leadership, you can take it up *after* we get the hell out of here."

"Oh, I'm making it an issue." Houston looked up to the open elevator hatch, and the cluster of shocked faces staring down at them. He raised his arm. "Show of hands. Who thinks this ship needs a new captain, starting now?"

Castillo leaped up from the floor, eyes glazed, and he let out a feral-cat screech before sinking his teeth into Houston's outstretched arm. He dug in just below the elbow, chomping through Houston's uniform shirt and into flesh and muscle. A dark stain spread down Houston's sleeve as he flailed wildly, trying to shake Castillo off.

Ricky put his pistol to Castillo's temple, pulled the trigger and painted the elevator panel with his brains.

Now there were two corpses sprawled on the floor of the elevator cage, cooling in a spreading puddle of scarlet. Harmony's hearing swam, bells ringing at the furthest edges of sound, the receding thunder of the echo from Ricky's gun. Houston thumped back against the far corner of the elevator cage, clutching his wounded arm, face pale and glistening with sweat.

"Tourniquet," he gasped. "I need some cloth, bandages, anything I can make a tourniquet with."

Ricky raised his gun and thumbed back the hammer.

"Ain't gonna help you none now."

"I'm fine," Houston gasped. "I'm fine! You don't even know if I'll turn or not!"

"I could pretend to give a shit," Ricky said, "but I think we're way past that part."

His gun had the final word. Houston slowly slid to the floor, eyes wide and staring at hell, his forehead cratered with a bullet.

No one said anything. No one moved. The last echoes settled, like a silent rain of dust. The air was thick with the coppery stench of spilled blood and butchered meat.

"Okay," Josh breathed. "We're gonna try this one more goddamn time. And if anyone else has issues with my leadership..."

He pointed at Houston's dead body.

"Have a word with him about it. Now pass that casket down to me and Ricky. *Gentle* with it. The floor down here is a little bit slippery."

Once the casket had been passed down, Harmony dropped through the elevator hatch, landing in a crouch. Jessie was right behind her, and she reached up to catch Franza by the hips, lifting her up and over the carnage. Bette and West were the last ones down.

While Josh surveyed the vaulted corridor up ahead, squinting into the puddles of darkness between wall-mounted amber lights, Harmony crouched down and shouldered Houston's knapsack. Metal clanked and shifted inside the pack, the load heavy enough to make her shoulder ache under its nylon strap.

She took something else when everyone's back was turned: the dead man's gun. As the crew prepared to move out, shouldering the casket like pallbearers, weapons ready, Harmony gently tugged on their hostage's sleeve.

Franza's eyebrows lifted as Harmony pressed the grip of Houston's pistol into her hand.

"Hide it," Harmony whispered. "Emergencies only, understand?"

Franza's hand visibly shook as she slipped the gun under her lab coat, tucking it behind her back.

"If this isn't an emergency, what is?"

"You'll know it when you see it," Harmony told her.

Jessie and Ricky carried the front of the casket, Bette and West taking up the rear, while Josh took point and Harmony covered their backs. The crew advanced cautiously down the concrete tunnel, the floor painted in yellow and orange lines to chart a trail through the bowels of the laboratory. Up ahead the way was a zebra-stripe pattern of shadow and light, with amber wall sconces trying to push back the darkness — but only so far. There were vast patches of gloom in between those safe harbors, question marks where anything could be lying in wait. Josh held up his phone and clicked on the flashlight mode, strobing a thin, weak beam along the walls.

West let out an irritated hiss of breath. Josh turned to look back at him.

"*Lights out*," West whispered. "The one upstairs was able to follow my penlight with his eyes. It was the only thing that got a rise out of him, at least until the cell doors opened."

"So?"

"I'll use words you can understand. They. React. To. Moving. Lights."

Josh cursed under his breath and turned off the flashlight.

They took it slow, footsteps soft as they carried their sleeping burden up the tunnel, eyes in all directions as they forded the patches of shadow.

A ragged screech sounded down the tunnel. Harmony spun, whirling on the ball of her foot and bringing up her Sig Sauer in both hands as one of the infected charged at the crew from behind, snatching for Harmony's throat with fingers twisted into broken claws. She shot him twice in the heart, sending him staggering as puffs of black-ruby blood blew out his back in a spray of hot mist. He was dead before he hit the ground.

As the echoes of the gunshots faded, Josh held up a finger for silence.

They weren't alone. They heard rustling, slithering, from up and down the concrete tunnel. Faint, sleepy groans that slowly became a chorus, rising in pitch, rising in hunger, playing counterpoint to the distant patter of running feet.

"Put the casket down," Jessie said.

Ricky looked her way.

"We're gonna need room to fight," she said.

The ivory casket thumped on the tunnel floor. Then the infected came. Two screamed down the tunnel ahead and Josh dropped to one knee, giving the shooters behind him an open lane as he, Jessie, and Ricky laid down a wall of fire. A whole pack was on the heels of the first two, mangled and bloody faces lit in the strobe of muzzle-flash. They stumbled and fell over their fallen comrades, loping on all fours like wolves as they raced to close the gap.

More rushed in from the opposite side and West squeezed his trigger as fast as he could, firing wild and blind until his hammer clicked down on an empty chamber. Harmony and Bette were sharpshooters. They picked their targets, checked their angles, and fired with deadly precision. A fast runner nearly closed on them before Bette blew out his knee, popping it like a rubber duck in a carnival game, and Harmony finished him with a skull shot.

Harmony recalled Jessie's assessment after the Gold Star raid, when she told Harmony about the employee Bette was "forced" to kill. *Cool as a cucumber from start to finish. I don't think her heartbeat even sped up.* As she and Bette fell into sync, nailing targets and filling the tunnel floor with sprawled and broken corpses, Harmony realized: *she's like me.*

In the other direction, a curtain of blistering fire tore into the oncoming pack, shredding them into raw meat. One kept coming, dragging herself on her fingernails, a broken spine jutting from the small of her back and her legs leaving a slithering worm-trail of wet scarlet behind her. Jessie finished her off.

That was the last of them. Josh held up a hand and hissed, *"Hold."*

They waited, and listened, but nothing was stirring. For now. They hoisted the casket up once more, and the crew advanced deeper into the tunnels.

CHAPTER THIRTY-SEVEN

There were warrens down here, nooks and crannies and side tunnels that squeezed between fat exposed pipes. The ductwork rattled like a stalled engine. The crew kept moving, sweeping every corner with the muzzles of their guns, escorting their prize to freedom.

A huge, heavy, open doorway of solid steel, like a bank's vault door, caught Josh's eye. He led the crew down a side corridor, past the door and its wide wheeled lock, but it didn't lead to freedom: the passage ended in a humming room filled with electrical boxes and a backup generator, all bathed in puddles of steady, cool amber light.

"All that protection for this?" Ricky sneered. "Thought there'd at least be something valuable down here."

"Safety measure," Bette said. "See that generator? That goes, everything in the building goes with it. No backup lights, no refrigeration, no power to the equipment upstairs, nada. Not that it makes much of a difference now, with the facility on lockdown and most of the staff either dead or infected. Let's double back; the way out must be further up the tunnel."

They found their target another fifty feet along the tunnel. A fat yellow stripe led the way, running straight to a solid wall of concrete and a metal-plated hatch with a combination eye-scanner, fingerprint reader, and keypad alongside it. Harmony crouched, silent and frowning. There was a crumpled shotgun slug on the ground, and chips gouged in the walls, as if someone had been firing into the tunnel from outside the hatch. Recently.

"That's it," Franza confirmed. "I remember from my orientation video. That's the emergency exit."

"Then if you would be so kind," Josh said with a wave of his gun, "move your butt and do the honors. Ten thousand dollars is waiting for you on the other side of that door. Time is money and the money is *waiting*."

Harmony's hand tensed on the grip of her weapon. While Franza made her way to the control panel, her eyes were fixed on Josh and Ricky. Obviously Franza wasn't getting a dime for her loyal service; none of them were. As a hostage, though, Josh didn't even need the pretense of keeping her alive until the end of the heist. He could gun her down the second she got that door open and justify it by pointing out the obvious: they couldn't trust her not to run to the cops.

Harmony had made a promise: no one else was dying here tonight. The corpses of Castillo and Houston, cooling back in a blood-soaked elevator, made a liar out of her. She was *not* going to let Franza down.

Decisions, then. Josh was the only person who knew where the handoff was supposed to go down. The handoff...and Nadine. Harmony's first chance in years to come face to face with the demon who'd tried to destroy her life. Her first chance in years for...*Catharsis? Closure?* she thought. *What do I want?*

Revenge was a good word. Simple. To the point. That would do.

This was a golden opportunity, but if Josh drew on Franza she'd have no choice but to let it slip away. Saving civilian lives came first. Had to, or she wouldn't be worthy of the mission. She side-stepped, quietly positioning herself behind him as the others set the casket down on the painted yellow line.

Franza squinted at the optical scanner, leaning back as it answered her with a strangled electronic squawk. The fingerprint pad flashed cherry-red under her thumb.

"It's...not working," she said.

"You probably punched in the code wrong," Josh suggested. "Try again."

Another try, another angry bleep. The door didn't budge.

"It's not the code," Franza said. "I'm locked out."

"You weren't locked out upstairs," Ricky said.

"Well, I am now! Lorne must have figured out we were trying to leave this way. He did something to the security system."

Bette brushed past her, dropping her backpack onto the floor and brandishing an electric screwdriver.

"Let me," she said.

After a few minutes of tinkering, frowning down at a tablet connected to the open guts of the control panel, she shook her head.

"No good. Franza's right: this door is on a totally different circuit from anything else in the building, as far as I can tell. And somebody told it not to open from the inside, even if we say 'please.' I can't override it from here. You know, I'll give him this much: most of the time, I can count on private companies cutting corners and cheaping out on security. Lorne actually invested money into this setup."

Ricky stared at her, his eyes cold as tombstones. "You tellin' me we went through all that back there for *nothing?*"

"Don't put words in my mouth. I said I can't bypass the electronic security. Doesn't mean we can't figure out another option. Bring Houston's knapsack over here. Let's see what he had in his toy box."

The deceased safecracker had come equipped for the job. Harmony crouched down beside Bette and they rifled through his bag, tugging out a heavy diamond-tipped drill mounted to a fat pair of battery packs, the custom rig literally held together with strips of duct tape. He had a fiberoptic camera, a few instruments for sounding out a vault's defenses...and two cone-shaped bricks wrapped in brown paper, fixed by red and blue wires to a pair of egg timers.

Jam shots, Harmony thought. Concentrated shaped charges of nitro designed to blow the door of a safe right off its hinges. She showed one to Bette.

"What do you think?"

Bette narrowed her eyes, then cast a glance up the tunnel at her back.

"Grave reservations," she said.

"Why?"

Bette pointed to the exposed pipes that ran the length of the tunnel, clinging to one wall and scaling the roof like black iron vines.

"Because I'm pretty sure one of those conduits is a gas main," Bette murmured. "We get any blowback from the charges, one ruptured pipe might be enough to turn this tunnel into a blast furnace."

Harmony checked the egg timers.

"These run up to three minutes," she said. "We can set the timers on maximum, sprint back down the hall and climb up the elevator shaft before the charges go off. We should be able to get clear in time."

"Barely. And you're only half-right. *We* could get to safety." She nodded at the white plastic casket on the floor at their backs. "Zero chance we make it with the package in tow. And even if we managed to haul it all the way to the elevator before the detonators blew, there's no way we can get it back up the shaft. That was a one-way trip."

Harmony lowered her voice to a conspiratorial whisper.

"Maybe that's the best outcome. Let it burn, deny it to the enemy."

"Unacceptable," Bette fired back. "Uncle Sam wants that casket. And I'm going to deliver it, because Uncle Sam is always right. This is bigger than us. The safety of the planet might depend on it."

Harmony tilted her head, trying to read her.

"When we first talked, you said you didn't even know what we were trying to steal."

"I never lied to you. All I knew was that it was over my pay grade, and my bosses gave me two choices: come back with the package, or don't come back at all. Now I know why. For the record, I think Franza is right: the alien in the box has some kind of communicable disease. Minor for its own kind, catastrophic for humans."

Facts and recollections floated around Bette's face, etched in blue light. Harmony twirled them in her mind's eye, drawing strings from point to point, tethering facts and locking them into one clear conclusion.

"You know this," Harmony breathed, "because the *other* aliens you've found didn't have that effect on people."

Bette tapped a fingertip against the side of her nose.

"I said no such thing. Just like I didn't say there's a grain of truth at the core of Lorne Murrough's madness. You want to know the whole reason Truman authorized the creation of Majestic? One of 'em is sleeping in that box over there. These little bastards have been scouting our planet since the nine-teen-forties."

Harmony thought about the creature in the box, then slowly raised an eyebrow.

"Don't say Roswell," she whispered.

"Fine," Bette replied, "I won't say it. I will tell you three things we know for certain, just to put everything in perspective: the Greys hail from a parallel Earth, one we haven't charted yet; their tech is bio-organic, we are talking *crazy* levels of genetic manipulation; and they absolutely, positively, do not come in peace. I lost eight good men learning that lesson. You don't want to know how they died. I wish I could forget."

Bette fixed her gaze on the casket, quietly seething.

"It's coming back with me," she said. "See, as long as it's still breathing, that's not just a test subject."

Harmony understood. "It's a hostage."

"I need to have a little chat with our next-door neighbors. With leverage this time."

She wasn't going to bend on this. They had to find another way. Harmony studied the floor plan in her mind's eye, retracing her steps. They could scout the opposite direction from the elevator shaft, the tunnel not taken, but they'd risk running into more infected and more dead ends. Then she got it.

"The generator room," she said. "That vault door is designed to hold back a small army. Think it'd muffle the blast?"

"Risky," Bette mused. "But I don't see any better options."

Josh had been carrying on a low-voiced conversation with Ricky. Now he looked up, turning their way. "You ladies having an ice cream social over there? Can you get the door open or not?"

Bette sighed and held her hand out.

"I'm demo-certified. Give me the drill and the jam shots. While I get these set, tell the others what we're planning."

As Harmony leaned over, digging into Houston's knapsack, she felt a slight tug on her hip pocket. She glanced over, seeing Bette's hand snake away empty. A strange extra weight pressed against her leg.

Bette had just slipped something into her pocket.

They made fleeting eye contact, as Harmony passed her the drill, and Bette gave a nearly imperceptible head-shake. Harmony kept her mouth shut.

The drill whined as it dug into the hatch, spitting white sparks and shredded bits of steel that clumped on the floor like molten pencil shavings. Harmony stood and walked back a few feet, gathering the rest of the crew around the casket.

"We think we can blow the door," she told them. "It's risky, though."

"Less risky than goin' back up," Ricky said. "Just one of those things took out Castillo before he even knew what happened and he turned freak in less than ten seconds. Topside, there's at least a baker's dozen of those mutants all piled up against the only door out. Zero chance we gun our way through that crowd without losing more people, and I don't plan on becoming a casualty tonight. Whatever we gotta do to *not* go through that hallway, I say we roll the dice and give it a shot."

Heads nodded silently, agreement all around.

"We're going to set the charges and fall back to the generator room," Harmony said. "We...should be safe behind the vault door. Hopefully."

"Least-worst option," Jessie said. "Let's do it."

"Okay," Josh said, "you heard her. Let's carry the package back to the generator room while Bette finishes placing the charges."

Harmony froze in mid-turn.

Bette. He didn't call her Cherry, her alias. He called her by her real name.

Josh gave Harmony a cherubic little-boy smile, all innocence.

"Oops," he said.

CHAPTER THIRTY-EIGHT

The tunnel bristled with guns. Harmony and Josh drew down on each other, Josh a split-second too slow, each of them standing point blank with their fingers on their triggers. Ricky drew on Jessie, who already had her Sig Sauer drawn and ready. Bette rose, leaving the diamond drill on autopilot where she'd clamped it to the door, and drew her own pistol.

She aimed it squarely at Harmony's heart.

"*Woo!*" Ricky hooted, grinning. "Looks like we got ourselves a genuine goddamn Mexican standoff. I love this shit! Looks like you're a li'l bit outnumbered though."

"Not for long." Harmony kept her gaze fixed on Josh. Her finger brushed the feather-light trigger. "Doctor West?"

West nodded firmly, drew his Luger...and walked over to stand beside Josh and the others, taking aim at Jessie from the far side of the casket.

"Big mistake," Jessie said through gritted teeth. "You know they're gonna kill you, right? Did you think I was lying?"

"Not in the slightest," the coroner sniffed. "But I believe the unfortunate death of Doctor Castillo has changed the dynamic. For me, that is. You see, I'm the only person left who can authenticate the seals on that containment unit, let alone keep it safe in transit."

"Doc's right," Josh said. "We need him."

"Only until the job's done." Jessie's gaze bore into West. "You just signed your own death warrant. We would have *protected* you."

"From what? Success? Prosperity?" Josh had an easy smile, his patter flowing as he slipped into salesman mode. "I talked to the boss, and she thinks a man of Doctor West's talents would be a perfect fit for the House of Dead Roses. She's going to make him a job offer. In person."

"Their 'boss,'" Harmony said to West, "is a demon. You know that, right?"

"And? Priests call me a blasphemer and men call me mad. I see no reason why I shouldn't take hell's coin instead. It spends just as well and it's blissfully unburdened with pious pomposity. I understand that Josh's employer is a patron of science and higher learning."

"What you 'understand' about this situation," Jessie said, "I could scribble on the back of a grocery store receipt and still have room for a game of hangman."

Harmony couldn't blame West for falling for the ruse. Josh was smooth, practiced at selling false hope, and if she had been in the coroner's shoes she might have even believed it herself.

Ricky gave them a lazy reptile grin. "Now it's four against two. Lookin' less like a standoff, more like a massacre."

"Four against three," Franza said. She whipped Houston's gun out from under her coat, holding it clasped in her trembling hands, the muzzle sweeping from target to target as she fought to control her fear.

"Ricky owes me five dollars," Josh said, pleased. "I bet him that you'd slip the hostage a gun. Of course, just one question...did you take the safety off?"

Harmony stared at him, blank. His smug expression brightened a notch.

"See, Houston — a pacifist to the end — kept his safety on at all times. I wasn't really worried when he held me at gunpoint: I knew my boy Ricky could drop him before he flicked the switch. I'm also wagering that science-girl here has never touched a firearm in her life. She doesn't even know what a safety looks like. And when she pulls that trigger...well, it's going to be a whole lot of nothing."

"Hell of a gamble," Jessie said.

"Now watch me double down. Hey, hey, eyes over here. Aim at me, okay?" Josh leered at Franza and tapped a fingertip against the middle of his forehead. "Go ahead. I'm not worried. I'll bet my life on it. How about you two? Are you willing to bet your lives that you remembered to switch the safety off before you gave a totally untrained civilian a gun?"

He was willing to bet his life. So was Harmony.

Because she hadn't forgotten.

She had been as surprised as anyone when the gun-averse Houston suddenly brandished a pistol, but under the circumstances she understood. He'd been pushed to the breaking point. Didn't mean he was comfortable waving a weapon around — something he'd avoided his entire criminal career — and Harmony knew he didn't really want to use it. When she scooped the fallen Smith & Wesson from the blood-soaked elevator carpet, she'd spotted the safety switch. And considering Franza probably wouldn't even know to check, she flicked it off before passing it over to her.

Apparently she had a tell. Or Josh was just that good. He saw something in Harmony's eyes and without a word passing between them, his resolve sprouted cracks. He took a step back and held up his open hand.

"Let's not be stupid," he said.

"Ship's sailed on that," Jessie replied. She looked to Bette. "Think you forgot something."

"Enlighten me."

Jessie reached up with her free hand and took her sunglasses off. Her eyes burned, radioactive in the amber shadows like pits of blue fire.

"I told you what happens to people who point guns at my partner."

"Oh, yeah," Josh said. "Partners. The illustrious Jessie Temple and Harmony Black. The shining stars of...what was their little outfit called?"

"Vigilant," Bette said, holding her aim on Harmony.

"See, the night we all first got together, Bette came to me in confidence. My girl here has quite the background in industrial espionage, but she's done some off-the-books government work too. She recognized you two from an old op she ran. Warned me what you were all about, and that you were here to rip me off."

"So you told your boss about us," Harmony said, "and she told you to play dumb until you could deliver us along with the package."

Josh's brow furrowed in surprise.

"Huh? Why the hell would I do that? I didn't get this far by bothering the boss with petty shit. She doesn't *like* being bothered with petty shit." He held up his left ring finger, showing off the smooth nub of skin over a severed joint. "Ask me how I know. Anyway, I was just using you until we got the casket out, because I needed the extra hands and I knew you'd play along. I was gonna bury both of you along with science-girl the second we breathed fresh air again. But now we've got control of the only way out so...we can call this close enough for government work."

"Besides," Bette added, "I told him the truth. Your sad excuse for a 'shadow agency' is a joke. What have you ever accomplished, rounding up a couple of rogue magicians? You've never even encountered a demon. You wouldn't know what to do if you did."

Games inside games, Harmony thought, puzzled.

The irony rankled her. All this time worrying about protecting Bette's cover, and they were the ones who'd been burned from the start. By her. Considering Josh was still talking about her like she was a rogue industrial spy — not a representative from a second shadow agency that wanted the package even more than they did — Bette had torn their stories apart while protecting her own. Harmony was tempted to fix that, to throw some chaos into this dangerously lopsided standoff...then she held her tongue.

All of the wrong answers suddenly pointed in the right direction. She knew exactly what Bette was up to.

"Now we could just start blasting," Josh conceded, "but I don't feel like getting shot today and I'm guessing you don't either. And we can't trust each other, so here's a solution that doesn't require any. We're going to keep these guns high and keep each other honest. We're going to back away from each other, slowly. Then my friends and I are going to walk this casket into the generator room and close the door between us."

"You're just going to let us go," Harmony said, her voice flat. She didn't buy that for one second.

"Not exactly. I'm giving you a chance. And by that I mean pure chance: this isn't poker, it's roulette. Maybe — maybe, if you run like you've never ran in your entire lives — you'll get clear of the blast in time. Maybe you'll get lucky and the charges won't rip open a gas line and turn this tunnel into a char-broil oven. Maybe you'll find a spot to take cover...you know, one that isn't infested with blood-barfing zombie freaks. What can I say? The house odds are not in your favor, sad to say. Then again, they never are. How are we doing on those holes for the charges, Bette?"

"Just about ready."

"Good. Set the timers for...oh, what the hell, I'm feeling generous tonight."

Josh grinned at Harmony over the sights of his gun.

"Let's give 'em ninety seconds on the clock. Ladies? You should run. It's about to get toasty down here."

CHAPTER THIRTY-NINE

Jessie took the lead, eyes glowing in the dark, loping up the corridor. Harmony had to half-drag Franza along, one hand on her pistol and the other on the scientist's sleeve.

"Stop looking back," Harmony snapped at her. "Listen to me: I'm not leaving you behind, but you've got to shake it off and keep up with us."

"Can't believe Bette fucked us over," Jessie growled on the move. "Correction: can't believe I fell for it. Should've known what she was from the jump. This is some serious scorpion-and-the-frog bullshit. My fault."

"We're dead anyway," Franza stammered. "Ninety seconds? We'll never make it."

"We don't have ninety seconds," Harmony said. "We have three minutes. And Bette didn't betray us. She saved our lives."

Jessie shot a look over her shoulder. "Gonna need you to explain that."

"I will just as soon as we get clear of the blast radius. Three minutes is still cutting it close and there's one thing Josh isn't wrong about: the odds are not in our favor."

Franza dug her heels in once they veered down the access corridor leading to the elevator. Up ahead, lights flickered in the open cage, shining down on three tangled corpses and a carpet soaked in cold blood.

"Are you crazy? We can't go back up there!" she stammered. "We couldn't get through that crowd of infected patients when we had a whole gang. They'll swamp the three of us in seconds!"

"We're not going back through the hallway."

In Harmony's mind, the road to victory was paved with contingency plans. She'd been working on hers since the moment everything went south. It was the reason she'd asked Franza about the architecture of the lab. There was always a chance they'd have to double back, with or without the rest of the heist crew.

Harmony cupped her hands, gesturing for Jessie to step up and pull herself through the open ceiling hatch. She hoisted herself up and wriggled through the gap like a fish. Franza was next. She hesitated.

"Come on," Harmony said, nodding at her hands. "I know you're scared. It's all right to be scared. But the only way we survive this is to *keep moving*."

The vault door sealed the generator room with a heavy clang and the wheel-lock spun until it was too stiff to budge. Josh waved his heisters back, away from the door and toward the far corner of the room.

"All right, one earth-shattering kaboom and we waltz right out of here. Dima should still be topside, minding the store. Let me tell you, I am *so* looking forward to finding out how two government agents ended up on her vetted list. I mean, it's almost like she's exactly the backstabbing bitch I always thought she was. I'll deal with her, we load the casket in the van, we saddle up, and we go get paid."

He stared at his watch, his ebullience fading.

"Bette, sweetheart, honey-darling? Where the fuck is my earth-shattering kaboom?"

She glared at him from across the room. "They were Houston's charges, remember? He probably did some weird tweaking to the timers. We could ask him, but, you know, he's dead."

"Are you sure you set them right?"

"You said ninety seconds," Bette replied. "So I set them for ninety seconds. Clearly, something's off. Blame Houston. I was using his equipment."

"So go out there and fix 'em," Ricky said.

Bette took a deep breath and pinched the bridge of her nose.

"You want me to open the blast door. And go outside. While two active charges are ready to blow at literally any second. Would you like to think that plan through again? Because I do have some notes."

"We can't stay locked up in here forever," Josh fired back.

"And we won't have to. Everyone who works with explosives develops their own quirks. Their own ways of wiring a charge, their own little tweaks. It's like a..."

She trailed off, pretending to think, inviting Josh to fill the silence.

"Like a poker tell."

"Exactly," Bette said. "Now, I know less than nothing about how Houston operated, but I do know his gear. Those off-the-shelf timers have a maximum setting of three minutes. I suspect he bypassed the crank and just set them both for the full duration."

"That don't make any sense," Ricky countered. "Why even have the option for less time if you're gonna go for the full wait anyhow?"

"Convenience. Far easier to go to the shop, buy a couple of five-dollar egg timers and tweak the insides than to try and build a timed trigger from scratch. And it fits what we know about him, doesn't it? Houston was...careful."

"You mean he was a wimp," Ricky said. Still glowering, but now he was back on her side.

"Let's say he was safety conscious. If I'm right, the detonators will go off once we hit the three-minute mark."

"And if they don't?" West demanded.

"Then I will be more than happy to go out there and take a look personally. Let's just wait another..." she glanced at her wrist. "...seventy seconds, yeah? A little patience won't kill anyone."

Harmony was first up the emergency ladder, clambering up the narrow rungs of the elevator shaft hand over hand, eyes on the thin rectangle of amber light from the open door high above their heads. Franza was second, and dragging her heels. Her moves were tremulous, her feet testing each individual rung before committing her weight, pulling herself up at a snail's pace.

Beneath her, Jessie looked up.

"*Listen*," she snapped, her voice like a whip. "You want to endanger yourself, that's cool. You're endangering *me*. Get your ass moving up that ladder or I will grab your ankle, climb *over* you, and let you take your chances with the bombs and the mutants all by yourself."

It was almost always best, Harmony knew, to handle a civilian with kid gloves. To be gentle, and soft, and let them find their inner strength on their own time. But by her reckoning they had half a minute left on the clock and softness was a luxury she couldn't afford. She looked down, locking eyes with Franza on the ladder below her.

"She'll do it," Harmony said, "and I can't stop her. So climb or don't."

She climbed.

They were three-quarters of the way up the shaft when the jam shots went off. At first there was a soft, distant rumble, so subtle that Harmony wondered if Houston's charges were a dud.

Then came the thunder, and the fire. A roaring fury shook the foundations of the lab like a freight train had crashed through the basement walls at full speed, burning as it barreled up the vaulted concrete tunnel. Harmony clung to the ladder's rungs while the elevator shaft shook, an earthquake trying to buck her off and fling her to the bottom of the shaft.

The hatch on the roof of the elevator's cage blasted open, flung back on its hinges as a gout of orange-hot flame boiled up from below, licking the air with breath-searing heat and charring the walls black. The fireball burst, curled and died in the air beneath Jessie's feet, falling back in a billowing cloud of acrid smoke. Harmony kept scrambling up the rungs, her face glistening with sweat as she craned her neck, fighting to reach breathable air.

She pulled herself clear at the top of the shaft, scrambling onto the vestibule floor and turning, quickly, to grab hold of Franza's outstretched arm. She pulled her up and through, both of them tumbling across the tile floor as plumes of vile smoke, the odor like charcoal mixed with the chemical tang of smoldering metal, wafted up from the open shaft. Jessie clawed her way through, heaving herself up and over the edge, rolling to land on her back at Harmony's side.

"Say this for Houston," Jessie wheezed, coughing into the crook of her arm, "man knew how to cook up a bomb."

"Is everyone okay?" Harmony said.

Franza rolled over onto her belly, coughing herself hoarse as she pushed herself onto her hands and knees. She managed a feeble thumbs-up. Jessie looked down at her feet and groaned. She showed Harmony the soles of her running shoes, the once-white rubber seared black and melted like burn tissue.

"Son of a bitch," Jessie muttered. "So much for my new kicks. I really liked these."

Franza gaped at her. "We almost *died.*"

"Yeah, well," Jessie said, patting Franza on the shoulder as she clambered to her feet. "If you think too much about dying, that's when death starts thinking about you."

Franza turned to Harmony. "We're still trapped. There's no way we can get through the cell block and that's the only way to reach the outer lab."

"I think there's another way. I asked you earlier about the outer shell—"

"Which we can't get through, right."

"—and any maintenance hatches, or anything construction workers might have used when they were building this place. I need you to think back for me, really hard, and try to remember where you saw one."

Franza pursed her lips, eyes to one side and distant as she combed her memory. Then she nodded, pushing herself to her feet.

"Follow me."

She led them back through the open mantrap doors and antiseptic hallways, through the empty surgical theater where machines beeped listlessly around an empty operating table and hoses, still slick and glistening with black alien ichor, coiled across the floor like sleeping snakes. They went all the way back to the beginning, the first honeycomb chamber of the inner labs. The path ended in a sealed door and death just beyond it, the infected prisoners still pounding on the battered steel from the other side.

Franza led them to the northwest face of the hexagon where, under a research table piled with folders and a softly whirring centrifuge, a long, fat square of the metal wall was held fast with painted-over bolts.

"I've never seen anyone open it," Franza said. "I mean, I don't know if it's even possible."

"Oh, it's possible." Jessie breezed past her, crouching to eye the panel. She reached out and ran her fingertip along the hair-thin seams.

Jessie sat down on the floor, level with the panel, and drew both of her legs up until her knees were bent double. Then she lashed out, driving her heels into the panel with brutal force and leaving a fist-sized dent in the thin metal sheet.

The infected in the hall heard the commotion and answered with a ragged-voiced chorus of animal growls, pitch rising to distorted shrieks as their sore-encrusted hands hammered the door between them and their prey.

One more kick and the panel buckled and broke, snapping from its bolts and spinning off into the darkness beyond the wall. A gust of stale air wafted through the gap, sweltering hot and carrying the stench of roadkill, like something had crawled into the space behind the walls and died there.

Jessie poked her head through the gap, then pulled back and shook her head.

"Good news is, I think we might be able to pull this off. Bad news is, you're both going to seriously hate it."

Harmony ventured past her, getting down on the floor and leaning close to the hole, squinting into the darkness beyond.

The upper floors of the lab were disembodied ghosts floating in a cube-shaped void, encased by the outer shell and held aloft on massive riveted support struts that made Harmony think of a child's construction toy. Thick rods and girders formed a sparse lattice suspending the honeycomb rooms and passages over a chasm so deep Harmony couldn't see the bottom. The only way forward was out, and up, across a steel beam barely one foot wide.

CHAPTER FORTY

At the back of the plant, down in the concrete drainage ditch, the escape hatch blew off its hinges in an eye-searing fireball, sputtering gouts of filthy black smoke. The hatch went spinning end over end along the ditch, finally landing in a heap of dead, smoking slag.

A few minutes later, long after the dust had settled and the smoke drifted up into the encroaching light of dawn, Josh was the first to emerge from the rubble. He waved his hand in front of his face, coughing wetly, followed by Ricky, Bette, and West lugging the ivory casket between them...and that was it.

Dima, crouched in her hiding spot behind a cement mixer, did what she did best as an infernal accountant: she ran the numbers. She didn't like how they added up. Eight members of the heist crew had gone into the restricted labs. Four came out. Agents Temple and Black were among the dead, and normally that would have elated her — that was certainly one way to get a pair of blackmailers off your back — but she had no idea how they died. And if Josh — or worse, Ricky — had figured out their true identities...

Josh was fiddling with his phone. Dima's cell vibrated softly and she scrambled to silence it. He had just sent her a text message: *Crew out w/ package, bring the truck around to the back of the plant.*

"How do you want to do it?" Ricky asked him, not realizing she could hear every word.

"I don't think we need a whole lot of conversation," Josh replied, idly scanning the lot and keeping an eye out. "Either she knowingly brought two government agents onto our crew, or she's so incompetent she let herself get played. Once we load the casket into the truck, just pop her in the back of the head. Nadine can decide what to do with her. In hell."

Keeping her head down, Dima texted a response: *Had to run, someone called cops over missing security guards. Stole a car and led them off so you could get away. Truck still in front lot.*

She watched Josh read his phone, scowling at the screen.

Where r u now? came his response.

Up by Midway Airport but still trying to lose the cops. Will rendezvous once I do. Where is the meeting point?

"Unbelievable," Josh muttered.

Can't wait 4 u, he texted back. *Will contact you after the handoff and tell u where 2 go.*

"She better hope the cops shoot her ass," he said, jamming his phone back in his pocket, "because I am *not* bailing her out. Okay, gang, let's saddle up. Time to get paid."

Dima pressed herself to the cold asphalt, a motionless lump in the shadows, as Josh led the crew — what was left of it — past her hiding place and into the parking lot.

"Explain to me," Jessie said, inching out along a one-foot-wide girder suspended above an inky void, "how Bette *didn't* screw us over."

Harmony was happy to oblige, thankful for the distraction. She was just a bit behind, crawling out on all fours to squirm through the open hatchway and clinging to the girder with both hands. There was no wind in the dark, nothing but stale air and that foul dead-animal stench, but she still felt like a stray gust of air or a trembling aftershock from the explosives might rise up at any moment. She imagined herself being knocked from the girder, plunging into the darkness at terminal velocity, her body and bones shattering on impact—

She gritted her teeth and kept crawling along the beam, carefully sliding her knees up under her and holding her balance.

"For starters, if she wanted us dead, she would have just obeyed Josh and set those timers for ninety seconds instead of three minutes. If she had, we'd be charcoal right now."

Jessie reached the far end of the girder. It connected to a tall rounded pillar ringed by a narrow ledge, maybe six inches wide at best. More girders veered in to connect with the support beam, some level like the one they were navigating, others sharply slanting up or down to connect to other parts of the laboratory's exposed guts. From the outside, the lab and its chambers looked like a strange steel-jacketed skeleton, exposed from a perspective that no one but the original builders were ever supposed to see.

"Right before the betrayal went down, she slipped something into my pocket."

Jessie craned her neck, gazing out across the tinker-toy architecture and plotting a path.

"Which was?" she asked.

"Don't know yet," Harmony said, pulling herself along the beam. "Under the circumstances, it has to wait. Need both hands at the moment. I'm pretty sure I know what she gave me, though. Did you catch what she did? She blew our cover, but she also lied to Josh."

"She made us sound like punks," Jessie groused. "'Never even encountered a demon,' my ass. Fair, we've never been able to take down an *incarnate* demon like Nadine, but neither has anybody else and we've racked up all kinds of other wins. Hell, we've faced off with the Kings of Man. Twice. Two wins, zero losses. She was there for one of 'em."

"Right," Harmony said, "now ask yourself why. Why would she...I believe the phrase is 'talk trash?' Why would she deliberately blow our cover, but at the same time do something that made us look less dangerous than we actually are?"

Franza poked her head through the gap and took one crawling step forward. She was half in and half out of the hole, locked up tight, staring down into the abyss.

"I...I don't think I can do this," she stammered.

"You can," Harmony urged her. "Just watch me and do exactly what I'm doing. Hand over hand, nice and slow, but steady. It's not as hard as it looks, I promise. I wouldn't ask you to try if I didn't know you were capable."

"Oh, son of a..." Jessie trailed off. "Because of Nadine. She knew that if Josh thought he had some kind of a golden ticket, something Nadine wanted — namely, you — he'd try to hand us over to her. So she downplayed us. Made it sound like we were some kind of trifle and that the boss-lady would get pissed off if he bugged her about it."

"You saw his hands," Harmony said. "Josh knows what happens when Nadine gets angry. It doesn't take a whole lot. And remember what he said? We were never going to make it to the end of the road. He planned on killing us as soon as that hatch opened."

"Which Bette knew." Jessie leaned against an upward-slanting beam, testing her weight and giving it a firm wriggle. "So she stepped up and improvised. Gave us the opportunity to draw down and even the playing field, then convinced Josh we'd burn up in the blast. Clever girl. If she wasn't such a duplicitous bitch, I'd think about recruiting her."

"Pretty sure she's happy with her current employers."

Harmony turned her head, squinting into the shadows and following the path of the up-slanting beam ahead. It veered back on a hard angle, welded into the side of a long metal-plated box: the cell block corridor, and the way back to the outer labs. And freedom.

"Up that way," Harmony said. "We're not going through the cells. We're going *over* the cells. We can find another access hatch and break through on the other side."

Jessie clambered up the steep girder like a squirrel. Harmony took her place at the central pillar, pulling herself up and clinging to the fat, painted pipe. Franza was still only halfway out onto the first beam, petrified.

"I can't do it," she stammered.

"You can." Harmony crouched as low as she dared, one arm hooked tight around the pipe as she looked back, meeting Franza's terrified eyes. "Hey. Do you have a family? Anyone at home, waiting for you?"

"I...I have a boyfriend."

"Tell me about him."

"His name is Peter," Franza stammered. "We've been dating for nine months next week. I think he's getting ready to pop the question."

"Okay, good, good," Harmony said, her voice soft. "Are you going to say yes?"

Franza's head bobbed, jittery.

"I'd like to."

Harmony held out her open hand, the other squeezing the pillar for dear life.

"Come on. Crawl to me. Just one inch after another. Jessie and I just did it, so you know it's possible. You can do it too."

"I *can't.*" Franza's eyes glistened in the dark.

"Don't do it for me. Do it for you and Peter. I want you think about that moment while you're crossing this girder. Just put your left hand out, grab tight, and put your right hand out. One hand, then the other. Do you have a favorite restaurant?"

Franza inched out along the beam, her gaze fixed on the abyss below.

"Rosebud on Randolph," she whispered.

"Okay," Harmony whispered. "You're at Rosebud on Randolph, with Peter. He's dressed nicely tonight. He's nervous. He doesn't think you can tell, but I bet you can."

Franza kept moving, a trembling smile rising to her lips.

"I can always tell."

"Of course you can. And tonight is the night your life changes. A new adventure, with the person you love. What could be better than that?"

Franza was halfway along the beam now, her paralysis broken but her body still trembling like a leaf. Her shoulders shook and she sniffed hard. Her eyes were wet with tears but she didn't dare try to brush them away, both hands clamped tight around the girder beneath her. Every time she moved her clammy palms left smears of sweat behind.

"You're going to get through this," Harmony said. "You're going to go to that restaurant with Peter, and he's going to get down on one knee and you're going to say yes, and this — all of this — will just fade like an old nightmare. Now come on. Take my hand."

Just a couple of feet away now, Franza looked up at her with freshly mounting fear. She clung to the girder for dear life, her hands frozen.

"You're almost there," Harmony urged her. She reached as far from the pipe as she dared, her own grip straining, her fingers outstretched. "I won't let anything happen to you. Just take my hand."

With something like a glimmer of hope in her eyes, Franza lifted one hand from the girder and reached out to her.

Her other hand, slick with sweat and trembling from the strain, slipped loose.

The breath froze in Harmony's throat as Franza tumbled over the edge. She fell, facing upward as she plummeted into the dark, one arm still outstretched and fingers grasping as if she thought, even now, that someone might catch her and make everything all right.

Then Franza hit a girder midway along her back and her spine cracked like a wooden ruler. She twisted in midair, bouncing off, veering toward a second steel beam. She hit it face-first and her neck snapped. What was left of her fell away into the dark, swallowed whole and gone.

Harmony stared down in silence, her lips quivering but no sound coming out, her hand still open and empty.

Chapter Forty-One

The cap on a fat ventilation duct rattled, warbling over the floor of the inner lab's silent workstations. Then it jolted hard, and again, before it was knocked loose and fell straight down, crushing a computer monitor in a crash of glass and twisted metal.

Jessie lowered herself from the duct, dangling by her hands before letting go and free-falling the last five feet to land in a crunch of debris on a cluttered desk. Harmony shimmied down after her, let go, and Jessie caught her in her arms.

"Harmony—"

"I promised." She shook her head and dug into her hip pocket. "I promised I'd get her out."

"You tried."

"Trying isn't good enough. Trying has never been good enough." She looked down at her prize, a thin black oblong about the size of a cell phone. A tap of the screen made it light up with a wireframe grid. "Bette followed through. Look."

She passed it over to Jessie, who arched an eyebrow at a slow-moving blip.

"GPS tracker," she said.

Harmony nodded. She hopped down from the desk and onto the floor, already on the move.

"I was right. She's on our side. Bette must have stashed a transponder on the truck. She's showing us where Josh is taking the casket. And since they all think we're dead..."

"We can thunder down like the fist of an angry god and they'll never see it coming." Jessie tilted her head and called out, "Hey, exit's in the other direction."

"Need something first," Harmony said.

The door to the firing range whistled open at her approach. She came out a moment later, arms laden with cardboard boxes.

"DOVE rounds?" Jessie asked. "Do you want those so our techs can study 'em, or are we taking prisoners tonight?"

Harmony stopped dead in her tracks. There was a coldness in her eyes that Jessie had never seen before.

"I think," she said, "I'll let Franza decide. If she tells me to show mercy, I'll show mercy."

She paused, tilting her chin upward, staring at nothing.

"Hear that?" Harmony said. "Dead quiet. Let's go."

The lobby was empty, barren save for the hidden corpses and the dry smears of blood under piles of newspaper. Harmony assumed Dima had left with the others, until they stepped out into the parking lot — dawn coming on strong, the horizon a bright dirty-blue — and she rushed up on them so fast that Jessie drew down, jamming her gun into Dima's face. Dima backpedaled, panicking, showing them her empty hands.

"Don't shoot! Dear sweet Lucifer don't shoot, I need *someone* to not want to shoot me right now."

"'Want' is asking a hell of a lot," Jessie said. "Try starting with 'don't shoot me because I'm useful,' and we'll see how things go from there."

"I assumed you were dead. What about Castillo and Houston?"

"Dead and very dead," Jessie said. "Why aren't you with the rest of the crew?"

"Josh knows who you really are—"

"We're aware."

"—and he's decided I'm a liability."

"For once," Jessie said, "I'm leaning toward his point of view."

"Wait! Just...just wait, all right? I need to show you something."

Dima led them to the scene of the breakout, showing them the brutalized, burned remnant of the hatch door and the corpses of the two security guards, still in their containment suits, scattered across the asphalt.

"Josh didn't do this," Dima said. "Lorne Murrough did. I watched him back an Ardentis delivery truck up to the hatch a little while before the crew busted out. These two helped him wrangle these...people onto the back of a delivery truck. I mean, I think they were people. They looked sick and they acted like wild animals."

Harmony and Jessie shared a look.

"And the dead men?" Harmony asked.

"Once they loaded four or so people onto the truck, they locked it up and Lorne said he was sealing this passage for good. Then he shot these two and drove off. He called it..." Dima scrunched up her nose, thinking hard. "He called it the 'Pyrrhus Contingency.'"

A cold, skeletal hand squeezed around Harmony's spine.

"So that's useful, right?" Dima said. "You're going to help me now? You're going to get me out of this and make things right with Nadine for me? I did everything you wanted!"

Jessie grabbed Harmony by the sleeve, tugging sharply. She pulled her a few feet away, keeping one eye on Dima while they decided her fate in low murmurs.

"Josh wants her dead, but if he hasn't told Nadine about us he probably hasn't blabbed about Dima either. If we can silence him fast enough, we can keep her in play."

Harmony pondered that. Normally she shared her strategies. Now she was silent as a graveyard as her hard stare bored into Dima's big puppy-dog eyes.

"If she's outlived her usefulness," Jessie added, "just say the word. We've had this talk, hon. You don't kill cold and that's fine, because I do. I'll drop her right here and now."

Her partner stared for one long, silent moment, then shook her head.

"Keep her in play," Harmony said. "If Nadine's onto her, she'll take care of Dima for us. If we manage to keep Dima's mistress in the dark, we might still get something out of her. No sense throwing away a tool that isn't broken."

Jessie turned to Dima. "You got a safe house in town? Somewhere you can go to ground for a little while?"

"A few such places," Dima said.

"Go there. Burrow deep, keep your mouth shut, talk to no one, and we'll contact you as soon as we know the score vis-a-vis your continued good graces with Nadine."

"Is there anything else I can do?" Dima asked, grasping at straws.

"I'd suggest prayer," Jessie said, "but...yeah, in your case, that's not gonna help. Now get gone before we change our mind."

She didn't need to be told twice. As she scurried off, Jessie squinted at Harmony's face.

"You look like somebody just walked over your grave. What's going on in that noggin?"

Harmony was lost on a trail of thought, the fingers of one hand rhythmically twitching at her side as she navigated a tangled string of clues and inferences.

"This isn't his plan," she said. "Attacking the Pentagon, turning Congress and the President into plague mutants...he wasn't going to load up a delivery truck in the middle of the night and wheel over to Washington DC."

"Have to ship the zombies somehow," Jessie said with a shrug.

"No, he told us his appointment with the Joint Chiefs of Staff was *next week*. You remember what dealing with the bureaucracy in DC is like: even if Lorne wanted to move the timetable up as a reaction to having his lab invaded, it'd be days before everyone's admin called everyone else's admin and set up a meeting to discuss rescheduling the meeting. He's a Washington insider. He *knows* this."

"Okay," Jessie said, "so he shifted gears. Where's he taking the zombies?"

"Pyrrhus Contingency. He's telling us; it's all in the name. Okay, so, his point of view: his sanctuary has been violated and a gang of strangers are out to steal his most treasured prize and undermine the moment of triumph that he thinks his entire life has been leading up to."

"He's shook," Jessie said. "And probably confused as hell, considering he first met the two of us under the guise of..."

Jessie's voice trailed off.

"Oh, motherfucker. He doesn't realize he got hit by *thieves* tonight. He thinks this was a government raid in disguise."

Harmony tapped her lips with her fingertip, frowning.

"I think someone wants him to come to that conclusion. Like the creature in that box. Lorne Murrough has been primed for paranoia, because it makes him easy to manipulate. Carving one of his own eyes out and replacing it with an alien organ? There's no way he came up with that on his own, let alone thought it was a rational or remotely sane idea."

"You think he's possessed?" Jessie asked.

"Sort of. Not like a demon: I don't think he's being puppeted. More like...influenced. The thing in the box is asleep. Dreaming, and dreaming loud. My coin went berserk the second I got near the casket. I suspect it's been working on Lorne since the day he brought it into the labs. Influencing him, subtly at first, while it dug its claws in nice and deep."

"Hence Lorne's bullshit delusions of grandeur," Jessie said. "This thing is whispering in his ear, telling him he's going to be the savior of the world, when it really wants him to spread the disease. So what's the fallback plan?"

"King Pyrrhus of Epirus," Harmony said.

"Going to need you to be a tiny bit more specific."

"Pyrrhus landed himself in a protracted war with the Roman Empire. Things came to a head at the Battle of Asculum, where he won by the skin of his teeth. The Romans lost six thousand men. Pyrrhus lost almost four thousand of his own, along with his most seasoned officers and generals. Allegedly he later said, 'If we're victorious against the Romans one more time, we'll be utterly ruined.' That's where we get the concept of a 'Pyrrhic victory.'"

Jessie nodded slowly, taking that in. "A victory that no commander wants."

"A victory Lorne doesn't want. But he thinks his back is up against the wall, so he'll take it. Look at what we know: he's convinced that he has to wake the public up and prove the alien threat is real. He also believes that he's out of time and that the end justifies the means."

Jessie took a deep breath.

"He's gonna let those things loose," she said. "Today. Someplace public."

"Somewhere with cameras and a ton of witnesses around, so at least a few people will escape to tell the story once the plague begins to spread."

"And meanwhile," Jessie said, "Josh and company are carrying the casket straight into Nadine's clutches. If she gets away and sells it on the black market, no telling where it winds up. Or who ends up *using* it."

Harmony looked down at the GPS tracker in her hand, flashing silently as it tracked the getaway van.

"So we divide and conquer. Which target do you want?"

"No."

Jessie put her hand on Harmony's shoulder.

"Which target do *you* want?"

She knew why Jessie was asking. If Lorne succeeded in his mad mission or the casket vanished into the underworld, the entire planet was in danger. Only one of those two trails ended at the grave of her worst nightmare. She *wanted* to go after Nadine, wanted it more than breathing. Harmony thought it over. Then she held the tracker out to Jessie, her voice firm.

"You take the casket. I'll stop Lorne."

"You're sure?" Jessie asked.

"Lorne's traveling alone. If I can intercept him in time, I can stop him. Maybe I can even get through to him somehow. On the other hand, Josh has Ricky and Doctor West on his side, and depending on where they go for the meet with Nadine there's a good chance this'll be a close-quarters battle."

"Have you *seen* me?" Jessie arched one eyebrow. "Every fight I'm in is a close-quarters battle."

"Exactly. You're better equipped for this. If I can cut Lorne off fast enough, I'll come and meet up with you. Just stay fluid. We're playing this whole endgame by ear, and we can't afford any mistakes. Not one."

Not one more, Harmony thought, thinking of Franza.

Jessie put an arm around her shoulder, walking with her into the parking lot. The cargo van was long gone, of course, but plenty of cars were scattered around, slumbering in the gathering dawn. A cold and hungry light broke over Chicago's South Side, glinting off mud puddles and the twisted boughs of half-dead trees along the broken sidewalks.

All over the city, Harmony thought, people were waking up. Brewing their morning coffee, making plans. Getting ready to face a bright and hopeful Sunday morning.

If she and Jessie failed, it would be the last bright and hopeful morning for a very long time.

"Saving the world twice in one day," Jessie mused. "Okay, guess there really is a first time for everything. Let's swipe some wheels and rally the troops."

Chapter Forty-Two

Jessie hotwired the fastest-looking ride in the lot, a sleek blue Miata they found in the reserved executive parking row. They hit the streets, cornering fast and flashing through yellow lights just before they strobed red, the chassis rocking over potholes while Jessie leaned on the gas. Harmony got in touch with Kevin and April, opening a line to the *Imperator*.

She brought them up to speed fast while Jessie made a beeline for their hotel.

"We're about to switch vehicles and split up," Harmony said. "We've got a line on Josh and his team, as long as Bette's tracker holds out. I need you to find Lorne Murrough, and fast. We know he's going someplace public, populated, with cameras. Preferably with live media on hand and a quick police response time. Remember, Lorne's going for maximum shock and awe, but he also thinks the plague can be contained."

And he's wrong, she thought. Not wrong. Misled. Lied to, by the withered gray thing in the casket. She had seen with her own eyes how fast the disease could spread: Castillo turned barely thirty seconds after exposure, going feral like a newborn berserker. One infected victim loose in a packed crowd, could — *would* — spread the sickness like wildfire. There'd be no containing it, not with anything less than the National Guard rolling in, and Lorne was right about one thing: when it came time to act, the government would move too slowly, take too long to assess the crisis.

By sundown, Chicago would be a city of the dead.

• • • ● ● • ● ● • •

Kevin kicked his heels against the *Imperator*'s shivering metal deck, sending his swivel chair spinning and sliding down to the far end of a bank of consoles. He caught himself on the edge of the desk and leaned into the cold blue glow of a monitor, windows of code blossoming while his fingers danced across the keyboard.

"Chicago's got a crazy red light camera network," Kevin muttered, huddled over his keyboard while status reports fluttered in from a half-dozen wall screens. "Crazy easy to hack into, I mean. Total amateur hour."

April rolled up to the next terminal over, adjusting her bifocals.

"I don't suppose we have a plate number," she said.

"No." Harmony's voice crackled over their headsets. "But we know Lorne's driving an Ardentis Solutions delivery van. It'll have company livery on the sides."

"We've gone searching for smaller needles in larger haystacks," April said. "Still, searching over a hundred camera feeds and hoping to spot one random truck is a fool's errand. We need to narrow down his list of potential targets."

The stolen Miata screeched to a stop halfway down the gallery of the Fairmont's parking garage.

"Take the wheel," Jessie said, hopping out and leaving the hotwired engine running. "I'm driving the Hemi."

Harmony scrambled out, racing around the front of the car. She and Jessie crossed paths. They paused, for just a second.

Without a word, Jessie grabbed her shoulders and yanked her into a tight, quick hug.

"Do something for me," Jessie murmured in her ear.

"Name it."

Jessie held her out at arm's length, squeezing Harmony's shoulders and looking her in the eye.

"Don't hesitate," she said.

They split up. Harmony took the Miata. She was just emerging from the parking garage when she heard tires squeal behind.

Jessie drove the ink-black Hemi Cuda, a knife on wheels. They rode convoy right up to the first highway on-ramp. Then Jessie veered south, hot on the casket's trail.

Lorne and his plagued cargo were in Harmony's hands now.

The gears of her mind locked steel teeth and spun, a machine racing at full throttle. It was Sunday. People would be out all over the city, enjoying the newborn sun after a week of dark clouds and cold rain. No shortage of soft targets for Lorne to attack.

She turned on the radio, flipping through stations so fast they came through in tiny bursts of static, snatches of song, cut-off words, her fingers pausing just long enough to register the sound before jumping to the next frequency. She was looking for something. Trying to jar a memory just at the edge of her recollection.

Then she found it.

Back on the night they'd abducted Castillo from his house out in the Michigan woods, on the way back to the hotel, Jessie had the radio on.

"*Forecast says we're looking at the storms clearing up and blue skies into the weekend,*" the DJ had said over the tail of a classic rock song. "*Don't forget to come down to Navy Pier for Live on the Lake, one of the biggest events of the season. We'll have bands from rock to reggae playing up in the Navy Pier beer garden, a fireworks show at sunset, and of course, yours truly as the master of ceremonies. Area parking will be limited so plan ahead—*"

Harmony snatched up her phone.

"Kevin. April. Focus your camera search on the area around Navy Pier. There's a big music festival happening today. They'll have massive crowds, press, cameras, emergency services on standby...it's everything Lorne wants."

"You want us both focused on the same part of the city?" Kevin asked. "I mean, there is other stuff going on downtown. We'll be putting all our eggs in one basket here."

Harmony nodded, resolute.

"It's the target I would have picked," she said.

• • • ● ● • ● ● • •

Lorne sat in standstill traffic on Park Drive, a looping road at Lake Michigan's shore on the east side of the city. A long line of canary-yellow cabs waited to feed into a stand by the curb, snug against the boardwalk of Navy Pier.

The festival wasn't set to start for a couple of hours, but the shoreline was a beehive of activity. Vendors and exhibitors were clogging up the access road, waiting to get into the festival hall. Lorne's truck blended right in, just another special delivery on its way.

He could hear the infected locked in behind his seat. They slapped at the truck's inner walls, battering themselves and letting out stray-cat screeches. Each tortured yowl made Lorne's pockmarked hands clutch tighter around the steering wheel.

While he waited for traffic to start inching along, he looked at the flood of pedestrians out on the sidewalk, faces lifted to the sun. Oblivious. For them, it was an ordinary day. Lorne watched a young woman breeze past his window in a sundress, pushing a baby stroller. She was headed for the pier.

He squeezed his human eye shut, fighting back tears.

"I don't want to do this," he whispered.

You have to, said the voice that wasn't quite his own. *You know this. This is your contingency plan. You came up with it because you knew it had to be done.*

"There has to be another way."

There isn't. If there was, you would have found it, wouldn't you? But healing can be a brutal thing, by necessity. How do you treat a cancer?

"You cut it out, you burn it out," Lorne said to his reflection in the rearview mirror. "You do whatever you can. You attack it and you destroy it."

Why? the voice asked, leading him on.

"Because if you don't, it'll kill the patient. Either the cancer dies or the host dies. There's no other outcome."

This nation has a cancer, the voice confidently, calmly assured him. *And you are the attending physician. The patient is counting on you to save its life. No one else can. You are the only one with the strength to do what must be done.*

Traffic began to crawl. Outside the driver-side window, Lorne watched a happy family walk past, young parents wrangling a pair of rambunctious kids.

This isn't murder, Lorne, the voice whispered in his ear. *This is chemotherapy.*

"We've got him," Kevin said.

"You're sure?" Harmony asked, her pulse quickening.

"Unless you can come up with another reason for an Ardentis truck to be sitting in traffic right outside Navy Pier on a Sunday morning, I'm pretty sure."

She took inventory. Her Sig Sauer was running on empty; she had one, maybe two bullets left in the mag. Her only backup weapon, the wristwatch Kevin had given her during the mission briefing with its concealed Taser barbs, rode on her right wrist. At this point she wasn't sure if it would even slow Lorne down.

"Change of plans," she said. "April, I want you to liaise with our civilian contacts. Do we have any friendlies at the local FBI office?"

"One," she said, though the hesitation in her voice said it wasn't anyone they could depend on.

"Reach out to our people embedded in CIRG. Tell the Critical Incident Response Group we've got a brewing situation here. No details, obviously, but get response teams on standby."

"Can you wait for backup?" April asked.

Harmony fixed her eyes on the road ahead.

"Negative. Every second counts; CIRG is our backup in case I fail. They'll be able to mount a resistance to the infected faster than the local cops will, but it's still a worst-case scenario plan. Kevin, while April's on that I need you to come and meet me as fast as you can."

"You need me," he said, "where the zombies are."

The stolen Miata rocketed under the eye of a yellow stoplight.

"You keep asking for more fieldwork," Harmony said. "I need some gear from the *Imperator*'s armory and I don't have time to drive out to the airport, so you have to come to me."

"It'll take a while, even in good traffic," he said.

"This isn't for Lorne. It's for what comes *after* I deal with Lorne."

Harmony was thinking three moves ahead.
Poker was Josh Orville's game. Hers was chess.

CHAPTER FORTY-THREE

Harmony had never been to Navy Pier. Whatever she'd pictured in her mind's eye, it was a circus tent compared to an entire carnival ground. The 'pier' was a massive, wide boardwalk jutting out over the water, over half a mile long, fronted by a park and a massive open-air building housing shops, restaurants, art galleries, and the Chicago Children's Museum. Behind it she saw the rise of the Centennial Wheel, a two-hundred-foot-tall Ferris wheel that dominated the skyline.

And beyond that, another building, this one an elegant curling rise of walls made from greenhouse glass. The festival hall and beer garden, where vendors and performers were setting up for the big show.

She cruised past the taxi stand and took a right on Grand Avenue, driving onto the road that stretched along the left side of the pier. She passed the first parking entrance, then the second one as she angled to get closer — then noticed a wide-open bay at the side of the festival hall. A delivery van chugged inside, followed by another. She slowly rolled up in their wake, only to slam on the brakes, jolting against her seatbelt as a man in a high-visibility vest and a hard hat jumped out in front of the bumper.

"Official traffic only," he snapped, waving a clipboard at her. "You need to drive up to the end of the pier, double back, and go in through the east parking entrance."

Harmony threw the car into park and got out, leaving it idling and abandoned in the mouth of the open bay doors. She flashed her FBI credentials at the man, snapping the folio shut and pocketing it in one smooth motion as she marched inside.

"Official business."

"You can't just—" he sputtered. "You can't just leave your car here! You're blocking the way in!"

That was the idea. She took out her phone.

"Jessie. Talk to me."

The highway was open and free and the steering wheel thrummed in Jessie's grip as she tore up the asphalt, the Hemi Cuda thundering like a torpedo. Bette's tracker sat on the passenger seat, tracing a neon blip as it slid along a scrolling wireframe map.

"I'm about ten miles out and making up for lost time," she said. "You find Murrough?"

"Traced his truck to Navy Pier. I'm following a—"

She fell silent.

"Harmony?" Jessie said.

Her response was a soft whisper: "*Contact.*"

The massive glass-walled festival hall was swarming with people, trucks and vans scattered across the wide-open floor while workers hammered and drilled, putting up stands and tents and firing up grills for an eager lunchtime crowd. The main doors were still closed, keeping the public at bay for the moment, but no shortage of victims.

And there was Lorne's truck, tucked in at a tight angle by the back of the hall. Still sealed, for the moment.

He's waiting for the festival to start, she realized. *More eyes, more cell phones and cameras, more victims, more fear.*

As she strode toward the truck, she eyed the cherry-red box of a fire alarm mounted on the wall. She grabbed the lever and yanked it. A klaxon split the air.

Lorne had been pacing, walking back and forth beside the parked truck, his mane of wild ivory hair cascading over half his face while he argued with himself. He couldn't do this. *He had to do this.* This was monstrous. *This was necessary.*

The fire alarm squealed, grating electronic sounds riding under a pre-recorded voice: "*Attention, patrons. Please proceed in a calm and orderly fashion to the nearest marked exit.*"

He froze in mid-stride. An accident? Coincidence?

No coincidences, the voice in his head whispered, curling gray and gnarled talons around his fevered brain. *This is the hand of the enemy.*

He turned. Harmony Black stood behind him. They were ten feet apart, facing one another like gunslingers at high noon. He squared his shoulders and widened his stance.

"I'm going to give you one last chance," Harmony said, "to do the right thing."

People were scattering behind her, flooding out of the festival hall and onto the boardwalk, while the man with the clipboard shouted at someone over a walkie-talkie. A moment later the fire alarm died, fading on a whine of static. Silence engulfed the cavernous hall.

"Stay out of my way," Lorne said, "and I'll do just that."

He turned and started walking toward the rear of the truck.

"Don't do this. Lorne, I'm begging you. You're a good man. But you're sick. And your sickness is...tricking you. It's luring you into making bad choices. You *know* this is wrong. You know you're going to kill a lot of innocent people."

"Necessary," he grunted, though his steps became slower, almost stumbling, like he had to force his legs to work.

Or like some part of him, buried deep down inside, was trying to stop himself.

"That isn't true. And you think you're alone, that you're fighting this war all by yourself, but you're not. I can help you. Please...let me help you, before anyone else gets hurt."

She held out her hand to him. Imploring, fingers stretched wide. Just like she had for Franza.

"Take my hand," she told him.

He stood there, frozen, silent, staring at her.

Then he turned his back and reached for the handle on the back door of the delivery truck.

She could have shot him, then and there, and ended it with a single bullet. Harmony was a crack shot; at this distance, she wouldn't miss. But she still thought she could save him. She closed the distance, lunging, grabbing his wrist before he could pull the handle and yanking it behind his back in an aikido joint-lock.

He was faster than he looked, stronger than a man his age should have been, his body fueled by desperation and the dark passenger in his brain. Lorne whipped his head back, cracking his skull against her forehead and blinding her in a starburst of pain. She felt hot blood trickling down between her eyes, wasn't sure if it was hers or his. He slipped her grip, spun on his heel and whipped his open hand around, backhanding her hard enough to send her sprawling to the festival-hall floor. She tasted blood, a loose tooth wobbling under her tongue.

She went for her gun and he pounced like a cat, landing on top of her, straddling her chest as he grappled with her. As he looked down at her, his veil of ivory hair fell away. She stared up into the jet-black orb of his alien eye, bulging from his mutated face. She saw her own reflection gazing back at her.

He hesitated, tilting his head, and spoke in a voice that was almost his own.

"*Bioforge unit. Here? Data...corrupted. Where is your overseer?*"

"Lorne," she gasped. He got his hands around her throat and started to squeeze, digging his thumbs into her trachea. "You're still in there. I know you are. *Fight* it. You're stronger than it is. You're strong enough to fight."

"*This host*," said the thing wearing Lorne Murrough's skin, "*is dead.*"

Harmony couldn't breathe, her throat strangled shut, eruptions of blood bursting in her blurry vision. She got her hands out from under his weight, scrambling for one last chance of survival.

"You know what happens when a parasite kills its host?" she managed to croak.

She twisted the face of her wristwatch and held it up to Lorne's face.

"Bad news for the parasite."

She pressed the watch's crown and fired.

The Taser's twin barbs were designed to fire up to ten feet away. They only needed three inches, both shining missiles launching straight into Lorne's alien eye. The black sphere ruptured like an egg, bursting in a spray of black ichor as the weapon delivered fifty thousand volts straight into his ravaged eye socket.

Kevin ran into the festival hall, a heavy olive canvas duffel bag slung over each shoulder, the special delivery clanking with every jogging step. He stopped, leaning against a green glass wall to catch his breath, and froze.

Harmony and Lorne were both down by the front wheel of the parked delivery truck. Harmony sat, her back resting against the wheel, staring vacantly. Lorne's head was on her lap. What was left of it, anyway. His alien eye was nothing but a gaping, jagged crater oozing a thin trickle of gray smoke, his human one squeezed shut and dribbling tears.

"I'm sorry," he wheezed.

"I know," Harmony said. She gently ran her fingers through his hair. "It's okay."

"I didn't mean it."

"I know."

Kevin looked between them, uncertain. "Harmony?"

She mouthed the words, though she didn't need to. They all knew the score. "He's dying."

The graft had run deeper, grown more roots, than she'd realized. Destroying the alien eye broke its hold over Lorne's mind, but now his body was shutting down. First he couldn't move his legs. Now his arms were slack at his sides, his speech slurring. He was dying, and he knew it.

"I meant..." he caught himself, drool running from one slack corner of his mouth as he let out a humorless chuckle. "Isn't that what they all say? Meant well. The road to hell is paved with good intentions."

He went limp, cradled in Harmony's arms. His good eye glazed over.

"Oh, hey," he said. "I think I see it now."

Then he took one last, rattling breath, and never let it out.

Harmony gently eased his body to the floor. She rose. Kevin nearly stumbled back as she fixed her eyes on his. He had seen her at her worst — down and out, despondent, depressed — but he had never seen her like this. She burned with a cold and silent fury, a lethal winter frost. She held out her hand and he gave her one of the duffel bags.

"I'm putting you in charge of cleanup," she said. "Coordinate with April. Make this body disappear, make the truck disappear, make any lingering questions disappear. Understood?"

A faint rattling sound thrummed against the inner belly of the truck. Kevin asked a question with his eyes.

"Infected. We'll take the truck to an open field somewhere, rake it with a machine gun from a safe distance and then burn the thing. For now, just keep it locked up tight and don't let anyone near it."

She took the other duffel bag and shouldered it. It clanked, heavy against her hip.

"What's that for, anyway?" he asked.

Big question, but she answered by spitting one single, venomous word.

"*Nadine.*"

Chapter Forty-Four

"Threat neutralized," Harmony said over the speaker of Jessie's phone. It sat snug in the center console of the Hemi Cuda, rattling a little as she poured on speed.

Jessie had the cargo van in sight, still clad in its Gold Star livery, up ahead in a tight patch of traffic. She slinked around a semi truck, shifting lanes, closing in on her prey.

"I've got eyes on the prize," she murmured, pushing her dark glasses up on her nose. "No idea how far they're planning to drive or where this meet-up is going down, though. No sign that they're looking for an off-ramp anytime soon. Right now we're cruising on I-65, southbound."

"I'm en route."

"Want me to wait for you?"

"No," Harmony said. "We shouldn't let them reach the meeting site. That's *their* playing field; we need to control the battleground. Don't give them the upper hand. Not for a second."

A sign flashed by on the side of the highway. *Rest Stop, 5 Miles.* Jessie's lips curled into a lopsided smile.

"Got it covered."

"What's the plan?" Harmony asked.

"Just gonna do what I do."

Bette was living on borrowed time.

She wasn't sure if the promise of a job offer for Dr. West was legitimate or just a ruse to keep him on Josh's team until they no longer needed him, but no one had extended her any such largesse. Just the promise of ten thousand dollars, cash — a promise she knew damn well Josh had no intention of honoring. He was under orders to murder all the loose ends once the heist was done.

And considering the casket was strapped down in the back, status lights green, nothing left to do but hand it over to the boss...the heist was done.

Josh was driving. Once he pulled over, sooner or later, she'd have to watch for the double-cross. It would be either him or Ricky behind the gun. Whichever one of them hung back, trying to get behind her...he'd be her designated killer.

She had made a string of calculated risks. Despair was a waste of time and processing power, but Bette was starting to think she'd chosen poorly. Everything — her life, but much more importantly, the creature in the casket — depended on Harmony and Jessie coming through for her. And at least for the moment, it didn't look like—

"Goddamn," Josh said, breaking her train of thought. "That is one sweet-ass ride. Ricky, check this out."

Ricky, who had been sitting uncomfortably close to Bette the entire ride, got up in a crouch and ambled to the front passenger seat. He let out a long low whistle at the sight ahead: a midnight-black muscle car, swerving into the lane just ahead of them.

"Oh damn," Ricky said. "That is some vintage Detroit steel right there."

In back, West had been riding in silence, staring at the casket between him and Bette like it held all the mysteries of the universe and he couldn't wait to dig in.

"Listen to me," Bette murmured through gritted teeth. "We have to work together, or we're going to die here."

"Speak for yourself," the coroner sniffed.

"I'm gonna get me one of those," Ricky said up front, pointing at the Hemi. "That's what I'm spending my cut on. Yes sir, time to ditch the ol' Camaro."

• • • ● ● • ● ● • •

Now's good, Jessie thought.

Aselia, their pilot and resident gearhead, had been tinkering with the Hemi Cuda over the past few months. She'd armored it up, bulked up the already massive engine to handle the added weight and — among other goodies — installed a little surprise on the exhaust pipe. Jessie had used it once before, on the Basilisk mission, to throw a pack of hunters off her trail.

Today she was the hunter. She reached for the small button concealed at the base of the gearshift, checked the rearview mirror, and pressed it down.

Oil sprayed onto the Hemi's exhaust pipe. The burning heat broiled it on the spot, turning the dark liquid into a billowing, choking cloud of black smoke that boiled out behind the muscle car and engulfed the road behind her in a torrent of swirling darkness.

"*Christ*," Josh squealed as inky smoke washed over the windshield, blotting out the world. He wrenched the wheel left, heard horns blare, then swung it hard to the right. Rumble strips at the side of the road made the van shake — just before it launched off the highway, jolting and bouncing as it fired down into a grassy ditch. The smoke cleared and Josh fought for control over the bucking wheel, throwing the passengers around as he stomped on the brakes. A front tire blew with the sound of a gunshot and the van jolted to a dead stop, the front bumper buckling against a low wall of tangled grass and mud.

"Casket," he said, but Bette and West were already on it, checking the display and tapping through a string of live feeds from the measuring instruments inside.

"Still green," Bette said. "We're good."

"We're a long goddamn way from good," Ricky growled, shoving his door open. He drew his revolver as he hopped down from the passenger seat.

Josh squinted through the windshield, the glass smeared with grime in the aftermath of the smoke. He pointed a shaky finger up ahead.

"There. Rest stop. New plan: we ditch the van, we carry the casket, we take cover in there."

He dug out his phone as he wrenched his door open, the tortured metal squealing until he shoved his heel against it.

"Who are you calling?" Bette asked.

"Getting us some reinforcements."

Nadine had been busy.

The second Josh — her sweet boy, her *dependable* boy — sent her the all-clear, she dispatched tendrils through the human underworld. Her devoted Roses ferried messages and carried word to smoky back rooms, to seedy dive bars, to windowless chambers with tacked-up plastic on the walls that stank of cigar smoke and blood. These were her people. Her *clients*.

She had decided to hold an auction. Highest bidder got to go home with their very own alien. What they did with it, after that, didn't overly concern her; she just wanted the money.

But first, she needed to see the package with her own eyes and verify the discovery. She had been waiting at the pickup spot for an hour, less patiently by the minute, when her phone lit up. Josh's voice gushed over the line before she could get a word out.

"We're under attack," he gasped.

"By whom?"

"Don't know. We had some hiccups with the crew—"

"Hiccups?" Nadine arched one delicate eyebrow. "Dima told me you ferreted out an impostor at the very start. A cambion from a rival court?"

"We had, uh, more trouble than that. Couple of government agents from some sad-ass attempt at a covert cell. Not a problem, I dealt with it, but they might have had friends."

Nadine's grip tightened on her phone. The sleek rose-gold case quivered in her hand.

"*Describe them.*"

"They were nobody, I was onto them by the — damn it, West, careful with that thing! That casket's worth more than your life."

He took a breath. "I was onto them from the start. I used them to get the job done, then I took them out. Easy. No stress."

"Joshua?" Nadine said. "You know I dislike repeating myself."

"Couple of chicks. One white, wore a suit and tie, one black, always had these dark glasses on..."

Nadine stormed toward the door. She paused just long enough to snatch an oversized pair of white plastic sunglasses and her favorite cashmere scarf, winding it around her throat as she walked out into the sunlight. She got behind the wheel of her car, a cloudburst-gray Lexus LC coupe with a buttery leather interior, and fired up the engine.

"You had Harmony Black and Jessie Temple. On your heist crew."

"You...know their names?"

She took a deep breath, inhaling through gritted teeth.

"Why am I just learning this now?" she demanded.

"Because I took care of it! It wasn't a big deal."

"I decide what's a big deal and what isn't. Not you."

"The last time I 'bothered' you with a problem you decided was beneath your attention," Josh fired back, "you *cut half my goddamn ring finger off.* And it's fine. We took them out as soon as we secured the casket."

Nadine rolled her eyes as she threw the purring coupe into gear.

"You shot them?"

"No, we burned 'em up in the blast when we detonated the lab's gas line."

"This is important: did you see the bodies? Did you actually look with your own eyes at their corpses and verify the kill?"

"No, but who cares? Nobody could have survived that."

Josh. Her sweet boy. Her sweet, moronic *imbecile.*

"Help is on the way," she said.

"You're sending backup?"

"No." She tapped a sharp, violet fingernail against her center console, bringing up the GPS. "I'm coming to deal with this myself. Where are you?"

"A rest stop just off I-65 southbound. The van is totaled, so we're going to hole up inside."

"Good. Mommy is coming. Do try to stay alive until I get there."

Nadine hung up on him. Her lips pursed into a tight, bloodless line.

"I just want perfection and absolute obedience," she said to the empty car.

Then she rained her hand on the steering wheel, punctuating every frustrated word with a bleat of the horn.

"Is that *so! Much!* To *fucking! Ask!*"

Chapter Forty-Five

The rest stop squatted on the edge of the highway, flat fields behind it, two parking lots — one for trucks and RVs, one for cars — flanking a visitor center with pebbled walls and a slanted wooden roof. It gave off a rustic campground vibe, or at least a theme park version of one. Travelers came and went, popping in to use the restroom or refuel at a line of vending machines. It was peaceful. Ordinary.

The glass doors burst open and Josh led the charge inside, gripping a corner of the casket in his right hand and brandishing a pistol in his left. He fired a shot in the air, blasting a timber beam into shards of shattered wood and sawdust.

"On the ground," Ricky roared, holding the other side of the casket and sweeping the fat barrel of his revolver across the room. "On the goddamn ground, now!"

People were screaming, running. A tubby guy in a Hawaiian shirt tried to make a break for it, barreling past them. Ricky whipped his revolver across the back of his skull, sending him crashing to the ground and rolling across the hardwood floor. A family huddled by the vending machines, parents putting themselves between their two little kids and the guns.

Bette and West brought up the rear, carrying the back half of the casket. They set it down in the middle of the room. Josh snapped his fingers and pointed at them.

"Bette, corral the hostages and calm them down. West, check the bathrooms. If anyone's in there, drag 'em out and sit them down with the others."

The coroner bit his bottom lip, fingers twitching at his sides.

"Could we switch jobs? I'm not really the 'drag people out' type."

"Nadine is on her way. She's not sending lackeys, she's coming to take care of business herself. Do you have any idea how rare that is? You know what's going to happen if we don't have our shit together when she gets here?"

"I'll do it," Ricky grunted. "How about you lock the doors, Doc? Think you can handle that, or is that too hard for your delicate constitution?"

Bette walked over to the huddled family. She crouched down, sweeping her gaze across the four of them. A couple in their late twenties, two children — a boy and a girl — all four of them visibly shaking as they held each other tight.

"Listen to me," Bette told them. "We aren't here for you. We don't want your money. We don't want anything from you. We're just waiting for a ride, and when it gets here we're going to leave. Just sit still, be quiet, don't make any sudden moves, and you'll be all right. No one will hurt you. I promise."

She was lying, of course. This heist had gone completely off the rails and things were getting worse by the second. They were leaving, all right, but there was no chance Josh and Ricky would leave witnesses behind. Her own life would basically be forfeit the second Nadine showed up and announced it was time to start cutting loose ends.

Kill Josh and Ricky now? she thought. She could get the jump on them — drill Josh right here, then gun down Ricky when he came out of the washroom — but that left the problem of the package. The casket was too heavy, too bulky for her to move on her own. *Maybe* she could cow West into helping, but she couldn't hold him at gunpoint while she had both hands on the prize. And even if they got it out, their van wasn't going anywhere without a tow truck.

She looked to the windows facing the south parking lot. Cars and cover were sparse out there. She caught a glimmer of movement out there, low and fast, loping from shadow to shadow like a wolf on the prowl.

•　•　•　●　•　●　●　•　•　•

Crouched low beside the bug-spattered grill of a Winnebago, Jessie had a vantage point on the visitor center. Not a great one — the most she could make out were blurs moving on the other side of the glass — but good enough to verify Josh and his crew were buttoned down in there.

At least they had an inside asset. Maybe. Jessie weighed the risks and sent Bette a one-word text: *SITREP*.

Bette approached the front windows, turning her body away from the others and holding her phone tight to her chest as she tapped out a terse response.

Multiple hostages, Nadine inbound.

The shimmery figure, half her face blotted out by sunlight on the glass, hesitated. Then she sent a second message.

Need help.

"That had to sting," Jessie murmured.

"—so we've got 'em cornered," Jessie was saying over the phone, "but if we start kicking in doors, those hostages are dead meat."

"And Nadine is coming," Harmony said, her voice flat.

The Miata's engine whined as she redlined it, pressing down on the gas until the car started to shake. She veered around a slow-moving semi on the highway, then another, gliding across lanes and closing in fast.

She forced herself to push Nadine out of her mind, just for a moment. The hostages took first priority, the casket second. Nothing bites as hard as a cornered rat; the trick was to flush Josh and his crew out of that corner, out where she and Jessie could take them all down, while making them think it was their own idea.

Harmony had to break their resolve. And she had to do it from a distance.

When the idea struck, a rare smile rose to her lips. She told Jessie she'd get back to her. Then she called Dima.

"Need you to do something for me."

"You want something. Again." Dima's exasperated sigh washed over the line. "So far you've endangered my life, not to mention

my *after*life, made me look like a fool, threatened my relation-
ship with the Roses, and Joshua Orville is planning to murder
me."

The rest stop was just ahead. She saw the crashed cargo van in
the ditch, and the Hemi parked a safe distance away. Harmony
slowed down and steered onto the off-ramp.

"Yes," she said. "I'm using you. And I'm going to keep using
you, because you're a demon-worshiping serial killer and the
only reason I haven't sent you straight to hell where you belong
is because I can use you to take down a bigger threat. I'm going
to tear the House of Dead Roses to the ground. I'm going to
destroy everything Nadine has ever built and everything she's
ever cared about. Now you can get with the agenda and *obey*
me, or you can end up as just another dead statistic. *Choose*."

Dima's response was sullen. "You sound more like her all the
time."

The first time she said that, it stung. This time, Harmony didn't
mind.

She didn't mind at all.

"I'll take that as a yes. Now: would you like me to remove Josh
Orville from the board before he can squawk to Nadine and tell
her how you screwed up the entire mission by letting a pair of
undercover agents onto the team?"

"I *didn't*—" Dima caught herself. "You're insufferable, you
know that? But yes. Yes. Please."

"Then you're going to call him, right now, and you're going to
tell him a story."

This is fine, Josh told himself. *This is fine*.

They had a bolthole they could defend, and they had guns.
They had hostages. The casket was intact and pristine, all systems go. And Nadine was on her way.

*She'll see. She'll see that I'm on top of things, that I held it
down, that I'm the best there is. She'll tell me I did a perfect job.
She'll tell me I'm a good boy.*

He suddenly needed that, more than he needed anything.

His phone buzzed. *Not* Nadine.

"Dima," he said, "I swear, if the cops caught up with you and you're calling me from jail right now—"

"Shut up," she snapped. "Are you near a television set?"

He looked up. There was a TV mounted in one corner of the visitor center on ceiling brackets, but it looked like it was playing a tape on loop, extolling the wonders of camping and fly-fishing. He waved to catch West's attention.

"Make yourself useful. See if you can find a remote or something," he whispered, then put the phone back to his ear. "Not at the moment, why?"

"Because you're fucked, that's why. When you raided Gold Star for those uniforms, why didn't you erase the security footage?"

"I *did*," he started to say. Then his breath caught in his throat as a winter frost bristled along his spine.

That wasn't how it happened at all.

He knew that Harmony and Jessie were undercover agents by then, of course, thanks to Bette ratting them out. He brought them along on the raid because he knew they'd do anything to keep their cover intact until the end of the mission; he told himself it was because they were useful, but he couldn't deny taking a certain perverse thrill in the idea of forcing a couple of feds to murder innocent civilians.

He remembered Harmony walking out with the recorder under her arm. He'd told her to wipe it clean.

I did, she told him. *That's not good enough. In case you haven't noticed, we just committed a mass murder. This will go federal, and the feds are going to bring in their forensic boys. You know, the kind of experts who can reconstruct data from an "erased" hard drive. All of our faces were recorded on the way in here. Do you really want to take any unnecessary risks right now?*

It made sense. Everything she said sounded true, sounded right. Bette promised him she could finish the job with a high-powered magnet and a drill back at the garage, and he didn't have any reason to doubt her, but he never checked to make sure the job got done. In all the excitement, all the planning for the real heist, the stray details just...faded into the background.

"You're burned," Dima told him. "You and Ricky both. They're showing the footage all over the news, along with Ricky's last mugshot and your championship photo from that last poker tournament. Warrants have been issued, you understand? The footage is crystal clear: they've got your ass in 4k."

"No," Josh breathed. "No, no, no. This...this is your fault. *You* let those two onto the team."

"And you *kept* them on it even after you knew what they were, because you were stupid enough to think you could control them," Dima shot back. "Josh Orville, the great 'mastermind.' The man with the plan. Well, I'll take my lumps from Nadine and I'll probably lose a finger or two, but you? You're worthless to her now."

His lips parted, trembling. His arm fell to his side, still clutching the phone, while his entire world quietly crumbled around him.

Chapter Forty-Six

A remote control, *indeed*.

Dr. West had one of the most brilliant minds in all of modern science. A polymath and a renaissance man. And Josh Orville, a puffed-up player of card games, wanted him to find a remote control for a television set.

That wasn't the real issue. He was miffed, certainly, but that was a daily tragedy when one was surrounded by inadequate minds. The issue was the sudden look of feral panic in Josh's eyes, the faint and breathy whine of his voice, the way the blood drained from his cheeks. West had no idea what his phone call was about, but Josh was flinging blame like burning meteorites, praying to make them land on anyone but himself.

He had no intention of standing in the impact zone. And he suddenly decided that no, he didn't want to meet Nadine after all.

This isn't a retreat, he told himself as he slipped into the men's room. *Discretion is simply the better part of valor.*

He wriggled through a tiny bathroom window, tumbled over the sill, and bruised his arm as he landed on the rocky grass outside with a thump and a muffled grunt. He popped up, looking left and right, pressing his back to the pebbled outer wall. No witnesses. Good. West had a cat's philosophy: if no one saw his momentary indignity, that meant it had never happened.

He bit back a momentary surge of panic, patting his pockets. Then he let out a sigh of relief. His precious cargo hadn't broken in the fall.

The Ardentis labs were a giant candy store, and considering how these fools barely paid him any heed no one could blame him for helping himself to a treat. Just a little one. He'd pocketed it in the surgical suite, when no one was looking.

He beamed as he held it up to his face. It was a syringe, the hypodermic needle protected under a plastic cap, its chamber filled with bubbling black blood. West had no interest in plagues — his life's work was a quest to destroy the very concept of death, not spread it — but there was no denying the "alien" ichor had qualities that could make his own necromantic reagents...more interesting.

"Herbert, old boy," he said to himself, "you've outdone yourself this time."

He pocketed the syringe and started walking, sticking his thumb out once he reached the highway.

"Um, need you to hold down the fort for a second," Josh said.

Ricky gave him a suspicious look. "What for, boss-man?"

"Nadine's going to be here any minute now." He swallowed hard, looking pale. "I want to go out there and, you know, see if I can spot her so I can flag her down."

"Whatever. No worries, I'll keep things tight."

Ricky turned, suddenly scowling.

"Hey, where's the Doc?"

Bette, still standing guard over the hostages, answered with a shrug. "West? I'm not his keeper. Check the bathrooms?"

"Eh, he's probably pissing himself in there." Ricky waved an idle hand. "You two are about to get a big honor, you know that, right? Nadine's gonna reward you *personally*."

Josh casually walked out of the visitor center, the door closing at his back, his safe harbor gone. Nowhere would be safe for him now, not in this world or any other. His own muscles fought him, jerking as he forced himself to keep a casual, calm gait until he was out of sight.

Then he ran.

He broke into a mad sprint, scrambling for the north parking lot, no destination in mind but *away*. He'd jack a car and he'd drive until the engine gave out and then he'd steal another car and keep going and maybe, just maybe, he'd figure out how to survive.

He barreled between a pair of parked semis, their long aluminum trailers catching heat and gathering dust in the afternoon heat. He was almost clear when a shadow, backlit by the sun, stepped out from around a truck's hood and stood in his path.

Jessie's fist lashed out like a sledgehammer, pulping his bottom lip and shattering teeth, dropping Josh to his knees. He groaned, drooling blood, and spat broken enamel onto the hot asphalt. He went for his gun, but she slapped it out of his hand like it was a toy. Then she hoisted him up, spun him around, and slammed him against the side of the truck.

"Nuh—" he stammered, trying to talk. "—you need me. You *need* me. I can help. I know things."

"You know things, huh? Like how Nadine's gonna tear you into itty-bitty pieces and scatter your bits all over flyover country? Or I mean...she would have, if we'd released that security footage."

He blinked.

"Would...have?"

Jessie took her sunglasses off. Her eyes were burning coals of neon light as she got up close, almost nose to nose with him, keeping him pinned against the truck with her forearm.

"Isn't that a riot?" she asked. "You just made the last gamble of your life, you went all-in...and you lost to a bluff."

"No," he whispered, realizing what he'd just done. "N-no, listen, you have to take me in. I surrender."

"I'm not a cop," Jessie said.

"I *surrender*," he whined, spitting blood.

"I'll tell you what," Jessie said. "I'll give you a fighting chance. One question. You answer it right, I stand aside and let you walk right out of here. Scout's honor."

He narrowed his eyes, uncertain, but he couldn't resist the chance at a lifeline.

"What was her name?" Jessie asked.

"Her...who?" he squinted, confused.

"The hostage, from the Ardentis lab. You know, 'science girl?' She died, by the way. My partner's feeling pretty fucked up over it. And when Harmony's upset, I get...well, I get to feeling a certain sort of way. Murdery, mostly. But I am a woman of my word, so here's your chance to get away with everything. You can walk away free and clear, right now. Just tell me her name."

"I..."

He trailed off. He didn't even have to say it: he had no idea. His shoulders sagged.

"Aw, Josh," she said. "I guess you're just not a detail-oriented kind of guy."

She grabbed his shoulders, spun him around, and snaked one arm tight around his throat.

His neck snapped like a twig. She dropped his corpse to the asphalt where it fell next to his own broken teeth. Then she stepped over him and got back to work.

"Who *is* this?" Bette said, loud enough to turn Ricky's head. "How did you—"

She fell silent, then held her phone out to Ricky.

"Got a call from Josh's number."

Ricky frowned at her. "Why's the boss-man callin' you and not me?"

"No," Bette said. "It's not Josh. It's for you."

Ricky snatched the phone out of her hand.

"This better be something I want to hear," he growled.

"How about a get-out-of-jail-free card?" Harmony asked.

He looked to the visitor center windows. Harmony stood alone, in the middle of the parking lot, staring at him through the glass.

"How'd you get my man's phone?"

"Because we've got your man."

Ricky cursed under his breath. "He all right?"

"Of course he is," Harmony said. "We're the good guys. We don't kill people. I'll get right to the point: I know you have hostages in there."

"Sure do. Got ourselves a whole happy family. Couple of sweet little tykes, too. Sure would be a shame if I had to pop 'em."

"I propose a trade."

Ricky snorted. "Oh, lemme guess. I send out all the hostages, give up my bargaining chips, and you pinky-swear-promise to hand Josh over? That's gotta be the most transparent fed bullshit I've ever heard."

"Let me sweeten the pot then," Harmony said. "I come in alone, unarmed. The civilians go out. If my partner doesn't follow through and give Josh back, you can kill me instead. Think about it: I'm with the FBI. Eventually this place is going to be swarming with agents and you know, just like I know, that the feds won't shoot one of their own. I'm a much more valuable hostage."

He chewed it over, licking his chapped lips.

"All right, then," he said. "C'mon in."

Harmony felt a certain sense of *deja vu* as she crossed the threshold into the visitor center and Ricky pressed the barrel of his revolver against the side of her head.

"We do keep meeting like this," he said. "Hold on, gonna pat you down real quick."

It wasn't real quick. She held still, glaring while he took his sweet time frisking her, starting with her chest and then sliding his hand slow along her inner thighs.

"Feel anything you like?" she asked.

"Maybe if you lose ten pounds." Ricky lowered his gun and nodded back over his shoulder. "*Walk.*"

Up ahead, she saw Bette standing over the hostages. Bette slightly moved her body, shuffling to one side, and Harmony knew what she was thinking because she would have done the exact same thing if their places were reversed.

She was blocking the kids, so they couldn't see what was about to happen.

Their path would lead them right past the row of vending machines. As they passed the first, Ricky walking right behind her, Harmony saw her own blurry reflection in the glass.

"Funny thing is," Ricky said, "we don't even need the hostages. Got a very special lady on her way, and she's gonna make everything right. We'll be long gone before any of your fed buddies get here."

Wait for it, Harmony commanded herself. She kept her muscles limber, ready, watching the vending machines in the corner of her eye.

"But I figure," Ricky added, "there's still time for me to earn a few brownie points."

His reflection raised a blurry gun, aiming at the back of her head.

She spun on her heel, grabbed his wrist and kept turning, yanking him off his feet and using his own momentum against him. With his arm locked she hoisted him up and over her shoulder in an aikido throw, sending him smashing against the closest vending machine. Its Plexiglas shroud shattered under his weight, lights flashing and burning out as he fell free and tumbled to the hardwood floor at Harmony's feet.

Like a magic trick, his revolver was in her hand now, pointed at his face as she stood over his fallen body.

"Whoa there, missy," he said, frantically showing his open hands. "You got me, okay? You got me. You ain't gonna shoot an unarmed man, right?"

"Normally? No. I wouldn't. But you taught me something, Ricky."

He blinked. "I...did?"

"Sure. I keep thinking about what you told me back at Gold Star, after you shot that innocent woman in the back. What was it? Let me see if I can remember. 'Anyone can shoot back when the lead starts flying. That's no great feat of courage. But the first time you stand in front of an unarmed man and you both know it's over, and he's got nowhere to run, nothing to fight back with, no power left and you just...'"

She trailed off. He finished the sentence for her.

"*Bang*," he whispered. "Yeah, you get it. I see it in your eyes. You're a natural born killer, just like me. You can't fake that."

"'It's the split second before you pull the trigger,'" she said, repeating his own words back to him. "'That's the moment you know what real power feels like.' That's what you told me, right?"

Ricky broke into a feral grin.

"You ain't just judge, jury, and executioner," he said. "You're God almighty. Okay, Hit-girl. Let's see if you've got the stones.

Do it. Pull the trigger. Do it. I *want* you to do it. What are you waiting for?"

Harmony held the gun on him, her grip tight and bone-dry, her finger on the trigger.

"Come on!" he barked. "Do it! *Do it, you fucking cun—*"

She put him down like a rabid dog. Then she walked outside, into the sunlight.

CHAPTER FORTY-SEVEN

A lone arrival rolled into the rest stop behind the wheel of a Lexus luxury coupe, her ride the color of a storm on the horizon. Nadine stepped out, her eyes shrouded behind oversized sunglasses, dressed for a Parisian catwalk with a breezy cashmere scarf trailing off one shoulder.

Harmony and Jessie were waiting for her. Harmony opened the trunk of the stolen Miata, barely looking at Nadine as she rummaged for something inside.

"Hello, puppy," Nadine said to Jessie.

"Hey, bitch. Good news and bad news. The good news is, the casket's right in there. Bad news is, you can't have it. Oh, and if you're looking for Josh and Ricky, try your own backyard, because we just sent their asses straight to hell."

Nadine's teeth clicked as she ground them together. Still, she forced a gracious smile that didn't come anywhere near her eyes.

"Insolent as always. Nice to see you haven't changed. I seem to recall promising to rip your tongue out and make you eat it. It's officially on this afternoon's to-do list, so...you have that to look forward to."

Jessie spread her empty hands. "Come and get it."

"In a minute." Nadine turned, putting her hands on her hips, and glared. Harmony was still digging in the trunk, not even looking at her. "*Harmony*. You *look* at Mommy when she's speaking to you. Don't you dare ignore me."

Harmony turned. They locked eyes. Staring, unblinking, the two women locked in a psychic duel.

Nadine was the first to flinch. She took a hesitant step backward.

"Here's what's going to happen," Nadine said, shaking off her momentary fluster. "I'm willing to spare the puppy's life, but only if I get you instead. You're going to come home with me."

"No," Harmony said, "I won't."

Nadine squinted at her and waved a hand at Jessie.

"Excuse me? I will rip her goddamn throat out with my teeth while you watch."

"No. You won't."

"Have you forgotten who you're dealing with?" Nadine stomped with one petulant foot. "I am an *incarnate demon*. The most powerful of my kind. Who do you talking monkeys think you are?"

"I haven't forgotten," Harmony said.

She took a deep breath and squared her footing.

"You broke me, Nadine."

Silence washed across the parking lot, punctuated by the rumble of tires from the freeway.

"I wish I could pretend it wasn't so," Harmony said. "I wish I could stand here and say that I toughed it out. That after all the hell you put me through, I never bent or buckled. I kept saying I was just damaged, not broken, but I was lying to myself. So congratulations. You won. You broke me. You shattered me. And along the way, I learned a special secret. Do you know what *kintsugi* is?"

Nadine shook her head.

"It's a Japanese art. See, they take broken pottery and use lacquer and golden powder to put it back together again. It's a lesson. It teaches us that broken things, even...even terribly broken things, hopelessly broken things, can be put back together again. And they're never the same after that. They don't look quite the same, don't work quite the same, but they're whole again. They're *new*. And sometimes broken things come back stronger than they ever were before."

"Sounds like you should be thanking me," Nadine said.

"You stole so goddamn much from me, Nadine." Harmony's eyes glinted wet, her voice tight as her hands curled into fists at her sides. "You assaulted me. Invaded my body. You tainted my magic and left a stain inside of me that I can never scrub clean. You stole my confidence, my dignity, my pride. Well, guess what? Today I'm taking it all *back*."

She grabbed the Benelli tactical shotgun from the Miata's trunk — part of Kevin's special delivery — shouldered it, and opened fire.

The DOVE slug hit Nadine in the stomach and blasted her off her feet, sending her tumbling across the pavement wreathed in an electric halo. She had barely recovered before Harmony pumped the slide and shot her again. Nadine screeched in fury, scrambling up on all fours and throwing herself at Jessie, the closest target.

Harmony plucked a second shotgun from the trunk and hurled it underhand, tossing it to Jessie. Her partner snatched it out of the air, spun around and yanked the trigger, blowing Nadine out of the air mid-pounce. She hit the ground again with a strangled grunt, her body spasming from impact after impact.

Harmony and Jessie locked eyes as Nadine clambered back to her feet. The demoness's eyes were spheres of jet black now, her lips pulled back to bare a maw of jagged shark teeth as she dropped her human disguise. They advanced on her, walking side by side, racking their shotguns and firing again and again. Nadine jolted backward as the high-voltage rounds ripped into her, breaking bones and spattering dark ichor.

Harmony's last slug caught Nadine square in the breastbone, just over her heart, and sent her sprawling to the pavement. She jerked, spasmodic, lightning washing over her skin until the last flickers died in a storm of tiny, glimmering sparks.

Her eyes were closed. She wasn't moving. Harmony and Jessie stood over her.

Jessie leaned close. "She dead?"

"No," Harmony said. "Let's get the—"

Nadine's eyes snapped open and she roared like a lioness, hurling herself at Harmony with her hands twisted into claws and her shark-teeth snapping at Harmony's throat. In that moment, Harmony didn't need a plan, or training. Her body knew what to do. She pressed her open palm over Nadine's heart.

Then she *pulled*.

Power ripped from Nadine's body and flooded Harmony's veins like lit gasoline. It was a euphoria like nothing she'd ever known, nothing she could have imagined. She was mainlining hellfire and her body wanted *more*. She could be anything with this kind of power. She could be a conqueror, a warlord, a *god*.

She ripped her hand away and broke the flow. It was enough. She had enough. Nadine's eyes rolled back in her head and she slumped back to the pavement at her feet, out cold for real this time.

Harmony walked to the open trunk of the Miata and hoisted the second duffel bag from Kevin's delivery. It rattled when she dropped it at Nadine's side. She unzipped it and dragged out an armload of heavy chains.

• • • ● ● • ● ● • • •

A convoy of SUVs with tinted windows rolled in. Bette's people. She met them in the parking lot, conversing with men in dark suits and earpieces, pointing in all directions as she handed down orders. Harmony and Jessie watched as they carried out the casket, carefully loading it into the middle truck.

Bette turned to face them from the far side of the lot. She hesitated a moment, deliberating, then walked over to speak with them.

"You made the right choice," she said, "letting us take the containment unit. We'll keep it safe. Safe, and buried so deep it'll never see the light of day."

"You'd better," Jessie told her, "or you'll be hearing from us again."

"I would expect nothing less. You should go. My people will handle the cleanup here. We'll take care of the witnesses."

"I don't know how Majestic 'takes care' of witnesses," Jessie said, "but my group has some firm rules on that. What I'm saying is, I had better see that family giving an interview on the news tonight, alive and well after their dramatic rescue."

Bette cracked a tiny smile.

"Message received," she said.

"Where's Doctor West?" Harmony asked.

Bette sighed. "Ran away just before the fireworks started. I think he slipped out a bathroom window. I'll have my people keeping an eye out, but...I'd say this mission is officially bagged and tagged. Well done out there."

She gave them one last look, then snapped a salute before dropping her hand to her side.

"I look forward to our continued coexistence," Bette said. "See you on the battlefield."

Riding together again, back in the Hemi Cuda with their prize locked in the trunk, Harmony and Jessie drove in silence for a while. There was nothing but the wind, the sound of the purring engine and the open road, and the wide-open horizon ahead of them.

"Stupid question," Jessie said, "but how are you feeling?"

Harmony had to contemplate that.

"I think I'm okay," she said. "Yeah. I think I'm okay."

Vigilant's field teams rallied to the Midwest, undercover operatives arriving in a flurry of commercial flights before converging on the *Imperator* for their marching orders. Then they hit the Ardentis plant hard and fast under the cover of a bogus search warrant. A tactical team tore through the ruins of the laboratory with flamethrowers, searching every last corner and burning the corpses to ash. Technical support infected the plant's mainframe with a handful of custom viruses, all authored by Kevin, that reduced their data to molten slag.

There were no samples left, no remnants of Lorne's mad experiments, nothing to rebuild and nothing to rebuild it with.

A story needed to be told, and Harmony wrote one. It was the story of how Lorne Murrough — entrepreneur, philanthropist, seeker of peace — died of a heart attack while working late one night. She wanted him to be remembered for the good that drove him, not the evil that led him astray. No one, no one who wasn't there on that long and terrible night, would ever know the truth.

The security tape from the Gold Star massacre was eventually released to the media, for real, via an anonymous leak — after carefully editing Harmony, Jessie, and Bette out of all the footage. Josh and Ricky were shamed in death, exposed as killers and thieves. No one could find a reason for the baffling crime, but Harmony hoped the tape would give the families of the dead some closure. It was all she could do for them.

Back at Vigilant's headquarters, down in an unfinished sub-basement that was all sheetrock and exposed guts, they had built a cage — like a bird cage, for one human-sized occupant — in the heart of an empty chamber. There were no guards stationed in the room; they were carefully kept up the hall, isolated, watching the room through camera feeds that monitored their prisoner from every angle at every moment of the day.

The door hissed open. Harmony walked in, alone. Nadine sat in her cage, perched on the edge of a prison cot, and smiled.

"Hello, sweetie."

CHAPTER FORTY-EIGHT

"You're chipper," Harmony said.

"Of course I am." Nadine hopped up, approaching Harmony from the other side of the bars. "I haven't had this much fun in a *century*. And it only gets better from here. You see, my people, my family...they're going to come for me. And they're going to come for you, too."

"They have to find us first."

"I don't think you appreciate just how skilled the Dead Roses really are."

"Are you talking about all the agents we've already terminated?" Harmony asked. "Or do you have some super-secret and extra-talented ones you just haven't thrown at us yet?"

Nadine's smile disappeared.

"My *daughter* will come for me," she said.

"Maybe," Harmony replied.

"And you brought me into your home. Of all the things you could have done, all the paths you could have chosen...be honest, Harmony. You know how foolish this is. You should have killed me when you had the chance."

"I thought about that," Harmony said. "But you're an incarnate. Back in hell, you'd just reform, even from a speck of dust."

"In a matter of decades. Decades upon decades. By the time I was back to anything resembling my old power, you'd be long-dead and buried. You could have made me someone else's problem, a generation from now."

"I thought about that too." Harmony shook her head. "But I don't ever want to be the kind of person who passes the buck or kicks the can down the road. That's not fair. You're my problem to deal with, no one else's."

"And you're mine," Nadine said.

"So here we are. Fates entwined. Until I find a way to destroy you for good, I'm keeping you on ice."

"You really believe you can hold me in this cage," the demoness said.

"I know that I have to," she replied.

"So...are you going to tell me how you did it?" Nadine curled her hands around the bars, leaning closer. "You've been holding out on me, little girl. Share the trick. Explain how a mortal with no demonic heritage, not even a trace of cambion blood, gained a tiny taste of *my* power."

"I hoped you would know. You did this to me."

One corner of Nadine's mouth quirked. She let go of the bars, stepped back, and sat down on her cot.

"I did, didn't I? Oh, I remember the first time we met. You were such a...goody fucking two-shoes. A noble crusader for the righteous and the just. Never saw a rule you wouldn't obey. And now?"

Nadine took a deep breath and let it out as a mischievous giggle.

"Look what I *made* of you, Harmony. I brought out the best in you. You know I'm right."

Harmony's phone buzzed against her hip. She checked the screen, pursed her lips, and slid it back into her pocket.

"We'll talk more later," she said. "Duty calls."

"Oh, I look forward to it." Nadine flashed a wicked grin. "Come back and chat again soon, darling. Don't keep Mommy waiting."

It wasn't a mission. April and Jessie were waiting for her in the conference room. April looked grim. Her wrinkled hands rested on a thick manila folder.

"What's this about?" Harmony asked.

"Please," April said, "sit down. After the Basilisk mission, I...found something. After you came back, well, you weren't in any condition to hear it. I think you are now, and Jessie agrees."

"Shouldn't have kept it from me either," Jessie said in a low voice, shooting her a sidelong glance.

April slid the folder across the glass table.

Harmony stood on the doorstep of her mother's house, her stomach twisted into knots, with Jessie at her side.

Her mother had hair like silver tinsel and eyes like Harmony's. The crow's feet at their corners crinkled as she opened the door, dressed in a long lavender robe.

"Harmony? You didn't tell me you were coming! I mean, you're always welcome, but I would have cleaned up the place."

"It's okay. You remember Jessie, right?"

"Of course," she said, giving Jessie a welcoming nod. She waved them both inside. "What's going on, hon?"

Harmony held up April's folder.

"We need to talk about great-great-grandma."

Not long after that, they were all sitting down in the living room, sipping coffee from mismatched mugs while her mother pored over the paperwork.

"I don't understand what I'm looking at," she said.

"My medical reports," Harmony said. "My real, unredacted, unaltered medical reports."

Her mother shook her head, not following. Jessie got up and ambled over, pointing to a pair of graphs at the top of a page.

"This here," she said, "is what normal, healthy human DNA looks like."

Her finger slid down the page.

"And that's your girl."

"I'm... I'm sorry, I still don't..."

"Mom," Harmony said, "you know that there are other worlds than this one, right?"

"Of course. Like—" she paused, but they all knew what she was going to say. *Like the place your sister went.*

"Every woman in our bloodline has the Black family magic. And I'll tell you something: I've met a lot of magicians since I started working with Vigilant. Know how many of them are anything like us? None. Zero. Magical abilities aren't hereditary. To say nothing of the weird side effects, the cramps, the way we manipulate the elements like nobody else can."

"Harmony says your great-grandmother was the first," Jessie added. "That true?"

Her mother nodded. "Yes. I mean, I barely even remember her, she died when I was very young, but that's what my mother always said."

"Mom," Harmony said, "there's no easy way to say this. We aren't *from* here."

"When you say 'here,' you're not talking about Talbot Cove, are you?"

"It's not like you're aliens or anything," Jessie said. "You're human by any measurable standard — I mean, if you weren't, great-great-grandma wouldn't have been able to make babies with great-great-grandpa in the first place."

Harmony nodded. "But that's the reason for all of it. I don't know if she was an explorer, a refugee, if she was looking for something or maybe she was on the run, but...she came here from a parallel world and brought her magic with her. Then I guess she met somebody, fell in love, and settled down to raise a family. And here we are."

"Well." Her mother stared down at the mug in her cupped hands. "I should have had decaf."

"There's more." Harmony inhaled, resting her hands on her knees and squeezing them tight. "I don't talk about my work, but...I've been going through some things. And I need to tell you. I need you to know where I've been, the things I've seen, the things I've done. I need you to understand."

Jessie stretched and nodded back over her shoulder.

"Nice day out," she said. "Think I'll finish my coffee on the deck and give you two some privacy."

It really was a nice day. Jessie leaned on the rustic wooden railing on the back deck, sipping her coffee, watching birds flit through the trees.

The patio door slid open behind her, then rattled shut. Harmony sidled up alongside her, eyes puffy from crying but dry and clear now. Jessie didn't have to ask.

"Well," Harmony said, "she doesn't think I'm a monster."

"Good. Because if she said otherwise, I'd go in there and show her what a real one looks like."

"Are we okay?"

Jessie slapped her arm. "Because someone in your family four generations removed came from one of the worlds next door and you've got a little wonky DNA? Bitch, please."

She tugged down her sunglasses and stared at her over the rims.

"I've got the blood of a *literal alien god*," she said, "and you're still *my* best friend. I should smack you upside the head just for thinking I'd have an issue with that."

"It's a lot, okay? This is just a lot to take in."

"Which is why I'm not smacking you upside the head. Yet."

"But my powers, mixed with Nadine's infection...I'm changing, Jessie. And we don't know what I'm changing into."

"So you know what we gotta do, right?"

Harmony nodded. "Mom's going to dig through the family archives. She'll send us everything she can find."

"Good. Because you and me have a new mission: we're going to find the world your family came from. Once we get some hard data, then we can figure out if what's going on with your magic is something we need to fix, or nip in the bud or...hell, if we should celebrate. I'm open to any and all possibilities here. Meanwhile, the work's piling up at HQ. You ready to get back in the field and kick some demon ass?"

Harmony stared out over the back yard. Over the trees, to the far horizon.

"Doesn't even matter if I'm not from here," she said. "Still my planet. Still my war."

AFTERWORD

Regular readers may know that I ran into a bit of a burnout patch during the great quarantine, and I've been spending the last year getting myself put back together and on track once more. As part of that process, I'm so happy to be working on Harmony again, and I hope you enjoyed this latest adventure! Things will be ramping up pretty darn quick around here and while Harmony and Jessie have a new mission ahead, some old foes are about to come knocking...

I couldn't do what I do without my team: this time around I'd like to give special thanks to Jay Ben Markson for editing, and Damonza for cover design. And of course, thank you for reading! You make this all possible and I'm so grateful for you.

To be notified of new releases, you can get onto my mailing list over at https://craigschaeferbooks.com/mailing-list. You can also find me on Facebook (https://www.facebook.com/CraigS chaeferBooks/) and Instagram (https://www.instagram.com/cr aigschaeferbooks/).

ALSO BY

The Daniel Faust Series
The Wisdom's Grave Trilogy
Any Minor World

Made in United States
Troutdale, OR
01/12/2024